Ask Me For Fire

Halli Starling

Halli Starling Books

CONTENTS

PRAISE FOR ꟻALLI STARLING'S BꝊKS

Praise for *Wilderwood*

> "Starling's novel...will shatter readers' expectations with its bewitching complexities... [her] characters are provocative and engaging. Bellemy Eislen is equal parts intriguing and vulnerable, while Octavia Wilder easily fills the role of a well-defended, tenacious heroine."- **The BookLife Prize**

Praise for *Twelfth Moon*

> "This book was perfect for cuddling up on the couch with a blanket and enjoying the ride. Sweet stories of

Chapter One

Winter

"Don't say I didn't warn you."

Ambrose huffed amicably at the older man. "I'm not worried about a taciturn neighbor, Brad. I used to live in the Flats. And I'm not exactly looking to be chummy."

Brad winced then laughed. "Well, godspeed, kid. Barrett's a bit of a loner and you'll probably never see him except to glimpse a bit of beard or flannel. Or if he's out on the lake."

The landlord left him with a pat on the shoulder and the keys to his new home. Ambrose took in a deep breath, smelling the pines and moss and dead leaves on the air, and then unlocked the front door to his new place.

His place. Alone. No more roommates blasting shitty music at three am or cooking tuna melts. No neighbors screaming through paper thin walls or babies shrieking, forcing him to wear headphones in his own house. No shared green spaces or driveways.

Just him in a little cabin on a plot of land near Lake Honor, where the internet was surprisingly fast and he could have a home office and a tiny recording studio. Brad was the landlord but they had an agreement. Ambrose would take care of the place until Brad retired, meaning all the upkeep, interior and exterior. And Brad would sell it to him for only the value of the building. Land was expensive everywhere and paying only for the building was a steal.

It was the perfect arrangement. The perfect place for a loner like him.

After he put down the first few boxes from his rented truck, Ambrose grinned and ran his fingertips over the kitchen countertops, adjusted his glasses that had slipped over the bridge of his nose. This was exactly what he needed.

Barrett didn't look up at the sound of tires on his gravel drive. Hardly anyone came out to the southern edge of Lake Honor, and only one person's truck rattled and sputtered so.

"Barrett."

"Brad." Barrett tossed another hunk of wood on the nearby pile then readied his ax. "How are you?"

"Ah, you know me, right as rain until it rains." Brad chuckled at his little joke and Barrett had to twitch a grin at the old man. Brad had sold Barrett his cabin years ago, having owned a string of them around the lake. Over the years Brad sold off the properties. Barrett had been his first buyer. "Offloading the extra weight for when it's cruise season," the old man always said. Barrett assumed it was a metaphor for something else, since Brad never seemed to leave Honor, let alone take a vacation.

Barrett grunted and swung the ax down. The log, now cleaved in two with a mighty crack, split to either side and Barrett tossed them both onto the pile. It was supposed to be a wet winter, and Barrett didn't fancy chopping wood in the heavy, damp snow while shivering. "You want some coffee?"

"Nah, I'm headed up to see Audra. They're having a little thing for Beckett, since she's not a big fan of parties."

Barrett smiled. Audra was the mayor of the next town over and Brad's relative. Audra's college-aged daughter, Beckett, came home every autumn for her birthday and Audra and their wife typically kept the celebration within the family. "Have a nice time, then."

"Yeah, thanks. But real quick." Brad held up an empty metal ring between two arthritis-crooked fingers. "Sold the last one. I'm officially on the countdown."

"Shit. Congratulations." Barrett forced the words out between a sudden shot of anxiety down his spine. The last cabin was the closest one to his, abandoned a few months back when the previous owner had passed away. He'd been neighbors with Perry for half a decade, and the son of a bitch kicked it before his sixtieth birthday. Barrett missed his friend, missed their nights drinking together and chatting. Missed going fishing, sharing vegetables and venison.

Fuck, he thought, swiping a hand down his face and probably smearing dirt over his forehead. But he was genuinely happy for Brad, knowing the old man had big plans. He'd worked his ass off at the docks for decades and finally had a nice little nest egg to show for it. Granted, that was to the point where he tried to give Barrett retirement advice, even though Barrett's job as a forest ranger was plenty fine to provide for him and he wasn't forty yet.

It wasn't all about someone else in Perry's house. Only about half. The other half was the unknown. "Who is..."

"He. Ambrose Tillifer. Nice lad, young." Brad eyed up Barrett's wild black hair and bushy beard. "Maybe about your age, if you shaved off that soup catcher."

Barrett sputtered a laugh, making Brad grin. "Haven't heard that one in a while."

"No? I got a few more stored in the ol' noggin, if you give me a few minutes."

"Or a few beers."

"Touché, my friend." Brad picked up a split log and tossed it on the pile for Barrett. "He works from home, said he wants to fish and write and work on some side hobbies he's got going on."

Barrett's ears perked up at *fish*, but the rest of it sounded all right. He breathed a silent sigh of relief. "Sounds good."

"You should go over there. Be neighborly. Say hello."

He snorted as he placed another log. "You're talking like I'm some kind of grumpy loner.

"This guy and you might get on, even if it's just to fish in silence." Brad looked away, his nose wrinkling. "With Perry gone -"

Barrett's heart lurched at someone else saying that name aloud. "Yeah. I get it. If I see him around, I'll say hello."

"More than I was hoping for."

"I'm not that grouchy," Barrett mumbled, making Brad laugh as he climbed into his truck. Brad said his goodbyes and peeled out, leaving Barrett standing in his front yard as the sun shone down through the autumn-dappled trees.

There was someone out on the dock.

There was *never* anyone out on the dock except him and Perry. And now it was just him. Barrett rubbed his chest when his heart contracted painfully, thinking about his friend. Fucking heart attack at fifty-nine. The world was completely unfair.

The person on the dock had their back turned, but from the slight angle at which he approached, Barrett could see black jean-clad legs dangling over the edge, feet in battered boots kicking slightly. The wind blew, stiff and chilly, and Barrett pulled the zipper up on his jacket with his free hand, keeping his grip tight on his tackle gear. He watched as that wind played with the figure's shaggy auburn curls. But they didn't shiver or tug their flannel shirt tighter around them. That's when Barrett noticed the guitar in their long-fingered hands; when he heard the first few chords strummed out. It was no cheesy pop song or acoustic classic. Whatever it was left him feeling melancholic, as if the person playing was pouring feeling into every note. The music practically danced out over the fading morning mist and gray skies and it made his fingers itch to go get his own guitars, as shoddy of a player as he was. He had no skill next to this mysterious maestro.

"Hello?"

Barrett jolted, the fishing pole in his hand slipping through his fingers. "Shit, sorry," he muttered, bending to retrieve the pole. "You're um...you're good."

The stranger blinked at him, then got to his feet, guitar held carefully in his hands. "Thanks. The mist and everything felt right this morning, had to get out here." He approached and stuck out his hand. "I'm Ambrose. I just moved in."

"Barrett. Guess we're neighbors."

Ambrose was tall and lanky; almost as tall as Barrett, which was impressive enough. There were some doors he had to duck to pass through. Ambrose probably had the same troubles. And the man before him was of some indeterminate age between twenty-five and forty, with the kind of face so open, it made you want to confess everything. Long auburn hair that curled at the ends, dark grey eyes that looked even darker in the thin morning sun. There was a slight scar across his chin and over the left side of his jaw, faded white with age, and Barrett spotted the edge of curling dark ink above the collar of his high necked sweater.

You're beautiful, Barrett thought as Ambrose replied, "Then it's nice to meet you. Honestly, I came up here for the quiet and you don't look like the party type, so I guess we're good there."

It was such a casual statement, in a vaguely Bostonian accent, that Barrett almost laughed. Something about Ambrose made him think the other man wouldn't appreciate that, though. His stance was stiff, even with the gentle way he was holding his guitar. And he kept looking toward his cabin. Like he wanted to be anywhere else.

And people called Barrett standoffish.

Deflated, Barrett nodded. "Just doing some fishing, if that's all right."

Ambrose waved a hand at the lake. "It's not my dock nor my lake. I was just heading inside anyways. Nice to meet you."

With a nod, the other man walked off, leaving Barrett to watch until Ambrose disappeared inside his house. After a few long moments where an inexplicable loneliness rose up in him, he sighed and began unpacking his fishing gear. Perry was gone, he had to remember that. And clearly Ambrose wasn't the overly friendly type.

"Polite neighbors" was just fine. It's not like he was looking to supplant Perry any time soon, even with that hollow echo in his bones.

Chapter Two

A week passed, and with it, autumn quickly, suddenly, fell into early winter. Work deadlines were met, chapters were written (then edited, disposed of, rewritten, and finally settled on), and copious amounts of tea was drunk. Settling into his new home felt far too easy and yet, Ambrose relished in that quiet, where the patter of rain lulled him to sleep and he woke in the mornings to mist rolling over Lake Honor. He unpacked boxes, moved furniture, and hung paintings.

But he didn't go back out to the dock. Barrett seemed nice enough and Ambrose wasn't *avoiding* him, per se. Writing poetry and prose and music, those were solitary activities, and between his accounting job and video game raid weekends with some friends, there was no time to go borrow a cup of sugar or whatever neighbors did. And he strangely felt like going back to the dock would be an invitation.

His mother would have a field day with his pernicious reluctance to meet new people, especially when one lived so close. But Lake Honor was as far away from her as anything and the distance helped him ease into his new routine.

He spotted Barrett a few times from his kitchen window, as he leaned against the counter and sipped scalding hot green tea. The man was....well, *massive*. He looked like someone who had lived in the woods all his life. Raised by wolves or bears or something. His wild, snarled black hair and untamed beard hid a lot of his features, so Ambrose had no idea how old he was. But his confident stride bore no signs of age or injury, no limp or slowness. Barrett walked like a man who knew his boots would keep him steady on muddy ground; as if he knew where he was going and what he was doing at all times. It was a confidence Ambrose envied, even as it sent a jolt of something *else* through him.

With a sigh, he pulled away from the window just as Barrett turned in his direction. He really needed to focus on his new song, pull his head out of the manuscript that seemed to go nowhere. The tiny recording studio - really just a repurposed closet - was all set. Waiting for him. But that spark, that bit of ignition he was waiting on, the thing that fueled his musical passion and desire, was missing.

"Damn," he muttered as he reached for his guitar. It was going to be another long day of staring at blank pages and fighting with snippets of chords that only made him frustrated.

Don't think so negatively, Ambrose. Negative thinking only clouds our creative energies and you'll never get anywhere with your craft if you don't focus on the positives.

He could hear her in his mind, clear as a bell. His mother, Angelica Avery, was a renowned musician; had played violin with many an orchestra, had sang opera on stages across the world, and was loved by all those in the arts scene in the big cities on the coast. But while talented and beautiful, she was a terrible mother. She treated Ambrose like a rowdy pupil instead of a son at best, and his childhood desire to try his hand at all kinds of art only disappointed her.

Not everyone has so many facets to their talent, Ambrose. Stick with what suits you best.

He gripped his pencil tightly as anger doused his system. It didn't matter. She wasn't here, he was alone, and he could create and fuck up and create again to his heart's desire. That was all that mattered.

Ambrose wiled away the afternoon composing, strumming his guitar, and piecing together bits of a song that had lingered in his dreams for several nights. It was a sad little thing; the story of a boy who sat at the edge of a cliff and wondered if he could fly. What if he could dream and wish hard enough to grow wings and let him soar over the water like a bird, free and happy as the wind took him wherever it pleased.

He had just finished the chorus when there was a knock at his door. Startled, he jumped and his pencil went flying, pinging off the wall and skidding to a stop under his desk. "Fuck," he muttered. *Who the hell was at the door?*

He opened the door and was immediately hit with a blast of cold wind, which snapped at the curtains just inside the front doorway. His neighbor stood there, a cheerful smile on his face despite the wind buffeting him. Ambrose frowned but said, "Hello again."

"Hi. Hey so uh..." Barrett held up a cooler. "Caught a bunch, and I used to share my catch with Per - the guy who lived here before. Wanted to see if you were interested."

There was an earnestness on that heavily bearded face and Ambrose found himself relenting. Hard not to when Barrett was staring at him so openly, dark brown eyes looking right at him and not past to see the house. "Yeah, sure." Ambrose stepped aside and then scrambled to close the door against that blistering, damnable wind.

The door caught in his grip and would have whipped outwards had it not been for the extra hand suddenly wrapped around the edge. "Wild out there now," Barrett rumbled at him. Entirely too close. Close enough that Ambrose could *smell* him, for fucks sake. Fish, yes, but Ambrose enjoyed fishing and didn't mind it. It was the whiff of clean laundry and rosemary that somehow fit the man and lingered in his nostrils.

Together, they got the door shut against the wind. When Ambrose turned, Barrett was standing behind him, tugging his boots off while the cooler sat on the floor. "Oh, no you don't have to do that."

Barrett smiled at him. "No, I do. The floors are nice in here and besides, I'm not one to go walking through someone else's house and track what-have-you everywhere."

Discomfited by the casual familiarity of Barrett's boots by his, Ambrose took his coat and then led him to the kitchen. "I've got coffee or tea or beer," he said flatly, really not wanting Barrett to stick around longer than to drop off the fish.

"Oh, nah, I gotta get back and finish up some maps. But here." One big hand flipped open the cooler and soon Ambrose's kitchen island was piled with vacuum sealed fish filets. "Most of them are plain but I've got a few with some spices, rosemary sprigs, that kind of thing. I grew all the herbs myself."

That explained the rosemary. "Really, just a couple of plain ones are fine. It's unexpected but appreciated."

There was that smile again and then Barrett huffed a laugh. "Yeah well, it's just me over there and I know how hard it is to cook for one. Thought I'd share the wealth."

He handed Ambrose a few packets of fish, then paused and picked up one more. "Do me a favor? It's a new spice rub I put together. Let me know how it is, and don't be shy."

Their fingers brushed as Ambrose took the packet with a nod. He felt foolish, finding this all a little too familiar, too *close*. He wasn't adverse to people or company in general. He simply needed more time than most to recharge the social batteries after interacting with others. He'd been in relationships (most of which had fizzled when the other party got tired of Ambrose needing time alone). He had friends.

Something about this big man with the soft eyes and kind smile was making him twitch. And that wasn't part of the plan. The plan was to stay in the hills and write and record and work and enjoy the quiet. It didn't have room for anyone, not even a nice neighbor.

Barrett seemed happy with his nod, saying, "All right. Appreciate it." And then he was snapping the cooler shut and tugging on his boots, carefully holding them over the rug so as not to drip on the hardwood floors. "Be careful if you head out past Route 3, icy as hell when I was out there this morning."

That caught his interest. The weather had been horrible all day, and from the number of times he'd seen Barrett out chopping wood, smoking meat, or tending to his property, he'd figured the man had stocked up well. He also didn't seem the type to head out into shit weather for no reason. "Wasn't planning on going out, but thank you. Did you go to town or...?"

One arm in his coat, Barrett twisted around to say, "Nah. I had to get up into the foothills to check the trails. There's always at least one person who thinks days like this are great for starting to learn to hike or cross-country ski. We usually pull two or three out during the winter, so I decided to be proactive and check the places I know people usually get stuck." He laughed, and then said, "I'm a forest ranger."

Pieces clicked in place. Hells, Barrett was a *professional loner*. Any kind of major outdoor career usually dealt with long hours in all kinds of weather, and usually alone. "Oh, I had no idea. I'm assuming no one was out."

"No, but I was ready for it." And now, coat, gloves, and hat back on, Barrett looked all the more rough and tough woodsman. Later, he might marvel at the disparity between Barrett's appearance and his calm, casual demeanor. Appearances were deceiving and all that. "Anyways, appreciate the let-in. Enjoy the fish, Ambrose."

And then he was gone with a wave, the blistering cold wind and beginning snowfall making Barrett disappear like so much smoke between their houses.

That night, Ambrose made that specially spiced fish and enjoyed the way the smoked paprika and garam masala rolled around on his tongue. The green tea wouldn't pair well with it, but his homemade beer did. He'd have to tell Barrett the next time he saw him.

Chapter Three

When Barrett awoke to snow covering his windows, he sighed. The best season, and the hardest, had begun. Lake Honor was a winter wonderland, Hallmark dream covered in snow and frost, but the natural beauty of the weather also brought out some rather frightening stupidity. He couldn't blame folks for wanting to learn outdoor activities, even in the cold temperatures, and everyone had to start somewhere. But no matter how many bulletins they posted or paths they closed off, there was always someone who pooh-poohed at the rules, as if they existed only to annoy and not for the safety of all.

As he was leaving the house in the pre-dawn hours, the kitchen light flickered. Hmmm. He'd best check the generator again when he got back from work; if it was snowing this hard in early November, chances were good the winter would be a long, cold one. Barrett made a mental note to double check his firewood and ask Ambrose if he needed any.

As he climbed into his truck, he spared a glance over at Ambrose's dark windows. He'd noticed Ambrose wasn't a morning person and he had to admit it was funny to see anyone around here sleep past sunrise. Those who lived around the lake tended to keep time with the sun, or what little there was along the coast in the winter.

He didn't know much about his new neighbor at all, and it rankled some part of him. He knew that was him grieving his friendship with Perry, like the cold making one's joints ache. But aside from knowing the man could play guitar and he was a writer or something like it, Ambrose was a mystery. And that was strange. They might all keep to themselves out here, but they all were there when someone needed help or had a cookout. If he was a suspicious person, he might think Ambrose had moved in at the start of winter to avoid getting chummy with folks.

If he was a suspicious person, and he wasn't.

He couldn't begrudge the man his privacy or solitude. Hell, he picked being a forest ranger largely for the chance at *more* peace and quiet. Perry's absence was just something he'd need to deal with on his own time, and not make presumptions on the man who now lived in his dead friend's house.

All thoughts of Ambrose and Perry and the lingering, raw wound on his heart were vanquished when Barrett pulled up to the ranger station to discover chaos unfolding. "Need you, B!" Meredith shouted as she darted by, med kit in hand. "Bridge collapse trapped a couple of trail runners and a few people tried to help, but it's worse."

Adrenaline shot through his system but he didn't waver. He'd been a paramedic before a forest ranger and he kept up on his various trainings and skills in order to be of greater use to the team. He and Meredith were the only certified paramedics on staff but they needed more. They always needed more - funding, supplies, vehicles, maps. On and on and on.

All thoughts of the inadequacies of his department aside, he dashed to the medical hut, grabbed his supplies, and hopped into Meredith's truck. Their radios crackled between updates and streams of information from Jacques, the ranger leader, who was already on site and trying to help the trapped runners. They were at the Logger Pass, one of the higher points in the forest and tricky in the best weather. It was part of Barrett's current route and while he enjoyed the challenge of hiking up the hills and driving around the twisty-turny bends of the access paths, he knew it was dangerous. It's why it was only assigned to seasoned rangers, and he was the most senior next to Jacques. Having something happen on his route made his heart plummet a little bit more.

It was a trail for experienced hikers and runners but doable if you knew what you were doing. Barrett could feel his heart pounding harder with every turn Meredith took, the snow chains on the truck's tires crunching and squealing against several inches of thick, heavy snow.

"Come on, fucker," she grunted as she spun the wheel and got them around the last corner. "Thank god." She gave him a gap-toothed grin. "Aw, look! You didn't even cling to the door like you usually do."

"Yeah, yeah," he muttered, but he had to smile back. It felt forced with all the worry coursing through him, but she didn't seem to take offense. They'd been coworkers and friends for nearly a decade, handling all sorts of shit on the job and closing out the bars in Elsie in their younger days. But he trusted Meredith with his life, and had at least a handful of times when shit got rough.

The moment Meredith parked as close as she dared next to the evac site, they both launched from the truck and raced over. The bridge he checked every week was nearly snapped in half. But whatever the cause wasn't important in the moment, because Jacques was heaving timber off a woman's leg. She was conscious but panic was written in every line of her face, and Barrett could hear her calling out to her companion. The man was flat on his stomach, pinned at the hips by a large piece of timber.

"Shit," Meredith said just as Jacques looked up at them. "Is he conscious?"

"No, but he's breathing. Barrett, I've got her. Help Meredith."

Barrett sprung into action, pulling timber and rocks off the unconscious man. He had a nasty gash on his head, another through his running tights. He'd have a concussion at best, brain damage at worst.

"Emergency services are already on their way, but they can't get up the trails," Meredith said quietly as she pulled rubble away. The man's hand was going purple and the skin at the index and middle fingers was tented grotesquely. A bad break then, but the least of their worries.

"Okay, friend," Barrett said near the unconscious man's ear, his free hand on the fluttering pulse at his neck. "We're going to get you out of here."

The keening of sirens caught his attention and Ambrose whipped around to see two ambulances racing down the service road parallel to the hiking trail. Startled, he hopped aside even though the vehicles were peeling up the hill where the road split, spraying snow as they sped by. He wondered idly what casualty had befallen someone up ahead, and then he remembered.

Barrett was a forest ranger. Would he be on call today? Was he at the scene? Was he okay?

Ambrose gave himself a little shake and adjusted his pack. It was a short hike, a mere six miles, but he'd awoken itchy and restless and not wanting to stare at his own walls for another day. Had the newness of home - *his* home - worn off so quickly? That wasn't possible. He awoke every morning to mist on the lake, made dinner by the dying light of spectacular sunsets, and spent his days in quiet contemplation and creation. Even if creation was another spreadsheet for work, or editing another chapter or verse or note.

So why was he worried about a stranger? Neighbor or not, he knew little about Barrett. And no matter how hard he tried, he could never shake the habit of looking up new people in his life. But could anyone blame him for wanting to check on *who* the neighbor was? So he dug around online. Barrett Miguel was thirty-eight, single, never married. No arrest or court records, owned his little home on the lake for the last decade. Worked for the forestry service for as long, before that was a paramedic. But previous to his mid-twenties, his history was far more scant. Born in Harperton, about twenty minutes down the road from Elsie, not quite an hour from Lake Honor. Divorced parents, one younger sister. A few random photos from Barrett when he was in high school, but they were that specific kind of grainy, yearbook style that made details hard to make out. Bachelor's degree in applied sciences. In the age where all kinds of information was available online, it wasn't the most scant early life profile, but it made him wonder.

He was wondering about his neighbor a little too often, and this morning as he watched Barrett's truck roll past his house, snow crunching under his tires, he figured enough was enough. He'd put off his running for too long and now the trails were *right there*. Ambrose had once been a pretty accomplished trail runner, even winning a few local races, and he needed to get his head set right.

And yet the whine of ambulance sirens was echoing in his ears and his first thought had been to Barrett. Dammit all.

Racing up there into gods knew what was a bad idea. He could turn around and go home, but how would that make any difference? Then again, he'd just hit his stride, music blasting in his ears, and his trail was a slight downward slope instead of up into the hills where the ambulances had disappeared. So back to his business it was.

But a twinge of guilt had him yanking off a glove with his teeth and pausing to type out a quick text to Barrett. They'd exchanged numbers that first week, more in the interest of an emergency than friendliness. And beyond an occasional message from his Paul Bunyan-esque neighbor about bad ice on the roads or to ask if he wanted more fish, they didn't chat. Just two loners in the woods, keeping to themselves while winter settled in around them like a blanket.

But even loners sometimes had to look out for someone else.

> **To: Barrett** *I'm out on the trails south of the Logger trailhead. Some ambulances went flying by. Everything okay?*

If it was an emergency, Barrett would be busy and answer when he could. But even the text message didn't assuage all his guilt, so he cranked up the music, tugged his glove back on, and set out determined to run himself to exhaustion in hopes of feeling better. He'd hit his stride again right before the big bridge over the creek, and he could really lean into the tougher climbs beyond that.

Think in increments, his coaches had said. *Make it to a point, then once you've arrived, set another point ahead. Bit by bit, you'll get there.* Except Ambrose had never done anything by halves in his life, even when everyone else told him to do so. Maybe it was in spite of them that he leaned in hard to everything - his work, his hobbies, his quiet lifestyle. Hell, saving for his house had taken dedication over nearly a decade; a decade of shitty paying jobs and counting every cent and never splurging. All so he could live in peace in the woods, far away from the noise and bustle.

His phone buzzed as the bridge loomed ahead and the jolt of it sent his right foot skidding on a patch of thin, muddy ice. Cursing, Ambrose righted himself and pushed harder into his stride. He'd check the phone once he was past the bridge, didn't want to get distracted and wind up face-first in the snow.

"Shit. Meredith, drop me off."

"What?" The smaller woman shook her head. "No, why? We're going with the ambulances. We're already halfway down, Bear."

Barrett clutched his phone tighter. "Got someone down on the Logger trail, and I need to tell them not to go any further."

"Well, text 'em!" she said over the blast of snow that dropped on them from the trees overhead.

"I did, but he didn't answer!" Barrett yelled back.

"Shit!" Meredith stomped on the brakes, sending him lurching for the dashboard. "Okay, keep me posted!"

"You do the same, let me know about those runners." Barrett snatched his bag from the utility chest on the back of the truck, gave her a wave, and then wrapped his hand around his phone in his pocket, picking up the pace. Ambrose wouldn't be too far ahead if he'd been able to see the ambulances from Logger. The Seesaw trail didn't start to curve out of view past Logger until the bridge and *that* was propelling him forward.

When he'd been digging the man out of the rubble, he'd caught sight of a set of strange marks in the remaining support beams, as cracked and splintered as they were. And the more he looked at those marks, the larger the ball of dread in his stomach grew. Those had been saw marks. Not all the way through the beam, but enough to weaken it. Add thousands of visitors every week crossing the bridge, even in the winter, and you had a trap that could spring at any moment.

He'd had a moment where he thought he was seeing things, but he'd taken a picture and another piece of wood with the same marks. Maybe he was just getting cynical and suspicious as he aged. Maybe he *was* seeing things. But his hackles were up. There hadn't been time, in the rush to get the runners down to the ambulances, to show Meredith or Jacques. And then Ambrose's text had come in and the implications of it - and the future it might hold - made panic shoot through him.

Add in the fact that they'd had some downed trees in certain parts of the forest of late and well... It wasn't, in and of itself, unusual; trees fell. But he'd found a few with obvious saw marks and had mentioned it to Jacques. People sometimes poached trees from the forest, or didn't realize it was forest land. The trees had been fairly young, so Jacques had written it up and filed it away. But he did want to check those saw marks on the trees to the saw marks on the bridges, just in case. It was very likely just a weird coincidence.

Barrett ducked as a set of branches tried to whip at him and pushed forward again. The skies were darkening and the wind was picking up, and whatever strange, ominous feeling he had seemed to be following his boot prints in the snow. It rattled branches and scattered dead leaves and echoed through the forest with a groan.

Barrett wasn't superstitious, but he wasn't stupid, either. A snowstorm was moving in and he needed to haul ass.

Recalling his old linebacker days, he barreled forward, propelled by that gnawing sense of dread. A branch cracked behind him and he jumped out of the way as it crashed to the ground not a few yards to his right. *Fuck.*

Blinking against the wind, Barrett narrowed his eyes as a shape appeared up ahead. Hi-vis jogger stripes on the pants and jacket reflected like a cat's eyes in the dark. They were almost to the bridge.

"Ambrose!" He yelled, voice booming out around them. "Wait!"

Acid rose in his gut as the figure ran onto the bridge and paused, turning back to him as he reached the bridge's handrail.

"Barrett?" It was Ambrose, and he was still jogging. Feet *pounding pounding pounding* on the bridge, the entire thing bouncing slightly with the force.

"Get off the bridge!"

Ambrose frowned and for a wild moment, he looked like he might argue. But the panic Barrett felt must have shown, because Ambrose started to jog toward him. "What's going on?"

"Now!"

The bridge creaked. Groaned. And then snapped, beams cracking, giving way, and Barrett dove for Ambrose.

CHAPTER FOUR

The river below didn't look particularly wide or deep, but when Ambrose found himself dangling above it just now, it looked like the kind of bottomless depths Jules Verne would have written about. His left hand was slipping against icy wooden planks and the other straining to grasp Barrett's forearm as he kicked his feet uselessly in the air.

"Fuck, okay, hold on." Barrett was gritting his teeth and pulling but someone's grip was going to give. His stomach gave a sickening lurch as his left hand slipped against the wood once again.

"Just drop me."

"No."

Stubborn fool. It wasn't so cold out that he'd get hypothermia from being dunked in a few feet of water. He could roll right out and get back to his car to warm up.

"Water's deeper than it looks," Barrett grunted out. The big man caught Ambrose's gaze; there was a reassuring calm in his brown eyes and Ambrose could imagine that same gaze steadying panicked patients or lost hikers. "Can you get your foot on a beam?"

"Yeah." Ambrose swung himself right, stretching his leg out in hopes the toe of his shoe would catch. Any leverage was better than this. He swung once, twice, and on the third swing, as his arms started to go numb, his shoe's spiked sole caught on a broken bit of lumber and then the world was rushing up at him, the ground included.

Ambrose hit the ground with his left arm buckled under his torso. "Fuck."

"You're telling me."

Barrett's big, deep voice sounded strained. Ambrose rolled to his right and saw Barrett was flat on his back, left arm folded over his stomach while the right and both legs were sprawled out, starfish style. "Shit. You okay?"

"Yeah. Just nearly pulled my shoulder out of place."

"Did you?"

"Nah. Gonna be sore tomorrow though."

Gods, his heart was *pounding* in his ears but the solid ground felt good under him, even cold and wet as it was. He looked up as big, fat snowflakes hit his cheeks. The cold that hadn't bothered him a moment ago suddenly burned. Barrett rolled up and onto his feet, hand out to Ambrose. But the moment his weight settled on his right ankle, Ambrose hissed and tipped into the other man. "Shit. That might be sprained. Most of the rangers are out dealing with another broken bridge but I can radio ahead, get a truck up here."

"I can walk."

Barrett huffed. His breath puffed out in a cloud, the frosty air cut with a motion from his hand. "See this? Add in the sudden shift in wind and barometric pressure. There's a storm moving in. And it wouldn't be wise to fuck around in that even with two good ankles." He reached for the radio in his jacket, leather of his gloves squeaking as he gripped the comically small device. "Radio 4, this is Bear. Is there anyone available to bring a truck down to the Logger trail where it crosses Seesaw? We've got another bridge out and I've got an injured civilian."

Ambrose watched, fascinated, as his broad, hairy neighbor changed in that instant to someone who practically rippled with authority. Even the *Bear* had sounded clipped and business-like. The radio was snarled with static as someone on the other end said, "Bear, we got two more bridge collapses, only minor injuries. Afraid I don't have anyone to spare. Where are you?"

Barrett frowned and gave the dispatcher their location. "You've got a storm moving in and you're too far from the public parking lots. Alpha FL is just over the ridge. It'll be all supplied up and have a dedicated line we can call you on when we can get someone out there."

"Done. Update Truck 3 and Jacques on my location?"

"You got it. Hurry your ass, Barrett."

"Love you too, Marge."

The woman chuckled then the radio snapped off with an audible click. "Can you walk?" Barrett's hands were on his shoulders now, warm and broad and the sensation nearly made him stumble again.

"How far?" Ambrose winced as he tried to put his foot down once more.

"About a quarter of a mile." Something flashed over Barrett's face. "Okay, you gotta forgive me for this."

And Ambrose was scooped off his feet and into Barrett's arms, his legs dangling over Barrett's right arm. "Wha - whoa!" He had to hook his left arm around a thick neck for balance but Barrett didn't seem to mind.

The bastard just laughed. "Sorry. You're tall but, as I thought, a lightweight."

His ego bristled but his rage sputtered when he saw the way Barrett's eyes were glittering at him. Daring him. "I don't see that I have a choice."

"You don't."

Feeling strangely light, Ambrose waved a hand and Barrett began walking.

The journey was slow and bumpy but quiet. He could get over the sensation of being carried like a child and the slow sloughing of Barrett's steps as the snow grew deeper. He even got wrapped up in how *warm* the other man was; it was tempting to curl up on his chest and sleep.

Until Barrett said, "There should be medical supplies and some food and water in the FL." Ambrose blinked at him. "Fire lookout. It's one of the nicer ones. I think Meredith was in that one for the summer."

"Hope she brought some books with her."

"I think she was writing one."

He had to nod at that. "I wrote my first book and my first real songs during a lookout summer."

"Wait, what?"

"Yeah." Ambrose smiled. "I spent my summer between sophomore and junior year in college in the fire tower near Port Blythe. It paid, it got me out of the house, and it was so damn quiet that I got a lot done."

"Sounds like it. All that *writing*."

Was Barrett....teasing him?

But the thought was dashed as Barrett said, "Up ahead. We'll get you seen to."

It was only then Ambrose remembered his throbbing ankle.

"That's a lot of stairs."

Chuckling, Barrett steadied Ambrose by tightening his grip on the man's shoulders. They were surprisingly muscular under his layers, though he wasn't sure why he was shocked. Granted, he hadn't spent a bunch of time analyzing his neighbor's physique. They saw so little of each other and it wasn't usually for longer than a wave or a quick "Hello, how are you, thanks for the fish" kind of thing. Barrett had thought about inviting the man over for a drink or sharing some stew by the fire, but he'd always dashed those thoughts away as no more than missing Perry and their bond.

He and *Perry* had shared bourbon and venison stew by Barrett's big hearth. He and *Perry* had swapped stories and bullshit and played cards. Ambrose wasn't Perry. But Ambrose was here, now, and injured. He needed someone to help him, even if the man grouched about it the whole time. Barrett had almost laughed when Ambrose batted at him like a child and grunted, "Put me down" when they approached the fire tower.

"You said you'd been in an FL before," Barrett countered. Ambrose's frown was worth his little jab.

Ambrose's grip on Barrett's arm was tight as he said, "Well, it was only four stories. How fucking high is this thing?"

Ambrose's Boston accent was stronger when he cursed, his words rolling and snapping harsher. "This one's six. Bit of a climb and your ankle -"

"I got it." Ambrose hopped up a couple of stairs and looked back as if to challenge him.

"You got it. But I'll stay close, in case."

"Fine."

They started the climb and Barrett stayed within a few stairs in case the man wobbled. By the third flight, snow had begun falling at a rapid rate. Ambrose's breaths came quickly but controlled and Barrett was only beginning to feel that strange, tilting sensation he got when climbing such heights.

"You look green," Ambrose said as they slowly rounded the fourth story landing.

"I'm good," Barrett huffed back, his breath roiling in the frosty air.

"You sure?" Barrett just raised an eyebrow at him and Ambrose snorted. "Okay, fine. I'm only checking."

"You're the one with a twisted ankle." It was more than twisted, it was likely a bad sprain. Barrett could see the swelling under Ambrose's running tights. They needed to get those off and relieve the pressure. "Need help?"

Ambrose shook his head and began hopping up the stairs once more. It was like being batted at by a grouchy old cat, Barrett mused as they neared the top. One moment the man was joking or reluctantly engaging in more than single sentence answers, then the claws came out and they were back to staring at each other.

Ambrose was the one looking a little green, like pea soup, when they finally reached the top. He leaned heavily against the clapboard siding while Barrett entered the door code. "Gonna be cold for a bit until I get the generator started. There's some blankets and I can get the kettle going for you, since the stove is gas."

"Great. Thank you." But instead of haughty over his successful climb, Ambrose sounded weak. Barrett glanced over and saw Ambrose hadn't moved from his post just outside the door. "Just a minute."

"Let me help."

"No, I got it."

"You look like you're going to puke." Barrett stood in the doorway and put out his hand. "Ain't nothing wrong with letting someone help. You climbed six flights with a bad ankle."

Ambrose huffed at him but the sound carried little heat. Dark circles made his grey eyes look even more weary, giving his face a gauntness that made concern tick in Barrett's chest. But the stubborn fool just pushed past him to collapse in a battered armchair near the electric fireplace. "See? I'm fine."

"Well, then you're fine."

"I am."

"I know. I believe you." If Ambrose was digging into his stubborn nature, then Barrett had work to do. "You'll want to get those tights off. The pressure on your ankle might be making any sprain or fracture worse. I gotta get the generator up and running." He motioned to the radio and phone setup on the desk on the north wall. "If it crackles or beeps, hit the red button and pick up the receiver. Tell them I'm out with the generator and ask when they can get a truck out. It'll be probably be Marge calling, if anyone does."

"Right. Red button, receiver, generator."

Ambrose didn't look like he was going to be moving, given how he'd deflated in the chair, but Barrett didn't have time to babysit someone so stubborn. "Good memory. I'll be fifteen minutes tops. Don't move other than to get your tights off."

Ambrose shivered in his seat, staring hard at the floor. Something about his expression made Barrett think he was almost embarrassed. "Is there a blanket or..."

"Yeah." Barrett dug through the supply chest and found two scratchy wool blankets, which Ambrose quickly unfolded without a single wrinkle of his nose. Good. They were probably musty from disuse but they were better than bare skin in the cold of the tower. While Ambrose fussed with the blankets, Barrett gave the tower a once over.

The fire tower was one big room save a bathroom just big enough for a shower and toilet. A fully stocked kitchen, some worn furniture, and in the middle was a massive table groaning with maps, guides, binders, and anything else a firewatch needed during their stay. Alpha tower was Barrett's favorite, and he'd spent enough seasons in it to replace the shitty bed with one that didn't make his back ache every morning. He'd even installed a curtain that ran around a large pipe bracketed to the ceiling. Great for keeping out light and even better for hanging mosquito nets during the summer.

There were cobwebs and dust, but the supplies were stored away. Barrett flung open a cabinet and grinned. "Water for tea, and there's a container of tea bags on the counter, mugs in the drawer." He held the green glazed teapot up with a smile. "And ol' Froggy here should be boiling soon."

To his shock, Ambrose cracked out a laugh as soon as he saw the handmade frog teapot. "Then leave me to ol' Froggy and get some heat on in this godsforsaken place."

Barrett gave him a sharp salute, put the teapot on the stove, and headed outside. The snow was falling hard and fast now, the wind chilling him to the bone, and Barrett had a feeling they were about to spend the night in the tower. It was far better than being stuck outside or in his truck, but this was not how he'd planned to spend his evening.

CHAPTER FIVE

His ankle was a bruised, swollen mess. Ambrose wasn't good with blood or injuries in general, and seeing the ball of his ankle doubled in size over the top edge of his shoe made the room spin sickeningly. He'd managed to get the shoe off but now, with some of the pressure relieved, the throbbing was intense. Almost too much.

And he was alone, with Barrett outside. It was like something switched in the other man and Ambrose thought over their conversation as he stared down at his ankle. He knew he'd been a stubborn asshole but letting people do things for him had always left him feeling off-kilter and strangely raw. Add in the injury and the cold and....

Ambrose sighed. He'd been a stubborn asshole. His worst trait exposed like a wound to a stranger who had given him fish and saved him from dropping into a freezing river. What the hell was he doing? When Barrett got back, Ambrose was going to have tea waiting for him. A tiny repayment for all the kindness he'd been shown. Fuck his ankle, he could get to it in a moment.

The frog teapot whistled a minute later, so Ambrose hobbled over to the stove and dug out two mugs from the drawers. The box of tea on the counter was the usual grocery store chain stuff and Ambrose thought of his carefully curated tea collection at home. All loose leaf and specialty blends, some of which he'd made himself. If Barrett was drinking stale leaves....

He shivered, dug out the least offensive-smelling green tea packets, and left them to steep. The kettle was nicely made and ever an admirer of unique things, Ambrose turned it in mid-air by the handle to see it better. The glaze was even and bright, a soft moss green that looked right at home in a fire tower six stories in the air. And the frog was kind of adorable; it was hard to not smile at the novelty of pouring steaming water from a frog's mouth. It was an object clearly made with loving care.

He was digging through the cupboards for sugar or honey when a heavy buzz filled the air. It set his hair on end, like static electricity over his skin and Ambrose jumped back from the little kitchen corner. His ankle throbbed hotly with the movement but he didn't dare look down at it. "What the fuck?"

The overhead light snapped on with a harsh click and he jumped again, heart jackrabbiting as steps sounded below. "Thank fuck," he muttered as he hobbled to the chair, flipping the electric fireplace on before sitting down. The steps grew closer, louder, and then Barrett burst inside. He was *covered* in snow. It adorned his wool hat, nestled in the long, unruly curls that rested on his shoulders, and dotted his beard like confetti. "Fuck," he said, eyes going right to Ambrose. "It's bad out."

And it was. Ambrose had been too wrapped up in not shivering to death or fainting at the sight of his ankle to take too much note, but even a quick glance outside the massive windows that lined all four walls of the tower showed snow falling in a thick sheet. It blinded any vision past the immediate line of pine trees, dousing the world in white.

While Barrett was shaking himself loose of the snow and his gear, Ambrose sucked in a few deep breaths before poking gently at his swollen, almost purple ankle. "I think it's broken, or at least fractured."

Barrett froze mid glove pull. His stare burned through Ambrose in a way he couldn't help but shift uncomfortably from. "Shit, you didn't get those tights off? Ambrose."

His name rolled softly out of Barrett's mouth and something twinged low in his gut. Ambrose pushed it aside with an irritated flick of his hand. "I was too busy shivering and making tea. You did leave me with a kettle on the stove."

"Yeah but..." Barrett's hand was now in his hair, pulling slightly. "Okay, we gotta get those off. Hope you're not attached to them."

"What the hell does that mean? They're new, if you must know."

Barrett stomped over and kneeled down before Ambrose. "We gotta cut them off, check your ankle, and if it is sprained, rewrap it. If it's fractured, we gotta elevate it."

Well, that didn't sound so bad. Except for the cutting his running tights off part. The thought of it made him itch, like when his skin got too dry. It wasn't the thought of *Barrett* touching him that made him want to curl up in the corner. The thought of anyone he didn't know well touching him did that just fine. It wasn't a trust issue, it was...just him. Weird Ambrose, with his weird, crooked nose and solitary nature and difficulty making friends.

He was an adult. He could do this.

"Fine." He smirked, tried for levity; even if just to make Barrett stop frowning. "Please don't tell me you're going to pull a knife from your boot."

Barrett snorted, his eyes flicking up to Ambrose in surprise. "Shit. I do look the type, don't I?"

"The knife in your boot type?"

"Yeah. Huh. Usually I get lumberjack."

Ambrose gave his heavy ranger gear a once over. "I'd say forest ranger but that seems like cheating."

Barrett barked out a laugh. "You're funny."

"Could you tell my friends and family that?" Ambrose didn't mean for it to sound bitter. He didn't mean to say it at all. But as soon as the words left his mouth, Barrett's face softened in sympathy. Fuck. He didn't want anyone's sympathy. "Can we do this?"

"Yep." Whatever had lingered so softly on Barrett's face was now gone and that air of authority was back. Apparently Barrett was the kind of guy to adjust temperament based on the task before him. It was hard not to admire that kind of flexibility. Didn't Brad say Barrett was grouchy? He seemed...the opposite.

After rooting around in the first aid kit he'd pulled from another footlocker, Barrett came back with bandages and a pair of angle-bladed scissors. "Do you want to do the honors? I can hold your leg up."

"I don't think I can bend down that far and not put pressure on it."

"Fair enough." Barrett held his left hand out and Ambrose slowly raised his leg.

"It's okay." It was the only way he had to tell Barrett he could touch him, but the bigger man seemed to understand.

Thankfully, the running tights kept a bit of a barrier between his skin and Barret's hand as it wrapped around, then under, his knee. "I'm gonna try not to bump your ankle but I'll apologize now just in case."

Already the fire-hot throbbing was back and it was worrying. He might have really fucked up his ankle. And what if not getting his running tights off sooner had made it worse? Ambrose swallowed hard and nodded.

Watching Barrett concentrate was a study in contradictions. He was too big, too burly of a person to do something as delicate as stick his tongue out. Hells, his face barely changed but then again, with all that hair, it was hard to tell for sure. He pulled the tights away from Ambrose's knee, stretching the material out until it faded white, then quickly cut a line down, following the tibia. As the cold blades skimmed harmlessly along the tights, Barrett quietly said, "This might hurt, but I'm going to do my best. I won't cut you or press on your ankle, but handling it might make it throb. Okay?"

His breath left him in a rush. Something in Barrett's tone was steady and comforting, but soft. A good book and a cup of tea on a cold day. Shit, the tea. "I left your tea back there," Ambrose said as he turned in the chair. "You should drink it before it goes cold."

"We'll worry about that in a few minutes. Still good?"

He was dizzy and a little nauseated, but he had no choice. "Yeah. Somewhat."

Barrett nodded. "If you feel lightheaded or suddenly too cold or hot, tell me immediately." He waited until Ambrose shook his head in agreement before continuing to cut lower.

As the tights fell away, Ambrose saw how bad his ankle was in its full glory. The bruising bled up his leg and over his shin, but when Barrett finally got to his ankle, his hiss was more of shock than pain. It was now twice its normal size and a deep, ugly blue-purple. His vision swam and he closed his eyes. "Could you...give me a moment?"

"Take all the time you need. It isn't getting any worse in the next few."

He shuddered and leaned back in his seat. The chair's rough fabric was strangely grounding under his fingertips. The air was still cold but he caught a waft of green tea and wool. Moments passed and all he heard was his heavy breathing slowly easing into a less terrifying harshness. "Okay."

"Okay."

Barrett was either endlessly patient or his ankle wasn't as bad as the swelling and bruising let on. Ambrose passed the next minute with eyes closed, focusing on his breathing, and then Barrett said, "Got you free. Can I take a closer look?"

Ambrose cracked his eyes open. Barrett was still kneeling at his feet but there was a little nick between his eyebrows, concern flaring in those dark brown eyes. "You an expert on busted ankles?"

He sounded horrifically cranky (which he felt like there was cause for), but Barrett didn't seem to mind his snippy tone. "I was a paramedic a while back. Still use the skills for the forestry service."

Like today.

That jived with what his online snooping had turned up. But it helped his panic ease a little. "Yeah, all right."

"All right." He knew Barrett was speaking gently, repeating his own words to help Ambrose relax. It was a good trick and one that, even if you were aware of it, did help. "I gotta poke a little, so this might suck."

He laughed blithely. *"Might?"*

Barrett grinned, teeth bright against his dark beard. It was a nice smile; friendly and open and gave you the impression you were safe at the same time. Ambrose sank deeper into the chair. "Well, I can't guarantee anything. From the swelling, I think you've got a nasty sprain. Probably from the fall and banging against the bridge. But we won't know about a fracture until we can get you into an x-ray."

Ambrose found he couldn't argue with any of that. He nodded, and Barrett began turning his ankle over in big, broad-palmed hands. Whenever Ambrose hissed or winced, Barrett smiled apologetically. There was the crackle of the fireplace and the hum of the generator over the roar of the wind outside, but neither man made a sound.

After a few long minutes, with Ambrose's ankle throbbing hotly with Barrett's careful attentions, Barrett finally spoke up. "Yeah, a bad sprain, like I thought. I'd still like to take you to get an x-ray done, but until the storm passes, I'm going to wrap this and we'll put a cold pack on it." With that, Barrett stood and crossed the room once more, rummaging in a small footlocker at the base of the bed. He came back with one of those stretchy medical wraps and a cold pack that he cracked between his hands to activate.

As Barrett wrapped his ankle, Ambrose finally relaxed a little. It wasn't the ankle that had been worrying him as much as the *being touched* part. But his neighbor had been nothing but kind and gentle, and this was after saving him from a fall. He felt like he owed something. Anything for the dignity shown to him, a total stranger. "Thank you again for the fish. And for everything today." Ambrose grimaced as soon as the words left his mouth. Gods, what a fucking stupid way to say thank you.

Apparently Barrett didn't think so. He turned soft brown eyes up to him just as he finished tying the wrap and pressed the now active cold pack into Ambrose's hands while he shoved a small footstool under his ankle. "Ain't even a worry, Ambrose. I'm just glad."

"Glad?"

"That you liked the fish. And that I was able to catch you today before you went any further." Barrett frowned and that expression didn't suit him nearly as well as the brightness that had been in his eyes a moment ago. "Something ain't right with those bridges. We had four collapse."

"Four? Fuck."

"Yeah." Carefully, Barrett took the ice pack back and maneuvered it to wrap around Ambrose's ankle. With that done, he sat back on his haunches and nodded, pleased. "Do me a favor and avoid the trails for a bit? At least until we sort this out."

"Yeah, sure. Not looking to repeat today."

They stared at each other for a long moment, Ambrose had a few things on the tip of his tongue - inviting Barrett over for dinner as an extended thank you, asking him if he knew of good ice fishing spots, asking him *anything* about himself. Just being friendly. He hadn't made a new friend in a long while and maybe it was time to shake off the dust.

The radio on the other end of the room blared to life and they both jumped. Chuckling, Barrett got to his feet and marched over, leaving Ambrose to stew in his pain-colored confusion. The conversation Barrett had was short: the roads were blocked, the storm was still raging, and they'd be lucky to get someone out to retrieve them by morning.

"Well, shit," Barrett said as he ended the conversation with Marge, the station head. "It could be way worse. We could be stuck in the truck."

That *did* sound a ton worse than being inside and safe and warm. "Guess we'll make the best of it," Ambrose replied lightly, trying to already calculate sleeping arrangements.

Barrett must have been a mind reader - or very good at tracking eye movement - because he waved Ambrose off. "There's a couple of pull out cots in storage. You need the bed, since you need the support." He motioned to the little bathroom tucked into the corner. "Do you want to shower?"

That made his anxiety ratchet back up. He did not need to be fumbling and slipping in a tub and have to call Barrett for help. He wasn't precious about his body but he also didn't take pains to show it off, either. "No, I'm all right. But if you..."

"I was gonna say." Barrett pressed a new cup of tea into Ambrose's hand. "Don't get into trouble, yeah? I'm disgusting and I do not want to make you suffer with me."

Ambrose hefted his tea cup at him with a small smile. "Obliged."

As Barrett messed around with his gear and kits of what looked like toiletries tucked inside another one of the seemingly endless boxes around the tower, Ambrose sighed and closed his eyes. Not the worst day. Not the best. Definitely a strange one.

CHAPTER SIX

Barrett couldn't sleep. The cot was fine enough. Not like he needed much to get to sleep after the sheer exhaustion of the day. When this happened, he would focus on one thing: a spot of light on the wall, a sound, his breathing. A therapist had taught him that trick years ago and it had served him well through random periods of insomnia. He hadn't felt like this since Perry died, and that month or so afterwards had felt like reversing course in some ways.

One death, one coffin, one tragedy, and some part of him unraveled. A piece of him he'd worked *so hard* to fit back together.

As he lay in the dark and listened to the wind and the sound of Ambrose breathing nearby, his thoughts drifted. Staring up into the blackness. He couldn't do the single focus trick and he couldn't block out his tumbleweed thoughts. Barrett's mind eventually drifted away from Perry and the pain he now associated with his friend (part of grieving, right?). He drifted into thoughts about the other person so close.

Ambrose was odd. Barrett didn't mind odd. Most of the folks who lived around Lake Honor had a bit of a strangeness to them. Most were loners; a little off the grid, a little awkward, sometimes a little *too* quirky. Gesh hoarded cans of beans and jerky and bottled water *in case of the end*. Shannen and her son hoarded scrap metal for strange, oddly geometric statues they sold online. Gemma liked beer and hunting and her chickens and rarely let anyone else come round except him. Brad was probably the most sociable out of all of them, and he was getting ready to move on.

Another loss. Another hit to the heart in a year when he'd already been punched too many times.

Barrett sighed and turned over to face the bed where Ambrose lay. The other man was out cold, ankle propped up on some pillows, and he was practically smothered in blankets. He'd given Ambrose an old pair of cargo pants that had been socked away in the bottom of one of the footlockers in the tower, and they'd been comically large on his tall, thin frame. Ambrose had cracked a dry joke about needing two belts and suspenders to hold up the pants, ducked behind the bathroom wall, and then came back out with one hand wrapped around the waistband.

Now he was sleeping like the dead and Barrett was both jealous and confused. He knew what it was like to be a loner, to think he was all right on his own. And most of the time that was true; the quiet was peaceful, and after a chaotic early life and upbringing, the lack of noise was soothing. His therapist said he had PTSD from both his childhood and the things he'd seen as a paramedic. He knew she was right.

But the breathing exercises and medications and meditations didn't quite fill the strange emptiness he sometimes felt. The same emptiness that reared up in those same quiet times he so often cherished. It was cold, that space, that *void*. It wouldn't let him be at...Barrett checked his phone. Three in the fucking morning. Meanwhile, Ambrose slept like a baby.

He wasn't really sure about Ambrose. The man sat like an unfinished question in the back of Barrett's mind. He was pensive and standoffish, but every now and then he'd whip out a dry, slightly unused wit that left Barrett gaping. He supposedly liked to fish, worked as an accountant, and could play guitar and sing rather nicely. Ambrose also liked to take photos of the lake as the mists rolled out with the sun's appearance, and he ran forest trails. His car was gray, his hair was auburn and wavy, growing longer by the day. Ambrose was also a man who didn't mind a bit of winter beard, as he was actively growing one.

That was it. All he knew of Ambrose Tillifer.

Fuck, he knew he wasn't the most open of neighbors but Barrett did know something significant about everyone who lived at Lake Honor. He'd let Brad get to him, the fucking gossip. Barrett loved the old man but Brad would win gold in the gossiping medal. If he hadn't paid attention to Brad, Barrett's first impression of Ambrose would have been the dock and the lake and the music he'd interrupted. Like something out of a bloody book.

Barrett sighed, then against likely his better judgment and free will, turned his head to look at Ambrose again. The man really did sleep through anything, including the kick of wind and snow against the windows as the blizzard's death throes sounded all around them. The cot and the bed were about six feet apart, both of them wanting to be close to the fireplace and Barrett wanting to make sure he was there if Ambrose needed something. This high up, even in winter, the tower was never fully dark. The ambient light off the radio and different bits of meteorological and survey equipment gave just enough to see a few details by.

Ambrose breathed evenly and softly, his hands folded over his stomach. Not a limb was askew and Barrett's bones ached in sympathy. It looked deeply uncomfortable to him, but if the guy wanted to sleep like a vampire in its coffin, so be it. Despite that thought - which made him snicker - the first thing he always thought of when he saw Ambrose was *fascinating*. The man's face was a lesson in how symmetry could be *hard*. From his sharp, wide jawline to his slightly crooked nose and high forehead, Ambrose had the kind of face that should have been on magazine covers. That face made Barrett want to hold a plane angle up to it and see how perfectly aligned the features were. But when he got past his fascination, he could see where the symmetry was thrown in sharp contrast to wide, heavily-lidded eyes and a plush mouth. Not a *pout*, but almost pillowy.

Ambrose could have made so much money with that face.

Shit, now his thoughts were all jumbled up. His mind did that sometimes, bouncing from thing to thing like a child on a sugar high. The quiet helped keep him from feeling so untethered. His job helped. Fishing, knitting, reading, hiking. Beers on Fridays with the other rangers. But in the dark, after the day he'd had? Well, no fucking wonder he couldn't sleep. If it wasn't snowing so hard, he might have gone out to the balcony and stared at the stars. No such luck there. With another sigh, this one feeling like lead in his chest, Barrett stared back up at the ceiling.

After a few minutes, as he shifted again, Ambrose's soft voice broke the silence. "I like fish."

Barrett jolted awake from the half doze he'd been dropping into. "Wha - *what?*"

"I like fish." Ambrose repeated himself with that little bit of a huffy tone, like he was patronizing Barrett. "When I can't sleep, I try to remember the scientific names for fish I've caught or read about."

He had no idea where to go with that. More baffled than confused, Barrett rolled onto his side and propped his head up on his hand. "Okay."

Ambrose shrugged. "I thought it might be a useful tip."

Screw baffled. Barrett was completely befuddled. "Okay, that is ....nevermind. What's the name for rainbow trout?"

"*Oncorhynchus mykiss.*"

"You're making that up."

"I absolutely am not."

"I've got a field guide to fish over there."

Ambrose stared at him. "And?"

Barrett's befuddlement grew. But so did his amusement. "You could be completely fabricating every name."

"But I'm not."

Were they arguing or *bantering*? This was weird. But yet Barrett said, "So you don't want to play the fish name game? Gotta say, if this is supposed to put me to sleep, it's failing."

Barrett swore he saw Ambrose's lip twitch. Otherwise, the man was a moss-covered boulder. "If you would lie back and let me continue -"

"Yeah, continue lying."

A huff and then, "Let me continue *speaking*, I can tell you more. You can verify their sanctity in the morning."

"Fair enough." He knew when he was beat. Plus it'd been pretty hilarious to watch Ambrose try not to smile. Hilarious, sure, for such a sourpuss. It'd also been nice. Barrett was never one to turn down *nice*.

"*Cyprinus carpio.*"

"Okay, that might be legit. Carp?"

"Correct."

The beast that was Barrett's love of cheesy trivia games, the ones he never got to play, rose up with a delighted roar. He also had a thing for praise but that was never getting near Ambrose.

"Go again."

"Hmmm. How about a tricky one?"

"Tricky bullshit, you mean."

Ambrose shoved another pillow under his head and turned to look at Barrett, the tiniest smirk on his face as he said softly, "*Corydoras leucomelas.*"

That was way too elegant for three in the goddamn morning. Barrett flopped back down on his cot. "I got no fucking clue. It's so...ridiculous sounding, I'm prone to believe it's real."

"And you would, again, be correct. And it's the false spotted catfish, in case you were curious."

It wasn't praise, not coming out of that strangely hard yet plush mouth. But it warmed Barrett a little. He yawned, his jaw cracking. "Holy shit, you were right."

As Barrett closed his eyes, his body now heavy with exhaustion, he swore he heard Ambrose mutter, "Can you tell my mother that?"

When the morning blew in with more cold but thankfully no more snow, Ambrose awoke to the smell of coffee. "It's instant, sorry," Barrett said as Ambrose sat up, rubbing his eyes. He felt disgusting, and his mouth tasted like wool shearing.

"Any caffeine is better than none," he said, throat raspy. He started to roll to his side and then remembered his ankle. It slammed into his other one as he lost his balance and landed, askew, on the bed.

Barrett was right there a moment later. "Shit, you okay?"

Ambrose flinched as hands drew near and then Barrett remembered, cursing softly. But not at Ambrose. "No, it's not....I'm not touch-averse. I'm..." He paused, waving his hand then letting it flop limply to the bed. "I'm just sensitive. Always have been."

He could see the big man physically as well as mentally pause. As if weighing Ambrose's words. It was something promising and wholly unexpected. "No worries. And I'm assuming yesterday was through necessity."

"That and probably leftover adrenaline."

Barrett shivered and Ambrose noticed he was wearing a different shirt. This was a thick waffle henley in a pine green. He'd never noticed how dark Barrett's eyes were; they nearly matched his hair in the early morning light. "But sensitive. I got it." He motioned to Ambrose's ankle, which was making itself well known by the deep throb that timed with his heartbeat. "I've got some over the counter painkillers, and we can put more ice on it. Plus, all the better to wash this down with." He plunked a granola bar down and walked back to the kitchenette.

They sipped terrible coffee and ate dry granola bars while Barrett put calls into the station. The first few fritzed out but he finally got through. "Can probably clear a route to you in a few hours. We're already at the bottom of Logger, but with the bridges out we have to go around."

"Yeah, about that." Barrett paused and Ambrose tried not to look like he was eavesdropping. "I get back to the station, got something for Jacques."

"Got it. I'll let him know. You two okay up there?"

"It's shockingly cozy!" Ambrose said loudly.

The voice on the other end laughed. "Right? Sleep like a baby up there."

"Okay, I'm off. I'm not sure who to scold here so talk to you later, Daveed."

"Stay warm, Bear."

There was that nickname again. Or handle. It made complete sense but still struck Ambrose as faintly juvenile for someone so sharp as Barrett. "Okay, couple of hours to kill. Thankfully, this is not the first time I've been stuck in an FL." He rooted around and dug out a battered box of crayons and two coloring books. "We've got *Sprinkle's Perfect Day* or *Rainbow Garden*. You're injured, you pick."

Ambrose almost laughed. This was the weird cherry on top of the strange sundae and he found he didn't mind too much. "Well, how does one say no to rainbows? Or gardens?"

And with nary a smirk, Barrett brought the coloring book and crayons over and then sat on the floor opposite the coffee table as Ambrose slowly moved to the little sofa. "I don't know, that Sprinkle looked mischievous."

"How does one measure the mischievousness of a candy-colored goat?"

Barrett's face was flat as a river stone as he said, "You have clearly never had goats. From the moment they can hobble around, they create chaos."

Unbidden, the image of a goat leading Barrett on a chase rose in his imagination and Ambrose snorted. "I have not, though if social media leads me to believe anything, it's that tiny goats are automatically granted pardons for their many, many crimes."

"Little thieves, every single one." Barrett plucked up a red crayon and started coloring in a tulip. "So, are you an amateur ichthyologist?"

"More like a very thorough fixator. I'll find a hobby, get in deep, and then when I surface I feel as though I've become more than well-versed." He shrugged. It really wasn't a big deal. His intelligence had made him a target for bullies and buffoons all his life, so he didn't go out of his way to talk about it. He could have gone on to law or medical school or been a research scientist. But that all sounded very stressful and so Ambrose wasn't interested.

When he said he was *sensitive*, he meant it. And stress made him jumpy and nervous (and then maybe he didn't sleep for three days in a row and nearly fell out of an open window. He'd hallucinated it was a door.)

"Still impressive." Barrett swapped his red for orange just as Ambrose finished coloring in a daisy with bright pink, so it looked more like a cosmos. "So fish, music -"

"The music isn't a hobby." Ambrose dropped his crayon and sat back on the sofa. "It's a passion." A fierce possessiveness rose up in him. His music was *his*. It wasn't the same as sharing the scientific name of the common carp. Anyone could look that up. Those notes, those chords, came from his mind. But he had to swat all of that away in order to say, "It's meaningful for me. An outlet of pure joy or sadness or whatever I'm feeling in the moment."

He looked away, not sure if Barrett's silence and nonjudgmental, but too dark eyes were expressing something Ambrose simply couldn't understand.

CHAPTER SEVEN

The ankle was sprained but not fractured or broken. Ambrose counted himself lucky, said as much, but Barrett still felt guilty. About what, he wasn't really sure. It's not as though he could have magically known Ambrose was on the trail below before seeing the man's text. And reflecting on that text that evening, he realized that Ambrose had *cared*. In as much to text him and ask if things were all right. So he'd remembered Barrett was a forest ranger, saw the ambulances, assumed Barrett would be in the middle of it.

He couldn't help but wonder what else his neighbor tucked away inside that brain. He seemed the kind of man to stand against a wall at parties, nursing one beer that went warm over hours, and listening to everyone else's conversations.

All of that piled into his head as he made up a massive thermos of coffee and took it, along with containers of oatmeal, eggs, and fruit over to Ambrose's. He knew the man was up, had seen him limping about salting his walk. Instead of fighting with him *again* over Barrett helping him with some tasks - like they had the night before when Barrett dropped him off - he decided food might pave a smoother path.

Fight was a strong word for it. Barrett had offered his help. Ambrose had shook his head and said no, thanks. And when Barrett offered again, something flashed in Ambrose's eyes and whatever it was told Barrett to shut the hell up.

He fired off a quick text.

> **From: Barrett** *Hey, I've got some coffee and oatmeal I can leave outside if you want. Had extra, thought you might be interested.*

His phone dinged thirty seconds later. Barrett had to laugh at the fact that Ambrose put his full name into Barrett's phone. Like he knew another *Ambrose.*

From: Ambrose Tillifer *You can come in. Front door's open. Don't mind the smell.*

That was a....surprisingly neighborly answer. Even with the threat of a mystery smell. A few minutes later he stuck his head inside Ambrose's front door. "Am I walking into a bomb range?"

Then it hit him. Something sweet but tart, buttery yet crisp. Saliva pooled in his mouth. It smelled just like -

"Sorry." Ambrose hobbled into view, wearing a red t-shirt, black track pants, and no socks. Flour dusted his bare forearms but the black apron over his front saved him from the worst of it. "Had to pull the pie out of the oven."

He stepped aside and let Barrett in. "No worries. But..." He was staring at the streak of flour on Ambrose's right arm. *"Mind the smell?* You mean the scent of fresh apple pie."

Ambrose huffed. "It's not a scent everyone likes."

"Maybe if they're insane. Or allergic to apples."

Something like vulnerability flickered in Ambrose's gray eyes. "Well, I'm going to take that as a compliment, I guess."

Barrett grinned. Watching Ambrose twitch even under faint praise was endearing in a way that sidetracked his thoughts for a second. But it was also like digging for treasure in sand. Sift a little, find more sand. Sift more. And eventually you'd find a piece of something pretty surrounded by yet more sand.

Ambrose waved him into the kitchen and he followed, taking the chance to look around. The place was shockingly more lived in than just a few weeks back. Not a box in sight. Art on the walls, countertops and floors gleaming. As he stared at the dove gray sofa dotted with a few orange and yellow pillows, a paisley blanket artfully thrown over one arm, a lump formed in his throat. Ambrose's sofa was almost exactly where Perry's had been. It made sense, facing the big windows and the fireplace, television mounted over the hearth.

They'd had some great nights in front of that hearth; just them and a bottle of bourbon and stories from their lives. Sometimes

Perry would tell him about a new fishing spot or how his herbs were coming in. Sometimes they'd play cards, something Perry sucked at but still enjoyed. His friend had never made him feel young or inexperienced. They were simply two neighbors - two friends - enjoying each other's company.

It was hard, being in this house without Perry.

Barrett sighed and turned to see Ambrose yank the apron over his head and toss it into where he knew the laundry room was. He held out the bag of food and thermos in silent offering, which Ambrose took with a nod and a small smile. "You really didn't have to."

He shrugged. "Made plenty, even after I prepped everything for the week."

"Meal prep is smart." Ambrose sat on one of the barstools on the other side of the counter. "Join me? You did make it, after all."

That got him a smile in return. "I didn't want to intrude."

"Hardly." Ambrose dug out two spoons from a drawer and Barrett took the seat opposite him, extremely grateful. Focusing on the food would keep him from staring at Ambrose's tight, *tight* t-shirt. Damn thing was nearly painted on and Barrett did not want to get caught ogling. Staring.

No, he'd been ogling. Fuck.

They were silent as they shuffled containers and cups and silverware around, as Barrett heaped blueberries into his oatmeal and watched Ambrose do the same. They ate in companionable silence for several long minutes.

Finally, he couldn't stand it anymore. "Hey, so I gotta go to town and get some supplies, groceries, what have you. Do you need anything?" He nodded at the counter. "I'm guessing driving might be tricky."

Ambrose's reply was quick and pointed. "You don't need to do that. I'm stocked enough for a few days."

Barrett winced. Ambrose was going to be laid up with a badly sprained ankle for more than "a few days". Should he push? Ask again? What were the rules in a situation like this? So he did the only thing he knew to do right then: run his mouth. "I'm guessing the doctor told you no driving, running, shoveling. Limited walking until the swelling goes down. It's no trouble to pick up some things -"

Ambrose plunked his coffee cup down and shook his head. "I'm good."

"Ambrose -"

"I'm *good*." The other man's stare was piercing, the set of his jaw firm. "Thank you for the breakfast. If you don't mind, I have some work to catch up on after spending all day at the doctor."

And just like that, he was dismissed, his things put back into the bag and thrust at him with a nod. "Right. I uh...well, yell if you need anything."

"I will."

Barrett knew Ambrose wouldn't. Whatever vulnerability he'd gleamed earlier was now gone and replaced with a cold decisiveness. It wasn't even stubbornness or pride, but something that cut deeper, bled slower. A wound years in the making.

His own pride was a little scuffed but he'd live. Whatever was bothering Ambrose was being pushed on in the moment. All he could do was back off. "All right, well, have a good one."

Ambrose nodded and turned his attention solely to the cooling pie on the counter. Barrett shoved his feet into his boots, his arms into his coat, and left his dead friend's old house. Wondering if making a new friend was worth it as the scent of apple pie lingered in his senses.

Two weeks later

The dead of winter brought with it a blistering cold, the kind that chapped noses and cheeks before it settled into one's bones. Ambrose didn't dare step outside the house without being completely bundled up, leaving only his eyes uncovered. He'd lived in this area his whole life but the snap of true cold always left his eyes and nose stinging. His ankle was better now, but it was still tender, so he made do with getting things delivered.

Music bled into the air, soft and lulling, floating from Barrett's house. Ambrose picked up on it as he hauled the trash bin to the road. His ankle protested the rubbing of his snow boot, but it was a short walk and it felt good getting back to normal. He paused in the driveway and listened. A guitar, played slowly with skill. But the fingering was a little unpracticed. Guitar was the first instrument of many he'd learned and it was still his go-to when he needed to breathe. Playing helped him calm down and focus, helped him drive away some of the anxieties that blew ghostly behind him.

Ambrose hadn't talked to Barrett since that abrupt end to their breakfast. He'd instantly regretted his actions but like any fallible person, hadn't found the courage to apologize. Yet. It had been an instantaneous reaction, a flare of pain and anger at being offered help. Like he was a small child.

And yet.

He knew it was unreasonable, cruel even. The look on Barrett's face had flickered briefly between confusion, disappointment, and hurt. But Ambrose had still pushed him away. Rejected his kindness and his generosity and after the big man was gone, hidden away in his house, the warm oatmeal and strong coffee souring in his mouth. He did this all the time, the shove away to gain some distance and regain traction. But it wasn't even traction, was it? That implied a steadiness, a surety. Ambrose didn't feel either of those things. He felt very alone, trapped in a situation of his own making.

He hadn't even given Barrett the pie. It still sat in the freezer, carefully wrapped and waiting. He'd been baking for him. His rescuer. A friend in the making, perhaps. And then he'd done a full Ambrose and pushed and here they were.

The guitar stopped and Ambrose froze in the driveway. Was he caught? He go could knock now, bring the pie over. He didn't need another excuse to hide; one he knew he'd readily take.

Shit.

Ambrose hurried as fast as the boot on his ankle would let him. He hobbled into the house, to the freezer, nearly knocking himself out with the freezer door as he slipped in a puddle on the floor. Biting back curses and trying to not drop the pie, he wheeled out of the kitchen and through the front door. It had been only a few minutes, but Barrett's house was dark and his big truck rumbled in the drive. Ambrose waved but if Barrett saw him, he didn't acknowledge him.

Ambrose hobbled over, heart thudding. The door to Barrett's house was flung open with a force that made Ambrose's teeth ache. Barrett was there, bag slung over his shoulder. "Ambrose. Sorry, I gotta -"

Ambrose held up the pie. "I was bringing this over."

Barrett flinched, looked away. Something got stuck between Ambrose's ribs at the way Barrett's gaze flicked to the pie, then to the ground. "I gotta go. My nephew's in the hospital." Barrett opened the driver door and flung the bag inside. "Keep it. Give it to me when I get back." With a hurried motion, he yanked at the keyring on his belt, then approached Ambrose with his palm out. "Watch the place for me? I don't know how long I'll be gone." He nodded at Ambrose, eyes going to the boot on his ankle. "If it's more than a few days, I've got a couple of plants in the kitchen that will need water. I'll text you." As Ambrose reached for the key, Barrett frowned and said softly, "I'm sorry to impose."

"It's not. At all." He plucked up the key from Barrett's gloved hand and wrapped his fist around it. "I hope everything's going to be okay."

"Yeah. Thanks. Sorry again."

And then he was gone with the thick scent of exhaust curling around Ambrose. Him and the pie and the muddy snow were left behind as the truck sped down the road and out of sight.

Chapter Eight

"I'm telling you, that's a mistake."

"We've processed it twice, ma'am."

"Don't *ma'am* me. My son is in a coma on the floor above our heads and you're telling me my insurance is invalid?"

Valena was an inch from doing something not good but Barrett caught her by the arm, softening his grip as his fingers encircled her thin wrist. "We'll figure it out," he murmured. The jangle of multiple phones, pens clicking, the intercom overhead buzzing was all getting to be a little too much. It was like the fuzz from the godawful fluorescent lights overhead. All of it overloading his senses. The lack of sleep in twenty-four hours, after a seven hour drive, wasn't helping.

"Bear -"

"Val." He took her phone, wrapped his free arm around her waist, and threw the nurse behind them a nod. She stared at him hard, baleful. Val's outburst probably wasn't even the worst thing she'd seen that morning, but it didn't excuse the behavior.

"Just because you're bigger than me doesn't mean you move me around like some....some...toy!" she snapped as soon as they found an empty waiting room. "That fucker knows he has to provide insurance for Forrest. He *knows*."

Forrest's father was a piece of shit. There'd been fantasies of punching him out a few times, but never had his gut burned with anger more than now; staring at his little sister and her tear-stained face and rumpled clothes, her fists balled in anger. "I'm sorry. I'm so sorry. I just...."

Val sagged in his arms, sobbing. Barrett felt helpless as she cried. He could find them better seats, get her food, keep her company. But that wasn't going to bring Forrest out of a coma or make him better. His entire life - all eight years of it - Forrest had been smaller, slight, pale. Sickly. Then some months ago came the mysterious bruising, anemia, joint pain.

The doctors didn't listen at first. They told Val to get her son outside more, have him run. Give him better food. He'd be fine. Months passed and Forrest grew more tired, more pale. He would be afraid to tell his mom when he was hurting, even when she insisted he speak up. There were more doctors, more questions, more tests, but no real answers.

And Barrett was hours away, torn between his job and his family. So he was there as much as possible. For Val's anger, hot but helpless, during midnight phone calls when she couldn't sleep but was past the point of exhaustion. To see the fragile smile on his nephew's face when they'd video call and Forrest would insist he was okay. To send care packages full of books and games and snacks. And to call Ken, Forrest's father, when he found out that fucker had thrown out the latest care package because his gifts were, "spoiling the boy".

Barrett wanted to throw *him* out a window.

And yesterday, Forrest had collapsed at the top of a staircase at his dad's, cracked his head, and was now comatose while his body tried to repair itself.

"And of course now the doctors are fuckin' scrambling," Val was saying, pulling Barrett back into the moment. She sniffled and wiped her face with the back of her hand; the one with a wedding band tattooed on. "I told them months ago I was worried it was leukemia but they just brushed me off. And now he's...he's..."

Barrett pulled her close and let her cry. She needed someone to help steady her, even though Val would never admit it. They were both stubborn but his sister's strain of it was forged in the fires of being a single mother and someone who had escaped a loveless, emotionally and financially abusive marriage. Forrest was her whole world and while Val was still *Val*, she saw her kid as her top priority.

"Have you unloaded on them yet?" he asked softly, pulling her closer as her sniffles slowed.

"No. But if you can be there when I am...." She trailed off and Barrett just *knew* what she was thinking. How she'd been sick and alone at sixteen, Barrett a tender nineteen and her only source of company while she recovered from surgery and the infection that had settled in afterwards. The surgery hadn't been serious but the rash and swelling and fever afterwards, her stitched wound looking like something you'd see on a plague victim? That had been brutal.

And while their parents tasked Barrett with Val's care while they fucked off to gods knew where, a resentment grew. It festered and boiled like Val's infection, symbiotic to this last, final heartbreak.

So yeah, he'd be there. He'd always be there for Val, and for Forrest. Fuck everyone else.

A nurse found them not minutes later, saying the doctor wanted to talk. Val stiffened beside him, the line of her mouth so tight her lips almost disappeared. "I'm gonna fucking kill them," she whispered, only loud enough for him.

"I know." He smirked, knowing the expression was ugly. "Want me to hold them down?"

"Would you?"

"Of course."

Barrett wrapped an arm around his sister as they took the elevator up, then walked the long hall to Forrest's room. The first glance of his nephew, tiny and so pale he was almost translucent, made his heart stutter. He wanted to rush forward, gather the boy in his arms, and sob. But Val's death grip on his hand pulled him into focus, steadied him.

The doctor waiting for them was tall and reedy and his glasses reflected almost too much light. Barrett didn't like that they couldn't see his eyes. The nurse with him was giving them the long, hard stare of a lifer who had seen too much.

"Ah, good. I wanted to talk about Forrest's blood tests." The doctor gave Barrett a look, one he was intimately familiar with. He was a big man with a scruffy beard and long, dark hair that curled too much at the ends. His clothes were never new enough, his nails never clean enough. "We should talk in private, Ms. Miguel."

"We are in private." Val motioned to the room full of machines beeping, bleating, keeping Forrest alive. "We're the only ones here. I don't think Forrest minds."

The doctor nodded, apparently not one to press an angry, upset mother. But Barrett knew that tone, cold as ancient stone and sharper than any dagger. He reevaluated; the doctor's instincts were shit. "There's no easy way to say this. Your son has leukemia. It's manageable, but he's been ill for some time, according to his records."

"Go on." Val leaned forward but her grip on Barrett's hand was so tight he swore he heard his bones protest. He couldn't get away now, even if he wanted to. He'd always be by Val's side, through everything. He wasn't going anywhere, but his hind brain was screaming to get away because Val had the countenance of someone ready to fuck shit up. And he didn't know that anyone would blame her.

The doctor's words were a blur of difficult to follow medical jargon and what sounded to Barrett like bullshit, but Val was nodding along, tapping her chin with a finger. Looking utterly nonplussed. That thing in the back of Barrett's mind sent up little red flags, so he gave her hand a gentle shake.

I know you're mad. More than mad. Think of Forrest.

"So we'll need to start treatment now, but I see your insurance has been denied. We'll need to clear that up sooner rather than later." The steely-eyed nurse thrust a clipboard at Val, who handed it to Barrett without taking her eyes off the doctor. "Any questions?"

"Just one, for now." Val put out her hand. "I want your cell number. Or pager. Or whatever I can have to get in touch with you immediately."

The startled look on the doctor's face was quickly followed up by, "I don't give out my personal information -"

Val leaned in. "You will for me. We're in the Spinley Ward of this hospital. August Spinley's daughter, the head of his vast business empire, is my boss. And she said if I ran into trouble, I should call her and she'd...hmmm, what was the phrase?" Her smile grew but he knew it wasn't the nice kind. It weighted the very air in the room until it sat like lead in his lungs. "I remember now. She'd *take care of it.*"

The nurse silently handed Val a scribbled on scrap of paper and he wanted to laugh *so badly*. Val never, ever used her boss as a crutch or a lynchpin but now, with her son's health and life on the line?

Val would have found a way to crack the planet in half to keep him safe.

"You can't do that," the doctor choked out, his eyes narrowed, mouth thin, as he swiped the paper from Val's hand. "That's personal and it's a breach of my privacy."

Val leaned in, teeth bared. "My son's health doesn't give a *fuck* about your privacy."

The doctor looked like he might lunge for Val, but Barrett stepped in front of her and crossed his arms. He knew what he looked like and, much like his sister, had learned a long time ago to pull that kind of shit only when it was *absolutely* necessary. "The best care. The best doctors," he rumbled, not breaking his stare with the man trying desperately to pull himself up to his full height. Barrett was still taller. Some twisted little part of him smiled in glee at the doctor's obvious discomfort. "I'm guessin' you don't get talked to like that often, huh?" He leaned a little harder on the coastal accent that had been trained out of him by "well-meaning" relatives after his parents left he and Val behind.

It'll make you sound inbred.

Just like your father, too backwards, too stupid. Straighten up, smarten up, and don't sound so goddamned redneck for once.

And his favorite, from his grandmother: *The world isn't kind to people like us, Barrett. Don't give 'em an excuse to look at you like you're worth less than the mud on their shoes. The mud that they pay people to wipe off for them.*

Silently, Val handed the doctor her phone and Barrett could hear Eleanor Spinley's rich, cultured voice on the other end. "I understand you're causing issues with my employee's son, Doctor...?"

"Robinson," the doctor bit out.

And the conversation was lost to his ears, though watching the doctor get redder in the face was prize enough. He realized Val had moved to Forrest's bedside, her hand wrapped in his little limp one as the nurse talked to her quietly.

As soon as the doctor thrust Val's phone back at her, he turned heel and left. "Ass," Val muttered.

"He is. He's also a really good oncologist." The nurse looked up from checking the clear, snaking IV lines; with every touch of her gloved hands, Barrett felt his gut clench. His little nephew looked so sick, so sunken and those plastic tubes stuck into that thin, papery skin made him shiver.

The nurse left with a pat to Val's shoulder and finally they were alone. The tether of the little boy who shared their blood stretched between them. "Val?"

She sniffled, not looking at him as she gripped Forrest's hand. "Ken's been blowing up my phone but I don't want him here."

Anger curled in him. Forrest's father had partial custody, so Val couldn't block him from seeing his son. But Barrett could sure as fuck play bodyguard. "You want me to stay?"

"Please."

Gone was the bright, furious woman who wanted to rip into that doctor with her bare hands, face twisted into a snarl. Now she was Val. His sister. His nephew's mother.

The person who had saved him when things were really dark. When he'd been wondering if any of it was worth sticking around for.

Barrett got them coffee and bags of pretzels from a vending machine down the hall, then took up a post outside Forrest's room. Val didn't say it but he knew she needed some time - quiet, alone - to spend by the kid's bedside. So he sat in the rickety chair that cut into his thighs and waited.

"Shit," he muttered about an hour later when he remembered Ambrose. He'd been content to watch the nurses scuttle about, dodging beds and doctors and patients and family members, lulled into a fog by their movement and the drone of the intercom. He owed the man an apology and from the frozen pie in Ambrose's hands, he was pretty sure the man had been on the same thought track.

So they were both shit at making friends. Hell, even being polite. Barrett had noticed how uncomfortable Ambrose seemed to be when anyone was kind to him and that made a fierce kind of protectiveness flare in his own chest. Everyone deserved kindnesses and thoughtful words and honest compliments. Ambrose damn near flinched when he'd offered to pick up some groceries. Barrett had his own damage, forged in the fire of a tumultuous childhood spent raising Val instead of being a child himself. He never regretted a thing, but that stuff left an indelible mark.

He wondered what marks Ambrose bore, and how deep they went.

> **From: Barrett** *Sorry about this morning. My nephew's sick and they live far away. I owe you a proper apology when I get back. And a meal because I'm gonna be gone for at least a few days. Sorry again for tossing all that on you.*

He sent it without overthinking too much (how proud Val would be), then fired off some texts to Meredith and Jacques to let them know he was going to be out. Jacques could easily switch up the team leads for a few days and Meredith would cover for him. She liked the time and a half pay and with the holidays coming up and a dozen or so nieces and nephews to buy for, the money would be welcome.

"Ah, so Valena called in her guard dog. Lovely."

Ken Morano was the kind of rich prick who thought top of the line gear would make him a great hiker with no practice of any kind. He was also the kind of arrogant asshole who never did any proper research or went out with a guide before attempting a high level trail, expecting his fancy gear to save his ass. Barrett knew because many years ago, he'd received a call to go rescue a hiker who had fallen and likely broken his arm. That hiker had been Ken, the arm had been broken in two places, and while they were getting Ken warmed up and tended to, Val had swung by to pick up more trail maps for some friends.

This had been over a dozen years ago, when Val lived within fifteen minutes of Lake Honor, and when Ken had just been a handsome but foolish stranger. Barrett regretted that their paths had ever crossed. Ken had been ideal for a long time, until he wasn't.

Barrett knew that Ken considered him the catalyst for he and Val's divorce. But with Ken it was never a simple issue. There had been moments over the years that rankled but he'd kept the peace for his sister and his nephew. Even if that meant buffering Ken's snide little comments about Val not dressing up for him anymore and then, when Barrett would stare at him, listening to Ken say, "I was just joking!"

But when Val had called him to come over and silently handed him a stack of papers, her face ashen, her hair limp, and bruised purple bags under her eyes, he'd known there was something else going on. They'd spent an entire evening bent over her expensive as hell dining room table, piecing together Ken's various deceptions, frauds, and schemes. Shell companies where he was socking away money. Handwritten notes from mistresses. Purchases of jewelry and flowers and lingerie.

"It's almost like a bad Jackie Collins book," Val had said in a whisper, her eyes so sad but the grim line of her mouth determined. Val wasn't anyone's tool or castaway, and he knew she wouldn't take this lightly. And in the end, it had been Ken's own narcissism to sink him during the divorce, along with police reports of trespassing on Barrett's property while Val and Forrest had stayed with him during those weeks. Ken hadn't been stupid enough to mess with Barrett's government truck, but he or someone he'd hired had keyed Val's car, slashed the tires, and left yowling screeds in Barrett's mailbox. The fucker had always blamed Barrett for the divorce, which was baffling. But then again, the man had no ability to look at his own deeds and see the wrongs piled up like so much trash.

"Ken," Barrett said stiffly, not moving from his seat and not putting his phone away. The recording app he kept in the background, at all times, required only the press of a button. He knew Val could hear them just outside the room but wasn't about to take the chance. Ken was a grade-A asshole, and a litigious one. He'd threatened to sue Barrett more than once when Val had left his sanctimonious, cheating ass. All while festering his anger in harrassment and property damage, though they could never fully prove Ken had been behind the slashed tires and keyed car doors. Likely because he'd hired someone to do the dirty work for him.

Val was there a moment later, Barrett sitting between them like some kind of unkempt wall. "I said in the morning," Val bit out in a harsh whisper as she crossed her arms and stood in front of Forrest's door. "Visiting hours are almost over. And you have papers to sign."

Ken mirrored her stance. His perfect, pretty face got a particular sneer on it when the man was feeling especially assholery. It made Barrett want to punch him. Years of Val fighting him in court, years of fighting for their kid, getting put through fifteen layers of hell. And yet that sneer was the only thing that made him see red.

He didn't remember shooting to his feet or putting himself physically between them. All he recognized was his own voice dropped into a growl. "You heard her, Ken."

The sneer dropped, taking Barrett's skyrocketing blood pressure with it. But Ken couldn't just let it go. "You know, Bartie, this really is a conversation between two adults who share a child. Why don't you..." And he thrust a one hundred dollar bill out. "Go get Dandelion from the kennel and take her home with you. This should cover it."

Barrett waited.

"It's that or my secretary picks her up, only to drop the mutt off at the pound. And then I'll have to hear her complain about going out in the snow." His sneer made Barrett's ire rise but he kept his focus, kept breathing.

Val exploded from behind Barrett. "That is Forrest's dog! You can't do that -"

"Ma'am. Ma'am." The same nurse from earlier was now in the fray, hands out placatingly. "This is the ICU and there are other patients here. We can't have yelling or shouting." She slapped Ken with an icy stare. "If you need to have a conversation, take it outside. Where it won't disturb the other patients and their families."

"Go." Val's entire being was tense; she was practically vibrating with anger at Barrett's side. "Forrest will want to know his dog's okay."

"Val..."

She flashed her phone screen at him and he recognized the name of her attorney pulled up in her contacts. "I got it."

With a deep breath, Barrett dropped the money to the ground, kissed his sister on the forehead, and walked down the hall toward the elevators. It was only after he was squashed into a corner of one of those metal boxes that he turned the recorder off on his phone. His worry over Val was never going to abate. She would always be his little punk, climbing trees, singing off key, throwing gummy bears at him; usually the same ones they'd stolen from the corner store when that was all they could manage to stick in their pockets.

"Gummy bears or go hungry," he'd said a few times, watching her little eyes grow wide at the sight of big bottles of soda and loaves of bread. Sometimes their parents left food for them, and sometimes they were left to scrounge. Or steal. He'd never felt *good* about doing that, but it was survival first, morality second.

And then their parents would return from wherever they'd gone and things would be all right for a while. Sometimes months, sometimes just days; days he tracked by marking his wall with a pen. And when he'd lived with his grandmother for too long after their parents' divorce, he emancipated himself from that "care" at sixteen. And he'd fought to take Val with him. No one put up a fuss, just shrugged and said, "Take her".

Not everyone should be a parent. His mother and father, his grandmother, Ken....worthless.

The rage that had long burrowed inside his chest, the thing he kept locked away lest it turn him into a monster, started to reappear. It made his hands tremble and his breathing shallow and the moment he was free of the antiseptic-smelling, cloying air of the hospital, Barrett collapsed onto a bench on the edge of the parking lot. It was too late to make the calls he needed to in order to help Val, but at least he could go get Dandelion and get her set up at Val's place.

He could be useful tonight. Tomorrow, his rage would fuel the next steps.

His phone dinged and a message from Ambrose appeared.

> **From: Ambrose** *I'm quite sorry about yesterday. I don't do well when people offer me assistance. It's a fatal flaw. But yes, I can check on your plants. I hope your nephew will be okay. Please text me if you need anything else.*

His neighbor's oddly formal message made something kick in his chest. The rage burrowed there was pushed back down for a moment. It took him a few tries to get his fingers to work, sliding across the smooth glass face of his phone.

> **From: Barrett** *Hey, no worries. We're all fucked up in some way or another. Some of us more so. We can swap war stories over the dinner I promised. You know I make a mean fish filet. Thank you for checking on the plants, and the house. I'm not sure how long I'll be gone. And Forrest, my nephew, is in a coma. I hope he'll be okay but we don't know anything yet.*

Barrett put his phone away and gave himself one minute to get his shaky breathing back under control before hopping in his truck and heading for the kennel. His phone didn't ding again, but that was okay.

Ambrose let Barrett's text sit. Worry focused on a child he didn't know wasn't helping, but he could worry about the man he wanted to get to know. His own hot-and-cold, back-and-forth attitude wasn't doing anyone any good. And it was unfair to Barrett, who seemed like a good man stuck in an untenable situation.

Gods, he let himself get in his own head too much. He was being old Ambrose, stuffy and curt and unkind. He'd moved to his own place to be alone, but alone didn't mean...

Deep in his heart, Ambrose knew he could love and be loved in return. He knew his hang-ups, his issues with his mother, all his flaws got in the way of most relationships. His friends were close but distant because they knew Ambrose needed his time and space. There were some dates, a few relationships that lasted months, maybe even half a year.

And then Preston and the four years afterwards. Bliss. Then not.

The cold shoulder. The lies. The hiding. The cheating. So much that neither of them could rectify when it all fell apart. Preston had cheated first, then Ambrose in revenge. He knew that made him an ugly person, a sad one.

He wasn't that Ambrose anymore. Angry at everyone and everything and lashing out where he could. He wasn't ugly or sad anymore. No more anger. No more noise, no more annoyances.

But he was *lonely*. He could see that now. He'd assumed himself irredeemable years ago, after that angry, sad fuck at a hotel with a stranger who had flirted with him at the bar and not ten minutes later had him against the bathroom wall, his mouth around Ambrose's cock.

He'd been so stupid. And then he'd confessed, and Preston had followed him down that very dark hole. All their sins out in the open, all utterances and secret touches with clammy hands admitted to. Forgiven. But it had broken *them*, and that was it.

Ambrose had felt himself withdraw in those days and weeks afterwards. Like a fucking crab with a too small shell, desperate to stay hidden among the reefs. And here he was four years later, still convinced that shell fit.

He pushed inside Barrett's cabin, scrounging for the switch he knew was nearby. Most of the cabins had the same or similar floor plan, so unless he was going into some kind of upside-down land, the switch would be...there.

Ambrose gazed around, astonished. Yes, it was the twin to his cabin in room size and layout but this was *gorgeous*. Barrett's cabin was a modern delight, all bare beams and gray wood floors, matte appliances and mounted records and bookshelves so packed they groaned. Okay, maybe it had been wrong of him to assume the cabin would be cozy but dated, maybe decked with one too many blankets knitted by arthritic hands and a fireplace that seemed to never run out of wood. But this was just visually fucking amazing. It looked lived in but clean, sleek but not slick. It invited his senses to play about, begging for his fingertips to run over nubby fabrics and leather book spines and trace over perfectly preserved record sleeves.

But the wall on the far side of the living room was what pulled him under. Three guitars, all pristine replicas of famous models, hung there. Waiting. So lovingly cared for it made him want to pick them up, but he would *never* without permission. A musician's instrument was sacred.

But he did ache with desire to know more about the man. His neighbor. Someone he maybe wanted to befriend.

The world felt a little askew. It wasn't a bad feeling, necessarily, but it did its damndest to knock the wind out of him as he walked over to the kitchen and found the plants. Two massive violets on their own stands, a few cacti that were certainly fine, and a stunning pink hibiscus, the flowers bigger than his own hand. Two of them were halfway open, with three more buds just waiting.

A quick check of the soil told him only the violets needed water, but as he stood before the hibiscus, unable to take his eyes from its beauty, he got out his phone and snapped a picture of it.

> **From: Ambrose** *The plants are watered. I left the cacti alone. What about this beauty?*

The reply came quickly.

> **From: Barrett** *Meet Stella. I've had her for ten years and it's my longest relationship. She's okay for a few days more. Thanks for swinging by. I owe you dinner.*

> **From: Ambrose** *You've said that twice now. You're really not indebted to me. Stella is glaring right now, if you can't tell.*

His phone rang and, startled, Ambrose fumbled with it for a moment before answering. "Barrett?"

The other man was chuckling into the phone. "Ah, shit. You have no idea how much I needed that laugh this morning. Thanks."

His face was getting too warm already. Praise always felt strange, both too foreign and too close. "Sure. Though I refrained from taking pictures of the three yet to flower and making bud jokes."

There was a snort, then, "Wait. You smoke?"

"For years. Every other night or so." He was biting his cheek at this point, torn between wanting to laugh until he fell over or cried. Surely Barrett was just playing Ambrose's game, avoiding mentions of something more obscene like *tightly furled buds*. He didn't know Barrett, or his preferences.

"Shit," Barrett said, more quietly now. "Well, look at us. Two lonely fuckers out in the woods smoking pot and enjoying the scenery."

"That....honestly sounds okay to me." He paused, the question weighing him down. He had to ask. "Lonely?"

The answer was immediate. "You're not? Cause I'm not one to usually make assumptions about people I don't know but uh...you don't move to Lake Honor unprepared to be in all that quiet. Alone. I think everyone around there is lonely on some level. I know I am."

This was too heavy a conversation for the phone. Too close to the truth. Ambrose stumbled over his words, trying to catch them even as they tumbled out of his mouth without his permission. "I think I am, too."

A sound, like a sigh or a breath being blown out. Ambrose could almost feel it over the phone. "Well, we're neighbors. I wouldn't mind being friends. Could use one right about now." And then Barrett chuckled and Ambrose realized he liked that sound; the rumbling bass of it, the echo in his bones that didn't feel so hollow. "I'll be gone another couple of days. Keep an eye on the house for me? The plants should be fine."

"Yeah, sure." What else could he say? It was a favor, an easy one, and it's not like Ambrose minded. "Are you okay? You left fast."

"Fuck, yeah, I uh...." There was a sound, like Barrett shifting the phone, and then the clear, deep bark of a dog. "I apparently now have a dog."

"A dog?"

"Yeah, she's my nephew's but he's sick so I suppose she's mine for the time being. Say hi, Dandi." Another bark, and then Barrett laughed. "Big dummy. She's huge but cuddly."

"I love dogs." The words came so fast again. Ambrose wanted to slap himself. What was it about Barrett that made him want to just talk and talk, ramble and confess? "What kind is she?"

"A massive mutt. Honestly, I think mostly Great Dane but she's not quite as big as one. Are you, Dandi?"

"Dandi?"

"Dandelion, but not easy to yell when she bolts. I'll introduce you two when I get back." Then Barrett fell quiet in that way that had Ambrose glancing at the phone screen as if the call dropped. "Thanks again. This shit sucks and I'm uh...a bit of a mess right now. I didn't mean to dump anything on you."

"It's not dumping. I promise."

"Okay. Good. Thanks. And I gotta go, but let me know what you like to eat." Barrett laughed lightly and something eased through Ambrose's chest. Relief, maybe? "Not fish, if you don't mind. I've had my fill."

Now that was a pity. Barrett's carefully vacuum-sealed fish, packed with spices that reminded Ambrose of the best jambalaya he'd ever had, had been perfect. "Fair enough. I'll text you." And instead of saying goodbye, Ambrose said softly, "Text or call if you need an ear. Sometimes it's hard to take all that on your own, Barrett."

"Shit." Ambrose liked the way he said it, the quiet rasp of it in his ear sending shivers down his spine. "That's kind. You sure you want a stranger dumping their shit on you?"

"You saved my life. We're not strangers."

"We ain't friends, either."

"No, we're not. Not yet."

Another sigh. "Fair enough. I'm not easy to be friends with, Ambrose."

"Me either."

"Well, look at us. Two lonely fuckers out in the woods smoking pot and enjoying the scenery." The repetition made Ambrose laugh and Barrett joined him after a few long seconds. "Thanks. Talk later?"

"Yeah, sounds good."

The line clicked in his ear and, chuckling to himself, Ambrose left Barrett's house and locked up. It was a lot for one day, but instead of feeling overwhelmed, he felt strangely better. Thinking about Preston had shoved things to the surface Ambrose would rather stay buried. Not the healthiest tactic, but he'd been in survival mode for so long, he wasn't sure how to do anything else. Be anything else.

Maybe this was an actual new start.

The day passed in a blur, work and chores making him move, making him forget for a while. Ambrose was prepared to go to bed feeling drained but hopeful. And when Barrett's text came in while Ambrose was curled up in a chair, reading, he jumped to answer. If he was being honest with himself, he'd been waiting for the phone to ding all day.

> **From: Barrett** *Sorry I can't talk more tonight. I was with my sister all day. My nephew woke up. I feel like someone hit me with a truck.*

What could he say to that? Congratulations? Glad to hear it? You must be so relieved? It all felt trite.

> **From: Ambrose** *No worries. I'm nearly falling asleep in my chair. Your nephew waking up must be a huge relief. I'm glad you were there for him and your sister.*

> **From: Barrett** *Me too. And thanks. Good night, Ambrose.*

> **From: Ambrose** *Good night*

And that was it. The floating lightness in his chest lifted once more and he felt better. More than he had in a long, long time. Ambrose fell asleep that night as soon as he hit the pillows, missing the text that came in from an unknown number.

> **From: Unknown** *Ambrose, it's Preston. I know we said we wouldn't contact each other again like this but I...need to see you. I miss you. I'm in the area, I want*

to swing by if that's all right. I admit I snooped and found you. Talk soon? Please?

Chapter Nine

T he text from Preston should have sent him into a tailspin but after more than four years apart, he could only feel a sense of apathy, but one mixed with a tiny spark of excitement. He knew someone would eventually track him down; it wasn't hard, given how public home purchase records were. He found himself grateful, in some strange way, that it was Preston and not his mother who had found him. Not that his mother would ever take the time to learn how to seek people out on the internet.

He and Preston had parted on bad terms but had, over the years, regained some equilibrium. It took a lot of therapy and soul searching on his part, but Ambrose had always been one to seek closure, even in small ways. He didn't dig through Preston's social media and obsess over every post, but Preston would occasionally "like" a line from a poem Ambrose posted. That very limited contact helped him maintain a sense of dignity.

The flutter in his belly at the thought of seeing Preston again was stayed by that deep desire to not have anyone from his "old life" get close to the bubble of safety he had built. So his message back wasn't terse but wasn't immediately accepting, either.

From: Ambrose *I'm not completely averse but why now? We made our peace years ago.*

From: Preston *I've been taking care of my shit. Therapy. Meditation. I still miss you, though. You were the only person I've ever loved like that. Part of my healing, I think, is to see you again.*

Something about that last sentence...like the tip of a knife over a scar. The cold edge of metal over still-sensitive skin. The memories came rushing back. Preston knew him like no one else, and even when they fought, when they forgave, when they fucked...it all was mixed up in some sealed part of him. He didn't want to open that door again, but nothing said he *had* to provide any real opening.

He would always love Preston. And he was lonely. He wasn't looking to bring his ex back into his life in any meaningful way. But maybe it would be a temporary balm for his loneliness.

From: Ambrose *I'm home all day but I'm working.*

From: Preston *That's more than I was hoping for.*

But unlike before, he wasn't going to wait around for Preston to show. Ambrose poured himself more coffee and sat at his desk, spreadsheets open and waiting for him. His bills wouldn't pay themselves and he sure as hell would never go back to relying on someone again.

By the time another client's work was done and the sun had started its downward path to the horizon, any nerves or worry he'd had over Preston's sudden reappearance had vanished. This client was particularly precise and it was the kind of work Ambrose enjoyed. And he charged well for it. The money coming in for this job and the next few would let him sock away some cash for the spring. The house needed new exterior doors and trim, on top of more aesthetic updates he wanted to make.

Ambrose thought back to Barrett's gorgeous interior. He remembered very clearly the clean lines and precise corners, the muted colors next to splashes of bright oranges and yellows and blues. Maybe Barrett could give him the names of the people he worked with to create such a stunning space. Ambrose had always yearned for something sparse but cozy, but anything done to the house would take a lot of cash.

The knock at the door came as he was pouring over his financial documents on his computer. He'd been vicious with cutting any unnecessary spending, but the holes in his socks and the worn, sometimes fraying cuffs of his sweaters were proof enough that he needed to give himself a little room.

His head was full when the knock came and he spun in his chair quickly, heart pounding.

From: Preston *Gods I hope I have the right house.*

From: Ambrose *Be right there. I heard you knock. Was head down in some documents.*

Ambrose could almost see the smile on Preston's face at his acknowledgement of being, once again, absorbed in a task. For all the man's faults, and all their flaws together, Preston was aware of how Ambrose's mind worked. Hyper-focused on a task until it was done and very little would move him from it.

Ambrose stood, straightened his sweater, pushed his hair from his face, and went to the front door. A queer sense of calm washed over him, driving nerves and worry to the edges of his mind. Were they not different? Older, wiser, smarter? He was not the same Ambrose, and he did not expect to see the same Preston on the other side of the door.

"Preston."

Preston stood there, open-mouthed. Blatantly gaping, staring. *Admiring.* It laid on his skin like a burn and then burrowed deep; the hot, almost intrusive way Preston's gaze raked over him. The selfish, arrogant part of him preened. But he was not blind to the way Preston's undercut drew the eye to his angular face. The glasses were new, too, thick rimmed and stylish. But Preston was still *him* in some ways: heavy fleece jacket open to hint at a dark red button-down tucked into tight jeans. The boots were a little hipster, trying too hard to be fashionable in a landscape that sneered at thin soles and fake leather. But the necklace lying on his chest was the same. Ambrose had given it to him, a pretty thing of silver and amber (joking it would remind Preston of him. *Ambrose. Amber.*)

"Fuck. I..."

Preston crashed into him. Ambrose accepted his weight easily, let him carry them through the doorway. His lips remembered the feel of the ones on him now, the taste of desperation and *want* heavy on the tongue that flicked against his.

He should push Preston away. He *should*.

He couldn't.

Preston's body remembered his. Ambrose's senses were jolted, shocked with the taste and smell of a man who had been at his side for years. He'd *missed this*. And he was terribly, horribly lonely.

And then his hands weren't his, grabbing at the thick ponytail of dark hair, shoving that cold fleece away, grasping at muscled shoulders. Ambrose's knees went weak as Preston pushed against him, into him. His back hit the wall and dimly, in the distance, he heard the door shut.

"Preston." He barely managed to mumble it against the lips pressing into his, but he needed to get it out.

Preston startled back with a jolt, dark brown eyes wide. Shock? Regret? "Shit. *Shit*. I..." His ex looked away. "I lost my mind. I grabbed you -"

"I let you."

Preston's gaze cut back to him, sharp but hopeful. "You have to mean that. I can't..."

"I do. And I know." Ambrose curled his fingers into that ponytail, the thing at just the right height for him to grab and yank on. He pulled gently and Preston's moan echoed through him, down his spine. A bolt of lightning his body remembered; that he remembered.

Preston leaned his forehead against Ambrose's. "Tell me. Please."

"Fuck. Fuck, Preston..." This was insane. He didn't care. He *needed* to feel this. "Touch me."

Preston groaned

"We don't need these," he said softly, pulling Preston's glasses down. "Get your shoes and coat off."

He let Preston shrug out of his fleece and toe his shoes off while he put those pretty frames aside, safe on the kitchen counter. "You smell so fucking good." The voice in his ear, the press of warm muscle behind him, hemming him in. He remembered this, too. His body responded, cock growing hard, pressed almost painfully into the edge of the counter. Preston traced the side of his neck with his tongue and Ambrose sagged, groaning. "So fucking good."

Preston knew his weak spots and was taking him apart by the seams. Plucking. Pulling. *Licking*. "Ah, fuck, Pres." Ambrose arched back and Preston grabbed him by the hips. A hard cock against his cleft and Ambrose was reduced to whimpering.

Ambrose reached back, trying to grab at Preston, wanting to pull that thick ponytail again. Maybe wrap it around his fist and crush their mouths together. Relearn Preston's taste, hold him still while he nipped at the sensitive spot under his jaw; the one that never failed to make the other man hiss in pleasure. Ambrose liked that hiss, liked what it belied with no words but always *always* made his blood heat.

Preston relented, pushing even harder, chest to back, wedging a thigh between his. A knee teased at his balls and that hard cock was pressed so tightly between his cheeks, Ambrose wanted to sob with need. "Did you come here to tease me or fuck me?"

The growl he got back for that sent shivers across his skin. Sharp teeth bit down on his earlobe. "I came here to see you, then I saw you and lost my mind. I always do around you."

Ambrose turned. "We're not together."

One dark eyebrow lifted. "We're not. Four years."

"Four years," he agreed. "What is this? A...fuck down memory lane?"

Preston's laugh was warm and rumbly and for a moment, Ambrose remembered Barrett's laugh. Similar but deeper, more hearty. More earnest. Preston's slipped and slid, sensual but distanced in its own way. The distance of four years. And then Preston's hands were on his face, palms sliding against Ambrose's jaw as he said, "I was thinking friends with benefits."

He couldn't help the snark. "We'd have to be friends first."

"We would." He leaned harder into Ambrose, almost to the point of pain. His nerves were already jangled but this was...different. Preston had never been so demanding, so desperate. He found he liked this side of his ex. A little strung out, a little thready breathing, a little more darkness in already dark eyes.

"I'm okay with benefits for now." And he was. Because he was lonely and desperate and wanting and weak and all of the things he hated about being a *goddamned human who needed others*. He hated that weakness, that swirling void waiting to be filled.

Silently, he pulled Preston upstairs, to his bedroom, and was shrugging out of his sweater when, suddenly, there was a pair of lips on his neck and a hand on each hip. He was rooted, frozen in place by a few warm, steady touches. How fucking desperate he was, how pathetic. Ambrose bit down on the self-hated, determined to shred it to pieces so he could enjoy this. To remember the way Preston felt; the way anyone felt.

"Let me."

"You don't -" Ambrose was cut off as Preston pushed his sweater up. Warm fingers trailed over the knobs of his spine and he shivered. "You don't have to be kind."

"This isn't that kind of game, Ambrose."

"I know." His sweater was dropped to the floor and then Preston's hands were on him once more and his thoughts *stopped*. He kissed Preston hard, surging up into it, fingers flying over buttons and zippers while Preston cupped the back of his head just right and licked into his mouth.

Another tug and Preston was over him, on him, both of them half naked with Ambrose pinned to the mattress. Preston was a little thicker in the chest and shoulders from what Ambrose remembered. The muscles shifted under smooth skin and wiry chest hair and he had to touch. Preston bit down on a curse, eyes dropping shut. "Fuck."

He wanted to unravel Preston, to take his time. But the burning under his skin screamed for release. "Fuck me."

That's all it took to get Preston moving. They shoved at jeans and boxers and socks until naked and panting and Preston was groaning at the sight of Ambrose spread out before him. Ambrose widened his legs and let Preston look his fill. "Not like you haven't seen it before."

"No, but I missed it." Preston fell onto him and Ambrose shivered at the feather-light touches on his chest, his thighs. The breath ghosting over his throbbing cock. "Still in the drawer?"

He was already diving to the side as Ambrose nodded. "I fixed it," he said as Preston made a pleased noise at the way the drawer slid open smoothly. "Drove me nuts."

"I'm not surprised." Preston came back with a small bottle of lube and two condoms. He dropped both to the bed so he could run his hands up Ambrose's legs. Gooseflesh raised everywhere he touched and Ambrose let his eyes slam shut, let himself *have this*. "I've missed this."

"What?"

And that warm hand with its slender fingers wrapped around his cock and began to stroke. It was so good, just those few passes of a palm, the brush of fingers, and Ambrose was already moaning.

"Been a while? Me, too." Preston thumbed at his slit, pressing in exactly like he knew was right; the exact way he knew made Ambrose shiver. "Just like this?"

"*Fuck*. Yes." He forced his eyes open so he could watch Preston watching him, watching his own hand squeeze and touch and stroke. "Come on, Pres, fuck me."

"So impatient." But Preston was finally dragging Ambrose's legs up, guiding them around his waist. When they'd first fucked (and it was *fucking*, making love came later), Ambrose didn't want to be face to face. It was cliche and stupid, but face to face meant staring at each other, maybe even kissing if the coordination worked. It had been far too personal at a time when his body burned with need. The need Ambrose had tried to wish away when he was younger and annoyed at how his body responded to a cute boy in his class or the college kid he passed on the street.

He should turn on his stomach and take the *personal* out of this situation but that time had passed. In more ways than one. He slipped deeper into the vee of Preston's thighs and blatantly put himself on display. "Lucky you."

Preston was quick to roll a condom down his fingers while Ambrose growled little curses at him to hurry up. But when he finally had fingers inside him, rubbing and stretching and working him open until he was ready to sob, he grabbed for Preston, hauled him down. Kissed him hard, bit his lower lip, fucked his tongue into that mouth he knew so well. Preston was trembling, torn between a moan and a filthy spit of words about how *good* and *warm* and *soft* Ambrose was deep inside.

"So soft, so unlike that shell you wear." Preston's mouth was on his ears now and there were three fingers inside him, crooking high and up and making stars pop behind Ambrose's eyes. He needed, wanted to come, but he wanted to come on a cock.

"Fuck me or get out," he snapped, unable to get Preston's fingers in any deeper.

"I love how bossy you are."

"You don't." It had been a big reason why they'd broken up, besides the cheating.

"I do right now." He dragged Ambrose to the edge of the bed and while Ambrose moved his pillows around, Preston put on a condom. The stretch and burn were welcome, mitigated by Preston's careful prep, and finally Ambrose could sink into pleasure he so rarely divulged in lately. Some days he was too tired to even paw at himself. It just felt like work. Now he could let Preston pound into him and take away his scrambled thoughts.

He could simply be for a little bit. No too-contained, too-busy mind. He could be a raw nerve of pleasure and only that. He let Preston take the lead, braced over him and panting in his face, his breath sweet on Ambrose's warm cheeks and sweaty forehead. Maybe Preston sensed or felt Ambrose relax because his pace picked up, his thrusts harder, sharper.

Ambrose saw stars sizzle and pop behind his eyes and he clung to Preston's neck. The kisses were sloppy, rough and raw and angled wrong and it didn't matter. It didn't matter one fucking bit because Preston knew how to fuck him and knew how to make him shout and burn and melt.

"She's okay?"

"She's okay, buddy. I promise. While you get better, I'm going to take her home with me and spoil her rotten."

Forrest's smile was soft, the edges of it trembling as he watched Dandi bounce around Barrett's feet through Barrett's phone camera. Everything around him was pale - the hospital pillows and sheets, the top of his gown poking out above where Val had tucked him in, even his papery skin pulled tight over his little head. Barrett's heart clenched. He wanted to be there, but Val needed him to watch Dandi, stop by the house, pick up the mail. Ken had gone off again, threatening to take Val back to court. But it was a hollow threat; he was the one blatantly ignoring a court order to keep health insurance on Forrest and now his ass was on the line.

Barrett snorted. Ken's *money* was on the line, and that's all the bastard cared about. Fucking prick.

"Okay kid, you gotta rest. Can't come over to fish if you don't get some sleep."

"I know, Uncle Bear."

"Love you."

"Love you, too. Kiss Dandi for me."

"Of course."

Val took her phone back, her face now prominent on the screen. "Thank you. You're the fucking best."

"Mom."

"Sorry, kid. I uh...my bad."

Barrett had to stifle his laugh. Even sleep deprived and worried out of her mind, Val was still his foul-mouthed sister. "Val."

"Bear."

"Come on, Val. You gotta sleep." He dropped his voice and put his hand on Dandi's massive head. She nudged him in the leg and he stooped, angling the phone so Val could still see him while he scratched the dog's ears. "You can't be there for him if you're depriving yourself."

"I know. Bea's coming over to stay with him."

That was a relief. Bea was Val's oldest friend; so much that they were sisters in every way except by blood. He remembered little Beatrice, bright-eyed and always talking, following them around when they were kids. But she'd grown into a hell of a person, smart as anything and now a biochemist in something Barrett had no way of understanding. And on top of all that, Bea was Forrest's godmother. "That's good. Shower, eat, sleep." He looked at her through the phone, dead serious. "One day at a time. And Jacques already knows I gotta be able to drop everything when you call."

"You don't need to -"

"Yeah, I do. Don't argue, Hopscotch."

She laughed. "You haven't called me that in years."

"Don't make me bring out the other names."

"Okay."

"Okay. I'm headed back now. If Ken shows his fucking face -"

"I'll let Bea handle him."

And with that, the tendrils of worry that had wrapped around him loosened a little. Enough to let him suck in a deep breath. "You call. For anything."

"I will. Love you, Bear."

"Love you too, hopscotch."

They hung up and Barrett was left with a dark phone screen and two big doggie eyes staring up at him. "Fuck. *Fuck.*" He wanted to sit down and just...be. But he couldn't. He'd made a promise and Dandi needed looking after. "Come on, Dandi. Let's go home."

Barrett drove it straight through, the long road full of potholes that ate tires and Dandi snoring on an old blanket in the seat next to him. Some classic rock station droned on as the miles passed and he couldn't even spare the brain cells to hum along. He wanted to get the dog sorted and sit in the quiet for a minute before sleeping in his own bed.

He knew it was unfair, that desire for peace and silence, when his nephew was in the hospital and Val was watching over him and the kid's dad off doing fuck all. But his skin crawled in that too-dry way it did every winter; even his scalp prickled. And there was no cure for unrest like home and one's own bed and the creak and shudder of familiar floorboards.

It was late afternoon when he pulled into his drive. It wasn't hard to notice another car, parked pin straight behind Ambrose's. It was a nice car, too, with a flashy brand name and likely high end leather seats and a heated steering wheel. But whoever it was....it wasn't any of Barrett's business.

And then that not-his-business was racing out behind Ambrose as his neighbor pointed at the flashy car and yelled, "Get the fuck out of here, Preston! You don't get to do that after -"

Ambrose stopped short, pulled up by the sight of Barrett angling out of his truck. Or maybe he was staring at the massive Great Dane lumbering out behind him. Either way, it brought Ambrose and the tall, lean man with him to a full stop. Barrett's red flag meter was going off strong. Ambrose looked rumpled (not unusual) and upset (very unusual); the ever-present dark circles under his eyes nearly obliterated by red, puffy skin. And as much as he hated himself for it, Barrett was instantly checking the man over for bruises or scrapes.

The other man, this Preston, was glaring a hole through Barrett's forehead. "You must be the neighbor," he said, voice smooth and low and almost too perfect to be real. "Ambrose actually talks about you like you're a friend. Says you rescued him."

Dandi stopped twirling in a circle to stare at Preston, making Barrett put a hand on her head. "I did. And we are." His gaze caught on Ambrose. "Friends. Was going to introduce the newest one to Ambrose here before I headed inside. If y'all are done, that is."

A solid, almost bland statement. But Preston was clearly smart enough to read the murder in Barrett's eyes, because he started to back up to his car. "Think about what I said, Ambrose. It's for your own good."

The ferocity with which Ambrose wheeled on the other man nearly made Barrett step back. Dandi growled softly under her breath and Barrett hooked three fingers into her collar. He didn't stand a chance against a dog that size but he could try. Fuck, her leash was in the back of the truck and he should have had it out, ready to go.

"Nothing, *nothing* about what you think is helpful is what I need, goddammit." Ambrose was swift, his quick steps putting him face to face with Preston. Barrett's stomach churned. He shouldn't be watching this, but he couldn't leave either. An unwitting bystander to some kind of domestic dispute. But Ambrose wasn't done, and so neither was he. "You and her, you're both so alike. *That's* why I left you. Not the cheating, not the bemoaning my nature even when I tried to fix things."

He was so close to the other man, close enough to kiss him or spit on him or punch him. Barrett wasn't sure what to brace for. "As usual, you're here for your own agenda. *Fix Ambrose, make him better. Make him less grumpy, less solitary, more interesting.* I don't *need* someone to fix me into a 'better version', Preston." Ambrose flung his hands into the air and Barrett was horrified at his own fascination as he watched those long, lean fingers spread wide. "I moved out here to get away from every single person who has wanted to *fix me* instead of loving me as I am! Goddammit, I am not perfect but I'm not a monster."

Preston, for his sake, looked crestfallen. He reached out. "Ambrose -"

"No, Preston. Don't." Ambrose jerked away like he'd touched a flame. "Don't touch me."

But Preston tried again, even when Ambrose dodged. Barrett stepped forward. "I think that might be time to move on."

They both stopped to stare at him, all six and a half feet and too much dark hair, wearing last night's sweater and hiking pants and standing by a black and white spotted dog bigger than some grown humans. Barrett managed to mouth *sorry* to Ambrose, feeling guilt upon guilt at seeing this whole thing. It roiled in him, that guilt. But it could be dealt with later.

With a nod, Preston opened his car door and got inside, leaving Barrett and Ambrose to watch him fling it into reverse and speed out of the driveway as fast as the snow and his shitty performance tires would allow.

His timing was bad, his delivery was even worse, and all Barrett could think to say was, "Come inside, you look like you could use a drink."

CHAPTER TEN

"That is a very large dog."

Barrett stared for one long, bright moment and then threw his head back and laughed. The sound of it cracked across the gray sky and bare branches and somehow, it made Ambrose feel a little bit better. "Yeah, she's my nephew's but they don't really have anywhere to keep her until he's better." He held a hand out and said, "Ambrose, Dandi. Dandi, Ambrose. You be nice, Dandi."

But Ambrose sunk to a squat and put out a flat palm. The massive animal stopped snuffling in a pile of snow to cock her head, then romp over, tongue lolling.

"She's friendly, but new place and too much excitement..." Barrett trailed off but he stepped closer to them. "I'm just making sure."

"And I appreciate it." He craned his head so he could look back at the bigger man. "Like I appreciate the intervention a moment ago."

Shit. Shit. He hadn't meant to say that, even if it was completely true. They were now caught in that awkward dance of *do I say anything, should I say anything* and despite the deeply personal situation Barrett had gotten caught in, Ambrose had been relieved of the timing.

Dandi lowered her massive head and gave Ambrose's palm a cursory sniff. Then a lick. Then she was bounding into him, taking him to the cold, hard ground.

"Dandi!" Barrett raced forward, arms outstretched, fingers grasping.

But Ambrose was laughing. That big, goofy dog was now bouncing around them, barking happily while he practically giggled. "I love dogs," he said between wheezing breaths. A hand was thrust into his vision and he took it gratefully. "I haven't had a dog in years. This is reminding me maybe I should once again."

Barrett hauled him to his feet with one strong pull and then they were close. Nearly chest to chest, with the scent of coffee and sugar curling off Barrett like cologne. Ambrose spotted a bit of powdered sugar in Barrett's beard and nearly grinned. He felt...strange. Light, even dizzy and he swayed on his feet. His ankle was much better but there was a weakness to it still, so as his balance buckled, he reached out to grab something to steady himself.

That thing he grabbed turned out to be a set of very broad, very hard shoulders. "Whoa, careful there." Barrett's voice had gone syrupy. "Let's get inside."

Not a question. Ambrose nodded silently and, with Barrett's help, made his way into that finely crafted home he envied so. "Take care of her," he said with a feeble wave. "I'm just going to sit on that lovely sofa, if it's all right."

"More than."

Ambrose looked up to see Barrett staring hard at him. There was calculation in those dark, dark eyes and it nearly made him shiver to feel so *seen*. As if he was sitting bare-assed on Barrett's couch and waiting for....

He dashed that away with a shake of his head. Letting Preston fuck him had left him addled. "Go on. I don't need a nursemaid."

And whatever had been there for a moment shattered. Barrett nodded and then was moving about, opening doors, rattling bags and whatnot. Even whistling. All while Ambrose stared at his hands in his lap and tried to find his equilibrium again.

But no matter what he focused on, his thoughts ran back to Preston. He should have known. He should have fucking *known* it couldn't just be a fuck and then "Goodbye, thanks for the orgasm, maybe we'll do it again sometime".

Gods, Preston had sounded just like his mother, the great and oh so multi-talented Angelica Avery. She who could do anything she set her mind to and hated that her son *couldn't*.

Their faces flashed before him and the curl of anxiety in his stomach unraveled, spiraling out.

Why can't you just be friendlier?

It's not hard, Ambrose. Just talk to people.

Gods, how many times are you going to practice that infernal instrument? You're horrible at it, you'll always be horrible at it, and I'm not paying for lessons anymore.

Come on, babe. Let's just go to the party and you can meet the rest of my friends. We'll have a good time. Madison didn't make a move on you, he swears up and down he was just drunk.

Why in the hells would you want to live by yourself in the woods?

Why can't you be nicer?

Why can't you be more charming?

Are you going to do anything with your life?

Why? Why, Ambrose?

You're pathetic. Worthless. How could I have given birth to a son with not an iota of talent?

Do you want to know why I cheated? Because I could. Because I knew you wouldn't notice.

Why? Why can't you?

It was a hot metal band around his throat, a lead weight in his lungs. The attack came on so fast he didn't even have time to stumble over to his own house, where he could be safe and away from prying eyes.

"Ambrose? Shit." He was gently moved until his back was pressed to the couch cushions. "Easy, easy. I'm here."

Warm hands squeezed his but as they moved away, he scrambled for them. He needed their weight, their warmth; an anchor for him against the narrowing tunnel of his vision. "Breathe, Ambrose. I know you feel hollow or too tight right now. It's okay. I'm not going anywhere."

His hand was drawn up and settled against soft fabric, under which beat a steady *thumpthumpthump*. That rhythm lulled some part of his screaming, aching mind into a safer, quieter space. "Breathe for me. Just breathe. Listen to me if you can, but don't worry about anything else other than that."

Watching Ambrose go nearly catatonic with anxiety or some kind of panic attack sent Barrett's blood pressure spiking. Behind them, Dandi whined and he blindly thrust out his free hand. It was met with a sloppy, wet tongue and a bump from a velvety head. "Good girl," he crooned softly. "Come sit with us."

If this was his nephew, he would have pulled Ambrose into his lap and held him until he shook loose of whatever trap his mind had laid out. Same went for Val. But Ambrose was neither; hells, he wasn't even a ...

Barrett paused. Well, he supposed he was a friend. It's not like he'd lied to the other man, the one who was apparently responsible for Ambrose's distress. That thought made him see red for a brief moment, until Ambrose inhaled shakily and blinked at him. There was a haziness to his eyes Barrett didn't like, so he squeezed the hand on his chest. "Just breathe for me. It'll pass, I promise."

He stayed like that for several minutes, crouched between long legs, bony knees pressing into his ribs, and Ambrose squeezing his hand for all he was worth. His eyes were closed, his body limp against the couch cushions. The fire, the anger, he'd seen earlier was gone and now there was a vulnerability to the other man. It hurt to look at. If he knew anything about Ambrose, he knew the man was quick to make decisions and stick with them, for good or ill. He was sturdy, almost unbending.

Something about him now made Barrett's protective instincts kick in. Maybe it was the rumpled blue sweater, the wrinkles in a pattern that made him think it had been on the floor, maybe stepped on a few times. The chinos were creased like they'd been at the bottom of a drawer for too long. The kind of thing you pull on in a hurry, half-blind in the dark and simply looking to be decent.

But what Barrett fixated on was the hair. Dark auburn waves that curled and snarled about Ambrose's fascinating, strange face. His hair looked soft, such a contrast to the sharp angles and swooping curves of cheekbones that seemed to defy logic. The beard Ambrose had been growing over the winter was a dark brown and it strangely suited him well. Barrett figured if you had an interesting face, one might as well let the world see it. But it wasn't *his* face.

So instead he tried not to stare or think about how Ambrose seemed to withdraw from everyone but him.

Dandi whined again and then her big head came to rest on Ambrose's knee. "Dandi, hey, no."

"She's okay."

Something in his chest crumpled with relief. "Hey."

Ambrose's mouth twitched, an aborted smile that was hidden in his beard. "Hey."

"Can I...?" He pointed at the couch and Ambrose nodded. Once he was seated - close but not touching, their only point of contact their linked hands - Barrett said, "Do you need some water or a cold rag?"

Ambrose shivered. "Water would be good."

"Back in a flash."

When he came back, Ambrose was stroking Dandi's lopsided, floppy ears, her face cradled so gently between his palms. "Good girl. You're a good girl." Barrett wanted to stand there in his hallway and watch. Instead, he walked over and offered the glass. Ambrose drained half before setting it to the side on the coffee table.

Barrett now only had to wait him out.

"I figured I had a fifty-fifty chance of a panic attack after Preston showed up at my door." Ambrose's next inhale was shaky. "I think I was too generous in my estimation."

He had to ask. "Ex?"

"Yeah."

"Recent?"

"No, thank fuck." Another shaky inhale. "Four years ago."

"I won't insult you by asking if I can help."

Barrett tracked the bob of Ambrose's throat as he swallowed hard. Again. And again, before Ambrose finally said, "I appreciate it. And the intervention. He would have left eventually but only after he stuck around to argue. Cajole might be a better word." He turned his head slowly, smashing a perfect auburn curl under his cheek. "Thank you."

Two simple words. Why did they feel like lead in the pit of his stomach? "You're welcome. Guess I have better timing this go around."

The careful, slow look Ambrose gave him was steady, but lingering. "Guess you do." He sat forward, leaning to the left to scratch Dandi under the chin. Her tail thumped against the floor with a solid *whack* and they both smiled. "I might already be a little in love. If you ever need someone to walk her or watch her, just ask."

It might have been the most genuine thing Ambrose had said in their short time together, aside from when Barrett rescued him and when he complimented the fish. He liked this Ambrose. Still quiet but... "earnest. It's nice."

FUCK.

Did he just say that out loud?

He did.

Motherfucker.

Barrett flinched but Ambrose's hand shot out to land on his knee. "No! It's okay, really. You just...took me by surprise."

"Took myself by surprise," he muttered. "You'll still have to excuse me, I'm running on three hours sleep a solid forty-eight hours ago."

"That's right." And just like that, the hand and the earnestness and soft grey eyes were gone, replaced by a thick worry of a different kind, silky with sadness and exhaustion. "Get some rest. And when you have the brain power, let me know what alcohol to bring over for dinner sometime." He got to his feet, waved, and slowly walked out.

It was only later that Ambrose's words fully sunk in, but by then Barrett had slept away the day and part of the night. But at the moment, all he said was, "Yeah, sure. And hey, yell if you start to feel like that again. I don't want you to be alone through another attack. It ain't fun, I know."

Ambrose's nod made him feel better, but not great. But he went to bed with a massive dog on his feet and the knowledge that Ambrose was a text and a thousand feet away.

One week later, now mid-February

The ice from last week's storm had finally melted in a burst of sunny, unseasonably warm days. Had it been fifteen degrees warmer, Barrett would have been itching for the scent of potting soil and fertilizer and the ground warming in the midday sun.

Instead, his house was full of the kind of cooking smells one would expect from an Sicilian grandmother. Basil and rosemary, garlic and onion, fresh baked bread and ripe tomatoes. He was going all out, but after the last couple of weeks through which he and Ambrose had been drug, he figured the effort was worth it. While homemade pasta sauce simmered on the stove, he got to work chopping more garlic. Dandi was asleep on her blanket on the couch, and soft classical music echoed through the first floor.

Then the doorbell rang. Dandi lifted her head and gave a warning huff. "Hold on!" Barrett wiped his hands on the towel over his shoulder and ambled to the door. "Wha - hey. You're early."

"And prepared to help." Ambrose thrust out a bottle. "Unless you're going to turn me and twenty year old port away."

Barrett chuckled. It was the only thing he could do in the face of genuine surprise. Surprise that Ambrose wanted to come over early, surprise at the generous bottle of port.

Surprise at the way Ambrose was dressed, looking like an outdoor magazine cover model in black jeans and hiking boots and a half-zip cardigan that most younger men couldn't pull off. But it looked soft and inviting and some part of Barrett wanted to touch the deep emerald fabric.

Fuck.

Instead, he made a grand, sweeping gesture with his hand, stepping back as Ambrose entered. As his guest got comfortable, Barrett went back to the stove and his stirring.

"Glasses?"

"Top left cabinet."

When Ambrose came back with two glasses of port and a small smile, Barrett had to grin. "You're looking better."

"I feel better. Been a hell of a winter." He sipped and Barrett paused to do the same. It was easier to eye the other man over the rim of his glass. "Do I pass inspection?"

Barrett spluttered a little and Ambrose chuckled; a throaty thing that sounded nice amidst the pots and pans boiling and the slow tick of the oven. "Sorry. But yeah, what you said." Barrett rubbed the back of his head. "Hell of a winter."

The sound of heavy paws and nails skittering on wood paused their conversation. "Prepare for it."

But Ambrose was already on the floor, arms out to greet the clearly enthusiastic dog and her lolling tongue and copious amounts of drool. He watched for a long moment, the two of them rolling about like little kids tussling.

It looked like home.

He shouldn't have thought that. Barrett sucked in a hard breath and reached for his glass. The deep sweetness chased by the tang of oak barrel and time curled on his tongue. "Holy shit."

"I thought you might appreciate it."

"I really do." He raised his glass. "Cheers."

Ambrose got to his feet, to his glass. "Cheers." He took a sip, eyes steady on Barrett. "And thank you again. I uh...probably owe an explanation."

"Nah. This winter...shit." He huffed as he stirred, filled with the need to look away. "Did Brad ever tell you I was friends with the guy who lived in your cabin before?"

"A little. Just mentioned his name and that he had passed." Ambrose didn't hesitate or hang on that word. *Passed.* It still bore weight but he didn't let it drag either of them down. "I can't imagine that was easy."

"Wasn't. Perry and I were good buddies for about five years. He was older than me, a loner too." Barrett had to chuckle. "First time I met him, he was also on the docks but fishing instead of playing guitar. He reminded me a bit of my boss, Jacques. Eternal bachelors, outdoorsy, always in the mud or snow or the lake." He moved one saucepan to the warmer and pulled another one over. The garlic and onions had gone translucent and he didn't want to overcook them. "So we fished and talked and then one day he brought over a book."

"Novel?"

Barrett shook his head. "It's over there. Far left bookcase, top shelf. Little green leather thing with a ribbon marker."

Ambrose got to his feet and was immediately followed by Dandelion. When he turned around at the sound of paws, he laughed and patted her head. "I went fifteen feet, you goof."

Damn. There went his traitorous heart again, watching Dandi with Ambrose. She liked people in general but every time Ambrose was in her vicinity, she became his shadow. The only other person she did that with was him.

He liked Ambrose. And it would be nice to have a friend. Every other little thought was discarded ribbon from a well-received gift. Just something to cast aside for now, pick up later and dump in the trash. Maybe reuse it if the time and purpose was right.

"May I?"

"Yeah, bring it over here though. I haven't looked through it in a while."

Ambrose came to stand at Barrett's right, his gaze flitting over the stove full of bubbling sauces. "You didn't have to do all this."

Without thinking, he bumped his shoulder into Ambrose's. "It's not a worry. I wanted to." He froze then sighed. "Shit, sorry. I'm a touchy guy, I shouldn't have done that."

"You're fine." A finely boned hand landed on his shoulder and squeezed, then retreated. "I don't mind it from you. You've saved my ass twice and seen me not at my best. A few friendly bumps are all right."

Ambrose flipped open the book and Barrett watched, transfixed, as those long fingers traced over the first few sketches. "Gorgeous."

"Yeah. Perry was talented. I kept telling him he should publish it."

Silence gathered around them as Ambrose leafed through page after page of charcoal sketches and soft watercolors. Leaves, berries, flowers, mushrooms, and all manner of local flora came to life once more, each one gracing pages that had been lovingly worked on. His heart did that funny little flip when Ambrose lingered over a soft gold daffodil and the light periwinkle of foxgloves.

"If you ever want to publish it, I know a few indie places that might be interested. There's one in particular that is always looking for artwork for coffee table books and reference guides."

His heart really wasn't going to let up tonight, was it? Thinking of Perry's artwork proudly displayed on glossy pages and sitting on someone else's table, in someone else's house, made him suck in a breath. "I can't ask that of you."

"I offered." Ambrose smiled. "And I mean it. These are really, really beautiful. Do you have any more?"

"Tons. Boxes of 'em. Mostly loose leaf notebooks."

That smile turned into a frown. "His family didn't want them?"

The little knot that was always present when he talked about Perry clenched; a fist in his lungs, like a punch. A direct hit. "No family, really. He's got a sister on the other side of the country but they were estranged. His parents are long gone."

"Lifelong bachelor." Ambrose shook his head, his mouth a tight line. "You took care of him, didn't you?"

Fuck, his throat was so tight he could barely swallow. "My nature, I guess. Tends to get me in trouble."

The way Ambrose slid next to him was almost imperceptible, it was so fluid. And the arm that wrapped around his shoulders was heavy, but honest. Comforting. "You're a kind man, Barrett."

He couldn't look up, couldn't look at Ambrose. It was too much. If he did, the walls would drop and everything he held in place by duct tape and purpose would fracture, then give completely. He'd be exposed, a raw nerve throbbing in time with the hard beating of his heart.

"Barrett."

Ambrose was closer now, leaning against him and the stove full of pots and pans. It was a lot. Too much. Too close, too soon, too personal.

He didn't know if he wanted this. If he was ready for it. It was foolish to ignore his attraction to Ambrose, but they were barely friends. Everything was as fragile as a glass placed too close to a table's edge. One bump, one push, one careless move and everything would shatter.

He didn't have time for romance. But he could make time for a friend.

"Thanks." With another, final nudge to Ambrose's shoulder, the moment released. Ambrose stepped back and Dandi was right there to take his place, pushing her big, wet nose against Barrett's thigh. "Kid, come on."

Ambrose laughed. If he was put out by whatever had sparked, and then fizzled, between them, he didn't show it. So it must have just been in his head. "I can let her out, or..."

"Good, because we're about ten minutes from dinner and she fusses over every mud hole and pile of snow."

"I got her. Come on, Dandi."

His whistle was sharp and clear, leaving Barrett's ears ringing as he stirred their dinner.

That happened.

Something *popped* between them. He felt it, and from the quick intake of breath when he'd placed his arm on Barrett's shoulder, the other man had, too. The thing with Preston was still too raw to think about any other entanglements. Except when it was late at night and he couldn't sleep and Barrett's face and big, bushy beard and kind voice came to him through the dark.

Maybe he'd imagined, once or twice, that warm body lying beside his. A heavy arm draped over his middle, or his chest. He wasn't picky. The comfort of having the other person so close, so *alive*, next to him was the dream; the little furl of hope he kept stored away when his world darkened.

Standing out in the damp cold, watching Barrett's truly massive dog romp through the backyard, Ambrose felt at home. He turned and looked at their porch lights glowing in the twilight, the slight flicker of his own in the distance drawing him in. As if with every beat of his heart, and every flicker of the light, he knew that one solid truth.

Home. Finally.

Whatever spark of desire had kindled in him for Barrett, he had to squash it down. Preston's cutting words, his oh-so-helpful suggestions, his cheating. Maybe Ambrose would never be fully over it, but if he couldn't trust, he couldn't head into something *more*. Not yet. And maybe the ugly truth that sometimes came to him in the dark was more than the visitation of his own fears and fallacies.

Maybe he just wasn't built for romantic companionship. It had been a bloody miracle that he and Preston had pulled four years out of each other and their hopelessly tangled knot of idiosyncrasies and flaws. All the fighting, the cold silences, the incredible makeup sex....none of it was worth losing the tenuous, fragile friendship he had with his neighbor.

If he wanted companionship, this was the way forward.

Ambrose squared his shoulders and headed back inside, Dandi at his heels. Barrett was just setting down the last bowl when they entered. "Hey. Dinner's ready."

"More like a feast. I'm..." He paused, taking in the scene. Barrett in his soft, slightly worn clothes, his hairline damp from the heat of the kitchen. The table spread out with food enough for a family holiday gathering. The shining glasses of port and water. Dandi curling up on her massive bed by the roaring fire.

This could be home, too. He could share his time and effort and care with Barrett.

Maybe this was what it took to heal. Finally.

When the night ended and he was nearly falling asleep in one of the plushest wingback chairs in which he'd ever had the honor to sit, Ambrose remembered. "Hold on!"

When he came back, Barrett was rinsing a pan and glancing curiously at him. He knew he was being odd but this felt right. "I'm afraid to ask what's behind your back." But Barrett was joking and grinning and warmth flooded his chest in a way that felt so good.

"I owed you a pie." Ambrose thrust the frozen dessert out. "I probably owe you about a dozen but I'll start with this one."

But Barrett just laughed and took the pie with a smile. He set it aside and, leaning now against the counter and wiping his hands on a dish towel, his face turned pensive. "I know you're not big on touching."

"Casual touching," he corrected. It was still so hard to explain. But he'd welcome Barrett's touch. He knew he would. "It's different when I know the person."

"Do we know each other enough for a hug?" Barrett looked down, cheeks going pink. Ambrose found it utterly endearing. "I uh...yeah. Sorry."

Ambrose stepped forward and wrapped his arms around Barrett. After a quick breath in and a moment's hesitation, his hug was returned. "Thanks."

"Thanks for asking."

Barrett pulled back, his look now keen. "I bet a lot of people don't give that kind of consideration. I'm sorry."

He shrugged. "It's all right. I'm used to defending myself from it."

"Ah, but you shouldn't have to." And then Barrett stepped back, taking his warmth and scent with him and some tiny part of Ambrose yearned. He wanted to ask Barrett to *stay*.

But that wasn't their path.

On his way out the door, he gave Dandelion another pat and ear scruffle. "Good girl," he said softly. "Such a good girl."

"Good night, Ambrose."

"Night, Barrett."

That night, Ambrose slept soundly, even though he was curled up on one side of his bed as though there was another with him.

Chapter Eleven

Spring

"I'm glad to see you again, Ambrose."

Ambrose shifted in his chair. Uncrossed and recrossed his legs. "I thought it prudent to return. I wasn't in the best state before I moved. And now, I'm..." He sighed. "I felt ready."

The woman across from him smiled. "Well, I'm very glad." Her boots, fine brown leather with subtle silver buckles, gave him something to focus on as he dreaded that first awful question. "I'm curious if you might want to talk about the move. What changed, what worked, what didn't. If anything." She tapped the laptop beside her. "You weren't terribly detailed in your therapy appointment request, but I'm not looking to push."

No, you never do. It's a big reason why when I come back to therapy, I come back to you. You let me talk in whatever order I need. You're helpful.

"I suppose I'm feeling a little off-center." He smoothed a hand over his knee. "The move gave me the physical space I needed but the mental space is...slow to come around."

He had an hour. An hour that was all his. He so rarely took the time to simply talk things out and yet here, he paid for it. But friends were busy and interjecting and while he loved people like Raf, who was actually a good listener, the man was incredibly busy. Just this morning they'd exchanged messages; Raf asking how he was and showing Ambrose a new art piece he thought would be appreciated. And it was, a gorgeous, hand-blown glass vase in a yellow so gold it reminded him of sunflowers and wheat and summer sun through thick green leaves.

Raf was kind and sweet but busy. Ambrose never expected any of his friends, no matter how close, to want to listen to him piece his thoughts together.

"It's a big adjustment you're trying to make."

"It is." He looked Dr. Fielding over, from her cat-eye glasses and bobbed blonde hair, to the gleaming silver buckles on her boots. She was every inch the polished professional and something about her easy countenance and mild demeanor always put him at ease. He realized it was very likely a crafted look for her patients, but he also liked to think this was simply *her*. A subtly stylish fifty-something woman who had seen and heard it all during her long career. When Ambrose had first considered becoming her patient, he'd done a deep dive into her background. Certificates, degrees, awards, volunteer work. It was all up to par with his standards but what had impressed him was her dedication to ethics.

Ten years ago, she'd had a patient who threatened the lives of others and, believing him capable of doing real harm, reported him to the authorities. She'd testified in court but never broke privilege where her career demanded it be kept. That had been the winning point for him; an understanding of what she wasn't - and was - willing to do. There was no way his petty problems could top someone planning to kill his family, but it was good to know he couldn't shock her. He so often had wondered if his thoughts were "normal". Well, he'd never planned to kill anyone, so that bar had been swiftly passed.

The next thirty minutes passed as he talked about those first few quiet nights in the new place. Then came around to meeting Barrett on the docks. Being saved by the man. How unkind he'd been to his new neighbor, the same one who had pulled him from the woods and kept him warm and got him medical attention.

"I was unfair," Ambrose admitted, looking down at his hands. "But we're friends now."

"That's great, Ambrose." Dr. Fielding's gaze was steady but not intrusive. Open to hearing him. "How does Barrett factor into your life, do you think?"

God, she was good. The perfect question. It was the exact thing he'd been trying to puzzle out for himself. "I think of him as a friend. Just a few weeks back we had a nice dinner. Talked about fishing and hiking. He's a forest ranger, so..."

"So your interests align. That's a good start." Dr. Fielding had deep hazel eyes, now half-hidden in the afternoon shadows cast across her office. Ambrose was aware, in every session they had, of that light in her eyes that made her seem interested but not prying. It was like she was made to be a therapist. "What about a deeper connection? There are all kinds of friends. Do you think Barrett is someone you'd enjoy spending time with?"

"Regularly? I do. He's ...."

Stable. Interesting. Funny. Kind. Generous.

Attractive

Ambrose shook that last one away. "He seems real. I like that, knowing there are still people in the world who keep their feet on the ground. It makes me hope we're not all self-absorbed monsters."

Fuck.

He smiled wanly. "You're gonna latch onto that, aren't you?"

"Onto what?"

He fluttered a hand in the air. "Me thinking most people are self-absorbed monsters. Ask me if I include myself in that statement."

"Do you?"

"Sometimes."

"The kicker is, we all are to some degree." She leaned forward and Ambrose watched the sway of tiger's eye earrings by her cheekbones. "I think almost all people are capable of great deeds of self-reflection and narcissism. But most people find a balance and they go forward in the world doing their best."

"I don't think I'm narcissistic. I do think I'm stuck in my own head too much." Ambrose looked up at her, smile gone. "I think Barrett is a little like that, too. Or at least what I've seen of him."

"You like him."

"I do."

"This might come later, but I want you to think about forming a bond with him. Maybe something deeper. If you're both amenable, of course."

Ambrose flashed back to the mornings when they'd wave at each other. Barrett giving him boxes of Perry's drawings to dig through. He *trusted* Ambrose with those precious pieces of paper on which little parts of his dead friend was inscribed. It had hurt his heart, that gesture, but not in the way he'd expected. The drawings and watercolors carried joy and life in them. So instead of mourning someone he'd never known - someone whose house he had bought and now lived in - Ambrose got to see the passion. The life. The spark.

"Yeah, I think he would be," he replied just as the session timer went off.

"So, wait. You can paint, draw, write, sing, play guitar, cook, and make a mean fucking apple pie. But you don't know how to roll a joint."

Ambrose flipped Barrett off. "You say that like it's a crime against weed."

"A crime against your impressionable youth, maybe." Ice clinked as he watched the dregs of the nice whisky Ambrose brought over cling to the glass. "Shit. Didn't you ever sneak out, swipe the keys and the cigarettes, and go meet your friends in the woods or a cornfield? And just sit around and tell stupid teenager jokes and learn how to inhale and blow it away from your face so you don't smell too bad. And it's cold and the moon's out and you just....shiver but you don't want to let on cause you're trying to catch someone's eye" He chuckled. "Or, in my case, it wasn't cigarettes and the car keys, it was weed from the stash we kept in my buddy Jay's shed and a bottle of that shitty table wine you get upcharged for at restaurants."

Ambrose's mouth twitched into a smile. "A bottle and not one of those jugs?"

Barrett pulled a face. "Oh god, never remind me."

Ambrose's laugh hit him square in the chest. "Might have snuck one or two of those jugs backstage between shows."

Cue the intrigue. Every bit of Ambrose's life he learned about, no matter how small the crumb, made the puzzle pieces begin to click into place. "Yeah? Music or theater?"

"Theater. Two shows on Friday and Saturday, and a Sunday matinee during October. It was freshman year in college." Ambrose leaned his head against his fist, the move making him slouch in the chair. The position showed off his long legs. It was like they went on forever and then the rest of Ambrose simply *appeared*. A crown of wavy auburn, dark grey eyes that looked like their own galaxies, and a long, lean neck into sloping shoulders.

The sight made Barrett's mouth water. Every time it happened, Barrett had to remember he was simply reacting to an attractive sight and it meant nothing. Just his very human need reacting to a very pretty sight. That was all.

If circumstances were different.

If he were a grouchy book hero, stoic and sullen and emotionally constipated, he'd shake off all the shiverings of something *else* only to, much later on, be shown what he'd been missing out on. There would be a spark he couldn't ignore, a kiss, and then fumblings in the dark while desire thrummed under his skin and warm hands caressed him.

"What was the show?" he asked, voice gone a little hoarse while his cock tried to do some thinking for him.

Wonder of wonder, Ambrose flushed. *"Little Shop of Horrors."*

He couldn't help but smile. "No way."

"Yep." With a sigh, Ambrose poured a little more whisky into his glass. "Finish it off?"

"Ooof. But yeah, fuck it. I don't have to work tomorrow."

"You'll sleep like a baby, then."

"Heh, yeah maybe. That would be a nice change." Barrett leaned even further back in his chair, letting his head settle on the thick, dark blue, velvety fabric. He loved these chairs; had bought them at an estate sale when he'd first moved to Lake Honor. They were massive, overstuffed wingbacks that looked like they belonged in the drawing room of an old castle in a moor. Somewhere foggy and slightly mysterious, where the stone was always cold and the wind damp but somehow it felt like home. Fires smelling like old, cracked wood and peat moss and halls that lay thick with memories.

"Are you all right, Barrett?"

He blinked, shaking from the stupor. Ambrose hadn't sat up from that lazy, almost careless pose, the lines of his body sensuous and enticing. But those grey eyes had snapped into focus and all of it bore down on him. It was difficult to not shiver under the weight of that stare. "Yeah. I uh..." He licked his lips, chased the taste of whisky there. "I don't know what I was really thinking about. Just drifting, I suppose."

It was a soft white lie, nothing devastating. If Ambrose noticed, he made no move of it. "It's a good night for that. I saw robins the other day and the air's getting that headiness to it." He cracked a toothy smile and Barrett had to tighten his grip on the arm of his chair. Fuck. This wasn't fair. "Spring's perfume, I suppose."

"Just wait," Barrett replied, voice thick. "It rains like crazy every spring. Best check your basement. I know Perry did a lot of work down there, but still. Roots, stones, all of it gets pretty adamant about cracking foundations."

"Good to know. Thank you." Ambrose drained his glass and tipped it at Barrett. "I was hoping you'd point me to some good spots to see the spring foliage from. I'm finding myself in need of some inspiration."

"New project?" Barrett leaned forward, curious. He'd come to find out, over casual dinners and drinks during the last month or so, that Ambrose was the modern era version of a renaissance man. A deft hand at many things, not excluding painting, music, photography, and writing. It was stunning, really, to meet someone so talented and yet so cautious about airing those skills to the world.

"Unfortunately, no." Ambrose went stiff in his seat by the fire. Barrett could practically see the chair vibrate from the force of his ramrod posture. "It may be a tad early in our friendship for me to expose such a deep character flaw -"

"Ambrose." He almost reached out, but thought better of it. He didn't want to make the man uncomfortable, any more than his downcast gaze seemed to bely. "You don't have to share anything you don't want to. I'm sorry, I shouldn't have asked."

Ambrose huffed but it wasn't an angry noise. "No, no. It's not that at all. I rather enjoy having someone to talk to about all this. I'm just not used to sharing except with Raf."

He'd mentioned the name Raf a few times and this seemed to be a diversion he was willing to walk down. "Yeah, you've said his name a bit. Good friend?"

"The best, honestly. We just don't see each other much. Twice a year, once on his birthday, once on mine." Ambrose's mouth twitched into a smile. "He comes to me for both. We've been friends since college. After a disastrous blind date."

Well, there was no leaving that story unfinished. Ambrose started the story with, "Let me tell you about the most charming person I've ever met." Ambrose and Raf (Lutz, his last name, to everyone else) had actually been set up on a blind date by some mutual friends. "The entire thing was a failure. My god, we were compatible intellectually but I was so nervous being stared at all night by this handsome man. We went down the boardwalk, he turned, I turned.

We tried to kiss..." He clapped his hands together and laughed. "I nearly broke his nose."

Barrett winced. "Hell of a first impression."

"Truly." Ambrose started scrolling through his phone. "I scanned a bunch of old photos in....ah, here."

There they were. A clearly young 20-something Ambrose, gawky and thin, uneven skin and wild auburn hair next to... "Did he model or something?"

"Now you know why I was nervous all night."

Raf was stunning. Between the kind of jawline people paid thousands to surgeons for to the hazel eyes that sparked with mischief, he was drop-dead gorgeous in a way that didn't feel intimidating. His hair was wild, too; probably kicked up by a late summer ocean breeze. But that overly-tousled mass of black curls looked sexy in the lazy kind of way. Like he'd just slipped out of the arms of a lover.

"And here's us on my birthday last May." Ambrose flipped to another photo album.

Barrett's throat went dry. Raf was even more beautiful, but now the hair was perfectly styled and brushed just enough away from his face to show off the winking emeralds in his ears; so you could see the long neck and a bit of gold at his throat. He and Ambrose were dressed in blazers and button-downs, except Ambrose's jacket was flung over one shoulder. It was such a casually masculine image, sleek and stylish, that it made Barrett realize he was glad he could never find suit jackets in his size. There was no way he was pulling off that kind of lean sensuality.

Not like Ambrose. Now, or in the photo, or a decade and a half ago.

Something twisted low in his gut and it made Barrett dig his fingers into his thigh. "Looks like fun," he rasped. "Dinner?"

"Dinner, drinks, and then he convinced me to go dancing. That man, I swear." Ambrose chuckled, the sound rich and dark. "He could sell a realtor their own house if he wanted to. It's too bad he has a heart of gold, he'd be a fabulous con man."

"You insult all your friends like that?" Barrett was teasing, so his tone was light.

"Ha, very funny. And no, just Raf. Mostly because it makes him laugh and he knows it's true."

"And you're sure he's not a model?"

"Raf owns four mixed media art galleries on the west coast and writes poetry. I think in one life he was a model, and in this life he chose to sell local art."

"So he has about ten spouses now, right?"

"Lifelong bachelor." Ambrose laughed with a shrug. "Always been of that mindset. Hell, he didn't buy a condo until about five years ago. Liked the thrill of moving from city to city, meeting new people." He motioned at his phone. "Which he's obviously very good at."

"And you two..."

"After that disastrous first date? No, never. It wasn't the way we clicked, and honestly, I'm luckier for it. He's the sibling I never had, trite as that sounds." Ambrose gave him a pointed look. "And you two would get on quite well, I think. He loves the outdoors. It's one of the first things we bonded over, sans nearly broken nose."

Barrett was joking again, with only a tiny splinter of self-consciousness. But the way Ambrose looked at him as he said, "Sure I wouldn't be too much? I'm not exactly the kind of company that can match in the appearance department," made him regret his words.

Ambrose leaned forward, the movement sharp, almost cutting. He cocked his head and Barrett watched his hair brush his shoulder. Auburn against a dark grey waffle henley that was soft and faded from years of washings. "Feel free to tell me to fuck off, Barrett, but do you not realize how you look to others?"

Barrett froze. Cold spread over the back of his neck and old, old memories he'd long shelved rushed back. He'd always been too big, too tall, too hairy. First to grow a beard in middle school. First to get over six feet tall. He never fit in the desks, so he had to sit at an old table on a slightly wobbly chair that creaked every time he breathed too hard.

"Depends on the adjectives you use," he muttered.

Now a hand settled on his and the intent, intense look in Ambrose's eyes made him snap his mouth shut. "I see someone who so easily reflects his generous nature, it's like it lives in every fiber of your being." He gestured to the table. "You give your time and your dedication to having drinks with someone you've only known a few months. You spend your days looking out for the well-being of others, human and animal. You visit your sister and nephew every weekend and let Dandi haul you around."

At that, Dandi lifted her head and softly boofed. They both laughed, though Barrett's was a little watery.

Ambrose wasn't done, however. "You spend so much time helping others. I see someone who could use a little care himself." And then he sat back in his chair, drained his drink, and said, "So unless you really want to fight me on all of that, or call me a liar, I think I'm right here, Barrett."

He swallowed against a thick feeling in his throat. "No, not going to fight you. Don't see what good it would do, you stubborn son of a bitch."

"Ouch. I see we are comfortable enough for insults," Ambrose teased back. "I'll have to think of a good one."

"Text it to me."

"Oh, texting insults? How modern. I might be too luddite for that, you know."

As their laughter faded and the pop of the fire overtook the silence that gathered afterwards, Barrett understood, swiftly and suddenly, how comfortable he was. Not just in the chair, which was fantastic. But with Ambrose. He hadn't felt that since Perry. But then again, he'd never been physically attracted to Perry. So that realization bit with an edge that left him feeling overly warm. It made something twitch low in his belly and he pushed it aside, but it would be there later. Waiting.

As he got up to get a cold water bottle from the fridge, Dandi stood and stretched before pattering after him. "This is nice," he said as he turned back. "For two grouchy loners, we're doing all right, I think."

"Just all right?"

Fuck. The way Ambrose was staring at him made that coil in his gut tighten more. He shook it off, but wondered how many more times he'd be able to do that before it was too much. In truth, he needed a friend like Ambrose: stern but real, funny in a dry, dark kind of way. Slow to open up, to trust, but when he did...it was like finding buried treasure. Barrett could see that as plain as day, even if Ambrose couldn't or wouldn't.

"Well, like I said, for two grouchy loners..." He came back to his chair and plopped down. Raised his bottle in a toast. "To lakeside living and being alone, until you don't want to be."

"Couldn't have said it better, my friend." Ambrose smiled and for one moment, Barrett felt its warmth like the brightest, hottest day in summer.

When Barrett's phone buzzed ten minutes later, he was in the middle of a story about the first time he and Meredith saw wolf pups. "Shit," Barrett said as he read the message. "Sorry, work emergency."

Ambrose immediately sat forward in his chair. "Not another bridge, I hope."

"No, and we still don't know who did it. But at least now the bridges are all reinforced." Barrett tapped his phone in disgust. "But someone stole the generator from the firewatch tower you and I holed up in during that storm. Fuck."

Ambrose's brow creased. "Do you think it's connected?"

"Who knows? Or it's some down on their luck resident that needs the generator and doesn't want to steal from a neighbor. Same thing happened when copper prices shot up a few years back. We had a lot of pipes stolen, a lot of damage." He sighed, swiped a hand down his face. "I can't blame 'em. The shit economy, no jobs unless you can drive to at least the next town over. But that's if your car works, or you have one." Barrett glanced at Dandi, who had one ear cocked his direction. "You gonna be good while I'm gone?"

Ambrose was on his feet instantly, much to his and Dandi's surprise. "I can take her. I've got a few edits to make on some poems and this." He dug in the bag that had held fresh greens from a local grower; greens he'd shared with Barrett. And now he held out a folded letter. "Raf's business partners with an indie publisher near him, and they're interested in Perry's illustrations. I was hoping to dig through that box again, see if there's any that might be fitting to scan and to send as samples." He nodded at Dandi, whose tail was thumping on the floor. "She can keep me company."

Barrett found himself, once again, incredibly grateful for Ambrose taking the lead on the illustration project. He'd lingered over those drawings for months but could never find the energy to let them go. Ambrose, when latched onto a project, was all business and it was freeing to have someone else take charge for once. "Thank you," he said softly before hustling to gather his things and pull on his gear. "She loves your house. Must be all those pie smells."

Ambrose flushed. "You say that like I'm making pies all day, every day."

"Enough that I can smell it on the regular."

He huffed and crossed his arms, but that angular, fascinating face was wide open. Barrett could be pressed to say it even looked a little like *pleasure* across perfectly symmetrical features. "I stress bake," he proclaimed, arms spread wide. "I can't help it. Carbs are known to help the brain process in times of focus."

"Uh huh." Barrett wasn't buying it for one minute, and he hoped his smile conveyed that. It was better than letting his face show how much he enjoyed watching Ambrose be playful. "Well, don't feed her too much pie crust or I'll be walking her at three am."

Ambrose pulled a face. "I wouldn't do that to you. Now go, I'll lock up. I want to grab her leash and a toy before we go home."

And just like that, Ambrose was stooping to grab a battered stuffie from under the coffee table while Dandi sniffed at his knee. It was so shockingly *domestic* Barrett paused to watch. Then his phone buzzed again, this message more urgent.

"Thanks," he said over his shoulder before heading out to his truck.

He trusted his dog and his home with someone who, just three months ago, was shrugging off any casual concern or affection. Someone who he'd rescued, someone who had reluctantly let him touch his swollen ankle. Someone he'd come to care about rather quickly. They had a long road ahead of them, but he trusted Ambrose and that was enough for now.

Barrett drove as fast as he dared in the dark, even along roads he knew like the back of his hand. Meredith called in over the radio when he was a few miles out. "How bad?" he asked as he navigated a particularly nasty turn.

"Generator's gone but they also shredded the lines into the tower. It's gonna be expensive to fix. And they did a nasty job on the door. Thank god it's not fire season." Her voice was strung tight, a wire of stress and worry. "You close?"

"Yeah, yeah. Sorry for the delay." His hands were tight on the wheel so he relaxed a little. No point in straining now when there was work to be done.

Meredith laughed softly at that. "You get stuck in a project?"

He flashed back to Ambrose, fire-warm and relaxed in that wingback chair, his hair a splash of red and brown against navy blue. Without meaning to, he sighed. "Nah, just shooting the shit with the neighbor."

"Oh, really?"

"Don't start, Mer."

She chuckled. "I won't tell a soul about your crush."

Barrett groaned. "Okay, I'm ignoring that completely."

"Whatever you say, Bear."

When he got to Alpha tower, Jacques was standing beside his truck talking to a shorter man with tortoiseshell glasses who was jabbing at a tablet screen. Clearly dressed for the winter chill with the right boots and coat, the man was surprisingly bare-headed and the wind played with the end of the long, dark hair that went past his shoulders. The man didn't seem to mind, his focus fully on Jacques as they talked. Barrett cracked open his door and Jacques motioned him forward.

"It can't be random anymore, Jacques," the man was saying as Barrett approached. "The bridges three months ago, the stolen supplies, now a generator and a barred door. It reeks of sabotage." The man had a melodic, easy voice but there was anger under his words.

"That's what I don't understand." Jacques motioned with a gloved hand to the fire watch tower. "Sabotaging the tower during fire season would make more sense if they were trying to cause harm. It could be someone needed that generator."

The man shrugged, then cut his gaze to Barrett. Barrett nodded but the man smiled back. "Never said it had to make sense, because if that was the case then the barred door doesn't fit in. But we're all gonna need to be on alert. I have permission from central command to stay in Lake Honor until we get this figured out." That gaze, dark brown and intense, landed on him again. "You're Barrett, right? Oz Hampstead. I'm an investigator with Ranger Command."

Barrett shook the hand that was thrust out at him. "Didn't know we had investigators."

"We don't," Jacques cut in. "They borrowed him from County Fire and EMS."

Oz grinned. "Guilty as charged. But it's in the contract that we can be 'borrowed' by other local authorities as the need arises." He dropped the firm, warm handshake but those dark eyes stayed fixed on Barrett. He saw a smattering of freckles over the bridge of Oz's nose, just under his glasses. "Jacques says you were the one who found the bridge sabotage. I've already talked to Meredith about the fire watch tower, since she found the issues while on her rotation tonight. But I'd like to hear about all of this from you. Jacques says Alpha is your usual haunt."

"And that's my cue to duck out." Jacques slapped Barrett on the back and handed him a thin folder as he passed by. "I've got a shit ton of paperwork to do before we can all sleep. Wish me luck."

"Bye, Jacques." Barrett turned back to the man before him, scrubbing a hand through his beard as he tried to put his thoughts in order. "So, Alpha and the bridges."

Oz squinted at him in the glare of the work lights around the tower. The expression drew Barrett's attention to sharp cheekbones. Apparently, he had a type. He pulled his head out of the gutter as Oz said, "Yeah, but we can do that in a moment. I was hoping to borrow your insights on the tower. You know it best, so maybe you'll see something they didn't."

"Fair enough." He led Oz up the stairs, passing a couple of field rangers as they stomped down. "Jacques got you all filled in?"

"Every last bit. And it all fucking stinks, pardon my language."

Barrett had to laugh. "No worries there. We're all a little rough around the edges. Being out past most of civilization will do that."

"Yeah well, you're more my type anyways." When Barrett gaped at him, Oz waved a hand. "Forest rangers, I mean. Never had a bad night when in the company of some of the crews up north."

"Oh. Right." *Is he flirting with me?*

Oz just smiled and Barrett felt heat up the back of his neck.

When they reached the entrance door, Barrett saw how badly it had been damaged. Not only had someone taken the time to nail in heavy wood planks from the outside - and bend the nails in a way that would make getting them out a pain in the ass - but they'd also jammed several very thin strips of metal into the deadbolt lock. There was something almost unhinged about the entire thing, like the person who had done it was fueled by rage. Those little strips of metal glinted in the harsh lights and Barrett winced. "Nasty. What in the hell would make someone do that?"

"They clearly weren't trying to get in. This place is ninety-percent windows." Oz stooped down to peer at the deadbolt. "We already had an officer out to take prints but I don't think they'll find anything. Can you look inside, see if anything looks strange? Just in case they entered before jamming the door."

"Yeah, sure." Barrett spared Oz a glance before going over to the bank of windows on their left. There wasn't much room on the little landing, so he made do with squashing himself against the railing and leaning in, against the cold glass. From the radio desk and map table to the bed and lockers, everything appeared to be in its rightful place. But there was a creeping sensation worming its way down the back of his neck and he shivered. "Don't see anything on the immediate. But there's a ton of supplies and such in there, so if they stole something, we'd need to go in and physically take inventory."

"Fair enough. Man, they really fucked up this door." A shutter clicked and Barrett saw the flash of a camera from the corner of his eye. "Stole the generator, too, so they probably had help."

"Maybe. But the generator's on wheels, so anyone with a ramp and a decent truck could haul it away." Barrett turned away from the windows and looked down. "No shoe prints or tracks?"

"Snowed over by the time Meredith was up here."

"Fuck."

"Agreed." And as suddenly as it came on before, Oz's grin was back, wide and toothy and friendly. "But we might get lucky. Jacques speaks very highly of you and you strike me as an observant man."

Barrett wanted to scoff but the compliment hit him right where Oz likely intended. Smart, this one, and good with people. He'd never worked with an investigator when he'd been a paramedic; too low on the hierarchy and too busy saving people's lives and, on occasion, dragging cats from trees.

(Okay, multiple occasions for Mrs. Scoffer, whose cat Trixie always got stuck in the same ancient oak on her property.)

He turned to Oz, whose expectant gaze went delightfully dark once Barrett's attention was on him. Something *crackled* in the air between them. Instant and heady. Ambrose wasn't dashed from his thoughts, but it had been a long damn time since he'd felt such instantaneous energy.

Barrett was quickly feeling a strange, swirling eddy building in his gut like fire. It was *not* appropriate to be feeling so pent-up at the scene of a crime. And he was well aware it was a very bad idea to fuck this man or even consider it, but he was *wanting* and it burned in his veins.

And that's *if* he was reading Oz's body language and tone right. "Ask me whatever you want," he said, daring to lean in a little. "But it's fucking cold out here. And it's late."

"It is." Oz's plush mouth quirked up. "Bit of a drive out of here."

"It is," he agreed, echoing. Some thread of sanity pulled him back into the present. "What are you wanting to know?"

"Gather your notes, any reports or field observations from any time you've been in the tower." Oz's voice had dropped a little and *fuck*, he had not been reading that wrong. Oz was staring at him hard. Barrett almost changed his mind before Oz said, "Meet for coffee in the morning?"

It was now or never. "Swing by my place. It's closer than the station, easier to navigate in the snow." He leaned in again, daring. Hoping. Fuck, how long had it been since he'd felt someone else's warmth, their hands? Their lips on his? Too long. Too fucking long and now that it was being dangled in front of him, he ached with it.

But the morning. If it didn't bring a clearer head, then maybe. Maybe.

"That sounds good." For one brief moment, Barrett swore he saw Oz's right hand clench against his thigh. "I should have all the reports from Jacques soon. We can compare notes. I'd also like to hear the bridge story from you personally, since you were heavily involved."

Barrett saw an opportunity to tease, to flirt. So he took it. "Meredith was there, too. Right there with me."

"Ah, but she didn't save a hiker from an icy plunge into the river. And then you and the hiker holed up in the firewatch tower for the night."

Barrett scoffed. "That was months ago."

Oz licked his lips. "It was. But I never leave a stone unturned."

And why did that sound like something *more*, coming from this man he'd just met? "Fair enough. But you have to bring pastries if you want them, I'm a shit baker."

Oz's laugh snapped like ice-covered branches in dying winter's chill. "That is entirely fair. I don't have much of a sweet tooth. I'm more of a savory person."

All of Barrett's replies died on his tongue as Oz waved him back down the stairs. "Be safe on the way out," Barrett said once they'd reached their vehicles. "That last turn on Pike Trail is nasty."

"Very considerate of you." Oz hopped into his truck. "See you tomorrow. Nine okay?"

"More than."

He waited until the truck lights disappeared around the bend before getting into his own vehicle and peeling out, head too full to do anything but wonder what the fuck he'd gotten himself into.

CHAPTER TWELVE

C oncern wrote itself on the faint lines on Ambrose's face when he answered Barrett's knock. "Sorry, I know it's early. Or late," Barrett said, his head ducked against the wind. "I didn't want you to have to watch her any longer."

Dandi was suddenly right there, her massive head nudging Ambrose's thigh as she peered up at Barrett. "Don't worry about it. I've not been to bed yet." He scratched at her soft ears and said, "Except, you could have warned me she snored."

He wasn't angry, not in the least, and his biting little comment made Barrett laugh; which had been the intention. Ambrose liked to think Barrett was coming to understand his strange, dark sense of humor. Dandi danced between them, her big brown eyes jolting from him to Barrett and back while Barrett laughed. "Figured you could discover that on your own. Like a freight engine, this one."

"Did you want to come in? I just put coffee on."

Ambrose stepped back, out of the doorway, but Barrett shook his head. "I'm gonna try to get a few hours of sleep before Oz swings by. The investigator assigned to...whatever the hell is going on."

He frowned. "That sounds serious. Is anyone hurt?"

Barrett shook that shaggy head of his head again, brows drawing down. "No, but between the bridge incidents and some stolen supplies and now the fire watch tower being sabotaged, they're wondering if it's connected."

The wind kicked up and Ambrose shivered. "Well, I've read enough mystery books to make me rather wary of coincidence in general. But it all sounds a little dangerous. Are you all right?"

Barrett swiped a hand down his face, his other hand stroking Dandi's head. "Yeah, yeah. Thanks. I've got to get at least a few hours of sleep before Oz comes over with reports to review."

"No rest for the wicked." But Ambrose was sympathetic; it sucked running on no sleep no matter what, but especially if you weren't an insomniac like he was. He was used to operating in that hazy, fuzzy space between waking and sleeping, most of his motions automatic. But Barrett looked bone tired, his eyes sunken and his normal color now more pallid. His heart gave a funny little flip at seeing his friend's exhaustion. "Do you want me to keep watching Dandi? She's no bother." He looked down, as if yanking his gaze from Barrett's would make the admission easier. "It's nice, having a dog around."

Barrett gave him a little sideways grin. "They're pretty great. But I think we're okay for now. Appreciate it."

"Sure." Silence fell over them, broken only by the crunch of loose snow under Dandi's feet. "I shouldn't keep you, you've been up all night and you're still working." He hitched a thumb over his shoulder. "One coffee to go?"

Fuck. Well, that was fucking cheesy. Shit. Ambrose winced but Barrett laughed. "Yeah, you know what? I could use it. But if it's okay, I'd like to talk about the tower sabotage. Get it right in my head. Could use a friendly ear and Oz is about an hour away."

Music to Ambrose's ears, honestly. Something about the way Barrett looked now - in dark, heavy winter gear, his nearly black beard and hair getting longer by the day, but those eyes... He could get lost in those eyes, as deep and dark as they were.

Shit. Shit.

He had a crush.

On his neighbor, his friend.

So stupid.

"Ambrose?"

"Wha -huh?"

Barrett was trying so hard not to smile but he was failing. Delightfully failing. His friend (*friendfriendfriend*, the word rang in his head) had a face made for little smirks and mischievous twists of the lips, but it was properly, fully used when he smiled wide and earnest and honest. That was what Ambrose got now, a slow, steady spread of lips, those eyes mirthful. Genuine. Not laughing *at* him. With him. For him.

Ambrose stepped back more and in they came. Barrett smelling of snow and diesel, his cheeks a little red and chapped from the cold. He wondered if his lips were chapped, too.

Fuck. Shit.

Ambrose shook himself one more time and focused on getting out cups and creamer. Dandi immediately took up the spot he'd made for her, on a few old blankets near the fire. He heard the couch squeak as Barrett sat. "So, what kept you up?"

"General insomnia, but also I'm..." He paused. Unsure. Did Barrett really want to hear about his writer's block? Whatever lashed out inside him - pride, maybe - he pushed down, stepped on it to say, "I took a freelance gig writing short fiction for a zine."

"Wait, really?" Barrett's grin was wide now as Ambrose brought two steaming cups over and sat down in the recliner opposite the couch. "That's fantastic! Val, my sister, did some gigs like that back in college. The competition was stiff. I bet you're damn good." He sipped his coffee while Ambrose tried not to squirm under his praise. "Any chance you'll divulge the name of the zine?"

Ambrose hadn't thought this far ahead. Hadn't really thought about it at all because, like so many things he did, he simply...did. Or, created. However one wanted to phrase it. He'd done that his whole life; the pouring of so much effort and sweat and stress into poems and songs, stories and articles. In every work, Ambrose left little bits of himself and over the years it wore down, dragging. He'd stepped away from most creative endeavors for a while, thinking it would recharge him. But he missed those bursts of inspiration, the way a new idea made his fingertips tingle and something swoop in his belly.

It was a lot like how he felt after a really good kiss. A little warm and shaky, the ground under his feet uneven enough to make him question his balance. Looking at Barrett now, one of Ambrose's stone coffee cups cradled in his hands, wasn't helping his balance currently.

Maybe he preferred uneven ground.

"It's a sci-fi and fantasy publication called *Nosferatu Starship*." Ambrose swallowed a little too hard against the next mouthful of coffee, winced against the sting. "I have one article a month, one story every quarter, until either they cancel my contract or I decide to stop. A year, minimum, though."

Barrett whistled, long and low. "Congrats. Seriously. That's amazing. I can't wait to see what you write." His gaze slid to the corner, where Ambrose's guitar sat. "You really are a man of many talents. I'm a little jealous."

"Jealous?" He frowned. "You're a forest ranger, and was a paramedic before. You save people. That's impressive. It takes guts." Ambrose squeezed the cup in his hands just for something to do with them. "I just make up shit in my head and try to put it down on paper."

"Ambrose."

"I'm serious. None of my little endeavors are equal to what you do day in and day out."

"Stop. Stop it." The bigger man slid to the edge of the couch and leaned into Ambrose's space as he hunched over his cup. "That's bullshit."

"It's not." He could feel anger begin to bubble in his gut. This was not the conversation he wanted to have today; now or later. Not tomorrow, not next week. Not ever. He was still picking apart the knots of his mother's career of slights and vitriol and maybe they'd never fully unravel. But that was his territory to claim, and nothing to do with Barrett. He got to his feet in a single huff, feeling his face twist out of a moue of distaste, to grab a small paperclipped bundle of pages from the kitchen table. Sharing good news was better than most things, especially his own fallacies and emotional hangups. "Here. From Raf."

Pages of rendered book layouts were thrust into Barrett's vision. "These ain't getting you off the hook, Ambrose," he muttered, but the little smile on his face as he flipped through the papers was its own story. "But hells. Really?" Barrett held up one of the page spreads; one Ambrose especially liked, as it featured long lines of wisteria and lilac paired with the pop of crocus and foxglove. Pretty in purples and blues and yellows, spring personified on two pages. "This is incredible. Huh."

"What?"

Barrett shook his head. His voice went quiet, almost stunned, as he said, "Perry would have loved this. You're doing right by him, and you didn't even know him."

If his heart could have sprouted wings and taken off in joyful flight, it would have. Barrett was staring at him hard now. Having all that attention focused on him in such a way usually made Ambrose want to find a dark corner in which to hide. But Barrett had a way at looking at you with raw, unfiltered emotion and it left him feeling...

Off-kilter. Off balance. A little bit as if he were on uneven ground.

"It's nothing," he said, trying not to be *Ambrose* and make his tone snap out of embarrassment.

"It's not." Barrett's tone had turned emphatic and now he was on his feet, the page hovering in front of Ambrose's face. There was no anger in the motion but Ambrose had to quell the urge to recoil anyways. "It's not 'nothing'." His voice broke. "Perry was a good man. A good friend. But he had no one."

"He had you." A solid knot of emotion was forming in his chest.

"He did. And then he had a heart attack and he was just gone and...." Barrett's eyes were wet as he turned away, motioning at the house. "And I thought coming back in here after someone else bought the place would be too much. But the house isn't his memory." He shook the page gently. "This is."

When Barrett stepped closer and looked down at him, Ambrose had to take in a shuddering breath. Carefully, his fingers trembling, Barrett handed back the pages. The rawness of the emotion on his face was nearly too much to bear, but Ambrose was rooted to the spot; sunken into dark brown eyes that swirled with unspoken emotion.

In his head, Ambrose was bolder, braver. Willing to lean in those last few inches and take the thing he was at least seventy-five percent sure Barrett was offering. He'd pull Barrett to him, hands cold with nerves but the rest of him on *fire*, and find out how that beard felt against the sensitive skin of his face.

He should do it.

But a hug was okay, too. Barrett pulled him in for the kind of touch that made some part of him curl up in a happy, sated ball. Maybe he was touch starved, maybe it was the slowly abating loneliness. Maybe it was because Barrett was a genuinely good guy and Ambrose was happy to have him near, no matter the context. But his friend (his *friend* and wasn't that an amazing thing to be able to say and think and *feel*, like a drumbeat) smelled like the outdoors and wood smoke and Dandi's warm fur and he wanted to keep that close to him. Wrap himself up in it.

Ambrose *wanted* and he practically burned with it. Being held in Barrett's arms as if it was the most natural thing in the world made his head spin. But then Barrett said, "Thanks, Ambrose," near his ear, beard brushing his jaw, and his knees turned to water.

"Yeah. Sure." That was all he could manage until Barrett stepped back and he saw the bit of red on the other man's cheeks. Maybe Barrett felt something similar?

"Ah, hell." Barrett held up his buzzing phone. "Time got away from me. I appreciate you listening. Really."

Ambrose swallowed away the lump in his throat. "Take your time with the pages. Anything you want to approve, just mark in the corner on the box that's there. Note any changes you want. Raf will send you the contract."

Barrett frowned, his thick eyebrows nearly drawing into a vee. "Contract? Shit, I didn't even think about that."

"He'll go over it with you, but I know he'll also recommend getting an attorney to review it."

Barrett chuckled. "Well that's awfully sporting of him."

"Raf's not interested in ripping people off, and he's pretty choosy who he works with."

That little smile was back. "Guessing your recommendation helps."

"Maybe." But he felt his own smile spread across his face, wide and open. Hopeful.

"Don't play coy, Tillifer." Barrett called for Dandi and moved toward the door. "Thanks again. I know that sounds like it's not enough appreciation, but I really mean it." He hooked a thumb over his shoulder. "I'm gonna go get about two hours of sleep and then drag myself through today. Get some sleep, Ambrose."

"Thanks." Ambrose meant it, wished he had more words to give Barrett more than just that.

And with the papers under one arm, Dandi's leash hooked in his right hand, Barrett gave him a cheeky salute and ambled out.

Barrett didn't fully get to sleep, staying in that strange place between dreaming and waking, lucidity and the slow daze of the sleepless. He jolted awake when his phone buzzed with a text from Oz, saying he was thirty minutes out.

Shit. He was a wreck, Dandi probably need a run, and there wasn't a big enough coffee pot in the world to deal with the dull thumping headache behind his eyes.

He managed to shake himself awake under the viciously hot spray of the shower and the bounding, endless energy of a very happy dog. By the time Oz pulled up, Dandi was appeased, his headache was nearly gone, and there was thankfully a full pot of coffee waiting and ready.

"Come on in," he said as he swung the door out for Oz to enter. "I hope you like really strong coffee."

"As a matter of fact..." Oz turned, tipped his chin up, and met Barrett's eyes. Something popped in the air between them and it had Barrett sucking in a sharp breath. "I find myself craving it this morning."

Oz slipped by him to get his coat and boots off, leaving Barrett fumbling with the door handle against a kick of wind. He moved to the kitchen while Oz seemed to take in the place in a slow, sweeping way that made Barrett prickle with awareness. There was an intensity to the man's dark gaze that had immediately sparked something in him, but now, in his own home, it felt more intimate. "Nice place," he drawled. "I really like the floors."

"Thanks." Oh god, were they at the small talk part? Barrett was always shit at that.

At Barrett's gesture, Oz brought his bag over to the kitchen table and settled, the battered old chair creaking under him. Oz wasn't a big guy in the least but those chairs groaned under even the slightest movement. Thankfully it didn't seem to bother Oz.

"Coffee?" Barrett cleared his throat, sparing a glance out the kitchen window that faced Ambrose's house. The chimney smoke swirled in the wind that had picked up, a gale blowing in while spring clawed its way through the remnants of winter. Thinking about Ambrose now was only going to be a distraction.

"Please." There was a charming quirk to Oz's smile and Barrett now noticed a thin, white scar from the corner of his mouth, curving up with his jaw. Oz busied himself with pulling out papers and a sleek laptop, his hands moving deftly. Barrett was thankful he had to turn away to finish the coffee, lest he be caught staring at golden-brown skin and the way dark ink peeked out from the cuffs of Oz's sweatshirt. He wondered how high it went. Did it twirl over hard-muscled forearms, maybe even slide over elbows and twist, higher and higher?

Ambrose's face appeared before him for a moment afterwards, those plush lips within distance, below stormy grey eyes staring up at Barrett as Perry's illustrations hovered in the space between them. Barrett had been torn. He wanted to lean in, pull the other man to him, and bury his face in the crook of that lean neck.

Ambrose made him tight, tense in a way that shocked him. These last few times they'd shared space, something electric had fizzed and snapped between them. He would readily admit Ambrose terrified him. Talented, smart, brooding, good looking. His neighbor, his friend, hit almost every button Barrett had, along with a few unexpected ones.

But he was a big believer in "moments". Perfect little bubbles of time where some stars aligned or a ley line connected, something in the universe *spoke*, and somewhere on their little planet, someone else listened.

Barrett had felt he and Ambrose were close to a *moment* just minutes before, standing in Ambrose's living room. But not close enough. Not perfect enough.

Val used to tease him for waiting for perfect, when they were both younger and more aligned ideologically. Not religious, per se. Maybe spiritual had been a better word. He'd let go of a lot of that over the years, but the older he got, the more he wanted to find that perfect moment in a bit of romance. He wanted to be like a hero in a novel, there to sweep someone off their feet and make them sigh. And...that's where the feel-good romance ended and the *fantasy* began. He was only human, after all.

But he and Ambrose kept missing a moment of their own and he wondered if he'd started falling too fast, too soon. What if that was where his hangups really were?

He glanced back at Oz as he shut his bag and stowed it under the kitchen table. His sleeves bunched up and Barrett lost himself in a two second fantasy of finding where that ink ended. Oz was strong. Had to be, the field they were in. But Barrett knew that swagger Oz had. It wasn't born of ego or overconfidence. It was the walk of someone who understood himself, his place with others and in the world. It was a rare kind of nirvana; and he would know, as he'd been chasing some semblance of it for nearly twenty years.

Not everything was about a perfect moment. Sometimes things were more *urgent* than that. A clash, a collision, hot and fierce and vital like the blood in his veins kind of *alive*. He wondered if Oz would be amenable, given the little spark between them last night.

"Ready?" Oz asked as they hunched over the laptop and a pile of papers and steaming coffee cups. "From the top, no detail too small."

"Got it," Barrett replied, reaching for his cup as Oz leaned forward. Their fingers brushed and he swore he heard Oz suck in a breath.

Maybe *alive* was okay for now.

He felt a continual hum under his skin as they spent hours pouring over very factual but very dry reports. Even Meredith had to stick to the structure rules, and her emails were full of playful uses of language and way too many emojis. They drained two pots of coffee and when Barrett made soup and salad for lunch, Oz tucked in like a man who enjoyed - and appreciated - good food. "You should swing by this little place in Nemesda, about an hour north of here. Called 'Patty's Place' and it looks like it should have a whole retro vibe, you know flickering neon sign and fried everything," Oz said as Barrett fed Dandi her afternoon meal. "But below there's a really awesome bar. Reservation only, bouncer at the door and everything, but it's super chill inside and all the art on the walls are pictures of tattoos. It's almost artsy, the way everything looks."

"Like purposefully a little messy?" Barrett hedged, retaking his seat. Was Oz a little closer now, or simply more relaxed? It was so small to almost be immeasurable, but Barrett would have sworn Oz's leg was closer to his.

He liked Oz. Sharp but funny, his wit fast and furious but never to make fun of someone. He was certainly a talker, but that wasn't a hardship as the man had a nice, even timbre; like a good narrator in an audiobook. He'd probably be a lot for Barrett day in and day out, but right now, as Oz leaned into him and their thighs brushed, he didn't care.

"I think that's it," Oz said as he flipped over the final piece of paper from their numerous stacks. "Thank you again, especially because I know you didn't get much sleep."

"Neither did you."

"Ha, no that is very true. I'm still buzzing though." Oz shivered and Barrett caught a whiff of faux-spicy deodorant, the kind of thing you could get at the drugstore for a couple of bucks. It was strangely charming on Oz, instead of cloying. "Something's definitely going on and this kind of malevolence is more than just costly."

"I was afraid you were going to say that," Barrett admitted. "Guessing you'll do up a report, send us the findings?"

"And make some suggestions for better security, tighter patrols. We don't have a clue if this is one person or a group. It could be a disgruntled ex-employee, a pissed off camper, some prankster who went too far. No idea yet, and without any evidence linking someone to all of this, it's impossible to know."

Barrett ran through his years of service in his memory, knowing he never encountered everyone who worked for the forestry service. There were twice as many admins, accountants, and department office staff as there were actual rangers, but there had certainly been some dramatic firings in the last several years. "So vigilance for now, yeah?"

"Yeah. It's the best we can do. That and a few hundred more security cameras."

He winced. There was no way they were getting permission from the state government for *that*. They could barely replace the trucks that became irreparable. "Yeah, everyone in our ranger department will do what we can to help with that, but it's gonna be an uphill battle."

Oz grinned at him. "I'm good with words. I'll impress upon them the importance of this. That, and how many lawsuits the government might face if they don't give us the tools to prevent future problems." He leaned in more and now they were inches apart, Oz looking at him with dark expectation. Barrett's stomach swooped. "I'm gonna take a chance here and tell you how attractive you are, Barrett. If I'm crossing a line, say so, and I'm done."

The timbre of that fine, even voice had gone soft, thoughtful, but edged with live-wire tension. Barrett's hand tensed on his own thigh. He was hanging on by a thread at this point. "I kinda thought the same about you," he admitted, drawing his words out slowly, watching every little flicker on Oz's face.

The tension was so good between them. It set his blood to boiling, *want* curling up from the bottom of his stomach like smoke. Promising fire and flame and heat. What lay between he and Ambrose was slower, broken up by a few near misses and some early mistakes.

He and Ambrose were friends.

He and Oz could be a really good fuck.

Daring a little, dreading a little, Barrett ran his palm under Oz's jaw and got a heavy breath in and a flare of nostrils. Dark eyes going even darker. And then Oz leaned up, head slanted.

Their lips met.

Oz groaned. Or maybe he did. Some heady, filthy noise before a tongue teased his bottom lip and he relented, letting Oz lick inside his mouth before pulling him to his feet.

"We doing this?" Oz asked, the question smashed, almost lost, between their mouths.

"Yeah. Fuck, yeah we are."

CHAPTER THIRTEEN

O z laughed the moment Barrett lifted him by the backs of his thighs and pinned him to the wall. "Holy fuck you're strong."

"I'm also not twenty any more." He kissed Oz hard as he dug his fingers in more. "So we've got about two minutes before my back gives out." Oz's answer was a quick tongue in Barrett's mouth, so he shut up and let himself *feel*. Everything. All of it. He was already hard, pressed into the vee of Oz's legs and thrusting against the cut of the other man's hip. With every thrust, his cock would brush up against Oz's and it felt so goddamn good.

"Let's not kill your back," Oz said. Reluctantly, Barrett put him down but he had no time to mourn the loss because Oz was asking, "Where's the bedroom?" and letting himself be tugged down the wide hallway leading to the back of the house. There was a bedroom upstairs in the loft, but Barrett mostly used it for another space to fill with books and trinkets, rocks and glass terrariums and his telescope.

He didn't care about any of that now. Oz slid into the room like he belonged there and immediately pulled his shirt off.

"So that's where all that ink goes."

Oz put his hands on his hips and let Barrett look his fill. The ink he'd spied under Oz's sleeve was a combination of thick, dark lines, almost vine-like, that twined up his entire right arm. The ink carried over his shoulder and ended in a rather delicate flourish near his right nipple. Barrett wanted to get his tongue on it. All of it. "I've got more but that involves nudity."

"So get naked."

"This isn't going to be a bad idea, right?" Barrett asked as he flung his shirt to a corner and yanked down his pants and boxers. "Like, there's no department code for -"

"Fucking a colleague?" Oz looked at him over his shoulder and then whatever he said next was obliterated by the sight of more dark ink curving over his left hip, over his ass, and down the back of one delightfully muscled thigh.

"Fuck. Oz."

"I know."

Barrett snorted. "You've got a healthy ego, I'll give you that."

"And you have a massive dick. Holy shit." Oz snatched Barrett's hand and pulled him to the bed. "I'm gonna need that in me about ten seconds ago."

"Only ten?"

"Give me a break, I was busy letting you stare at my ass."

While Barrett dove for the nightstand drawer, Oz started licking a wet path down his neck. Goosebumps erupted over his entire body. It had been a long goddamn time since anyone had touched him beyond platonically and Oz had thick, rough hands and a talented mouth that felt divine on his own weather-beaten spots and the more sensitive places covered by his gear.

Barrett shoved the condoms and lube under a pillow, then turned back to Oz, who was staring up at him with a pleased smirk. "No, there's no policy forbidding two colleagues in different government offices from fucking each other's brains out." His gaze slid south. "Or, in my case, letting you fuck me stupid on that massive cock."

"Jesus Christ," he muttered, but Oz's words were getting to him. He wasn't usually so vulgar in bed but if it got Oz going, then so be it. "This is a fuck, right?"

Oz shrugged. "If it's good, I'd be up for doing it again when the need arises."

"Guess we should figure that out."

"If it'll be good?"

"Yeah." Barrett ran his hands up Oz's chest, watching those dark eyes flutter shut at that simple touch. It spurred him on, those closed eyes and slick, parted lips, so when he pulled Oz into another kiss, he busied his fingers with stiff-peaked nipples. "Good?"

"Fuck. Fuck *yes*. You have great hands. Keep going."

He pinched and scraped his way down Oz's chest, emboldened by the near wild noises his partner was making. Oz seemed the type to like being catered to, and Barrett had a lot of pent-up energy to give. He followed the path of his hands with his mouth, skating over ribs and nipping at sensitive spots just above Oz's hip. Those legs he'd been admiring hooked around his waist as Oz slid closer and wrapped his hand around them both.

Heat roared through him at the touch of another's hand on his cock. But Oz kept talking, rambling, panting. "Fuck. Oh, fuck you Barrett. I can't even get my *hand* around us and you're going to break me open on that goddamn thing..."

Barrett was already sweating. But so was Oz, at his hairline and his neck. He licked the hollow of Oz's throat, feeling more than hearing the other man's groan. "You prepped?"

Oz yanked him forward, setting his teeth in Barrett's shoulder before saying, "Yeah, yeah. Just need stretched a little."

So Barrett slid his hand down the back of that tattooed thigh, keeping his touch light. "I'm good at that."

"Fuck. You're gonna kill me."

As Oz flipped over, Barrett pulled a condom down the first two fingers of his right hand and coated it all in lube. Then he looked down. "Aren't you a sight." Barrett ran his free hand up Oz's back, watching the shiver that ran up a supple spine. "Ready?"

"Yeah. Please." Oz looked back at him with wide, dark eyes. His bottom lip was red. Barrett wanted to push his thumb into that flesh and make it flush even darker.

That was the move of a lover. Not a fuck.

But the full body pulse of *want* was his reward for patience - and perseverance - when he gently pushed his index finger into Oz's body. Oz groaned, slumping forward to cradle his head on stacked forearms.

There was very little more physically intimate than being allowed to do this to someone else, pushing into a sensitive, delicate place that always felt like intrusion at first. But Oz knew what he was doing, and knew his body, because he spread his knees wider, canting his ass higher into the air. Asking for more, panting and thrusting back.

Barrett put a soothing hand in the middle of Oz's back. "More?"

"Goddammit, Barret. *Yes.*"

"I didn't forget you, promise," Barrett said after he put a condom on himself and then returned to spear Oz on three fingers. "Not gonna come if I touch you, right?" Oz tried to huff or make some other contemptuous noise, but Barrett twisted, then spread his fingers just right. Oz threw himself forward, hips jolting forward to thrust his cock into Barrett's fist. "Got my answer."

"Fuck you."

"Gladly."

As perverse as it might have been, watching his cock slowly disappear inside Oz nearly overwhelmed him. He pulled back on the urge to slam in, but even through the condom he could feel that silky heat and some part of him hungered. It had been so fucking long. He was no believer in denial, like some kind of weird, medieval punishment that denying yourself earthly pleasures was how you gained nirvana or what have you.

Life simply hadn't cooperated. And now life - or luck - had changed course.

"If you...go any slower...I'm gonna die of old age," Oz panted.

"So tell me what you want." Barrett gripped slim hips harder.

"In, all the way, now."

He sucked in a deep breath and let himself collapse a little forward, giving over to gravity and the velvet clutch of Oz's body. Oz didn't speak for a long moment when they were ass to hip and Barrett was barely hanging on to any semblance of sanity. He wanted to *move now*, every thrust and bump dragging little sounds out of Oz. But Oz needed the time to adjust, so he would get it. As long as he needed.

Then came the command, maybe three seconds and one eternity later. "Move." Oz slammed his hands down on the low wood headboard, fingers tight on the dark oak.

Barrett moved. It was slow at first but as deep as he could get at this angle, this speed. Though *deep* wasn't necessarily a problem. There had been a few potential lovers who had gone running for the hills when they saw what he carried around and that had been the only time he'd been aware it was *different* in a bad way. Mostly they were like Oz: impressed at first, and left pleasantly sore afterwards. Oz was all tight, silky heat and Barrett knew he wasn't going to last long.

The moment Oz began to reach for his own cock, Barrett got serious about chasing his own pleasure, that rush of stars exploding behind his eyes and heat through his body and the distinct feeling of contentment after really good sex. There was nothing else quite like it. Drugs, alcohol, none of it could match. He bore down on Oz, throwing his weight forward more and delighting in the surprised moan he got in response.

"Yes, yes, yes," Oz murmured, right arm flexing as he worked his cock. Gods he was a beautiful sight, all sweat-shined skin where long, black hair began to stick and curl; tattoos dark against grey flannel sheets. He was letting Barrett *unleash* a little, groans and *fuck yous* spurring him on, driving him higher while he sank deeper.

"Close," Barrett managed to say.

Oz swatted limply at him. "You're wrapped, just go."

Barrett came seconds later with a stifled groan, feeling as though he were one raw, pulsing nerve. He wasn't made of individual bones and sinews and old scars and bruises. He was solid, whole. Everything flared and flashed with pleasure, the kind he knew would leave him sated and asleep soon after. He fumbled near Oz's hip, wanting to bring him off.

"Is good. *Ah god fuck.*" And then Oz went rigid under him and Barrett heard a whisper-soft gasp. *"Fuck."*

After several long seconds, Barrett very carefully peeled himself off Oz and pulled out. He collapsed on the bed with a sigh. "Goddamn."

"Yeah." Oz flopped onto his back, face red and sweaty, eyes screwed shut and his left arm flung over his head. "Shit."

Barrett had to laugh. He was exhausted but some part of him was elated, rolling around in the afterglow. "Verdict?"

The bed shifted and then Oz was pulling him into a slick kiss, his tongue clever and quick against Barrett's. "I'd be good to do it again."

"Same."

"Then it's that easy."

Barrett sighed and nodded, letting his eyes fall shut. "Glad to hear it." He pointed vaguely in the direction of the bathroom before patting the spot beside him. "Shower's there if you need it. Or if you wanna stay..."

"I gotta get going. But maybe next time."

The bed shifted again and then bounced and when Barrett opened his eyes, Oz was on his feet, swiping at his body with a handful of tissues from the box on the nightstand. Barrett knew it was a hookup, a way to fill a very human need for physical intimacy and release. No shame in it, no concerns outside safety and consent. As long as everyone was fulfilled and all in, what did it matter if his bed partner didn't stay to cuddle through the afterglow?

It was sex. It wasn't a relationship. Shit, they barely knew each other.

He forced a smile on his face, ignoring the way his chest tightened. "So colleagues first, fuck buddies second? You cool with that?"

Oz yanked his shirt down, eyes narrowed in calculation. "Are you?"

"Yeah. Just no late night booty calls, I'm too old for that."

Oz laughed and just like that, the tension in the air lifted. "Yeah I got you. No worries." He finished zipping his pants before coming around to Barrett and leaning down to kiss him. "We figure out who the asshole is doing this shit around the parks, maybe I'll blow you as part of the celebration."

"Maybe?"

"Maybe." Oz winked. "I'm very good with my mouth."

"Jesus Christ."

Another laugh. "See you around, Barrett."

"Yeah. See ya."

And then Oz was gone and Dandi was snuffling at the rug in the hallway and Barrett was alone in a cold room, his bed smelling like sex and sweat.

Two weeks later

Ambrose was strangely nervous for this week's dinner with Barrett. As long as they were both available and feeling up for it, the routine was nice. Another stabilizing force in the wake of disruptions and aggravations. It also meant Ambrose was socializing, and doing so with Barrett was far less stressful than doing things like going to parties and standing in the corner all night. But tonight felt off somehow. Barrett hadn't been around much these last two weeks and when Ambrose did see him, Barrett sometimes would jog over, Dandi at his side, for a few minutes of catch-up. A few more times, he just waved and smiled. He never felt ignored, per se. But something felt *off*. Ambrose was aware enough to know when someone was putting distance between him and them.

He allowed himself one moment to reflect on the rumpled, sweaty man who had emerged yesterday afternoon from Barrett's, as Ambrose was fixing a pot of tea and listening to a podcast about forgotten history. While the water boiled, he began texting Barrett a link to the show, thinking as a reader, his friend might enjoy it. And then he saw the man jog to his truck. Hair messy and tangled, gait a little off. Cheeks flushed.

Looking for all accounts like a man who'd just come back from a hard run. Or a good fuck.

He'd turned away, suddenly feeling nauseated. He wasn't the jealous kind. He wasn't. But something about knowing *this*, right after Ambrose had nearly kissed Barrett, was sending him spiraling. And then Barrett's distant look and little waves but few words...

No, tonight wasn't off. He was just being an idiot.

Resolved with a deep breath (the ones his therapist constantly reminded him to take) and dinner, Ambrose flipped on the little portable speaker and set his phone to play some lo-fi. Opening the wine, fussing with the silverware, and straightening the tablecloth helped. But that slight undercurrent of nerves was still there. An itch he couldn't quite scratch between his shoulder blades, slowly driving him mad.

Barrett's knock, a *thumpthumpthump* gentle against the worn front door. When Ambrose answered, Barrett was smiling and holding out an unlit blunt, bottle of tequila under his arm, and Dandi fiercely wagging her tag. "Peace offering?"

"For?" His fingers hovered over the blunt.

"I know I haven't been around as much for talking and such, and I missed last week's dinner." Those soft brown eyes matched the sad little twist to lips hidden in his beard. "Felt weird, having a week like that. Didn't want you to think I was ignoring you or anything."

Oh. Ambrose blinked, then moved out of the way so they could enter. "You really do just...spell it out, don't you?" Dandi nudged at his hand and he gave her velvety head several pats.

"Too much? Yeah, been told that." Barrett tugged off one boot, then the other. "Sorry. I'm a little frayed." He hooked a thumb at the door. "I can go."

"No, don't!" Ambrose didn't mean to say it that loud but Barrett's face only showed concern, not shock. "It was weird, not having you around last Friday night."

That face broke open in a smile. It hit him in the chest, that bright thing, and made him suck in a breath. Ambrose hoped Barrett didn't notice. "Yeah, yeah. I was getting caught up with Val and Forrest, and then I had company. The company was kind of spur of the moment, but it worked out."

"How is your family?" Ambrose went over to the oven to check on the food as Barrett settled on the couch, Dandi in her designated area by the fire only after sniffing at Ambrose's hair as he bent down to greet her properly. It was almost amusing that he and Dandi were so physically affectionate, like they were old friends.

Barrett blew out a hard breath. "Forrest is stable for now, but the kid's got a long road ahead. Leukemia treatments have come a ways but..." He trailed off, gaze distant.

"Sorry." He turned his face away from the blast of hot air from the oven. "I shouldn't have asked." Ambrose gave the crust of the chicken pot pie a solid once over. It was done, but a couple more minutes wouldn't hurt. Letting Barrett talk about his family worries and then him blithely announcing dinner was done would be jarring to say the least.

"No, it's fine. I need to talk about it and I appreciate you listening."

"Any time. I hope you know that."

Whatever lay in those dark eyes of his friend seemed grateful now, instead of focused somewhere on a far horizon. "I do. But you got shit going on, too. Anything going on with the zine?"

"Actually, yes." A flush of pride went through him. "The first story's with the editor."

"Already?" Barrett placed two glasses of tequila on the table and now moved to the other side of the kitchen. Warm and comforting, voice rumbling in Ambrose's ears. Gods, he had it bad. He wanted to touch. More than just curiosity, more than pushing away any remnant of Preston. He simply *wanted*, that unscratchable itch now burrowed deeper under his skin. "Damn, you work fast! That's impressive as hell."

He tried not to flush. "Just got some inspiration late one night, spent the next few days writing when I wasn't working."

Barrett laughed. "Man, when you focus, you really dig in. I love that."

There was no hiding his startle or his sharp intake of breath. Ambrose stared at Barrett, his brain trying to unscramble what he'd just heard. "Compliments" like that were always backhanded. Always. A nod to Ambrose's dedication and focus, and a slap of the other cheek meant to wound him shallowly. But years and years of shallow, an entire childhood's world of shallow, meant there were a thousand and one little cuts across his skin. The back of his hands, the sides of his neck, his throat, his chest. Skating over his scalp, even hooking tiny claws into the grey wrinkles of his brain.

"Ambrose." Barrett shifted, scratched at his beard. Scratched again. Cursed.

And then his brain sped back up with time and he blinked. "Usually, when I've heard things like that from other people, it wasn't meant so kindly." Ambrose's voice was tight-strung; wire on a holiday decoration threatening to give at any minute and send the entire chain of lights crashing down. "But you were kind. It was an actual compliment."

Barrett looked stunned but Ambrose kept talking. "I don't make friends easily, as you can imagine. A lifetime's worth of things have made me skeptical. And the therapy's only now cracking through. Working, I guess." He tore his gaze away. "I take patience."

The worming, squirming thing in his chest made him want to hide. He couldn't, not really, so he settled for reaching into the oven and pulling the food out. Soft footfalls echoed across the floor and then Barrett was there and he smelled so good and Ambrose couldn't take it any more.

Chapter Fourteen

B arrett was reaching for him when Ambrose caved. He knew he was trembling. He knew he was weak. He liked Barrett; every rough edge and worn flannel shirt and the love and care he showed for his neighbors and friends and family. That willingness to help a stranger in need. How he didn't push, didn't antagonize.

He liked Barrett. Desired him, even. But right now, this very moment where he felt flayed open but so distressingly, blindingly *alive*? Ambrose needed someone to touch him like he mattered. He hoped Barrett was willing to give just a little.

Barrett didn't startle. Didn't move back in shock. Somehow he knew. He knew Ambrose would fold into him so Barrett's arms were open; solid and real and warm and perfect. There was too much of his own beard in the way and Ambrose wanted to rip the thing off, only so he could feel Barrett's prickle against his face.

Finally, after the silence turned soft and Barrett's hug tightened, little by little, Ambrose heard him say, "Get me a list."

"Of?" He absolutely didn't want to move away from the crook of Barrett's neck and that warmth.

"Anyone who's made you feel like that. I got a bone to pick with them."

His laugh was too watery by several degrees, but he was glad he didn't sound like he was crying as he said, "If it's the same to you, I'd rather not. As much as I appreciate it."

The broad hands on his back slowly moved up and down. "Why not?"

Now Ambrose pulled back. He needed to look Barrett in the eyes as he said, "Part of my journey. Learning to leave the past in the past, bit by bit. There was a time when I would have gladly taken you up on that but, one, I don't need a white knight, and two, it would only set me back." He squeezed Barrett's shoulders then let go. "You're a lovely person, Barrett."

Ambrose was beginning to learn that Barrett was a man with dozens of little expressions. Thin, tight lips, a tiny squint. Fingers scratching at a thick beard or the back of his neck. His words were careful, calculated after these expressions and Ambrose had been around him long enough to know Barrett wasn't one to fire off without reason. "Okay. Okay. But uh, promise not to get pissed at me?"

"I promise." He could do that much.

"You gotta be better to yourself." Barrett was now gripping Ambrose's shoulders, each finger an indent in his skin, like a brand. "You gotta, Ambrose. I'm really glad you've got help, someone to talk to. You can come to me, too." His face fell and Ambrose wanted to fix it, wipe it away. Replace it with something better. Someone better. "I know these last couple weeks have been kind of scattered, but I am here."

His weakness was going to do him in.

Hands hovering around Barrett's jaw, he said, "Thank you."

He meant to pull back, but then Barrett was leaning into that ghostly touch, left cheek turned into Ambrose's palm. "I'd let you."

Ambrose's words died on his tongue.

"I would. Thought about it a few times." Barrett's confession sounded like it hurt, pulled up from a throat and lungs and heart that weren't fully sure if they should help him speak it aloud. "Wondered what it felt like."

His weakness wasn't only his, apparently. Ambrose fixed his eyes on Barrett's mouth, expecting to see chapped, red skin, worn from the cold and wind he worked in. Instead, those lips were smooth and pink and slightly damp from where Barrett had licked them moments ago.

"You....wondered," Ambrose managed to say, feeling frozen, stuck. His hand cradling Barrett's cheek, the other sliding up a thick neck. His heart thudded in his ears, his mind stuffed full of twisting, combative emotions. He should pull away. But he didn't want to.

"Yeah, more than a few times." Oh gods, now there was a hand on the back of his neck, gently suggesting more than pushing. No demands. No expectations. Barrett was letting Ambrose figure himself out. Figure out the moment. "Turns out I have a thing for handsome, talented men who can match me drink for drink and know the scientific names of fish."

The words fell from him faster than he could stop them. "What about your uh....friend?"

Barrett's brow dipped in confusion, then he laughed. "Oh, Oz? That's just fucking. He's too chatty for me. A little too full of himself."

Oh gods. Ambrose considered perishing on the spot. *He* wasn't chatty, or full of himself. In fact doubt racked him so badly he was finding all kinds of ways to ruin this *goddamned moment*. When he should be kissing Barrett.

"Kiss me." He whispered it but he couldn't pack more bald-faced *desire* into those two words. "Find out."

He stopped before he could say please, but Barrett would have swallowed the word up in that first brush of lips. Ambrose let his eyes fall shut, could feel his body stiffen as Barrett carefully - reverently - kissed him. Lips against his, just a press of warmth and softness.

And then it was over. He hadn't even had the chance to shiver, to melt into Barrett's arms.

"It's not right." Barrett's low voice shook him loose.

Dread pooled in his stomach and he didn't want to look but he had to. But concern was the only thing written in those broad, blunt features. "Ambrose. I know." Barrett smoothed his hands over Ambrose's shoulders. "I think...no, I get it. You've got need written all over that *incredible* face of yours. And something in me thinks I ain't worthy of your attentions." Ambrose frowned, opened his mouth to protest (maybe even to beg for more, more touching, more kissing, more of Barrett's hands on him), but Barrett held up a finger. "Hold on. Let me get this out. Cause I have a feeling I'm right here. But I'm thinking this winter, and this new place, and everything going on has you wanting. Right?"

Barrett was right, and Ambrose hated it. There was something else far buried inside, nestled against his heart and trying to mimic *hope*. "Are you psychic?"

Barrett laughed, the sound loud and echoing but just right in its' full-bellied honesty. "Winter's rough out here. I'm sorry I haven't been around more -"

"Stop saying that."

"No, you're getting an apology." Barrett smiled. "I mean it. But this...you and me...I think we gotta work up to it." And then there was a hand on his face, a calloused thumb stroking his cheek and

Ambrose remembered Barrett calling his face *incredible*, saying he was *handsome* and *talented*. "Cause here's the thing. I like you. A lot. But I haven't made room in my life for someone in a real fucking long time but I want to. But I also think you and I gotta go slow."

Barrett was right. He was absolutely right and Ambrose knew it. Some part of him ached for more touching, more kissing. From the darkness at the edges of Barrett's brown eyes, he was pretty sure his friend felt something similar. "To what end? What are we working up to?"

Barrett's gaze locked on Ambrose's mouth and the world stopped. Hope, that thing in his chest, cracked open an eye and shook its head in acknowledgment. "I want to be friends. Good friends, Ambrose." The hand on his cheek dropped away but it was replaced by fingertips down his neck, tracking the tendons and freckles like Barrett was just now seeing them. "I want to share things with you. Meals and drinks and chasing the mutt around. I want to share stories and moments and long, easy silences. But there's something here. Something real. And I don't want to fuck that up." Barrett dropped his hands away and Ambrose nearly whimpered. "I've fucked up enough things in my life. I want to share something special." He looked away. "So to what end is whatever is right for us."

Sharing...yeah. Sharing space and breath and touches like they mean something because they do, they mean so much and it could be more. It could be need and desire and sweat and sex and intimacy like I've never had before and it's all right in front of me if I just take the time to hold onto it.

"Yes."

In the end, it was that easy. Ambrose didn't have to overthink it. "Just like that?" There was a twist to Barrett's lips, playful. Hopeful. "Even if it requires both of us to be patient. I don't dive in and as much as I like you, it's been a long damn time."

"Tell me about it sometime. When you're ready."

Barrett nodded. "When I'm ready. And when you're ready to hear it."

Deep breath pulled into his lungs, Ambrose stepped back, away from the protective circle of his friend's arms. Back into his own space, even while his brain felt too full for anything more. "So no labels, just....friends."

"Not just." That smirk grew and Ambrose found it adorable. "You kiss all your friends?"

That got a laugh, surprised and delighted at the same time. Something in Ambrose's chest lifted, lightened. "Never. Except you."

Dinner wasn't awkward like Barrett thought it would be. There was a moment, seconds long and split between the first cut of a truly professional looking chicken pot pie and the placement of that piece on his plate, where Barrett thought Ambrose might back out. And that was okay. He'd be disappointed for sure, but he was asking a lot. Mostly he was asking for forbearance. A little forgiveness. A lot of patience. The thoughts and doubt that clogged his mind rose, twirling like the steam off his plate. But he knew this was the correct path forward.

The kicker was what he couldn't tell Ambrose right now but really wanted to. It was some kind of gnawing, gnashing maw inside him. Culturally, people like him didn't "make sense" to a lot of queer folk. Hells, he was already on the outside, a gay man who looked like he belonged in a commercial for deodorant aggressively marketed at *manly men*. There were quite a few gay men who thought Barrett bottomed and *only* bottomed. He'd been told more than a few times he had an ass anyone would like to plough (which wasn't the compliment most thought it was).

Then you had people like Oz, who figured Barrett would be a good fuck (accurate) and would want more. They never expected him to enjoy the sex and the cuddle, and then be just fine left alone. Or appear to be fine with it.

And then there was the real him. A gay forest ranger who was a good cook, a guy with a high sex drive, and someone who was a brother, an uncle, a friend, a lover, a good neighbor, but someone who had never been in love.

Barrett loved love. He loved the whole concept of being swept off your feet, falling madly in love (or lust) at the first pass of a hand, trembling under the fragile potential of a first kiss. He was a massive sap and proudly bore that badge, but he'd never been more than a step or two further out. Val said he was a relationship sprinter: a burst of speed, and then done. Over. No family holidays, no moving in together, certainly no long term commitments because quite simply, he didn't feel it. That squishy, gooey, molten caramel core of love and devotion and thinking of the future and wanting to...hell, sample wedding cakes or some shit like that.

Barrett wanted at least some of that. The thought of not being alone the rest of his life sounded pretty great. But getting there seemed like a chore, too white picket fence and cutesy for his liking. He knew, realistically, he could define love however he wished. And thinking back on his relationships, he knew he probably had come the closest with Marcos. But they'd been fresh out of college and still riding the high of first big jobs after school. Long hours tore them apart and they could never quite fit back together after that. And now, a decade and a half later, Barrett was still waiting to be swept off his feet.

Ambrose had changed a lot of that. And the worst thing was, he'd given Barrett hope. He didn't know whether to cradle it close, or let it drop and dash against the rocks of his cynicism. But he knew everything in him screamed for more. More touching, more soft words, more kindness. He wanted to be smothered with it, safe and warm and sure that nothing bad could find its way through.

But now as they sat in Ambrose's loft, each two tequilas in and feeling pleasantly warm (at least that's how Barrett was feeling), he felt that flare of hope again. Bird wings against his heart. "I had a question but I didn't want to impose," Barrett said as he leaned back in his chair.

"No imposition." Ambrose's smile was small but genuine. Did he ever not look good? He was a little rumpled, his hair thick and wavy and gorgeous in the flickering light. Two thin, long fingers were curling around a lock of it. The sight made Barrett's teeth itch.

"You're really good on the guitar. I was hoping you might show me a few things." He held up his own broad, rough hands. "I've got some chords I haven't quite gotten yet."

Ambrose leaned forward quickly, tequila sloshing in his glass as he smiled. A big, open smile that made the corners of his eyes crinkle. "I'd love to show you."

"You sure? I know it's - "

"It's not. An imposition or a lot to ask or whatever other idiom you were about to use." Ambrose was *teasing him*. The stark truth of it slapped him in the face. The man continued to surprise and delight him and Barrett wondered what else was buried under freckled skin and auburn hair and clothes at least a size too big on his lanky frame.

The image of Ambrose dressed like he'd been in that picture with Raf flashed before his eyes and Barrett had to bite back a groan. "Okay, yeah, great," he finally managed after clearing his throat and giving himself a little shake.

"But I get to do something for you."

Oh. Interesting. There was a gleam in Ambrose's gray eyes and he wondered where this was going to lead. "That's not me returning a favor, Ambrose. That's me getting twice the kindness."

"And? I want to offer, at least, before you turn me down."

"Okay but..."

"Let me fix your hair. And your beard."

"Wait. What?"

Ambrose laughed and Barrett liked the sound instantly. It was a pleased little noise and the happy consequence of it was an expression of delight on Ambrose's gorgeous face. "I know you're out in the wind and cold and rain and whatnot day in and out. But..." He watched Ambrose's hands tense on the armrests. "Self care shouldn't go out the window. I've seen you scratching at your beard."

"Can't say I've ever had anyone offer that," he replied, catching himself only after he'd dug his fingers into his beard. The knowing little smirk on Ambrose's face made his self-consciousness worth it. "Is this you telling me I look like I climbed down from the mountains?"

A shrug. "You said it. Spoke it aloud and made it real."

"Ass. You a trained barber, too?"

Ambrose took it for the gentle jab it was. "Just years of experimenting with my own face and hair, honestly. Figuring out the best combinations of oils, finding good combs and soaps. That kind of thing."

"Do I get a hot towel and a beverage?"

"Of course." Ambrose wiggled his fingers on the armrests. "Full service."

Barrett's mouth went dry. "You flirtin' with me, Tillifer?"

The laugh and lip bite Barrett got in reply sent a bolt of heat through his entire body. "Maybe." Then reluctance, a spark going out. "Too much, too soon? I know we're not.." He turned away and Barrett hated that.

"No, it's fine. More than, really. Just so we know where we stand, and we're comfortable." Barrett leaned back in his chair. "It's good. Good way for us to work out some things. Set some boundaries. And speaking of, this you and me thing." Ambrose turned back, gaze expectant but wary. "Are we drawing lines with exclusivity now? Is that something you need or want?"

Ambrose immediately shook his head. "No. I'm not looking around. Never was like that."

He might as well just ask. "I've got a sometimes fuck buddy, just a side thing. You might have seen him around recently, but he doesn't stay." Barrett sucked in a deep breath. "Does that bother you at all?"

"Gods no." Ambrose was back at his side now, grey gaze serious. "I would never get in the way. We're friendly flirting, figuring each other out. Going slow."

"All right. Just making sure cause it's definitely not anything more than that."

Ambrose nodded. "I understand that. A filling of a physical need."

"Yeah. Yes. Exactly." It felt good to air that out. He didn't take Ambrose for the jealous type but people constantly surprised him. "It won't be a thing that lasts."

Ambrose leaned down and brushed the pad of his thumb over Barrett's cheek. It made him shiver. "We're just testing waters right now. I appreciate your honesty, Barrett. More than I can convey. But we're good." His gaze dropped to Barrett's mouth. "Needs have to be met. And you and I aren't there yet."

He let his gaze scrape over Ambrose. Wanted to let the other man feel it like a hand on his body, in his hair, tracing tendons in finely boned hands. The hands of a painter and a musician and a writer. An artist. Lust flickered on the edges of his mind, swirling with the tequila in his system and making him too warm. Something lingered, unsaid. "Yet?"

"Unless you're looking to *test* a few boundaries. Because I've always loved doing that." And as he passed by, he squeezed Barrett's arm. "Another drink?"

It wasn't until Ambrose was downstairs, making ice clink and bottles rattle, that Barrett laughed and shook his head. It was, apparently, always the quiet ones.

CHAPTER FIFTEEN

END OF MARCH

"**N**othing?"

Oz shrugged. "It's not nothing." He pointed to the monitor that he, Meredith, and Barrett were huddled around. "See, cameras two and four go out. Conveniently the ones pointed at the storage shed. And then next..." He hit a couple of keys and a new camera feed popped up. "Fire."

"That shed was about ten years old and we'd just replaced the roof." Meredith spun in her chair, boot heels squeaking on the cracked linoleum. "There are five sheds in a ten mile radius, and they picked the one we'd just done a bunch of work on."

"Not accidental," Oz agreed. He nudged Barrett with an elbow. As he did, he leaned forward, shirt gaping until Barrett could see the dark edge of a bruise. Fucking tease. The bruise was barely twelve hours old, left at three in the morning when Oz begged for Barrett to fuck him into next week. They hadn't hooked up in a few weeks, Oz's county job dragging him back as the sabotage investigation sputtered. With no evidence of the perpetrator and no other incidents since early February, there was nothing for him to do.

But he'd shown up on Barrett's doorstep with a bottle of bourbon and while he might have minded a quiet Sunday getting interrupted, Barrett knew Oz's cocky smile promised a fun, sweaty evening.

"Ah, gods, fuck, you're so fucking tight."

"Been....been a while."

"Do you need -"

"No. Keep going. Oz. Fuck.

Heat zipped down his spine and he pushed back from the table. Out of Oz's reach. Couldn't get distracted now, and he was more than a little annoyed seeing their lead investigator - their only investigator

- not giving the tapes his full focus. The bridges, the fire tower sabotage, and now arson. People had already gotten hurt and it was by sheer luck that it hadn't happened again.

His stomach clenched thinking of what might have happened if he hadn't caught Ambrose before he'd crossed that bridge.

"It's not an accident. We all know that." His words snapped out, harsher than he meant, but maybe harsh wasn't a bad thing by now. "It's all circumstantial, but either this person is well researched, or they know us. Our safety measures. The placement of the cameras. The ranger rotations. It's too convenient."

Oz's face had gone blank and Barrett thought *good*. Maybe that would wake the man up. "Well, there's little I can do without evidence, Barrett. They're smart enough to not get caught on the cameras, smart enough to track your squad's movements. Seems like you might want to take some precautions, switch things up." Oz stood up in one smooth motion and smiled down at them. That smile was tight and Barrett heard Meredith shift in her chair. He didn't blame her; it wasn't a nice smile by any means.

"I have to get back to County," Oz said as he zipped up his jacket. "Send over any plans you make so we have them on record. But until we have evidence - anything - I'm not going to be able to help. Cut wires and a burned shed and some broken bridges don't lead to anything until we have something substantial."

"So we just wait until they do something else and hope it doesn't get anyone else hurt?" Meredith's voice grew louder, anger flushing her cheeks. Barrett watched her ponytail bounce as she stalked toward Oz. "So what, County won't care until something headline-grabbing happens? That's some bullshit and you know it, Oz. Grow some fucking balls."

She stomped out of the room, leaving them to stare at each other. "Might not want to get that one pissed off," Barrett said, trying to lighten the air.

"It's not a joke, Barrett." The flat, hard stare Oz gave him ruffled more than a few of Barrett's feathers.

"Whoa, okay. Hold on." Now he was up and moving, but he kept space between them. "I was a little miffed earlier because it felt like you weren't fully focused. But we're all stressed because of this. I'll go to Jacques and we'll figure out something."

Oz sucked in a deep breath through his nose. "You're right, you're right. And I get it. But I actually can't do anything here, Barrett. You know that. My hands are tied." He smirked. "Something we can try later, if you want."

Barrett's wheels were spinning, his mind bouncing from idea to idea to present to Jacques, when he caught up with Oz's comment. "Hey, not now," he hissed, eyes darting to the partially open door. "And not here. I don't want that getting in the way."

"I know." Hands up in a placating motion, Oz stepped toward him. Chin tipped up invitingly. "Later?"

"I can't. Busy."

"Too busy for me to come over?"

"Yeah. I won't be home. It's Friday, I'm having dinner with Ambrose."

He got an arched eyebrow at that. "You two seem cozy. What's the story there?"

"What does it matter?" Barrett glared down at Oz, something protective rising up in him. His time with Ambrose was *theirs*. Time slowly spent getting to know each other, building a tapestry of story between that *meant something*. Because Barrett really, really liked Ambrose and as much as that hair called to his fingers and he wanted to know what that mouth tasted like, he was enjoying taking his time. *Their time*. Together.

"Sorry I asked."

"No, it isn't that, I just..." But Oz had already backed away. "Oz."

Barrett licked his lips, tried again. Somewhere in the back of his mind, he wondered what he was trying to salvage here. He liked Oz, but while the fucking was good, they didn't really have anything in common. They weren't even friends. It was all physical. Oz came over to his place, they fucked, and then he left. It was hollow on a level Barrett never expected to be bothered by. Until now. Because Ambrose was in the picture and even though Ambrose knew the deal with him and Oz, somehow it still bothered Barrett.

"Send over anything you come up with, just mark it urgent so it doesn't get buried in my inbox." The smile that flickered over Oz's face felt like a hand on his shoulder, shoving a dislocation back into place. "And sorry, Barrett. I didn't know. If you get bored, text me."

And he was gone and Barrett was left to stare at the security camera footage, watching the storage shed go up in flames over and over again.

"You should lure them out."

"This isn't a spy movie, Ambrose."

Despite Barrett's snippy tone, Ambrose didn't blink. He had both hands wrapped around the slobbery, frayed rope Dandi was tugging the other end of. He was giving her a pretty good fight, but it was tough to hold your own against a one hundred and fifty pound Great Dane. "I know that," he said between heavy breaths. "But what other options do you have?"

Ambrose was right. Barrett gave the wooden spoon a few taps on the edge of the pan and set it down. But there was a big difference between what Ambrose was suggesting and what the department was capable of. Jacques had managed to wheedle more money out of County for additional security cameras, and they'd set up a guard rotation on likely targets; the sheds, supply drops, the fire watch towers. But it wouldn't be enough. His gut told him it wouldn't be.

"No, you're right." Barrett put the lid on the pot and set a fifteen minute timer. "Dinner's soon."

"It smells amazing." Dandi woofed softly and Ambrose laughed. "Dandi agrees."

"Dandi isn't getting table scraps and she knows it." Barrett gestured to the dog as he sat down on the couch. "She begs something awful."

"That's because she's precious," Ambrose cooed, leaning forward to rub the dog's velvety ears. As he did, his long sleeved shirt rode up and Barrett could see a swath of pale, creamy skin dotted with freckles. No hair that he could see but he did spot a dimple at the base of his tailbone and Jesus fucking Christ....

He dug his fingers into the throw pillow beside him. This *agreement* between him and Ambrose, to let things naturally progress, was killing his restraint. Especially since he and Oz weren't fucking anymore.

From: Oz *Sorry about today. The whole situation's fucked up.*

From: Barrett *The sabotage...or you and me?*

From: Oz *You and me aren't fucked up. We're just fucking. But what you want and what I want I think are two different things.*

From: Barrett *Yeah, I get that. Still keep you on call in case?*

From: Oz *You know it. That ass is too good to turn down.*

And like that, it was done. Sure, they could get a beer. They could be friendly. And it was easy to walk away like this. As easy as it had been to hook up.

"How's work?" he asked, desperate for a distraction that didn't involve ogling Ambrose's back.

"Same as ever. Dandi, seriously." Ambrose laughed as the dog shook his grip on the slobbery rope and flung it from side to side. "How many of these does she go through?"

"In a week or a month?"

"Forget I asked." A keen look on his face, Ambrose pulled his knees to his chest and wrapped his arms around them, his chin now resting on top. He looked younger that way, the fine lines of his face wiped away, his hair tumbling to almost mid bicep now. For all the man touted his hair care routine, Barrett could see it had been a while since his last haircut. But the winter beard was gone, leaving Ambrose's face bare and smooth and making Barrett want to lick along his jaw.

"Raf said you and he worked out an agreement for Perry's illustrations."

"Yeah, actually. Good guy, your friend. Super chill."

"I told you." Ambrose smiled softly at him and something inside Barrett's chest melted. Some hard exterior wall, left over after decades by bitterness and anger and isolation. Something was giving in. "Perry's illustrations deserve to be seen. He was really talented."

Dandi huffed at them both and threw herself onto her massive dog bed, instantly on her side with her eyes closed. "Dramatic," Barrett said, getting a tail wag in response. "She's ridiculous."

"She is, but she's worth it."

The timer on the stove beeped a minute warning and Barrett thrust a hand down to pull Ambrose up. As he stood, Ambrose put a hand on Barrett's shoulder to steady himself. Barrett really liked that Ambrose was as tall as he and now, this close, he could let a grin flicker over his face. An expression he absolutely hadn't practiced in the mirror a few dozen times, trying to get it right. Intriguing, but not suggestive.

"I'm really glad Raf was able to help," Ambrose said, his voice quiet amidst the pop of the fire and the patter of rain outside. Spring was in full force at Lake Honor, and that meant loads of rain. Grey eyes fixed on Barrett's mouth, then moved to his beard. "When are you gonna let me help you with that?"

"When I master the chords you're gonna teach me tonight."

"Fair enough." Ambrose's lips twitched into a smile.

After dinner, Ambrose set up in the corner closest to the fire while Barrett let Dandi outside. He was excited to show Barrett new chords but the excitement came tinged with nervousness. It was one thing for him to fumble around at home or in his tiny recording studio. He could fuck up as much as he wanted, curse, agonize, tear his hair out. But Barrett was genuinely asking for help and Ambrose wanted to be a good teacher.

The next thought was he wanted to be *good for Barrett* but that context had sent his thoughts spiraling.

This thing between them lay quietly slumbering. A reminder that they were going slowly, but not ignoring what was clearly mutual attraction. He'd seen Barrett staring and then quickly turn away. In any other context, with anyone else, he might have thought it a ham-fisted attempt at flirting or getting his attention. But after living next to each other for several months, Ambrose had picked up on Barrett's situational and surrounding awareness. He was pretty sure the man didn't miss much. So if he was looking, it was for a reason.

Barrett looked at him like Ambrose was *interesting*. Sometimes, like just before dinner, there was a flicker of heat to that gaze that upped *interesting* to *intriguing*, and it made his heart race. But feeling seen in such a way was also foreign to him. Letting anyone in after Preston was difficult.

He wandered over to the giant hibiscus in the living room nook window. Barrett was outside, illuminated by the back porch light and the fuzzy blue of his phone screen. He was talking animatedly to someone, occasionally swiveling the phone and laughing as Dandi barked. He stepped forward, trying to see more, when his foot bumped Stella's pot.

"Sorry, Stella." Ambrose touched a tightly closed pink bud with his fingertip. When he looked again, Barrett and Dandi were gone. The back door slammed and he jumped away from Stella, his finger tingling with aftershocks from her softness.

Barrett appeared around the doorway from the kitchen. He put a hand over the phone and said, "Hey, sorry. It's my nephew, I'll only be a few. He misses Dandi."

Ambrose's heart strings were properly tugged on. "Of course, of course."

He only got a few feet closer to the fire when Barrett said, "Unless you wanna say hi? No pressure. He only knows your name and sometimes you watch her, I didn't say anything else."

There was something vulnerable, almost fragile, on Barrett's face and it hit him in the chest. He had no reason to refuse. "Yeah, sure. No worries."

"Okay." Barrett pulled the phone back and flipped on video mode again. "Hey Forrest, remember I mentioned my neighbor?"

A small voice came from the other end and that damnable thing kicked him in the chest again. "Yeah!"

"Do you want to say hi?"

"Sure!"

Torn between heartbroken and amused, Ambrose let Barrett beckon him closer. And then the warm, comforting weight of an arm landed on his shoulder and that touch alone made him shiver. It was just an arm. "Ambrose, my nephew Forrest. Forrest, this is my neighbor and my friend, the one who watches Dandi sometimes."

The little boy through the video was tiny, pale, and bald. His dark brown eyes were large in his face, but they were clear and bright as he smiled. "Hi!"

"Hi." Shit, he wasn't good with kids. Barrett said he was eight but the leukemia and lingering sickness made him look smaller, weaker. But he figured the kid likely had a lot of people looking at him like he was made of glass, so he smiled. "Thanks for letting me hang with Dandi sometimes. She's really great."

"Yeah she is!" Forrest's smile dropped. "Mom says she might have to stay with you longer, Uncle B. Is that okay?"

Barrett cast a quick glance at Ambrose and all he could do was nod encouragingly. "Yeah, yeah. You're mom and I already talked about that, all good here. Dandi's gonna be so da - *dang* spoiled."

In the background, Dandi boofed and they all laughed.

Ambrose chatted with Forrest for a few more moments, asking him about the book on his bedside table. "Oh, it's *The Island of Doctor Moreau*. I haven't started it yet but Uncle B gave it to me. Said I'd like it."

"You will. I read that and *Treasure Island* when I was about your age and they remain some of my favorites."

Forrest giggled. "I like books a lot."

Ambrose leaned in, charmed. "Good. That'll serve you well as you get older, too."

There was the barest squeeze of fingers on the ball of his shoulder and Ambrose looked over to see Barrett grinning, wide and happy. "I'll pick up some more books when I swing into town, okay?"

As Barrett said his goodbyes after Ambrose waved to Forrest, he circled back to the kitchen to pour more wine. Children always seemed so foreign to him, even when he was a teenager. What did you *do* with them? As a gay man and a loner, he wasn't ever on the children train. Preston hadn't been either. Children never came up in conversation other than to reaffirm they weren't interested.

While his outlook on relationships might be swung around to the positive, children were a solid no. He wondered how Barrett would feel about that. And then wondered why he was thinking like that to begin with.

Ambrose shook his head and took a healthy sip of wine, letting the flavors burst on his tongue. "Thanks," Barrett said as he joined Ambrose at the kitchen island. Ambrose pushed the other glass forward and Barrett picked it up with a nod. "Kid's not so worried about Dandi now but at first he was a mess. It was all he was focused on. That first night after he was awake enough to talk, me and his mom took time with him to explain what was going on. He's always been too smart for his own good."

Ambrose studied Barrett for a moment, not liking how tired and worn he looked. Maybe tonight wasn't for guitar lessons. "I didn't want to pry."

"You're fine, Ambrose, I swear. More than fine now that Forrest knows who you are." Barrett took a sip. "He's been asking, wanting to know who the *nice man* was helping me take care of Dandi."

He nearly choked, the wine burning the back of his throat and even up into his nostrils as he coughed. "Shit," Barrett said, coming around the island to pat him on the back. "Fuck, you okay?"

"Nice man?" Ambrose croaked, torn between laughing and wincing. "He got that from where?"

Barrett got him a glass of water and while Ambrose coughed out the wine and probably part of a lung, his friend stared at him, big smile on his face. "From me, Ambrose," Barrett eventually said, leaning against the counter.

He laughed, still a little hoarse from coughing. "Well, I'm glad he's okay with it." He paused, trying to get back on track. "Still want to learn guitar?"

When they were seated by the fire a few minutes later, Ambrose took the time to ask for a few simple chords from Barrett. Nothing too wild. E and A major and minor, D major. He watched Barret's fingers move, his brow lower in concentration. "Good, good. I know it's beginner stuff but I figured the basics are the easiest to shore up and if those are good, we can move on."

Barrett's smile was soft. "How'd I do?"

With the heat of the fire at his back, Ambrose leaned forward, tipped his face up. Barrett's eyes caught on the fall of his hair, the way Ambrose's arm moved as he put his hand on Barrett's knee. "You did great."

That hungry, aching thing inside him shook itself awake. He wanted, despite everything, to crawl into Barrett's lap and kiss him. Spread his thighs over Barrett's thick ones, slide forward, and smooth his palms over that unruly black beard so he could kiss him hard and lick into that soft, warm mouth. Ambrose's gut tightened and blood roared in his ears.

He *wanted*. Desperately.

His face must have borne some expression because Barrett sat up straighter, one hand gripping the guitar's neck. "Ambrose. You okay?"

Reality doused him and his lust with bitter cold water. "Yeah. I'm good. You just..." He blinked hard a few times and shook his head. "Truth?"

"Yeah." Barrett's nod was quick but sure. "Always. That's how we build this thing between us. Trust, friendship, maybe -"

"I wanted to kiss you. Just crawl into your lap and kiss you until you were all I could taste." The words fell from him faster than he could stop them and Ambrose slammed his eyes shut. "Fuck. Fuck."

"Come here, Ambrose." That voice, the snap and crack of it, made his breath catch. "Is that what you still want?" And all the gods help him, Barrett put the guitar aside to lean back on the couch and spread his legs. "I won't stop you or say no."

"You have to..." Ambrose wet his lips. "You have to want it. There's a line between not saying no and wanting it."

fuck. The movement made him pant a little but what made his cock throb was that sight. Barrett was comfortable, relaxed on his grey sofa, arms now propped up on the padded back, and a cocky tilt to his chin as he let his gaze lazily stake its claim all over Ambrose's body and face. Worn black jeans, form-fitting t-shirt molded around thick pecs like he was begging for Ambrose's hands to squeeze him there.

If he kissed Barrett now, he'd fuck him. And if they fucked, Ambrose would dive headlong into something he probably wasn't quite ready for. Barrett had been right: wait, build, learn, then if everything lined up, they could take another step forward, the one rickety step past friendship and into something *more*.

But goddammit.

"We should probably keep going with the lesson?" It was a hedge, not an easy one to make, but the little smile on Barrett's face made it worth it. Ambrose didn't feel like he was being tested, made to perform for someone else's pleasure. And that alone made Barrett so much of a better person than most others who were in Ambrose's life.

"You got it. And thanks." The heat dropped from Barrett's expression.

"For?"

"For taking a moment to check in with yourself before thinking this was the only thing I wanted."

"Did you?"

"Want it?"

"Yeah."

"Enough to do everything but ask you to come over and sit in my lap and be a good boy."

Barrett was joking. But the reaction Ambrose had to *good boy* was no laughing matter. He had to duck into the bathroom to will away the semi-hard and when he came back, he asked. "Wanna try that one song everyone knows at like one in the morning at the bar?"

Barrett groaned. "No. But yes."

Ambrose sat down in his chair and pulled the guitar into his lap. "On three. We'll take it slow."

CHAPTER SIXTEEN

Ambrose's whistle was low, breaking the steady silence of the forest around them. "Who does something like that?"

Barrett shrugged. "No idea."

Always the sharp one, Ambrose leaned on the railing of the overlook as they stared down at the black spot where the ranger storage shed had been. "And it's in the middle of nowhere. Which I guess would be good for not getting caught. "

"Yeah, except now we have cameras pointed at all the storage sheds and the FLs instead of just a few." Barrett pointed to the cameras above the spot where the shed had been. "And even then, whoever did it managed to keep us from seeing them."

"Smart. Or lucky."

He huffed. "Or they know how we operate."

There was a light in Ambrose's eyes, some spark of mischief and interest as he replied, "So an inside job? How very bestselling thriller of them."

Barrett couldn't help but laugh. "Honestly, yeah. But I think it's maybe someone we fired or left in a snit fit." Ambrose raised his eyebrows and he said, "Call it a gut instinct. One of the first things you do as a rookie is memorize the trail patrols and all the locations of the hiker and ranger stations." Barrett held up a hand and ticked off the points in a sharp, quick voice. "Two to a truck from Snake River Point and up, one to a truck at sea level. Patrols from 5 a.m. to 11 p.m., never more than eight hours a day on the trails, summers are 24/7. All stations stocked with water and rations and heating and cooling blankets. Never let a station go empty. Never let a hiker stay lost."

"Couldn't someone learn that themselves, though?" Ambrose pressed. "I'm not trying to be recalcitrant here."

"No, no, I get it." Barrett sighed and leaned on the railing, mirroring Ambrose's pose. "And you're right. So the stations don't move and anyone used to this area would know roughly where to find a ranger. But add in the knowledge of the cameras and the..." Something inside him grated, skidding to a rough stop as anger welled in his chest. "The sabotage of the FL took time. To shove all that metal through the lock, take the time to board up the door and bend the nails? You'd have to be pretty sure you wouldn't get spotted by a patrol or go out in the pitch dark and operate by flashlight. Getting a truck up there is next to impossible without the right gear."

Ambrose snorted. "Everyone around here has tire chains."

"Not just chains. The trailer and hitch, enough power to get up by the FL? To know exactly where to turn off and know how to work the gate that blocks off the path from tourists?" Barrett curled his fingers around the railing, feeling the weathered wood bite into his palms. He'd told Jacques and Meredith of his suspicions, but kept it out of the official reports.

Because there was nothing to report. He couldn't document a hunch. But he'd seen the brutal angles of those metal strips, the angry bend to the nails sticking out of the moss-covered boards nailed over the FL tower door. It would have been so easy for anyone to break a few windows, spray paint the interior, run off with thousands of dollars of equipment. This wasn't some random asshole; it was someone with a grudge. But a grudge against who? It hadn't escaped his notice that it was the bridges on his route sabotaged, the fire tower he was in the most.

So he'd pulled the files of everyone fired from the ranger department in the last five years. Only four, but he'd worked with all of them. Two weren't likely, as one was an older woman who had worked in administration and refused to do anything more complicated than make coffee. Another was a "cartographer" who had lied about their skill set. And the other two had been forest rangers. But only Vincent had been angry enough to threaten a lawsuit and other blusterous outbursts as he was escorted from the building and to his car.

Barrett and another ranger had walked with Vincent and gotten cussed out as a thank you. Vincent had always been a little quick to anger, a little rough around the edges type with a chip on his shoulder about not getting promoted (a promotion that went to Jacques). If pressed, Barrett would have bet a little money Vincent had been angry enough to damage some ranger property. But he'd been fired three years ago and last Barrett had heard, he'd moved inland to be with family.

"And then we've got that same FL that needs a firewatch smack dab in the middle of the season. No one wants to take it cause it's around the summer holidays and the big boating festivals and fairs." He gave Ambrose a small smile. "So I volunteered."

"I can watch the house, no worries." Ambrose's response was so immediate Barrett wasn't sure if he hallucinated the words. "And anything else you need."

"Ambrose, I can't ask that of you."

"You didn't." A bony shoulder nudged his. Barrett watched as a careful hand was placed on top of his rough, weathered own. Ambrose wasn't looking away, gaze sure, strong. It was so steady, so warm, and Barrett could see the little flecks of green in Ambrose's grey eyes.

It didn't get much more romantic, he thought as he breathed Ambrose in. The forest smelled of fresh dirt and the fuzzy budding promise of spring and the ozone of last night's rain. They stood close to each other; touching at the shoulder, the hand, the hip. The wind bit with blunt teeth, teasing but not threatening. And they were talking like they did this every day. As if their lives were already so enmeshed that laying out his worries was normal. Easy.

"Unless you don't want me to watch the place." Ambrose's voice, softer now, shook Barrett from his thousand yard stare directly into those grey eyes.

"No, it ain't that. Not that all." He waved a hand artlessly. "You're busy, you've got what...four projects in the hopper? Five? I'm shocked you sleep."

"I do. But not well."

Should let me help you with that. I want to help you with that.

The words rose in his mind, unbidden, like they had in his dream last night. Dreaming of a slightly hazy figure that looked like Ambrose and talked like him, dressed like him. One who was lounging on Barrett's bed and watching while he struggled with a zipper or button. Hazy dream Ambrose said the same thing to dream Barrett, but instead of denying himself the scent of leather and tea, he fell in head first.

He'd woken up with a hard-on and no time to handle it. The closer he stood to Ambrose, the hotter the flame he carried flared. He wanted a friend and got one, but it came with an infatuation. No, not an infatuation. A *need*. "Guessing you've tried all the tricks?" he said, voice rough.

"Most of them. Even some odder ones."

"Such as?"

Ambrose laughed. "You only get to make fun of me today."

"Wouldn't do that and you know it."

When Ambrose looked down at the leaves around their boots, Barrett got to see a hint of self-consciousness peek through as he bit his lip. "Gods, vitamin shots. Medicated sleep masks. Do not try those, they leave a rash. Meditation. These weird bandage looking things you put on the soles of your feet and smell like rotten mint."

"Eugh. Why?"

"Because I'm a sucker, apparently. Or just desperate for a decent night's sleep."

"Ambrose. That isn't good. Does anything help?"

Barrett was not expecting Ambrose to raise his head and say rather simply, "When naming fish doesn't? Sex."

He couldn't stop his lips from twitching into a smile. Ambrose wasn't flirting with him, he was being factual. The difference wouldn't have been easy to spot for someone who hadn't spent the last several months in the man's company, but now Barrett understood. When Ambrose was flirting, he was quick at the mouth, combining humor and a straightforwardness that Barrett admired. When he had blood in his brain to do so, because Ambrose's flirting set his cock to stiffening immediately. But the humor didn't exist in his words when Ambrose was simply being *Ambrose*.

So he tried to be honest and forthright back as he replied, "And your hand isn't enough. I get it. The old stereotype of guys falling asleep after sex holds true, straight or not."

Ambrose's laugh cracked open across the wide space between them and the cliff and the burned out supply station below and Barrett felt it like a palm running down his spine. He couldn't even fool himself into thinking it was the wind making him shiver. Eventually he said, "You sure about watching the house this summer? It's only for four weeks but I can get a house sitter."

Ambrose's expression was so consternated Barrett worried his eyes would cross. "Barrett. I've got you. I live next door, Stella and I are quite fond of each other, and you have a guitar that needs restringing." The hand was back on his, but squeezing his fingers now. "I've got it."

"Okay, I get it," Barrett replied with a laugh. "A guitar that needs restringing? Ouch."

"I say it like it is."

"You do. I like that." He motioned Ambrose forward and they walked further uphill, following the trail. Barrett had offered to show Ambrose where the patches of wildflowers grew and with spring now fully upon them, he'd been itching to get up above the river. The views over the valley were incredible and on a day like this one, sunny and bright, Lake Honor would be sparkling in the distance. "And you should swing by the FL when I'm up there. It's not like I can't have visitors."

"As long as it doesn't involve me spraining my ankle again, I'm game." Ambrose shot him a bright smile and Barrett wanted to melt. Did he not realize how gorgeous he was? But the thought of Ambrose up there in the fire lookout tower with him and Dandi was more than tempting. Watching the sun disappear below the horizon, sharing some drinks. Barrett finally gathering up the courage to pull Ambrose from those too big clothes and take and give in the only way he knew how: with all his focus and attention and a touch that maybe meant *something*.

As they climbed the last rise to the cliff overlooking the valley, Ambrose stopped in his tracks. "Holy shit."

Spring wind, cool but promising, kicked up and pulled at his collar, his hair, but Barrett didn't care. The look on Ambrose's face as he stared out over the rolling carpet of tiny white and blue flowers would be seared in his memory for the rest of his life. Those angular, symmetrical features, so unique and fascinating up close, were now melted into an expression of pure wonderment. Barrett had taken many a hiker and mountain climber up to some truly beautiful spots over the thousands of acres which he and his fellow rangers carefully guarded, but there was no other place like this one. It was a pity the flowers would only last a few days, and Barrett had been so hoping they'd be ready for today.

"Barrett. I can't even..." Ambrose turned to him, a helpless little smile on his face. His grey eyes were huge against his pale skin and with the sun shining down on that auburn hair, Barrett was certain he'd never seen anything more beautiful.

And then he moved with purpose, toward Barrett. Barrett welcomed him into his arms. "This is the kindest thing anyone's ever done for me," Ambrose muttered into his neck. Barrett felt every word, every syllable, every breath on his skin. Something in him yearned for more: more closeness, more whispers against his pulse, more pressure from the fingertips pressed into the small of his back.

"Hey." He nudged Ambrose's head up with a curled finger until he could meet those eyes. "You're welcome. I'm glad you like it." Gods, his heart was racing but in his mind, he was calm, rational. And everything in him screamed for contact. But even now he knew that it was easier if Ambrose initiated. Some part of him would feel guilty for even this, pressing against him as if they did this all the time.

Ambrose swallowed hard, the effort of it making his throat click. And then he sucked in a breath and slowly, carefully, stepped back. "Finding even ground," he said, voice a little hoarse. "Something I'm working on."

The word *yearning* came to mind while they stood in that field of tiny wildflowers. It was perfect in some ways, and yet Ambrose made his heart pound so hard, Barrett feared it would give out. "I know it's not fair," Ambrose continued as he shoved his hands into his pockets. "I know we could easily fall into bed together."

He had to laugh, needed some kind of tension release from the moment where his body ached with want. "You're right. We could." Barrett motioned Ambrose forward down the path until they came to a few boulders. He felt like they should be sitting for this. "You game for some truth time?"

"Of course." There was no hesitation in Ambrose's answer and as they settled on the flatter part of the boulders, the carpet of flowers before them, Barrett took a deep breath. He'd practiced this but it still felt raw. "So everyone's got a past, right? Mine's not terribly complicated. I like sex and I like men, so finding someone to take to bed wasn't too difficult a lot of the time." He waved a hand at himself and smiled. "I'm a type, apparently."

"I have never once thought of you that way, Barrett."

"No, no, sorry." He smiled so Ambrose knew he wasn't offended or assuming. "You're good, trust me. But what I mean is my past is kind of boring in some ways when it comes to relationships and shit. It's also been something that's made people shy away. They wanted a commitment I wasn't ready to give, or I didn't feel more than physical attraction. I wanted - *want* - something more." Gods, his heart was pounding in his ears because as many times as he'd imagined saying this to Ambrose, being presented with the chance now felt like he was standing at the edge of a cliff. "You and I, there's a connection."

He waited, watching Ambrose's face carefully. Any little sign of the negative would make all this for naught, but he had to be sure.

"Yeah. Yeah, there is." A smile flickered over Ambrose's face and Barrett felt something relax in his chest. "Even though by rights you should think I'm a prick from the way I acted."

"I did, for a minute. But it was kind of clear from the start you were still finding your footing. I wasn't one to press."

Ambrose put his hand on top of Barrett's and those long fingers squeezed. Barrett felt grounded once more. Barrett liked the look of Ambrose's pale hand against his tawny, weather-beaten one. "You have no idea what that means. Everyone presses and it's exhausting. But you were talking, sorry."

"All good." And it was, because he had finally found someone worth telling this to. "So long and short, I've done flings and had a few relationships but nothing more than about a year. Me and Marcos were all caught up in the after college, real world job and life thing and it worked for a while. But I'm still waiting on that spark. You know, more than just oh hey, he's hot, let's bang, and then you keep doing it."

"And get takeout and go on dates and then it gets boring?"

"For a bit, yeah." Ambrose had no idea how on the nose he was. "But now comes the part where I get all real honest and I don't want to make you uncomfortable."

To Barrett's surprise, Ambrose shook his head and smiled. But he didn't remove his hand from Barrett's. "You've met my ex and saved my life and brought me to a field of wildflowers. Unless you're about to tell me you're Hannibal Lecter, I think we're good."

"Fair enough." Barrett's smile matched Ambrose's. "Not Hannibal Lecter, for the record."

"Good enough for me."

"Such high standards. Okay, but straight up, I like sex. A lot. Finding partners was never difficult, like I said. Around five years ago, I started thinking it just wasn't worth it for the most part. I got promoted, I had plans for the house, could feel myself getting older and my priorities shifting. Life shit. So I kind of gave up on something that would keep it from being boring. But I never gave up hope that I might find that thing, that *more*, that would make it special."

The word he was avoiding saying sat on his tongue, heavy like lead but more valuable than anything he could imagine. Ambrose filled it in for him. "Spark. Connection." He looked down at their hands, swallowed hard again. "And you're not pushing me because..."

"Because despite everything I know about people, you defy that in a good way. You're a fascinating man, Ambrose, and spending time getting to know you is important to me. More important than just fucking, cause I feel like there's more here." He waved a hand at the field. "I did bring you to a field of wildflowers to confess, if that's any evidence."

"Plenty. More than enough." Ambrose's eyes had gone soft and he licked his lips before saying, "Me telling you I like you too feels a little grade school, especially right now."

But that was what Barrett was hoping to hear. Whatever sat before them, or down the road apace, was meant for *them*. No one made him feel like Ambrose did, and he wanted to protect it, savor it, fucking roll around in bed with it.

With him.

Heat flared through his veins but it was tempered with patience and longing. The kinds of things he'd read about in those gothic romances about creepy old houses and manners and pining. It made sense now, except for the manners part. He leaned in and as if pulled by a string, so did Ambrose. "If I kiss you right now," Barrett said, tipping his head down, "right here? I might be in trouble."

They were so close and it made his body feel *alive*. But then Ambrose, quick as a snake and twice as clever, hauled him down by the back of his neck. That mouth, that body, met his. The world fell away. And Barrett couldn't imagine anything better than the taste, the scent, the feel of this man. He wanted to bottle it, douse himself in it, carry it around with him all day, every day.

"You are....very good at that," Ambrose panted after untold moments folded against Barrett like he held up the world for them both. There'd been nothing hard or demanding about Ambrose's kiss, but it had definitely made his head spin.

"Keep complimenting me. I won't get sick of it." A statement, a plea, a confession, all while something warm and soft swirled through him. Wanting someone, and wanting to be with someone, were two different things and yet with Ambrose, Barrett felt both. So deeply, tightly entwined that he couldn't separate them if he tried. He didn't want to.

"Problem is," Ambrose said, leaning in again, "everything I'm thinking right now is particularly filthy."

"In the middle of a field of wildflowers, when I just cracked myself open to you?" He let a smile play about his face, and saw it matched with one of Ambrose's own. "Is this about the whole comment I made about myself?"

"That you're a massive bear and people want to take you for a spin?"

"Yeah, that."

Ambrose tilted his head, smile growing. "Is that all? That's not nearly as filthy as I was expecting." They were both trying so hard not to laugh and Barrett was shaking with the effort of holding back. "But if I must restrain myself..." Ambrose tipped his head up, the invitation clear. "You're a fabulous kisser. Is that PG enough for you?"

"For now." Barrett brushed his lips over Ambrose's, let his fingers trail over that cut-glass jaw. Ambrose shivered in response and that yearning, aching thing in him rose up once more.

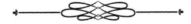

"So when do we get to meet him?"

"Forrest."

"No, it's okay, Val." Barrett had to laugh at the earnestness in Forrest's face and the smile on Val's lips. "So I was gonna ask you about that, kiddo. Your mom says you're doing better."

"I am!"

"And, even more importantly, that you've been doing really well with school. So I thought we'd celebrate that." He reached for the book sitting next to his elbow and held it up. "Apparently these are really popular with kids your age."

The *squeal* Forrest let out could have cracked glass and yet, for Barrett, it was the best sound in the world. For the briefest moment, he saw his nephew again - whole and healthy and excited over the prospect of a gift from his uncle. It twisted up in his heart and the sadness he felt as he realized, again, that the kid would maybe never be the same. If this was how he felt, he could only imagine what Val was going through. They talked about it sometimes, when she was especially drained or stressed. She was in therapy, she was getting help. And yet Barrett felt disconnected from them both. Distance was one thing; he could easily drive to them, stay for a weekend, hang out. They had to be careful introducing new people and all their germs into the apartment, but it was doable.

Instead, he was making do with a virtual story time while Val worked on bills and paperwork in the background. He knew this arrangement was the best they all could do in the circumstances, but some little part of Barrett wondered if he really was doing everything he could to support his family.

Barrett hid his sigh and held the book up higher. "I'm glad I picked right. You ready to start?"

Forrest nodded, hugging a pillow tighter to his chest. His gaunt little face was still pale but there was life behind his eyes and a smile through cracked lips. Barrett saw Val shift in her chair and cast a glance at her son, her smile matching his.

"Okay, here we go." Barrett flipped open the book, *Greenleaf Galaxies*, and began to read. The book was the first in a new series about a group of kids who travel from planet to planet, saving creatures and restoring habitats. He wasn't sure about the title, but he was no book editor. To him, it read a lot like the books he grew up on, full of heroics and friendship, bravery and humor. Some of it was clearly aimed at kids Forrest's age, but the author had done their homework on conservation efforts and managing diminishing species. He made a mental note to look them up later.

After chapter two, Barrett paused. Forrest was starting to nod off, his little head drooping. "Hey kid."

"Yeah?" Forrest blinked at him and smiled once more.

"Probably time for a nap."

"But the book!"

"The book will be there whenever you call your Uncle Bear, okay?" Val came into frame and put her hands on Forrest's shoulders. "Maybe we can set up a schedule, yeah?"

"Yeah!" Forrest brightened, now sitting up straight in the padded rocking chair Val had prepared for him. "Can you read to me when you're in the fire tower, Uncle Bear?"

Gods, where had spring gone? His tour in the FL was mere weeks away. He added that prep to his mental list. There was a significant amount of planning and packing to do. "I absolutely can do that. I should find a way to set up my tablet against the window where the sun sets."

"Oooo! Yes, please!"

He couldn't say no to his nephew. "Okay, you get some rest and make sure you eat when you're hungry, all right?"

"He will," Val said. She leaned down to better come into view and Barrett saw the dampness gathering at the corners of her eyes. "Now I'm not gonna do that thing where I cry, and then you cry, and it's all over. Not happening. I've got too much to do. But we love you, Bear."

"I love you!" Forrest chimed, but Barrett knew they both meant it with all of their hearts.

"Love you both. Get some sleep."

Barrett hung up, laid his tablet in his lap, and leaned back in his chair, eyes closed. "Shit," he muttered, rubbing his palms over his cheeks. His beard was officially out of control and his face felt permanently itchy and dry. He needed a haircut. Dandi needed another bag of food to replace the one he just opened. He should check the roster for work, see if Meredith was going back up to Alpha FL.

All of that became a ten car pile up in his mind, but when he opened his eyes, all Barrett could do was stare out at the lake. Evening was just starting to show on the horizon, the sun sinking lower in the sky and the edges of that beautiful blue turning slightly red and pink. Twilight would be in about an hour and he debated sitting there until the daylight died and he was forced to go inside.

"Hey, Barrett."

Ambrose's voice came to him from across their shared backyard and Barrett turned in his chair. Ambrose was standing a bit away, an uneasy look on his face. "Hey. You okay?"

"Yeah." His hands were jammed in his pockets and he looked like he wanted to rabbit back into his house. "I uh...I came back from a walk and heard you talking. When I realized you were reading to your nephew, I didn't want to interrupt."

Lightbulb moment. "Did you just stand out here the whole time?"

Ambrose laughed and walked closer, one hand going to the back of his neck. "Yeah."

Something in Barrett's heart melted. It was deeply endearing that Ambrose hadn't wanted to move for many long minutes while Barrett read to his nephew. As if Ambrose worried any little noise or movement in the camera's periphery would break the spell. "And this has nothing to do with you wanting to hear me read out loud?"

Ambrose shrugged but Barrett spotted the flush of pink up his neck. "No idea what you're talking about."

"Oh, okay. Got it." He heaved to his feet and tucked his tablet under one arm. "I was thinking about making some dinner. Hungry?"

"Keep spoiling me and I'll never leave." But Ambrose fell in step with Barrett and together they walked through the back door. Dandi woofed at them but refused to leave her spot on the couch. "I thought you were training her to stay down off the furniture."

"Ever tried to tell a Great Dane what to do?"

"Point taken."

Barrett chuckled and started to pull out utensils and pots. "How does chicken marsala sound?"

Ambrose slid up next to him, grey eyes intent on Barrett's face. Then his mouth. "Like I definitely owe the chef a kiss. If he's amenable."

Warmth bloomed in his belly and he leaned in. Barrett let Ambrose make the final calculation, the final move, and found himself being kissed gently. Ambrose didn't pull on him or let his hands wander. The feel of his hands on Barrett's shoulders was almost prim, as was the way Ambrose held himself slightly away from Barrett.

"I should start asking for payment like that," Barrett said as they broke apart. Ambrose gave him a shy grin and that warmth sparked again.

"Can I put a deposit in on the next one if I bring you another pie?"

Very carefully, Barrett put his hands on Ambrose's hips and steered him until his back hit the kitchen counter. "That's pretty domestic of you."

"Says the man cooking me dinner on the fly." But Ambrose was smiling and the way he wrapped his arms around Barrett's neck made him shiver with anticipation. "Sorry again for listening to your story time session with Forrest. You have a great voice. You should do narration work."

"Make you a deal." Barrett traced his fingers over the cut of Ambrose's jaw. "You bring me a piece of your writing you really like, and I'll narrate for you. You can do whatever you want with it. Sell it, give it away, whatever."

Ambrose studied him for a long moment. The gears were turning, Barrett could almost see them clank and slide together. "Counteroffer?"

"Negotiating. I like it."

"Ha. But I'm serious. My writing doesn't really work in audiobooks. But the nature writer Raf paired with you to do Perry's book would be perfect. You should read that."

It wasn't a bad idea. It was a great one, in fact. He couldn't stop the smile on his face. "I like it. I'll talk to Raf."

Now it was Ambrose's turn to laugh. "You're terribly agreeable."

"And you're used to fighting tooth and nail over every decision, even the little ones." Barrett ghosted his fingertips down Ambrose's throat. Sensation sparked under his skin at that small touch. "I'm a pretty laid back guy, Ambrose. You don't have to hedge bets with me."

Whatever pain lived behind those grey eyes was extinguished and Ambrose leaned in, this time kissing Barrett with a soft urgency that left him shivering. "I know. It'll take some getting used to, I think."

"I'm more than fine with that. But if we're gonna do this, this thing between us, you gotta just go for it. You don't have to hide with me."

Ambrose closed his eyes as Barrett carded his fingers through those auburn waves. "Thank you."

Those words were whispered against his mouth and yet they hit him right in the vulnerable, bruised part of his heart still raw from his time with Forrest. Barrett sucked in a deep breath and let his kiss turn needy for a few seconds, then backed away. "Ain't even a thing, Ambrose."

"And yet, *thank you.*"

CHAPTER SEVENTEEN

W hen the letter arrived in the early morning mail, Ambrose's heart sank. He'd know it was her even without a return address boldly declaring her stage name. Angelica Avery, in her looping, slanted hand. His mother said letters were a lost art, one that should be cherished. She also thought she was single-handedly bringing back the art of the letter.

Because *Angelica Avery* was timeless.

She was a product of art and history, story and time, and a God-given talent. And her mantle in the brownstone she shared with her partner, Thessla, was decorated with the awards she'd won because of that talent.

"It's a lack, Ambrose," his mother said, one bejeweled hand glittering as she waved it at the mantle in his little rented townhouse.

He knew the answer before the question fell from his lips. "Of?

"Ambition."

Ambrose had to laugh. "I've plenty of ambition, but not the will to run headlong after it. I prefer my life as it is."

Her smile was a thing of daggers. It had been aimed at him over the years in many regards, so much that he was nearly immune to it. But Angelica Avery never liked to let go of something that had brought her success in the past. "Ambition is only good if you've the talent to back it." She trailed her fingers over the tiny glass sculpture on the mantle, the one she knew he had made with his own hands. "Sold any stories yet, darling?"

Something his therapist had taught him was refusal to engage. Granted, he had just shot back at her but that was a warning shot across her bow, not a direct hit. And yes, he had sold plenty of stories and he could show them to her, relish in the way she'd silently steam at seeing A.E. Tillifer as the nom de plume. But he wasn't going to engage because doing so would make her victor.

Instead, he leaned back against the kitchen counter and kept his face as neutral as possible. "I've things to do, Mother."

Ah, there was the flinty gaze he'd been waiting on. Her eyes as dark and flat as a snake. "You could be a better host. Offer me a drink, a seat, take a moment to ask how I am."

Ambrose stared at her, as impassive as stone. She was looking for a fight, and he would deny her that. He would. He could do this: wipe the slate clean, get the fuck out of town. The contract for the house at Lake Honor was already signed and he was moving in two weeks. All the evidence of his move was packed away in the spare bedroom, specifically in case she decided to "pop by". Because Angelica Avery's timing was always impeccable.

Finally, his mother huffed and gracefully sank down on the sofa, her face a moue of distaste as she picked a piece of lint from near her knee. "I raised you better, you know. Ambrose." His stare didn't waver but didn't try to intimidate. His heart was pounding (he could do this, he could, he could write her off after this and be done) but he felt more confident than he ever had before.

"Ambrose." She snapped her fingers and his only response was to raise an eyebrow. "What kind of treatment is this? I'm your mother."

Her voice was rising ever so slightly; she wasn't used to being ignored. Point for him. "I'm waiting for you to find your manners, as you're in my house. Mother."

And like he had figured, she was unmoved. "This is not a house, Ambrose. It's a rental. And you know what I think about rentals."

He did, indeed. Thinly veiled classism at its finest. Heart in his throat but his hand steady, Ambrose gestured to the door. "You know the way out. And I do need to get back to what I was doing."

"Which was?"

The smile he gave her was so thin and brittle it could have shattered from the breath of a whisper. "None of your goddamn business. I'm done asking nicely. Leave." He walked over to the door and flung it open.

The look on his mother's face was possibly the most honest emotion he'd ever seen reflected on those features. The ones so like his own, with a narrow chin and hollow cheeks and cheekbones that stood up and out. A face called interesting or beguiling, one his mother had resculpted over the years so she never aged. He didn't begrudge her that, but he did still taste the bitterness at how she weaponized the features they shared. Long ago he'd learned to ignore the biting comments, but even shallow wounds could scar.

She did finally leave, no parting shot aimed at him through words. Just a disdainful sniff followed by a sneer, and then she was gone, locked away outside where he didn't have to see her any longer.

He moved two weeks later and left no forwarding address.

He left the envelope on the kitchen table, unsure if he wanted to open it. It was thick, heavy, creamy paper, his name and address in bold black ink. Hell, the paper even smelled like her and it made his stomach twist. He hated the scent of lavender, even now, but hers was a powdery thing laced with amber and pepper and it reminded him of slammed doors and backhanded compliments and being ignored for days on end as punishment.

Instead, he turned back to his work for the day; balancing books for a client who paid well and on time. Diving into numbers was soothing. Numbers didn't need interpretation beyond the rule systems laid down for each operation. Direct questions with direct answers. As the morning wore on and he was head down in work, he didn't hear his phone ding until he got up to make tea.

The screen was lit up with a slew of messages, all from the other person he didn't want to ever speak to again. He should just block Preston and be done, but every time he tried, hesitation stayed his hand.

From: Preston *Can we talk?*

From: Preston *I miss you.*

From: Preston *I'm sorry about before. I shouldn't have pushed. You are your own man, Ambrose. I just want what's best for you.*

From: Preston *Please talk to me.*

Ambrose closed his eyes and willed his heart to stop racing. Preston drudged up memories, and some of them were tied to his mother. Angelica *loved* Preston, loved how driven and dedicated he was. She swore time and again that Preston's desires and dreams would rub off on Ambrose and together they'd be unstoppable. And even when he admitted to her that Preston had cheated, she said it was no reason to break up.

"It's just sex, Ambrose. Honestly, if he was fooling around, then he must need something he's not getting at home. Have you tried new things? Told him no when he wanted to do something different?"

"I should burn you and never look back," he said as he touched the corner of the envelope.

Instead, he texted Barrett. He needed someone who would understand. Who would be kind.

Thinking about Barrett's deep voice and big hands and unruly hair (hair he wanted to take care of and swore he would, maybe he should tonight, maybe he should go over there and be good to a man he really, really liked)...it sent a surge of longing through him. His hands itched to map Barrett's body, following bone and sinew and skin like he could memorize every bump and scar and the smooth spaces perfect for his fingers and mouth.

> **From: Ambrose** *I hate to be a bother, but something distressing has happened. I know it's not our Friday night dinner date, but could we talk if you're free tonight?*

The reply came back immediately, despite knowing Barrett was out in the truck with Jacques. They were checking all the cameras around the supply stations and fire lookouts again, inspecting wires and lenses for tampering. Just in case, Barrett had said. With tourist season quickly approaching, they didn't want to miss any sign of sabotage, no matter how small.

> **From: Barrett** *Any chance I could get some tea when I come over? I might have already drank through that oolong mix you gave me.*

Despite the ball of anxiety in his chest, Ambrose laughed. Barrett was so damn honest and sweet and it made him want the man even more.

From: Ambrose *I'll mix it up now.*

From: Barrett *How's 3 sound? Sorry to make you wait, our shifts go a little longer now with the weather warming up.*

From: Ambrose *I appreciate you more than I can say. Three's fine. Bring Dandi, I have something for her. And don't be too worried about any music you hear, I just might be channeling my rage into a new piece.*

From: Barrett *Don't play too hard. I'm rather fond of your hands intact. And yeah, I'll bring her.*

Ambrose left the envelope on the kitchen counter and Preston's text on "read". Fuck them both.

Ambrose didn't start pacing until he showed Barrett the letter. "It's completely unfair and yet, that's how she does everything." He sighed and ran his hands through his hair, his face twisted into a bitter, sad mask. "It's a long story."

"Try me." Barrett gave him a soft smile. He didn't like seeing Ambrose in this way, caught in a riptide of anxiety and sadness. "I'm no stranger to family bullshit."

That pulled Ambrose up short, stopping mid-pace to stare at him. Barrett leaned back on the couch, let his hand fall onto Dandi's head as she sat at his feet. Ambrose needed him now, and not in the way they'd fallen together of late, with whispered promises to take it slow and drugged kisses that made his heart hurt. He needed an ear. A friend. A companion. An ally.

"I'm dumping on you." Ambrose made it a statement, but Barrett heard the ask there, too. The seeking of permission.

"You're not."

And then Ambrose twisted his hands together, lacing those long, agile fingers into a weave. That made his stomach clench. But worse than that, it made Barrett angry. Whatever Ambrose's past with his mother, watching this little sign of his upset made him see red. It made him want to defend Ambrose with every breath he had. The force of it sent the air from Barrett's lungs and his heavy exhale caught Ambrose's attention. His dark eyebrows shot up, grey eyes wide, and he strode toward Barrett with concern all over his beautiful face.

"I'm all right. I'm just..." Barrett looked down at the floor. "I'm mad on your behalf."

Something dark left Ambrose's eyes and with it, a bit of his own anger lifted, too. "I'm dumping on you," Ambrose repeated, his voice now sadder, softer.

He couldn't help but smile. "You're not, and I'm telling you that to make sure you understand something, Ambrose." Barrett leaned in, hoping Ambrose would do the same. That line between them tugged, drawing them closer with Ambrose looking at him with undisguised hope. "I'll never lie to you. I might not dress up hard truths to keep the blows from hurting. But I'm not false. I hate people who are."

And gods, when Ambrose kneeled so Barrett could touch his cheek, the shiver he got in response sent a jolt of gentle desire through him. This was no hot and heavy throb of wanting, leaving Barrett to imagine how Ambrose would look with his legs wrapped around his waist, sweaty and red-cheeked and begging. This was...deeper. Fonder. Somehow more possessive and honest than raw lust. He wanted to care for Ambrose. Wanted to know him. Wanted to let him peel back his layers a bit at a time and show Barrett who he was at the center.

Finally Ambrose said, "I know. And I wouldn't lie to you, either. It's just...this shit is buried so deep in me, it's like it's gone septic. I thought space, physical space, would help. And it has. But then she shows back up like a cancer."

"Do you want to read it?"

"No." Ambrose blinked hard and Barrett saw a glimmer of dampness at the corners of his eyes. "I want it to stop. I want to live my life free of her."

He nodded. This he completely understood. And one day he'd tell Ambrose about it. Right now wasn't his time, though. Ambrose needed help and Barrett was going to be there, no matter what it took. "What does that mean to you?"

Ambrose's laugh was dry, humorless. "It used to mean getting fucked six ways from Sunday so I didn't have to think for a while."

As appealing as that sounded to Barrett, he also knew it would be a mistake. He was pretty sure Ambrose knew it too. His face bore no sign of hope or expectation, just raw honesty. "Anything else help you get out of your head for a bit? Music, a book? We can cook or take Dandi on a walk."

Ambrose contemplated that for a long moment, and then he moved toward his back door. "Can we head up into the hills with Dandi? A little more physical space from the letter couldn't hurt."

"Of course. What if I showed you my first ranger trail?"

Ambrose was already shrugging into his fleece jacket. "I'd love to see it."

Barrett led Ambrose up into the western hills. The spring sun was warm and they were soon shedding their jackets to better soak it in. Dandi ran ahead of them only to come back minutes later with a massive stick, the ends of it covered in mud and leaves. "Good thing there's a river up ahead," Barrett said as they both laughed. "Gods, she's filthy."

"Did you hear him, Dandi? He said you're filthy." Ambrose didn't mind scratching the dog's dirt-streaked ears. Dandi dropped the stick and spun circles in front of Ambrose, whacking him on the thigh with her tail. "How many rivers are there around here?"

"Depends on your definition of river." Barrett pointed further west, where the land sloped up gently. "There's a little valley below that hill with a stream. In the drier summers, it gets down to nothing but a trickle. It's mostly fed from runoff. But since we don't classify that as a river, then..." He paused, gaze going skyward. "Officially there are four. A couple of the streams have widened over the years due to erosion and all the rain, so I'd say it's actually six."

Ambrose followed Barrett through a set of budding oaks as Dandi darted ahead once more, her massive paws sending leaves flying. "And this river was part of your first ranger trail?"

"Yeah." Barrett drew out his phone and pulled up an app. Soon a topographical map of the area in which they stood appeared on the screen. "So from that road we cut up, then west, down into the valley and across the river." He traced the path on the screen with his finger, lighting up the area in green. "Then over, looping back east. My old stomping grounds as a baby ranger."

Ambrose smiled. He could almost see Barrett then, a decade and a half younger but maybe with the same beard and hair. Fewer lines around his eyes and a tendency to smile more. It wasn't that Barrett didn't smile now, but there were layers to most of them. A fond one for his neighbors, a big open one for his sister and nephew. The one he used when talking about his job, as if his smile could express the volumes of enjoyment and exasperation he faced on a daily basis.

And then there was the one he was giving Ambrose now. "What's that look for?"

Ambrose tipped his head up and slowly reached out to touch Barrett's beard. A silent request for permission, one that was granted as Barrett angled his chin down. The smile didn't waver, but its edges grew curious. "You're a man of many emotions and expressions. I like pondering them. I don't want to ascribe meaning to them that doesn't exist and yet here I am, wondering if the smile you're giving me now has any specific meaning."

That seemed to bring Barrett up short, something Ambrose had never seen before. "Guess I don't think about it in those terms," he said slowly, still leaning into Ambrose's touch. His beard was wiry and Ambrose wanted to coat it in balms and lotions after giving it better shape. Or maybe Barrett would let him shave it off completely. "But I think this one is just happiness. The kind that I only get around you."

"Oh." The air left his lungs in a gust. "Is that a confession?"

"Confession implies it's something I'm ashamed of."

With a wink, Barrett pulled away and Ambrose almost dragged him back. But they trekked on, following in Dandi's scattershot path as she chased after chipmunks and squirrels. "She won't actually catch anything, will she?" Ambrose asked, suddenly very concerned that the dog would bring them a tiny, mangled body.

"Nah. She's never shown any inclination to actually hunt. I think it's more the noise she likes than anything." Barrett whistled and immediately Dandi was romping back through the forest toward them. But now her feet were wet. "Looks like she found the river. Come on, girl!"

Ambrose found himself tugged along in Barrett's wake, the forest spinning by as they ran toward the sound of rushing water. Barrett's grip was firm and sure and they slipped between trees with the confidence of a man who knew the land and trusted in his footing. Confidence was always attractive, but Barrett's was the kind that came naturally. As if he and the forest shared a private, protective bond. If he took good care of it, it would pay that kindness back.

Ambrose breathed in the scent of fresh dirt and river water and the bright promise of spring and let Barrett steer them downhill. His steps quickened, the sole of one boot slid, and he was crashing into Barrett's back with all the gracefulness of a drunken horse.

"Whoa, steady!" Those warm hands he'd come to love were now on him, stilling his forward momentum. "I got you."

They paused, face to face and breathing hard. Barrett's cheeks were rosy, his smile wide and open, and the grip he had on Ambrose's arms helped make the world stop spinning. "Thanks."

A splash behind them drew their attention to where Dandi was prancing in the shallow water at the river's edge. The landscape still bore the marks of winter, the ground too muddy for greenery to poke through, but beyond the river there were bits of yellow and green sprouting across the ground. Even the air was losing its bite. "Hell of a winter," Barrett said. "And yet still one of the best in a long time."

Something giddy rose in Ambrose's chest. He leaned into Barrett's touch, hoping the other man would read his silent signal. A request, and a token of permission.

Lean in and kiss me.

"You're making it harder and harder for me, you know."

Ambrose raised an eyebrow, teasing. "Harder for...?"

Barrett snorted. "Everything. Learning to take my time. Learning what you need. I want all of that. Old habits die hard, though." He smoothed his palms over Ambrose's sides, following the seams of his sweater until he could rest his hands on slim hips. "Guess that's part of my smile. What you were asking earlier."

Ambrose leaned in more. Aching. The sweetness, the desire, the yearning were getting all tangled up in one big ball that he didn't want to undo. This was like nothing he'd ever, ever experienced and it made everything in him light up under Barrett's attentions. "I don't understand."

Barrett shrugged. "Honestly, me neither. But I know I like it. And I think that's part of this." He leaned in, rested his forehead against Ambrose's. Their shared breath warmed the air between them. "The learning. Understanding each other. Taking our time."

"I don't *always* want to take my time."

"No?" His lips were so close; Ambrose could almost taste his kiss. He wanted to warm Barrett's lips with his, hold him close and breathe him in. "Would this be one of those times?"

With a groan, Ambrose surged up. Desire echoed through him but Barrett kept him steady, kept him true. Steered them into a kiss that lingered instead of tearing with teeth and soothing with tongues. It was as brilliant and bright and sure as Barrett's smile.

When they returned to Ambrose's house, Barrett's nerves had stopped jangling. But some part of him still teetered on a fragile knife edge. They'd held hands on the way back down, as much as the trail facilitated such closeness. Sometimes he ran his hand down Ambrose's back, earning him a shiver or the sight of teeth sunk into a plush lower lip.

But Ambrose was the one to make the first move.

"Let me take care of you." Ambrose slid into Barrett's lap, hands smoothing up Barrett's chest, then up over his shoulders, his neck, until those long fingers tugged gently at his beard. "I did promise. I want to." He leaned down, his mouth so close to Barrett's. "I like giving."

Barrett couldn't stop his groan in time and Ambrose knew he'd won. He wasn't attached to the beard and Ambrose seemed hellbent on helping him. It's not like he could deny the man anything, anyways. "You're gonna kill me, you know that?"

"Making you wonder why we're going slow?"

"Tease." But Barrett kept his grip gentle as he wrapped his hands around Ambrose's hips. "Fine. You win."

"Lucky me."

Barrett could have easily leaned up just a little and kissed Ambrose. He wanted to. But it wasn't what Ambrose needed right now; because as he was quickly learning, Ambrose understood his own needs pretty damn well and was willing to let Barrett see that vulnerable side of him. He trusted Ambrose to do the right thing for himself, right now. "What should I do?"

Ambrose had Barrett follow him to the master bathroom while he puttered around gathering bottles and jars. "I'd dunk you in the tub if I thought you'd be amenable to that," Ambrose said over his shoulder, a playful grin tugging at his lips.

"Who said I wouldn't be?"

That got Ambrose's attention. Well, probably a combination of Barrett's teasing tone and the way he licked his lips slowly, his gaze traveling down Ambrose's body. He wasn't being too lascivious but he wanted Ambrose to *feel it*. Just a little. "Appealing, but I think we'll save that for another day. It's more...intimate in the tub."

"Fair enough." But they were smiling at each other and Barrett felt the fizzy pop of happiness bubble through him, just knowing Ambrose's mind was settling. Ambrose took them into the spare bathroom where, in the corner, sat a slightly battered chair with a tall back and a footrest. It looked kind of like a barber chair but almost more like a gaming chair. Barrett was intrigued. "Should I..."

Ambrose smiled and waved him forward. Barrett settled in the heavy chair and let his arms hang off the armrests while he watched Ambrose move. Every step, every flutter of his hand, every jar he picked up from a small table on the side of the room, made Ambrose look sexy. A settled, even-keeled Ambrose was possibly the most attractive thing he'd ever seen.

If he didn't stop thinking like this, his body was going to turn traitor and start showing off his *interest*. Barrett took a deep breath and bit down on the urge to run his palm over his groin.

Ambrose wheeled over a small cart, the little casters clicking over the dark blue tiles. "Hmmm, almost there." He leaned forward, face so close to Barrett's, and then there was a click. The chair back sank and Barrett was staring up at the ceiling. "Better?" Ambrose asked with a grin.

"Do this often?" Barrett replied with a startled laugh. "Special chair and all."

"I actually picked it up at an estate sale." There was a spark of mischief in grey eyes as Ambrose loomed over him. "For a while, I got very invested in barber lessons."

"No shit." Barrett could almost see it now - Ambrose rattling bright glass jars and dark brown or blue bottles, his glorious hair tied away from his face as he took his time with each client. His gaze focused but still expressive, listening while the client talked. And savoring the moments where the client had to stay silent, with a blade to their throat or hot towel over their face. He could see those hands flashing, movements confident, sure. "Did you pursue it?"

"Just for friends." Gentle fingertips traced over his jaw, sinking into the thick hair of his beard and skimming the incredibly sensitive skin underneath. Of course, Barrett had no idea *how* sensitive he'd be but Ambrose's touch lit him up from the inside. "So, what am I allowed to do here?"

"Depends on the offer." Barrett let his eyes drop shut as Ambrose ran his fingertips over his throat. "But if you want to shave the whole thing off, I won't object."

Ambrose made a little choking sound that had Barrett staring up at him, worried. "I'm good. I'm fine. But...how long have you had the beard?"

"Dunno. Three years? I usually grow it out in the fall, keep it long until May or June, then trim it back." He shrugged. "I just let it get away these last few years."

Those fingers were back in his beard, distracting in their gentleness. But Barrett couldn't look away from those eyes and how they crinkled at the corners. "You trust me that much."

Again, not a question. A statement looking for surety, seeking permission. It sent him spiraling. It made him think about Ambrose on his knees. Hunger written as a sonnet on his face while his hands drifted. Asking for permission in that easy, silent way of his. "You're killing me, you know that?"

And now there were blunt fingernails running over his cheeks, down his jaw; just on the edge of tickling but firmer. "So if I keep this up..."

Barrett tried not to laugh but Ambrose's smile had him chuckling. "I'm going to have to worry about other parts of my anatomy."

"Then I guess I should behave." When Ambrose pulled his touch and presence away, Barrett wanted to chase after him. Instead, he watched. He liked watching Ambrose, liked seeing those cogs turn as he went through his personal methodologies. His hands moved, but that was such a plan, uninteresting verb for what they did. They grasped and fluttered, gripped and danced, slid and twisted and *touched*. Barrett could almost feel them on his skin, as if they'd never left.

Once they got a ratty blue towel around his neck and Ambrose pulled an old broom from the closet, he stood close, a pair of scissors dangling from his fingertips. "Ready?"

"Yes." He gave Ambrose a smirk that meant trouble. "Sure you won't miss the beard?"

"Why do you think I'm not touching your hair?"

"Fair enough." Barrett laughed and lay back in the chair. "Do your worst."

Cutting off the long, scraggly ends of his beard went quickly. When Ambrose focused, it was almost entrancing to watch. His eyes narrowed, he pursed his lips, and he fell silent in a way that felt meditative. Ambrose's touch was easy and Barrett let himself sink into the feeling of being cared for. It was strange at first but when Ambrose touched his shoulder and said, "Relax. I've got you," Barrett finally let his spine press into the chair's pillowy back and eased the tension from his neck.

The scissors clicked and clicked, the only other background noises were Dandi's soft snoring and the pop of the fireplace. He felt the weight of his own hair lift from his face, the air in the bathroom warm on skin that hadn't seen the light of day in years. "We might have to do a couple of rounds to get your skin soft enough to shave." A palm ran up his cheek then down, over his jaw, and it made him suck in a deep breath. Those fingertips left little tingling trails in their wake, sending goosebumps down his arms.

He knew things like this could be *intimate*. But he'd never attributed the word *erotic* to anything like this. Hell, had he ever even used that word before now? But there was a flash of silver in his periphery and he saw the towel over his chest covered in his own thick, curly beard hair and Ambrose standing above him, holding up a straight razor. A simple, incredibly sharp blade, the dark green lacquered handle poking out above and below his fist.

Barrett couldn't take his eyes off that gleaming blade. "I'm suddenly questioning my sanity here."

Ambrose's laugh was warm and comforting, even if he was poking fun at him a little. "I've done this before, just never on someone with so much hair. So..." He tapped his chin with the other hand, gaze going from Barrett to the little cart, then to the sink. "Let's do this. Take off your shirt and tie your hair up, so I don't accidentally cut your hair when I'm doing your neck."

A blade against his neck. Held by those long, thin fingers. That absolutely should not be hot and yet... "Right, okay." Barrett shoved out of the chair and set about following instructions while Ambrose filled the sink with hot water and started pouring thick, gold oil into little bowls. Gods, he could watch Ambrose do this all day, tinkering around with pots and jars and bottles, every movement elegant but precise.

"So, gin or bourbon?"

Barrett yanked his head out of the neck of his sweatshirt and turned to see Ambrose swirling a brush through something thick and white in a small pot. "What now?"

"After we get your skin warmed up with a hot towel and we wait for the oil to settle into the pores, I was going to offer a drink." His smile turned sheepish, unsure. "But I've only got gin and bourbon and I know you usually go for whisky."

That hand moved in slow, even circles and something zipped down Barrett's spine. He was not going to survive this. With another yank, he pulled his arms out of his shirt. "Gin's more than fine."

"Tonic water and lime?" Ambrose's words came slower now as he raked his gaze over Barrett's chest.

"Yeah, that's good." He took the little stretchy band Ambrose offered him and reached up, pulling his hair out of his face and off his neck.

"Jesus Christ." It was no more than a mutter but he heard it nonetheless. Ambrose's stare was blatant now. Hungry. "I didn't know you had those tattoos."

"Oh, yeah. They're so old I usually forget about them." Barrett pulled on the ends of his hair, tightening the queue. He looked down at the coiled blue dragon on his right ribs and, without thinking, hitched the edge of his waistband down a few inches so Ambrose could see the tail disappear into it. "This was the first one and Val said it was gonna suck getting it on my ribs and hip." He shot Ambrose a wide smile. "It sucked. Like ten times worse than I thought it would. But it's true what they say."

He tracked the bob of Ambrose's throat before he responded with, "What's that?"

"You get one, you'll get another. And another." He ran his right hand up over his left shoulder, following the darkly shaded wing there. "Turns out one becomes...eight at this point."

The way Ambrose was looking at him made a shiver skate down his spine. Normally he was the one teasing, leading. And he was definitely teasing, but in his own matter-of-fact kind of way. Ambrose was looking at him like he was a goddamn meal and it made him feel *wanted*. "I see four. I spotted the ones on your wrists before."

"Oh yeah, got one on each calf and each thigh." He pointed to Ambrose's neck. "I'm curious about that one myself."

"I'll let you continue to be curious." Did Ambrose's next breath shudder? Just a bit? Barrett felt something click into place in his gut; a little self-satisfaction that felt *good*. "We were in the middle of something."

And Ambrose became all business, getting Barrett back into the chair, clipping off more facial hair, as close as he dared to get to the skin. Every time Ambrose leaned down and Barrett got a whiff of clean laundry and the little drops of soft, citrusy oil that had sunk into Ambrose's fingertips, he had to grip the armrests. If he touched Ambrose now, that would be it. End of story, fade to black, and he wouldn't be satisfied until he got his mouth and hands on every inch of that lean body.

So he let the other man be kind and focused and careful. The scissors were eventually put away and Ambrose brought over a hot towel. "I'm gonna set this on you and then go get your drink."

"Okay."

Ambrose's smile was some kind of sensuous, indulgent thing that made his stomach swoop. "Relax. This will feel so good."

Barrett closed his eyes and felt the towel, just on the edge of too warm, be placed over his cheeks and chin and mouth, leaving his nose uncovered. Ambrose pressed the cloth down, wrapping the ends loosely around his neck and draping them over his shoulders. He sighed and slumped more into the chair and then Ambrose was gone with a pat to his shoulder.

When Ambrose's footsteps grew distant, Barrett sighed heavily. He needed these minutes to let his ardor cool the fuck down. There was no way Ambrose hadn't seen the growing ridge in his jeans but he'd mercifully not said anything.

Shit. Or maybe that's why he'd pulled focus back to the task at hand, not wanting to rile Barrett anymore. Shit. Shit. Had he fucked this up? What if he'd scared Ambrose off with his teasing? He'd been showing off, touching his tattoos like that, letting Ambrose stare.

Fuck. He might have overdone it.

"I can see you thinking." Ambrose's words were a light tease through his sudden flare of panic. "Relax, Barrett."

Gods, he wanted to sit up and assuage his worry but Ambrose's hand was back on his shoulder. Now the other hand on the other shoulder. And ....those were really strong fingers pressing into his muscles. Barrett groaned, making the heavy towel suction against his mouth. He plucked it away and Ambrose laughed. "We can take that off now." The towel was gone and Barrett blinked against the light. "Hold this for me?"

He could smell the juniper and lime, heard the clink of ice, and then he had a gin and tonic in hand. "Thank you," he said after sitting up slightly to take a few sips. "It's perfect."

"And thankfully not hard to mix up."

"Where's yours?"

"No caffeine or alcohol while doing this." Ambrose slathered his hands in that same golden oil Barrett had seen earlier. He flexed his fingers and wiggled them at Barrett. "This isn't dangerous but the straight razor is. And here, let's sit you up."

He got Barrett reclining at an angle where he could drink and not choke, but Ambrose could still reach him. "You're gonna spoil me," he huffed, making Ambrose smile again. He liked that smile. He liked Ambrose. Something about this man pulled Barrett forward, toward the terrifying unknown in a way that should have made him feel unsure, unsteady. Unsafe.

The opposite was true, and Barrett didn't know what to think. But he knew how his body responded to Ambrose, how he felt around him.

Just two grouchy loners living next to each other in the middle of the wilderness. That's how it was supposed to be. He wasn't supposed to fall for the neighbor. The friend. The ally. He wasn't supposed to want Ambrose with him; in his house, on his boat, in his bed. In his life.

When Ambrose touched his jaw with both hands, Barrett wrapped his fingers around those delicate wrists. "Wait."

Ambrose froze immediately. "I'm sorry. What did I -"

"You and I. There's something here."

Ambrose frowned. "Is that a question? I thought we worked that out."

"No, I didn't mean that." Barrett slid his hands up Ambrose's arms, until the sleeves of his t-shirt got in the way but he kept pushing, kept touching. He needed this. He needed to feel Ambrose's skin, pull him close. "This tension is good, right? You can feel it."

He heard the effort it took for Ambrose to swallow. "From almost the minute we met."

Fuck. Fuck. "You can't say stuff like that and expect me to not want you even more. Fuck, Ambrose." His fingertips were sliding over muscled shoulders but Ambrose was locked in place, staring hard at Barrett's face. That plush set of lips was damp from where he'd licked them and it would take nothing at all to pull Ambrose down and bite and lick into that mouth.

"You look a little wild, Barrett." Gods, Ambrose's voice, that gorgeous tenor, was strained. And when Barrett looked down, he saw the distinct ridge of Ambrose's erection through his black jeans.

"Like I want to eat you?"

"Yeah. Something like that."

Slowly, so Ambrose could stop him at any point, Barrett pulled his touch back. Down, down, down Ambrose's arm until he had those fingers linked with his. Then down again, together, until Ambrose could see Barrett's intention. "Stop me and we stop." He was breathing hard now, his brain going fuzzy, his skin too warm.

The sound Ambrose made when Barrett pulled their joined hands down a little more, over Barrett's hard cock, made him surge up. "Fuck, Barrett." Ambrose's needy little growl was cut off as Barrett kissed him hard. For a moment, he feared Ambrose would pull back, but then Ambrose was climbing into his lap, straddling his waist, sliding slick hands up his chest.

Barrett felt as if he were unwinding at every touch, with every moan, and the heartbeat of want that had lain quietly in the background all night was now center stage, pounding through him. "Fuck." He tore his mouth away, panting, and Ambrose immediately tucked his face into Barrett's neck and began laying wet, open-mouthed kisses on his skin.

He let himself *feel* Ambrose. Let himself get lost in the soft skin of his lower back, tracing the bumps of his spine. Let himself grow dizzy with every whimper and moan he pulled from the man above him.

And then there were blunt teeth in the meat of his shoulder and Barrett hissed, lurching up. "Shit. Shit. Sorry!" Ambrose immediately tried to scramble back.

Barrett didn't have oil all over his hands, so he could hold Ambrose steady by the hips, then yank him down. He thrust up against Ambrose's cock, making the other man whine. "Don't apologize. This is what you do to me. You're driving me fucking nuts, Ambrose." He let his head fall back against the chair, the move exposing his throat. "But I also want you enough that if we keep going, I'm going to back you against a wall. And we agreed to go slow."

Ambrose shook his head and Barrett watched, enraptured, at the sight of those messy auburn waves shifting in the light. "We did. We did." He drew Barrett's hand over the tent in his pants. "But this is slow."

Barrett had to snort at that. "We've not even been on a date."

"Haven't we?" He pushed Barrett's hand lower, his hips twitching at their joined touch. "Every Friday night for months now. I'd say that's a goddamn record for most people."

He was right. He was absolutely right.

While they'd been spending all that time getting to know each other, it had been a little bit like dating. He felt stunned. "Fuck."

"Yeah." Laughing, Ambrose leaned forward again and placed several small kisses along Barrett's jaw, making him shiver. "I fucked up your shave but I can't keep going like this." He held his hand out for Barrett's inspection. "Too shaky."

If he thought about his next words any more, he'd never say them. Swallowing hard, Barrett said, "Will you let me take you to bed?"

"Yes." Ambrose ran his fingertips over Barrett's cheek, then his jaw. "I've got some disposable razors, if you want to -"

"Yeah. Give me five minutes."

There was a spark in Ambrose's eyes as he replied, "Or you can just do it later."

With one great lurch (and not an unimpressive show of strength), Barrett hefted them both to their feet. Ambrose's delighted laugh was a little wild and sharp and he clung to Barrett even once he was back on the ground. Barrett kissed him again, winding that hair between his fingers and listening to Ambrose moan against his mouth.

CHAPTER EIGHTEEN

A s soon as Ambrose peeled off his shirt, Barrett pushed him into the wall, caging him in between thick forearms while an even thicker thigh notched between his own. Barrett's chest and neck and jaw glistened with oil (the oil Ambrose had made just for the other man, smelling lightly of cold pines and citrus and wood smoke) and he reached up, eager to rub it into warm skin and wiry hair. The shave was incomplete and some exacting part of him wanted to fix it, to go get the straight razor and watch shaving cream and hair be whisked away by that sharp, sharp blade.

What he had was a million times better, because Barrett was kissing him. No mere kiss, this thing that curled a tongue around his, that sent callused fingers into his hair and scraping along his scalp, that moaned into his mouth. Ambrose heard the plea for *more* in every hitch of Barrett's breathing. So he let his hands wander, searching over skin and muscle, rubbing the oil in.

Barrett yanked his head away only to come back with lips and tongue and teeth on Ambrose's neck and now he groaned softly, tipping his head to the left. "This is gorgeous," Barrett purred at him, another set of fingertips skating over the tattoo on his neck and shoulder. Ambrose used to rub his fingers over the swirling vines when he was thinking or nervous; a habit he'd broken long ago. But no one had touched his tattoo quite like this. Reverently, gently, with curiosity and wonder.

And then Barrett chuckled, the sound making Ambrose's insides quiver with expectation. "I was supposed to be supporting you with all the stuff going on. The letter and everything." He cupped Ambrose's jaw with one big palm, turning him back until they could look at each other. "You sure? I shouldn't have -"

"Barrett. Shut up." He touched Barrett's forearm with a finger, let that touch slide up. A mimicry of what Barrett had done just moments earlier. "Kiss me and hold me and take me to bed and fuck me so hard I forget to put clothes back on."

Those lips that had been on his twitched, accompanied by mountainous shoulders shaking with laughter. "You don't sleep naked?"

"You do?" He shot back.

"Course."

Ambrose let his gaze drift, hungry, over Barrett's shirtless body. "Hell, if I looked like that, I guess I would too." He'd figured out pretty early on that Barrett wasn't barrel-chested - as early as being crushed to the man as Barrett pulled him from a collapsing trail bridge. *Barrel-chested* brought to mind wide and thick all over, like the ridiculously huge men who did those strongmen contests. Barrett was broad but tapered, his shoulders easily the widest part of him, then his body slowly, almost carefully, narrowed into a trim waist that led to powerful legs.

Barrett's body had made him think vicious, filthy little things from the moment they'd met. First it had been the tight ass in dark, worn jeans as he'd walked away with a wave after finding Ambrose at the boat dock. The feel of hard - and hard won - muscles under Ambrose's hands as they tumbled to the cold forest floor. The warmth of his hands patting Ambrose's swollen ankle. The sight of his biceps flexing in a henley as he chopped wood.

But it wasn't difficult to appreciate the lines and art of a body. Ambrose had quickly started to see *more* in Barrett. Dark hair curling out of control, thick beard so dark it was nearly black. Molten brown eyes, deep set and framed with expressive eyebrows. The delicate tattoos on his wrists: a pine tree on the left, a compass on the right. That laugh. The smile. The *mind* and *heart*.

If he was really, really lucky, Ambrose would get to appreciate all of it and show Barrett the depth and strength of his appreciation. His affections. Ambrose was a physical creature and now he understood Barrett was, too. His might be a pining, pinching, needy kind of thing while Barrett's was for the physical pleasure of sex and touch and his tongue in another's mouth, but that didn't make their needs opposing. It was simply a puzzle to work out, to find how they fit together.

Ambrose lurched forward and pressed his palms into Barrett's stomach, taking in the man's soft gasp and how his fingers grasped Ambrose's shoulders. "Show me what you like. Or tell me. Just...."

His hands slid up, higher, brushing over Barrett's nipples and pulling a groan out as a reward. That was a good touch, a wanted touch. "You're so beautiful, I can't stand it."

"Ambrose." His name was choked out from between Barrett's lips. "Beauty's not....*you're* gorgeous. I've never met anyone like you. So gorgeous, and your mind is incredible." Barrett's expression twisted and Ambrose worried it was concern even as *gorgeous* rattled through his brain like loose change.

But the expression was blinked away and then Barrett was placing his hands over Ambrose's as he grabbed. Ambrose dug his fingertips into Barrett's pecs, squeezing, watching the bigger man shiver in his grip. Pride flushed through him, interrupted only by Barrett saying, "Keep doing that and we are actually going to fuck against this wall."

Ambrose laughed. A full-flighted sound that made Barrett smile in return. "I'm too old for that."

"So am I and yet I'm willing to try."

He stepped back, grabbed Barrett's hand, their fingers slippery from the leftover oil but leaving them smelling like forest and stone and *themselves*. Ambrose wanted to roll around in that scent but knew it would be better if spiked with sweat and musk.

His bedroom was simple in layout, with the center focused on a massive rug, on top of which sat a bed big enough for four people. He loved that bed. Custom-made, a splurge after he'd gotten hired at his most recent employer. He'd kept it in storage until the deal for the house went through, but he'd always hoped it would be appreciated by someone other than him. And Barrett was running a hand over the intricately carved footboard, a small smile curving on his face.

"This is gorgeous, holy shit."

The response was immediate. He didn't even want to stop himself from saying, "So are you."

Barrett's smile became a smirk right as he climbed on the bed and hung his legs off the edge. He spread them wide. Inviting Ambrose in.

How could he say no to such a generous offering?

Ambrose slipped between those massive thighs, felt them squeeze lightly, and then Barrett was pulling him down by the shoulders. On top of him. Letting Ambrose slither up his body and do as he pleased.

He was offering Ambrose permission and power to hold Barrett as he chose. To lay down kisses and caress oil-slick skin. To explore as his desire dictated. And Barrett gifted him these things gently, as if they were worthy of tender care and understanding and yes, passion. The revelation left Ambrose sucking in a shaky breath.

"You okay?"

Barrett was looking at him with those deep, dark eyes, the concerned twist of his mouth no longer hidden by thick hair. He looked ten years younger and yet still the same. There was a small scar on his chin and that's where Ambrose chose to press a soft kiss. Barrett inhaled and curled his fingers into Ambrose's hair as it fell over them.

"I'm okay." He pulled back to sit on Barrett's thighs and run his hands over that incredible chest. "I'm okay. Really. You rattle me."

"In a good way, I hope."

"In the best way." Ambrose couldn't find his voice above a whisper but into that he poured his lust, the *need* for the man lying beneath him.

Barrett heard it. He yanked Ambrose down, no longer careful with his touches. No longer caging his own pleasure for worry of making Ambrose flinch. Barrett knew he wouldn't. Not with him. Not ever with him.

This kiss bit. There were teeth in his lower lip, then a tongue in his mouth, and large hands roaming his bare back. Sliding down. Teasing the waistband of his jeans. Then two fingers slid in, directly over his tailbone, then down the swell of his ass. Ambrose let out a filthy moan and *bit back*.

"Fuck. Minx." Barrett tore away from the battle they were waging with their mouths to run his tongue along Ambrose's jaw. "Fuck. Fuck. I knew you'd be dirty in bed."

"Thought about that often?"

"More than I....*goddammit Ambrose...*"

Ambrose chuckled against his chest, leaned back to admire the already fading teeth marks he'd left on one pec. "Too rough for you?"

The world spun, his belly swooping with shocked delight, and then he was staring up at Barrett's pleased smile. "Not enough." Barrett pushed a thumb into Ambrose's lower lip and Ambrose sucked it into his mouth. "Can I fuck you?"

"Thought that's what we were doing."

Barrett shook that shaggy head. "Yeah but I gotta check."

What Ambrose heard rang like the clearest church bell: *I have to check you still want this. That you want me. Please want me.*

He pulled one hand away from Barrett's chest, where he'd been swirling his fingertips in chest hair as if finger painting, and undid the button on his own jeans. Shoved them down, took his briefs with the worn denim. Shoved them further, as far as he could reach, so his cock sprang up and he could get a hand around it. "I need you to fuck me," he growled, his gaze never leaving Barrett's. "I need it." Emotion swelled in the hollow of his throat, rose up to strangle him. "I need you."

That already smoldering gaze went pitch black and the expression on Barrett's strong features turned into something calculating. As if Ambrose were an equation and Barrett could figure it out. It hollowed him out, that look. Speared him, spread him open, left him vulnerable. It left him trembling, his shaky breaths filling what little space there was between them.

"Jesus Christ, Ambrose." Barrett swiped his thumbs over Ambrose's cheeks, his cheekbones. Up, over his temples and then into his hairline. Down around the sensitive curves of his ears, then along his jaw until Barrett could wrap one big hand around the back of his neck and pull him into a kiss.

The other hand wrapped around his cock and Ambrose *keened*. Some strangled, high-pitched noise in the back of his throat that sounded like a sob of relief. His back bowed with it, his hands gripped Barrett's shoulders with its power, and his voice rang with the sound of his own furious desire as he said Barrett's name.

"I was gonna ask you what you like but I think I figured it out." Ambrose had to roll his eyes forward and up, away from the backs of his eyelids, to see Barrett staring at him with fierce concentration. Barrett swiped a thumb over the head of Ambrose's cock and it made him shudder. "Oh, your face. Fuck. Like this?" A twist of his wrist, fingers grasping, and Ambrose gasped. "You're sensitive."

"To everything," he managed to gasp. His thighs were already shaking. Ambrose flung an arm over his head and grabbed the headboard. "Do it again. Please."

"This?" Another twist, somehow teasing in its touch now, and Ambrose groaned. "Fuck, you're so beautiful." His words were stuck in his throat and it was all he could do to gasp and moan. "Bedside table?"

Ambrose nodded but scrambled after Barrett as he moved to the edge of the bed. "Not yet. Just get them out but..." He gripped Barrett's arm, pulled him back. "Take the rest of your clothes off.

Let me see you." His other hand was on Barrett's chest and sliding down, dragging blunt nails over his skin. "Unless you need help."

Barrett laughed, the sound weak, but he immediately started undoing the button and zipper on his jeans. Ambrose went for the bedside table instead, his shaking fingers barely able to grab the condoms and lube. When he turned back, Barrett pushed him down gently and slid up his body, until his thighs were bracketing the middle of Ambrose's torso.

He couldn't even be shocked by how quickly Barrett got naked. He was too busy staring. "Can I..." Ambrose reached out but stopped inches from the black and red stripes tattooed on Barrett's thighs.

"Not what you were expecting?" There was teasing in that voice, but also a note of halting concern.

Ambrose immediately looked up. "Better. Even better and I didn't think that was possible." At Barrett's nod, he smoothed his palms over the tattoos, his touch even but gentle. "They go all the way around?"

Barrett shifted his hips to give Ambrose a look at the side of his right thigh. "Yeah. Stung like a son of a bitch. Worth it, though."

"Tell me the story later?"

There was that wry, softly delighted twist to Barrett's lips again. It was quickly becoming one of Ambrose's favorite expressions on that face. And he could see it better now that the beard was gone. "There's a story?"

"Make one up if there isn't." His touch turned firmer, more confident, and Ambrose lifted his head. Tongue out to lick his lips. Daring.

Barrett groaned and fell forward, into Ambrose. He slid along Ambrose's body, pressing their chests and hips and cocks together. Tucking his face into Ambrose's neck and inhaling before overwhelming Ambrose's senses with open mouthed kisses along his jaw, rough hands roaming. Ambrose slid his palms down Barrett's back, content with holding on and reveling in the sensations.

They lay together for several long moments, the sound of their intertwined breathing and the feel of Barrett on him, above him left him wishing this could last. That sudden punch of sadness, realizing that nothing good ever lasted, made him freeze. Barrett immediately pulled back and put a hand to Ambrose's face. "Hey. What's up?"

Not *You okay* or *What's wrong*. Barrett probably didn't realize it but his open-ended, bleeding-heart sweetness of a question meant a lot. "Overwhelmed, I think." Ambrose dug the heel of his palm into his forehead. "Sorry."

"Don't apologize. Ever. What you feel is real, Ambrose." Barrett gave him a little smile and Ambrose watched, fascinated, as some of that darkness in Barrett's eyes receded, replaced by warmth; the kind of warmth Ambrose wanted to huddle by and let seep into his bones. "We can stop."

That was the last thing Ambrose wanted. But doubt crept in as he said, "I don't think this was what you were hoping for a while ago."

"No, it's not. It's better." Barrett kissed his forehead, right where Ambrose's hand had been moments before. "Fucking's fun but this is much better."

With a groan, Barrett rolled off Ambrose and onto his side, his arm held out in silent invitation. "Are you sure?"

"Ambrose. Come here."

Ambrose let himself drink in the sight of Barrett naked in his bed before scooting close. They shifted around, the contact sparking along Ambrose's skin. Eventually he got a leg in between Barrett's, one arm under his head and the other flung over that broad chest. They were a good fit for each other, Barrett's muscular frame nearly swallowing Ambrose's lean one. But he didn't feel smothered. He felt content, like being wrapped in the world's most perfect blanket. "Barrett."

"Yeah?" Barrett leaned back to look down at Ambrose. "Anything you want to say is good, except an apology. Don't apologize. This is amazing."

Ambrose swallowed hard. "What is?"

Barrett pushed the hair out of Ambrose's eyes, kissed his forehead. "The closeness. I don't...." His voice broke. "Can't say I've had that in a long while."

That answer settled in Ambrose's chest and he took it to heart. Barrett meant what he said. "Me either."

Barrett lay in the quiet cocoon of darkness, his arms wrapped tightly around Ambrose. His ardor had died down long ago, left simmering in the background. Ambrose was warm and limp and Barrett could feel every breath he took as it settled on his neck. He hadn't felt so safe, so sure, in a very long time. With the turmoil of work, the sabotage, the ongoing health issues Forrest and Val were dealing with...hell, even Oz was a stressor.

But here, in the quiet, in the dark, holding Ambrose against him, Barrett felt settled. Back on solid ground. And more than anything, he wanted to give Ambrose *everything*. He'd been right; they'd been dating for months. They just hadn't thought of it that way because they'd been focused on getting to know each other. To get past their rocky start and work on a relationship.

And now that relationship had turned physical. But it was an inclusion, instead of a substitute. It felt right, natural. Perfect. As perfect as something like this could be between two grouchy loners living in the middle of nowhere.

In that fuzzy darkness, Barrett understood. He understood himself and Ambrose and their connection. More than the physical pleasure of having Ambrose naked and spooned against him. More than running his fingertips down Ambrose's arm and through that hair he was obsessed with. There was a spark between them, something fragile but brilliant, and he wanted to help it grow.

He would have done anything Ambrose had asked when they were naked and kissing and panting against each other. A thousand scenarios had entered his mind - him between Ambrose's thighs, his lips wrapped around that pretty pink cock; the sight of his fingers disappearing into Ambrose's tight body; holding Ambrose close as they rocked together slowly, their sweat staining the sheets.

But more than that, Barrett now understood *Ambrose*. He saw the passion and intelligence, the wry humor and the way storm clouds could gather over that head of auburn waves, and the fierce devotion that overwhelmed someone who felt *everything*. Ambrose had learned to build walls to protect himself from those who would hurt him, and it had been a lesson learned the hardest of ways, from the people he had trusted the most. He didn't need to read the letter from Ambrose's mom to know the sting of those bladed words. They'd both been hurt enough.

He wanted to help Ambrose heal.

Barrett closed his eyes and breathed Ambrose in and slowly, softly let that darkness take him, with a tattoo of yearning blossoming under his skin.

CHAPTER NINETEEN

A mbrose awoke to the smell of coffee but as he rolled over, following his nose, he ran into a warm, hard wall. Barrett made a rumbling sound of contentment and immediately pulled Ambrose close. "Morning."

"Hey." The prior night rushed back and Ambrose winced. Shit. Shit.

"I can hear you thinking." Barrett slid a palm under Ambrose's jaw, tilted his head up until their eyes met. Ambrose could feel every inch of Barrett pressed against him and it felt like heaven. "Lemme clear it up real quick. I stayed because I wanted to, I slept great, I made coffee cause I figured we'd both need it, and I still find you insanely attractive." That liquid darkness crept in around the edges of his brown eyes and Ambrose could feel its magnetic pull. "And I had a thought about the physical side of things, for which you do not ever have to apologize for."

His breath left him in a rush, heart swelling with shocked adoration. "You really thought you'd wake up alone, didn't you? Ambrose." Barrett carded his fingers through Ambrose's hair and he leaned into that touch. His whole body warmed; a flicker of lust slowly kindling in his gut. "Last night was perfect."

Then it dawned on him that Barrett had shaved completely and while he'd wanted to do it for him, Ambrose knew it had probably been itchy after the incomplete job he'd made of it the night before. His fingers sought to touch.

Barrett smiled at him, seeming to understand, and Ambrose reached up to let his fingers trail over smooth skin. "You did a good job," he murmured, following the line of that strong jaw. Barrett looked ten years younger without his beard and while that should have been a shock, it was just nice to see his face. "Your skin's dry. I have something for that."

"Later." Barrett leaned in, paused, and when Ambrose followed him, the kiss they shared was the sweetest thing he'd ever tasted. It made no demands on him, as Barrett's lips pressed gently against his own. He felt a hand smooth down his bare arm, leaving goosebumps in its tracks. It moved back up, dragging through his hair, making his scalp tingle.

Ambrose made a contented noise against Barrett's mouth. He wanted this, but he wanted more, and that war that raged in him left aching lust in its wake. It left him strewn across its battlefield, torn asunder. Arching against Barrett and murmuring soft words of praise into a mouth that worshipped him, and it felt natural and right.

He wanted more.

Ambrose made a needy noise, more whine than solid sound, and Barrett responded by rolling them and nudging his knee high up between Ambrose's thighs. "Is this okay?"

"Yes." Ambrose groaned. This was different. If last night had been a foundation of trust, stopped only by Ambrose's insecurities, this morning's bright light brought on new hope. Another chance. Barrett was still here and that meant something.

The look on Barrett's face was hopeful. "I really want to get my mouth on you."

Sparks flared behind his eyes and need pooled in the bottom of his belly. Ambrose flung a hand out, digging his fingers into Barrett's hair, yanking him down for another kiss. This one with teeth and tongue and all the pent-up desire he could pour into it. Barrett thrust against him with a roll of his hips. That easy, simple motion made him ache. "Please."

They fumbled with the condom, trembling fingers igniting a fire under Ambrose's skin like he'd never felt before. And Barrett was looking at him with the kind of reverence that bordered on too much, too intense. "I don't mind, trust me," Barrett said once the condom was in place. Just the care in his voice made Ambrose's cock twitch. "The only person I've slept with in the last..." He broke off. "A long damn time. Was Oz. And we both were clean before, got tested afterwards. But gotta be careful."

"Same," he gasped. Fuck, his body was already on fire and he watched while Barrett let his touch trail across Ambrose's skin.

"You slept with Oz, too?" That smile he was coming to adore cracked open. "Damn. Had no idea."

Ambrose snorted, making Barrett laugh. "You know what I mean. Testing, making sure. But I'd rather not say his name."

Gods, watching Barrett's eyes go almost black as quick as turning on a light switch was a heady thrill he didn't ever want to grow tired of. "Rather you start saying mine."

The thin latex did nothing to hide the wet warmth of Barrett's mouth. His hands were guided to rest in Barrett's hair and Ambrose got the message: *hold, don't pull.* He had no desire to do so. It waterfalled between his fingers, tickled the sensitive skin of his thighs, and rested in the cut of his hips. And as he arched into Barrett's mouth, he watched that hair fall around him. So dark against his pale skin; a myriad of brown and near-black strands that shone a muted copper in the faint sunlight splashing over them.

Ambrose would have closed his eyes, overwhelmed by the pleasure racing through him. But he didn't want to. Couldn't. And the singular experience of watching Barrett made something crumple inside him, leaving him gasping and groaning but never, ever looking away.

"God, you're gorgeous." Barrett was staring at him, lips shining with spit. "How does that feel?"

"So good. Fuck, so good, your mouth..."

Barrett's smile was full of teeth and lust. "Think how it would feel without the condom."

Ambrose heard the implication. If they went further. Became exclusive, monogamous. Yoked only to each other and knowing that skin on skin wouldn't be dangerous because there would be no one else. That realization was lightning down his spine. He held on as Barrett sucked him down and relinquished himself to the sensation.

When Barrett's touch slid down, caressing his sac, Ambrose nearly shot up. "Sensitive," Barrett teased and Ambrose groaned again, slumping against the pillows. "Do you want to come like this?"

The question rattled through his brain. He was so close already. It would be easy to let Barrett tip him over the edge. But he wanted what they'd started last night. "No." Ambrose grabbed and Barrett latched on, letting himself be hauled up into a bruising kiss that tasted like Barrett and latex and Ambrose didn't give a *fuck* because it was perfect.

When faced with the lube and another condom, it brought a question to Barrett's face. "Yes, yes, please." Ambrose punctuated his words with a long lick across Barrett's throat, leaving the other man shaking. "Just like this."

Just like this. Barrett folded over Ambrose while they shared breath and sweat and heat and an intimacy that colored his vision with lust and need. The spark, the light, between them grew with every touch. Barrett was incredibly gentle in his exploration, one hand petting Ambrose's shoulder and chest while the other moved down. "We'll go slow," Barrett said, voice hushed. "I don't want to hurt you."

"I know. I know." Ambrose was clenching in anticipation of that first touch. He willed his body to relax. "I won't break."

Barrett chuckled. "That I am very aware of. But I want this to be good." His hand lingered near Ambrose's hip. "Pull your leg up for me?

Ambrose drew his left leg to his chest and got a wolf whistle in response. He felt the heat in his cheeks while Barrett was gazing at the curve of his thigh and ass. "Gorgeous."

"You don't need to say that." *Don't stop, ever. I just don't know how to take compliments.*

"Mmmm, but I really do." Barrett rested his hand on the swell of Ambrose's ass. "Ready?"

"Please."

The lubed condom was lukewarm and Ambrose hissed automatically. Barrett didn't stop but he did lock eyes with Ambrose. He circled Ambrose's hole with one finger, almost a suggestion of a touch without any pressure. He remembered to breathe. He remembered how to melt into the mattress and let someone touch him so intimately. Ambrose remembered he was home. He remembered he was safe with Barrett. So he closed his eyes and focused on that pain-pleasure of being entered.

Barrett's touch was delicate but his words less so. *"Fuck."* Ambrose cracked an eye open and saw the open-mouthed desire painted across Barrett's face. He was watching Ambrose's body accept his finger, that intimate act making his heavy brows draw down, his lip be pulled between his teeth. It was a strangely coquettish expression on such a strongly featured face and if Ambrose didn't have a finger in his ass, he would have teased his lover.

"That okay?" Barrett was panting and those shaky breaths felt like his own.

"So good." And it was. Barrett's other hand began playing about his chest again and Ambrose grabbed it, planted it over his right pec. "You can pinch them, I like it."

"Goddamnit. You're gonna ruin me."

But Barrett's words were at opposites with his touch because everything he did to Ambrose was gentle. Even the little pinch he gave Ambrose's nipple was more teasing than testing. That finger slipped in deeper as Ambrose relaxed and soon Barrett was second knuckle deep in him and Ambrose was writhing. He pulled up his other leg and wrapped it around Barrett's waist. "Another. Fuck. Please."

Barrett pulled all the way out, leaving Ambrose feeling empty, only to push back in with two fingers. And the deeper he went, the more Barrett bent over him, the more kisses were planted along his neck and shoulders, trailing hot and slick up to his mouth. Ambrose was nothing more than a live wire of pleasure. It curled his toes and made him gasp and left him grabbing the sheets, grabbing Barrett, wanting to swallow the world into a void of pure bliss.

Barrett peppered his face and neck with kisses, his soft groans filling Ambrose's ears. But Ambrose couldn't find the brain cells to say more than *please* and *yes* and *Barrett.*

As slowly as he'd entered Ambrose, Barrett began stretching him. Ambrose reached for Barrett's cock, eager to feel that warm, thin skin and the pump of blood through thick veins. "Do that and I'm gonna spill before we get to the main deal here." Barrett was trying to chuckle but the sound strained from his throat.

"Where should I..." Ambrose licked his lips. He wanted to please Barrett. "Where should I touch you?"

"Kiss me."

That Ambrose could do.

Over slow, pleasure-drenched minutes, Barrett filled Ambrose's body while Ambrose devoured his mouth and tugged at his hair. His cheeks and chin burned from a bit of stubble but it was nothing compared to the heavy throb of desire between his legs. Barrett was *so careful* and that easy, gentle touch kept twisting the coil of need in the bottom of Ambrose's belly. And those fingers were clever, stroking and slipping inside him, nudging so close to that nerve he knew would make his sight go blinding white and his body taut like a bowstring.

And when Barrett did bump his prostate, Ambrose gasped like he'd been punched. So Barrett did it again and he sobbed and clawed and thrashed.

When he couldn't take it anymore, he said, "I'm good, I'm good. Barrett."

And Barrett was there, sliding on a condom and then rolling them until he was against the headboard and Ambrose was perched on his lap and that slick, heavy cock was sliding between his cheeks. Ambrose wanted to cry with how good it was. "This okay?" Barrett asked.

Oh, that darkness was back, drowning out all the light in Barrett's eyes. It made Ambrose want to see how lost he could get in it; wanted to see if it would swallow him whole. Devour him until nothing was left. "More than," he whispered back. That thick cock nudged at his hole and Ambrose trembled. Barrett gripped him at the hips but the touch tightened as Ambrose let his body open to take Barrett in.

The slide of Barrett's cock inside him set his heart hammering but Ambrose needed more. He wiggled and twisted, driving that cock deeper while Barrett held on for dear life.

When he bottomed out, Ambrose leaned forward with a grin, bracing himself on the headboard. "You feel *so good*," he moaned, capturing Barrett's mouth in a slow, drugged kiss. Barrett whimpered - *whimpered* - against him as his hips twitched. His body wanted in more, deeper, harder. Ambrose wanted to give it to him. "I need more."

The scent of sex and sweat and coffee permeated his nostrils, and all Ambrose could feel was *Barrett*. It felt right and good and perfect in the world-tilting kind of way he used to scoff at in well-thumbed books full of billowing sleeves and rocky cliffs and gusty sighs. But there was some truth to those yellowed pages and if he'd ever felt anything like it in the past, it was obliterated by the present. By the way Barrett clutched and clung to him, by the way he was kissed and held and *fucked*. Slow. Sure. Right.

The pleasure that had raced up his spine now spread and as he and Barrett moved together, their hands slipping on slick skin and the kisses they shared messy and wanton, Ambrose gave himself over. He let it consume him. He wanted to be taken by something more powerful than anything he'd ever experienced.

Barrett's thrusts quickened and he felt, rather than heard, his name whispered against his throat. "I'm close. You feel so good.

Ambrose." Barrett pulled back and Ambrose saw nothing but the devouring void in those eyes. "I need you."

"You perfect man." He pulled Barrett in by the back of the neck and slammed himself down. That thick, hard cock inside him pressed just right and Barrett went rigid under him with a moan that could have rattled the house's foundation. The warmth spilling inside him was muted and some part of him (the needy, greedy, grabby, wild part) wanted to feel that without the condom. He wanted to feel Barrett's warmth deep inside him while they traded spit and sweat and swears and filled each other with pleasure.

Ambrose fumbled for his own cock but Barrett was there with him, shivering and shaking and groaning. Together they pulled Ambrose off the cliff, his climax ripping through him as he spilled on Barrett's stomach.

When his senses returned, Ambrose pressed his sweaty forehead against Barrett's. "You're incredible."

Barrett kissed him again with a palm under Ambrose's jaw and fingers dug into his hair, all the way to the base of his skull. "So are you."

Barrett didn't know what to expect after their bodies cooled, but it wasn't for Ambrose to snuggle up to him and sigh happily. He'd hoped something like that would happen, but everything was so new and raw. Sex could go from good to bad in a blink and yet, here they were. Sticky and sated and curled together on Ambrose's bed.

He looked down at that fascinating, beautiful face, grey eyes hidden by closed lids, and smiled. Whatever this was between them, whatever lived in the spaces they shared, was making a home near his heart and Barrett welcomed it with open arms. He could see himself falling for Ambrose quickly. Probably already was.

"I can hear you." Ambrose's voice was a sleepy, heel-dragging thing.

"Can hear me what?"

"Smiling."

He laughed. "Caught me."

Ambrose lifted his head to place a kiss on the corner of Barrett's mouth. It wasn't enough, so Barrett pulled him up and over, until

Ambrose's lean frame was half sprawled over Barrett and neither had to strain their necks. "I forgot how good morning sex was," he murmured between kisses, already feeling lightheaded and giddy. That fizzy feeling in his chest was a nice contrast to the smooth muscles under his hands. And Ambrose looked *content*, the lines of his forehead and around his mouth faded into pale skin.

"Do you have to get up?"

"Nah. It's Sunday and I already let Dandi out. She's snoring by the fireplace."

Ambrose hummed and put his head back down on Barrett's chest while his fingers danced across his skin. "I have a favor to ask," he said quietly after several long minutes.

"Sure."

"You say that like it's easy."

Barrett shrugged. "It is easy."

He heard Ambrose swallow hard. "I am, admittedly, not good at taking people at their word."

That Barrett understood on a very basic level. People were complicated, twisting things and a certain number of them thought words had as much meaning as action. Words had power for sure, but actions had complete consequences. You could try to take back your words and apologize, but actions were more difficult - if not impossible - to undo. "Well, I'm not going to make big, sweeping promises," he replied, making sure to connect gazes with Ambrose. "But I hope you know by now that I'm a pretty open book. Ask whatever you want, Ambrose. And if I'm not comfortable or I can't, I'll tell you."

Ambrose took that in. Barrett could almost see the slow drip of realization and understanding erode another wall. "Well, okay." He shuffled closer, a small smile flickering on his face. "I still have to open that letter from my mother. I was hoping you'd be willing to stay with me as I did. Let me complain or vent or whatever strong feeling I'm sure she'll evoke." His smile twitched. "I can owe you a beer or a bottle of something."

"You don't *owe* me anything. We're friends." He trailed his fingertip over Ambrose's sternum. "Lovers."

There was no hesitation in the reply. "We are. But still."

"I got you." When Ambrose blinked at him, Barrett smiled. "Family shit is tough, doubly, maybe triply so when it's that close to the heart. I get you." He tipped Ambrose's chin up with a finger and kissed him. Softly. Quietly. Not intending to make Ambrose moan but there suddenly were fingers curled around his bicep; not clinging, but holding on. "I'll bring us some coffee. You want me to get the letter, too?"

That got him a laugh. "Oh the look on my mother's face if she knew I was reading her oh-so important letter in bed with my lover."

Lover slipped off Ambrose's tongue easily. Barrett liked the sound of it. "Be right back." He threw on pants and left the warm bed, shivering as the cold morning air hit bare skin. Dandi woofed at him softly, an acknowledgement of his presence, before closing her eyes once more.

The envelope smelled faintly of lavender and instantly Barrett hated it. He hated that this simple bit of paper and ink had made Ambrose upset. The urge to crumple it in his fist overtook him for only a moment, but he did squash it between the coffee mugs and lifted the entire thing to carry into the bedroom. Ambrose hadn't moved except to slide his briefs back on and drape an edge of the thick, dark green quilt over his legs. Barrett handed over a mug and the envelope before folding himself into bed.

"I won't bore you with the long details. My therapist has had to deal with all that at one time or another. But my mother is...unhappy with me."

That hit a little close to home for Barrett. The indifference to his existence, and Val's, had been the hallmark of their upbringing until their grandmother got ahold of them. And then it had been *you're not enough be better no wonder your parents dumped you on me.*

"I won't pretend to know. But I'm not lying when I say I understand on a level."

Whatever Ambrose was looking for on Barrett's face, he must have found it. With a nod and a long drink of steaming coffee, he said, "She's rather *famous* in the *well-heeled* parts of society."

He snorted. "A nice word for snobby?"

"Exactly. So being her only child came with a set of expectations. Expectations I have never, ever met." His mouth thinned and he sought out Barrett's hand. The faint note in his voice slowly eased away. "I know, poor me. But it's all to say that I'm guessing this," and he whipped the envelope in the air, "is her polite way of yelling at me for moving and not leaving a forwarding address. So she shouldn't have been able to find me."

It wasn't a hard leap to make. "The ex?"

"Fucking Preston. Has to be." Ambrose gripped the envelope tighter. "He'd better never come around here again." He snuggled closer, hooked his foot around Barrett's ankle. "He's ex. Permanently."

Something like nerves fluttered in his belly. Did he dare? "No ex here. And Oz was just a distraction." He grinned. "A physical one. And that gets boring."

"You're looking for something else."

Ambrose was trying hard to look nonchalant. Desperately. And failing. Carefully, Barrett took the mug from his hands and put it aside with his own. Then rolled them until Ambrose was half on top. He was quickly discovering that Ambrose under him (*on top beside with him*) was his favorite. Ambrose hummed happily, not the least perturbed at the shift. "I am," he replied, placing a kiss under Ambrose's jaw. "Thinking maybe I found it."

They fell into each other again and that damned envelope was shoved to the floor to make room for them.

Barrett was an incredibly giving lover. Thoughtful, attentive, *responsive*. And he liked hearing Ambrose say, "Please". He said it again and again, tasting Barrett on his tongue and their commingled sweat and musk somewhere behind his teeth. And the long, hot slide of Barrett inside him left Ambrose gripping the sheets, fingers seeking traction.

"Ambrose. Fuck. Gods." Barrett was plastered against his back, heavy and damp and perfect. Hands slid down Ambrose's arms and then circled his wrists briefly. He thought of being pinned, tied up, left to Barrett's mercy and it made him ache in a way he'd never known. Those hands pressed into his, letting their fingers intertwine, and Barrett's next thrust took them both over, leaving behind shaking limbs and harsh gasps echoing in the still of the room.

Ambrose could get used to this. Being taken. Cared for. Feeling Barrett's sloppy kisses to the back of his neck and the pause between them as he inhaled. Like Barrett wanted to trap Ambrose's scent in his lungs.

"Fucking hells." Barrett now had his forehead pressed between Ambrose's shoulder blades. "I've never had this much sex in one day."

Ambrose's laugh was squeezed out of his raspy throat. Barrett was *proportional everywhere* and the moment Ambrose had wrapped his lips around that length not ten minutes earlier, he knew the ruination of his throat was a fine price to pay. "Me neither."

Barrett hummed thoughtfully, pressed another kiss to his shoulder, and rolled off. But Ambrose had quickly learned that Barrett's touch didn't stop after the sweat cooled on their bodies. He *gathered* and *cuddled* and *lingered* and Ambrose felt adored. He wanted Barrett to feel the same. He turned in Barrett's arms and pressed several soft kisses to the sloping arch of his collarbone.

They laid in the quiet, watching the sun slide across the room and listening to the click of Dandi's nails and the churn of the washing machine. The domesticity of it should have scared him. He'd had this before. The love and care, the quiet, the closeness. The inextricable link between himself and another, the physical and the spiritual and something beyond definition.

Life was different now. He could make it different. Had already made it different.

Ambrose's breath left him in a gust, getting him a questioning look from Barrett. "It's a good thing. Trust me." He dragged the back of his fingers over Barrett's cheek. "I made choices this time. Things that were mine. The house. The job." Ambrose let his fingertips trace the line of that jaw. "I wanted to say thank you."

Barrett's throat bobbed. "For?"

"For letting me choose you." His fingertips drifted again, across strong shoulders. "Preston felt like a choice but I've reexamined some things lately. I wasn't ready, I wasn't spending enough time on me to figure out what I wanted."

"And now you have."

"Exactly." Ambrose let his touch skate around a nipple, drawing a soft gasp between still kiss-swollen lips.

CHAPTER TWENTY

"**I**f it isn't my favorite new author. How's the woods in your neck of them?"

Barrett laughed. "Doing okay. Nice to have the sun out for longer."

"I'll bet. Ambrose said you've been taking him to some truly lovely spots." Raf sighed. "I'm sad to get there too late to see all the wildflowers."

"Oh there's plenty of places that pop in May, if you know where to look."

"And I assume you bear this knowledge?"

His grin grew. "Might."

Raf's laughter grew, now a smooth wave that washed over the line. "Then I'm moving *hike with Ambrose and Barrett* to the top of my to-do list."

A thread of guilt wormed its way into his belly. "Nah, you just worry about Ambrose. I'm not about to get in the way of -"

"Barrett. My friend. We have not met in person but it's easy for me to see the kind of human I'm dealing with here." Raf shifted in his chair and gave Barrett an intense look, one he could almost feel through their video call. "In the vein of all best friends who suddenly find their nearest and dearest being swept off their feet, I will say I've known Ambrose a long time and he's never talked about someone like you. He's particular. To a fault." Raf held up a hand and Barrett saw the glint of silver on his fingers. "He's stubborn, self-effacing, and a loner at heart. There is no bigger seal of approval, in my mind, than how he speaks when he mentions you."

He couldn't do anything but give a weak smile. He hadn't expected to get the best friend gold star so quickly. "No talk about how I better not hurt him and how I should move at his pace?"

"No, because I know you understand that intrinsically. Your caution around him and care for him speak volumes. From even your very first interaction." Raf's hazel eyes softened. "Be good to him and he'll respond in turn. Oh, and watch out because once he likes you, he tends to spoil."

"Shit, I don't need anything."

Raf shrugged and Barrett watched his off-shoulder, dark blue sweater slide down further. Raf was a fascinating, beautiful creature and he knew seeing Ambrose and Raf together was going to destroy him. Ambrose's birthday was next week and Raf was coming into town. Barrett had planned to make himself scarce but both of them had squashed that almost immediately. They would have their traditional hike and dinner, and then Barrett was coming along for the remainder of the long weekend.

Except for Sunday night. Raf had "plans" that night, leaving Barrett and Ambrose alone the day after Ambrose's birthday.

"Well, expect it anyways. And it's not always tangible things, mind you. That boy's generous nature comes in all forms. But we're not here to only talk about Ambrose."

He snorted. "We're not?"

"Shocking, I know. But this," and Raf held up a thick stack of papers, "is what I'm mailing to you today. Final proofs for the page spreads."

Barrett felt something constrict in his chest. Perry's illustrations. "You move fast."

"I do. Especially when I've got an audience clamoring for content like this and we're working for a good cause." All joviality dropped off Raf's face. "You're sure? It's not a small sum of money and I get that you're not the kind to care about that. But it would make a good nest egg for the future."

Barrett shook his head. "I'm sure. That money should go to kids who need it. Perry would have wanted that."

Something shifted on Raf's face and Barrett saw the respect for his decision loud and clear. "Got it. The scholarship fund paperwork will be in the packet, too. And you'll want to set up a secondary executor, just in case."

Barrett had already talked to Val about that, and she'd been overjoyed to assist with overseeing the wilderness scholarship fund set up in Perry's name. Barrett's part of the proceeds from the book were funding the scholarship, with the money being given out to students interested in college-level environmental studies and attending wilderness camps.

He hadn't given it all away, though. The signing bonus had gone straight into an account for Forrest. His way of helping Val out, and as an apology. His call with his nephew a few days ago had gone about as well as expected, but it still fucking sucked to tell a kid he had to give up his dog. Dandi was too big, too full of energy, and too rambunctious even for him some days. But Val and Forrest were downsizing into an apartment, one closer to the children's hospital where Forrest went for treatments. It also put them closer to Barrett by about an hour, but cost of living in the city was higher and an apartment was no place for a massive beast like Dandelion.

Forrest didn't blame his Uncle Bear, but he was still just a kid. A sick kid going through some serious shit and even with a high remission rate as a light at the end of the tunnel, the journey was going to suck. He sighed and dropped one hand from his lap, caressing Dandi's soft ears. "Second executor's in place, just gotta get the papers to sign."

With a smile that read as utterly pleased, Raf leaned back in his chair. "So."

"Oh no."

"Please." Raf waved a hand, then pushed his stylish dark hair out of his face. "I'm just excited to meet you properly."

Barrett gaped. "That's it? No remarks about how..." He motioned to himself, old doubts creeping back in. "How different Ambrose and I are?"

"Not at all. I find that kind of talk a little crass, to be honest. Crass and tired. And like I said, I've no need to wave the theoretical knife under your nose. I am truly, honestly excited to meet you in person."

Something eased out of Barrett's chest. A knot undoing itself. "Yeah, me too."

"Then it's settled. I'll see you and Ambrose on Friday." Mischief glimmered in hazel eyes. "Should I text before I arrive?"

"Don't want to walk in on anything untoward?"

"Mercy, no. Untoward all you like. I just didn't take you for an exhibitionist."

Barrett barked out a laugh, waved, and signed off. It was nice to meet a best friend who wasn't an overprotective asshole. And any worry he'd had that Raf might look down on him and his worn clothes and simple life had been obliterated.

Raf's text came later with a recommendation of a "lovely little spot" to take Ambrose on Sunday. He hadn't been dancing in *forever*, not since those sweaty summer nights between college semesters where he and a group of friends had been drunk on cheap vodka and heard only their heartbeats and the pulsing music in their ears. As long as Ambrose enjoyed it, that was all that mattered.

And with his plans for Ambrose's birthday set, Barrett cast an eye at the afternoon sun gathering above trees boldly proclaiming their spring greenery. He hadn't been out on the boat in a while and Ambrose was in town on business for one of his clients. No time like the present.

He clipped Dandi and himself into their life vests and gathered his supplies. And when he stepped outside and looked at the dock, that memory of meeting Ambrose for the first time rushed him headlong. That had felt like years ago, but had only been six months. A lot had changed. A lot of good had come out of a budding friendship that was now something *more*. Something real and honest and full of warmth that filled a hole in his life.

But his boat was gone.

Frowning, Barrett walked around the edge of the water, looking for any sign of a snapped dock line. Nothing. No footprints outside his own and Dandi's and the occasional deer. There hadn't been any storms in the last week, just some rain and fog. So a snapped line, and the boat being carried away into one of the lake's eddys, didn't make much sense. Plus he knew his knots and the standing end was always tied securely to the dock. Barrett scaled back his memory, trying to remember when he'd last seen the boat.

> **From: Barrett** *Do you remember when you saw my boat the last time? I was gonna get out on the lake this afternoon, but the boat's gone.*

> **From: Ambrose** *Well that's not good. I remember seeing it from the bedroom window on Sunday night.*

That made him grin, despite the confusion churning in his gut. Sunday night they'd been in his bed. Then Ambrose's. Then on the couch. Back to Barrett's bed. *Terribly convenient having two beds so close*, Ambrose had said.

From: Barrett *You'll have to specify.*

From: Ambrose *My mistake. From your bed, around maybe 8 pm? It was after we had showered.*

From: Barrett *Okay, that makes sense. Shit that was three days ago. Why didn't I notice the boat was gone?*

From: Ambrose *I'm guessing you were distracted. But also it's that thing where we stop paying attention to items in our surroundings until they're out of place or missing.*

Ambrose was likely dead-on about that. But it nagged at him, that feeling he was missing something and couldn't pin it down.

From: Barrett *I'm going to keep looking, got Dandi with me. If I'm not home when you get back, text me? I might be lakeside, a ways up, checking with the neighbors.*

From: Ambrose *Aye, aye captain. Be safe. I look forward to you when I get back.*

Ambrose's endearments were, like him, breathtakingly unique and honest at the same time. Each one wrapped around Barrett's heart like protective vines. Like the vines tattooed on Ambrose's neck.

Dandi had wandered about thirty feet away, nose stuck firmly to the ground, so he whistled and she trotted back, tongue lolling.

She stayed with him as he followed the muddy line of the bank, occasionally perking up when some woodland critter scampered by. They were working on more training but Barrett had quickly discovered that the dog school Val had enrolled her in early on paid dividends in shockingly good behavior, especially from such a massive animal.

They continued to walk east but the further he got from home, the more his confusion bled into worry. Something tingled in the back of his mind. An awareness. The kind of sixth sense he knew meant trouble; even danger. The same strange feeling he'd had before rescuing Ambrose from the bridge. The same unease that wormed through him when he found an abandoned backpack near a trail. Most of the time the unease turned into relief. Barrett hoped that would be the case now. He paused to make notes in his phone - when he saw the boat was missing, screenshots of Ambrose's texts, his journey around the lake. Just in case. He blamed his ranger training.

He rounded behind the back of Gemma's property, gaze cast about in hopes of spotting the kindly old woman. She might be elderly, but Gemma was from the Canadian backwoods and built like an aged bodybuilder. She was as much a staple of Lake Honor as any of them, as if one day the land had spat her out and she decided to stay.

"Barrett!"

Gemma came around the corner, arms full of cut logs, and Barrett rushed to help her. She batted him away but he insisted; because as soon as she saw Dandi, Gemma didn't care if Barrett helped her. "What a beauty," she said, setting aside the wood and crouching to offer her hand. "I've seen y'all out hiking but didn't want to interrupt. Gods, what a good girl."

And Dandi, ever the attention-seeker, boofed softly and licked Gemma's hand. The old lady laughed, swinging her long gray braid over one shoulder. Barrett noticed a bandage on her right hand. "You can interrupt whenever you want, Gem," he replied, amused by how taken the woman and the dog seemed to be with each other. Dandi was bouncing, Gemma was laughing, and the whole scene made Barrett feel a little bit better.

"So what brings you by, Barrett?" Gemma stood and brushed dirt off her thick coveralls. "I know we're all a bit solitary out here, so don't think I'm criticizing."

Barrett explained his search for the boat and watched Gemma's frown grow, the lines on her face settling more into her windburned skin. "So if you see it, give me a call?"

"That's the thing, hon. I think I saw it, but it was foggy the other morning and the sun was right in my eyes. And every other person has a little motorboat like yours, but all I could think was how odd someone being out on the lake in that fog was. No one around here would do that." Gemma shook her head. "You want some tea?"

Something was bothering the woman. He'd seen that look on the faces of witnesses. "All right."

"Good, good."

As Gemma bustled around her homey kitchen, Barrett settled on the sofa with Dandi at his feet. If he tried to help, she'd smack his hand like an exasperated matriarch wanting the kids out of her kitchen. Gemma didn't speak while she made the tea, so Barrett looked around. Gemma's place was clean and tidy, but had a hill witch vibe to it; the bundles of herbs drying by the fire, the handmade pottery and candles, the fraying but warm blankets thrown over every chair.

She'd barely passed him a chipped cup of black tea that smelled of chai spices before she said, "I'm not sure what's going on, but something's got my hackles up." Gemma looked down at her cup, then back up at him. He'd always liked her directness and he braced himself for whatever was coming. "The other day I came out to find the roof on my chicken coop damaged."

Barrett sat forward, steaming cup cradled in his hands. "Damaged how?"

"Fucked up the shingles, tried to pry the whole roof off." She held up her bandaged hand. "And then I sliced my hand on one of the nails, trying to unbend it."

His ranger instincts kicked in and Barrett was asking what else she remembered, when this happened, the time, if she noticed anything else.

"The boat was odd enough," Gemma said, draining her cup. "But I noticed the damage to the coop the same morning. But coincidence is a tricky dick." She shrugged, the movement stiff and Barrett remembered she was in her seventies and healthier than most people half her age. But that stiffness made him worry anyways. "But what am I supposed to do? Call the police? Pffttt, what have they ever done for any of us? They'd take one look at me and say *now old lady, you sure you didn't imagine it?* Fuck that. And you know, it's funny cause I haven't thought about Marvin in *ages*."

"Shit, I forgot about that." At the time it hadn't been funny, but one of the original cabin owners, Marvin Gilbert, had complained long and loud about Gemma's roosters waking him up at the crack of dawn and making quite a bit of noise through the day. It had been one of those neighbor tiffs that Marvin really wanted to turn into a Hatfield/McCoy situation. Gemma hadn't stood for any of it, and since she had every legal right to her chickens, had ignored Marvin's increasingly angry phone calls and persistent doorbell ringing. It hadn't lasted more than a summer, and by fall, Marvin was gone and, according to rumor, angry at the town for forcing him to stop building cabins and making a fuckton of money.

He didn't bother to hide his laughter. "Fucking Marvin. Jesus, haven't thought about him in a long time. But your birds are okay?"

"Completely fine. I'm more shook up than them." Gemma looked down into her empty cup. "Fuck it. You want some bourbon?"

Barrett definitely wanted some bourbon. When Gemma brought the bottle back, he said, "You remember anything else? I know it's cliche, but even a little detail could help."

"Even if I don't think it's important?"

He laughed. Her tone was so dry but it wasn't aimed at him. "Even that."

Gemma stared at a spot on the wall above his head, eyes narrowed. After a few sips of bourbon, she said, "Now, this ain't anything. But I remember seeing they had on one of those stupid puffy vests. The ones the townies wear cause they think that's what real outdoorsmen run around in." She shot him a look that dripped with disdain. "Now, it was in the fog, from a distance, but those vests have a certain profile. So yeah, pretty sure it was one of those vests. And it was either a tall woman, or a man."

That was better than nothing. No one around the lake wore those vests, they did shit all to actually warm your core. So chances were good it wasn't a local. Which meant he had even more questions than answers, but it was a starting point.

As the conversation shifted and Barrett put his notebook away, Gemma leaned in, eyes glittering. "So word 'round the lake is you and the new neighbor are getting on all right. You gonna tell me what's really going on?"

Gemma would have been a good cop in her day. Her stare made him want to confess everything immediately. "We're uh...we're good. I thought it would be weird having someone new in Perry's place but Ambrose has made it his."

"A looker, your neighbor." She smiled. "Bet you two are cute together."

The flush making a mad dash up his neck was also making him sweat. Fuck, she was good. "Okay, come off it."

Gemma cackled. "I knew it."

"You didn't know anything."

"Didn't I? Don't get me wrong, there's some speculation about you two but it's more like arguing between the old coots who live around here. And then thirty seconds in they're so busy yelling about who is right and who didn't return what hammer and it all devolves into chaos." But she nudged his knee with hers and, with a softer smile, said, "Good for you."

Barrett was going to leave after taking some pictures of the chicken coop, but Gemma held out a handful of bent nails. Immediately that thing in the back of his mind sparked with awareness. That bend was the same. The same angry twist to the metal, the same marks around the nail head. All the same like the ones in the nails they took out of the ruined door to Alpha fire tower. He took his pictures and the nails back to his house, leaving Gemma with a kiss on the cheek and a promise to bring Ambrose by for dinner.

Fuck. Fuck. It was one thing to have sabotage creating issues - major ones - at work. There were files and reports, evidence and logs, and lots of people involved. It was another for it to hit so close to home, with just him and a dog and a notebook and a handful of nails. But somehow in his mind, the ferocity behind each of those bent nails didn't match up to the stuff-shirt snobbery of one of those stupid puffer vests.

It left him feeling queasy. Having the sanctity of his home and the little neighborhood of weirdos he'd known for a decade threatened wasn't right. His boat was gone, Gemma's chicken coop had been damaged, and someone or several people were wandering around the lake looking to cause trouble. Hackles raised, Barrett headed home, phone gripped tightly as he texted Ambrose.

From: Barrett *Come see me when you can? Got some weird news and I just...want to know you're okay.*

There was no answer, even by the time he unlocked his door. Unease turned into worry and he'd never been good at compartmentalizing his worry. So he texted Val.

From: Barrett *How's the kid? How are you?*

From: Hopscotch *He's all right today. Read a few comic books, we watched a movie, and now he's asleep.*

From: Barrett *You free to talk? Kind of need to hear your voice right now.*

His phone rang a moment later. "Hey, Bear. You okay?"

"Honestly, I don't know." Barrett sighed and leaned back into the sofa, rubbing his forehead with the heel of his palm. "Can I vent?"

She laughed. "I'm pretty sure I owe you about a day's worth of venting. Go for it. And don't let me forget to send you the video Forrest made earlier today. He felt pretty good, so he was fiddling with this little handheld camera a friend loaned him. He wanted to make a video diary about what it's like to have leukemia, so other kids who have just been diagnosed can have facts coming from someone like them."

His nephew's ingenuity and selflessness had no boundaries. "Jesus."

"I know. I'm so proud of him. He was hoping you'd watch them and give him some input. Asked about Ambrose, too."

"Shit, Ambrose knows his way around a video editor. I know he'd _"

"No, Bear, that's not what I was saying." Val sounded exasperated. Or maybe it was just the exhaustion he knew she was feeling. They weren't twins but they could have been, for all the times they felt each other's pain; some visceral, gnawing thing ready to chew on their bones. "He was just asking if Ambrose and you were doing okay. He's excited, he's never seen his Uncle Bear with someone."

"One, I'm asking Ambrose anyway. And two, you tell the kid I'm happy and so is Ambrose."

There was a clink of glass and ice cubes. "And what's your real answer?"

He smiled, and that warm feeling spreading in his chest knocked that pain away. "That we're happy and it's been good. You two do know it's only been a few weeks?"

"Bear. You big loveable dumbbell. It's been months. You only made it official a few weeks ago. You've been dating for months."

"That's what Ambrose said."

"And then you kissed him after that, right? Cause that's -"

"Val!"

"Some Hollywood shit," she finished. He knew she was smiling, could hear it in every syllable. "Anyways, I'm glad. But I better get to meet him this summer."

"I'm already thinking about that. Us coming out to see you two."

"Can't come soon enough."

It wasn't until the end of their call that realization struck Barrett like a train. Val was asking about the wild bird and raptor cameras his department hooked up every spring, noting that Forrest's favorite was the osprey camera.

Cameras

"Hey, Val, sorry. Work thing."

"No worries, I'm going to head to bed. Night, Bear."

"Night."

As he hung up, he saw Ambrose's car pull in next door. He was on his feet instantly. From the door he could tell something was wrong and he raced over, ready to help, with Dandi hot on his heels.

Chapter Twenty-one

The town of Honor was quaint and cobblestoned and quiet. A single main street, a few side streets with small houses, a post office, a library. A lot of people settled in or around the town to take advantage of the vast wilderness; to hike and fish and garden. But what he loved most about going into town was how quickly he'd gotten used to it. City living had been fun for a while, but you could only frequent so many bars and restaurants before either going broke, getting bored, or becoming an alcoholic. And there simply wasn't enough *quiet* between the billboards and neon and bustling streets. People were as diverse here as they'd been in the city, with the lake and forests feeding all manner of opportunities. But there was no light pollution, the air was clean, and he felt at home.

Ambrose had already swung by the hardware store for tomato seeds and a few other things he needed for around the cabin. So he parked in front of the grocery store, handwritten list in hand.

"Ambrose."

He froze on the sidewalk, feet from his car. His brain stopped but his heart immediately started jackhammering in his chest. Therapy was a wonder, but there was nothing to do about his fight-or-flight response at that voice.

Fucking Preston. In his designer jeans and his stupid fake leather boots and oversized sunglasses, looking like an aging boy band member and thinking he knew what was best at all times. Well, fuck him. Anger began to sweep over him, and he turned to fully face his ex, knowing this could go badly.

It was worse.

Preston was there, on the other side of his car, hands jammed into his pockets and looking rather unhappy. His gaze didn't stay on Ambrose long, darting away like a scared rabbit.

Because of her.

Angelica Avery was standing next to Preston. Ten feet from Ambrose. Maybe it was nine feet, which felt even more invasive. She should at least be double-digit feet away at all times. The salt in the wound was made even worse by the fact that she was, as usual, picture-perfect in a shin-length black dress, her signature peacock brooch high on her left shoulder.

Black, in spring. Like she was in mourning or some shit. The only pop of color was the absence of it; there was a gauzy white scarf, like something out of a 1950s movie, covering her auburn curls.

The only way anyone could think we're related, Ambrose dear. This hair. You really should find a way to tame it, darling.

And in the middle of this strange stand-off, Ambrose's phone buzzed against his palm .

From: Barrett *Come see me when you can? Got some weird news and I just...want to know you're okay.*

Worry flared in his gut. And he made his decision the moment he reached for the car door handle. That anger that had bled through was now fully flared; a fire made from years of his inability to walk away. "Fuck off."

"I raised you better than that, Ambrose."

There was the snake in the tall, fragrant grass. Always waiting, ready to strike. The patented Angelica Avery - no, Angel Tillifer - style of parenting. She'd always said *Angel Tillifer* was the name of an uneducated baby factory making the rounds through men. Because somehow the name Angel was beneath her.

Ambrose's gaze snapped up and locked on his mother. He'd worked *hard*, for *years*, to learn when and where to channel his anger. Most of him had hoped a day like this one never reared its ugly face, because that would mean she found him and decided to not let it be. But if he knew anything about his mother, it was that she didn't like having things beyond her control. Ambrose had decided to extricate himself from her and on some level, he knew there would be blowback. Abusers didn't like losing a part of their flock.

The words didn't come easily, but at least they showed up with a therapist-approved ticket. He'd practiced this, over and over again, dragging himself through a proverbial mudslide of emotions. For years. It was a little like training for a marathon, his therapist had said. A slow build of resistance and endurance, until thinking about a day like this one no longer made him want to hide from the world and shut off all his emotions.

Ambrose stared at his mother, then Preston. The fucker wouldn't even meet his eyes, but his mother had no issues there. He took a deep breath and it helped keep the tremor out of his voice. "You would have had to raise me to be able to say that, Angelica." Ambrose swung open the driver door and saw Preston move toward him. "Come any closer to me and you're both getting slapped with restraining orders." He held his arms out wide. "So go right ahead, because there's a camera above us and one across the street. Plus the grocery store owner has her own set."

Preston looked disappointed, his mouth twisted down, but his mother. Oh, the shock on his mother's face. The first and only time he'd ever seen her break character. He would revel in it later, want to roll in the memory of her open mouth and wide eyes. With his heart in his ears and his throat tight, Ambrose slid into his car, turned over the engine, and peeled out.

He didn't look back.

The anxiety attack didn't hit him until he was parked in his own driveway. His driveway. His house. She knew where he lived and he'd moved hours away to prevent that. But Angelica had Preston wrapped around her little finger, apparently, and they were both invading his space, his privacy, his fucking *sanity*. His gaze dropped to his hands, pale and tight on the steering wheel of his little utility wagon. The anger was still there, churning through him, burning up his lungs and making his breaths uneven and harsh. He could still feel his body and had some part of his mind left unscrambled, but this attack *hurt* on a level he'd never experienced.

Ambrose didn't hear Dandi's high-pitched barks or the scrabble of her paws against his window. There was a bright, painful flare of sunlight in his eyes and then he smelled lemon and clean laundry and let himself fall into Barrett's arms.

"I told her to fuck off," he said, pressing his forehead into Barrett's shoulder. "Both of them, actually."

"Ambrose. Ambrose. Fuck. Look at me." Barrett slid his palms under Ambrose's jaw, his eyes darting back and forth. "Are you okay? Jesus."

"Anxiety attack. Saw my mom, Preston."

He heard Barrett mutter, "Shit," before saying, "Okay. Do you have meds for this?" Ambrose could tell he was trying to keep his voice steady. It trembled at the edges, not unlike his own had done upon telling Angelica and Preston to go fuck themselves.

"Yeah, yeah."

Barrett led him by the hand inside his house, then on Ambrose's direction, rummaged in the master bathroom cabinets until he found a small bottle of tiny white pills. "Haven't had to take these in about a year," he said as Barrett gave him a pill and a glass of water. "Guess I have to set that timer back."

"Tell me where it is and I'll flip it to zero." Barrett's tone was as flat as a river stone, but his mouth was pursed, as if he were repressing a smile. Ambrose appreciated the gesture; humor in a moment of gravity.

"As if I'd tell you where my super secret timer is."

"Oh, we playing this game?" Barrett sat down beside him, his hand on Ambrose's knee, squeezing gently. "You really want to go up against a forest ranger? We're good interrogators."

Ambrose laughed, coughed. He pulled air into his lungs, hoping it would beat back the darkness swarming in his chest. "How advanced are your techniques? Because I'm no interrogation virgin."

Barrett snorted. "This is like out of a bad porno. What's my next line, something about I'm *very advanced* in the sexual arts?"

"That's so stupid." But he was laughing. Ambrose leaned into Barrett and got pulled into the bigger man's side as a reward. He slumped into that warmth and closed his eyes. "So out of curiosity ....how advanced *are* we talking?"

"You got expectations?"

"Curiosity only."

"So does that mean I keep up the St. Andrew's cross in the basement, or take it down?" Ambrose looked up and saw Barrett's smile, unhindered by what Ambrose would think of his answer. Or him, as a person. He flashed back to his mother; dozens and dozens of those shallow cuts delivered over decades. Judgments rendered based on her opinions and perceptions, and hers alone. No seeing Ambrose as his own person, as a human being with his own desires and fears. He was to be an extension of her, and that's where her care began and ended. But with Barrett, none of that mattered. Barrett cared about him as a whole, as another human being, and as a lover. Ambrose only wanted to do right by him.

"I can't tell if you're fucking with me or not," he finally said, laughter bubbling up from his chest.

"Good, that means I'm keeping you on your toes." Barrett kissed the side of his head, pulled him closer, and said, "Was this because of the letter?

"Maybe. Probably. She doesn't like being ignored, and me not seeking her out would have driven her mad, though she'd never admit it." Ambrose balled the hand on his thigh into a fist. "But fucking Preston. I should have known."

"What can I do to help?"

For that, and so many other reasons, Barrett got a swift, but hard, kiss, Ambrose's free hand wrapped into his collar to haul him down. "Grab the letter and a lighter for me?"

It wasn't until they were standing over the little rusted fire pit - the one that had been Perry's - when Barrett said, "This it?"

"It is." The tremor in his fingers was gone, and he could once again breathe; the cool spring air, smelling of twilight and moss, easing all those old emotional burns and scars. "You and I get the pleasure of watching this burn and I get double the satisfaction of knowing her words never reached me where she wanted them to." Ambrose held out the lighter. "Do the honors for me?"

"You sure?" Barrett looked unsure. "I can hold it, or we can get something to prop it up over the lip of the fire pit."

"I insist. Please." Ambrose held out the letter, his fingers curled around lavender-scented paper. Maybe this year he'd grow lavender and enjoy it. "New beginnings."

"New beginnings." With a deft flick of his thumb, flame sprang to life and Ambrose dipped the far corner of the letter into it. The paper caught, flared, then curled as the fire raced across it. Moments before it touched his fingertips, Ambrose dropped the letter into the fire pit, then silently held out his hand to Barrett.

The warmth of the fingers intertwined with his gave Ambrose back that last bit of solid ground he'd needed after today. Home, and all its comforts, had new meaning and a proper place in his life.

After the letter was reduced to ash, Barrett led him next door, to a roaring fireplace and Dandi asleep in the corner and a neatly made bed. "Proud of you," Barrett said against his mouth as he steered them back. His kiss was gentle and the press of that body against his made flickerings of warmth curl in his gut. But there was no frenzied tearing off of clothes. No spit-slick kisses and wandering hands. He wanted something else, and he could tell Barrett did, too.

Ambrose pulled Barrett down to the bed, turning so they were face to face. "I know," he said. "I know you are and yet hearing it feels good."

Barrett slid his fingertips down Ambrose's chest, let them catch on his belt. "Gonna let me keep doing that? Cause I can make you feel even better."

Ambrose didn't bother to hold back his smile. "Are we back to bad porno lines?"

"Yeah, actually I have one I wanted to try. Hold on." After clearing his throat rather dramatically, Barrett fluttered his eyelashes. Gone was the forest ranger, the voice of authority, and suddenly there was a coquettish ingenue in bed. Ambrose raised his eyebrows while Barrett softly said, "I don't know what you mean. I haven't watched a pornography -"

Ambrose snorted. "*A pornography?*"

Goddamn bastard didn't drop the act once. "I said what I said! I have never seen this *pornography*. I am a proper gentleman..."

Shit. He needed to remember how to act. Or what porn scripts sounded like. "Oh my god. It's a cock, darling. You have one and I have one."

"And I do not refer to *that*," and he motioned to Ambrose's groin, "as anything other than a penis."

Ambrose was torn between laughing and wanting to play along. "No dirty words? *Ever?*"

"I am untouched by such filth."

Swift as a snake, Ambrose rolled on top of Barrett and let his weight settle solidly. His thighs bracketed on top of Barrett's, his hands on either side of that shaggy head. "Filth, huh?" He slid down, grabbed for Barrett's jeans. Cast his gaze up to check for the head nod and got it. Seconds later, he had Barrett's jeans around his ankles and was mouthing at the head of his cock through his boxers. "Filthy enough yet?"

Nostrils flared, cheeks going red, Barrett fumbled for the bedside drawer. A condom packet smacked Ambrose on the shoulder. "Not enough, you cad!" Barrett said. "Oh, you dirty man, convincing me to do filthy, nasty things with you!" With a snort-laugh that ended with Ambrose wheezing for air as he pressed his forehead into Barrett's thigh, Barrett said, "Theater practice didn't exactly cover porn." But he reached forward, all teasing pretense dropped.

The fingers in Ambrose's hair felt heavenly and he let his eyes slide shut. The temptation to rub his cheek on the inside of Barrett's palm was ruined only by the way those thick thighs were flexing under him. "Shame. We could make our own."

"Ooo, I'm up for a lot of things, but that might not be one of them."

"Same." Ambrose tugged at the waistband of Barrett's boxers. "Though I'm still half convinced you actually have a St. Andrew's cross in the basement."

"I don't." Barrett drew his face up with a soft touch, two fingers under his chin. "But if you want to work up to it..."

"Kinky bitch."

"Yours, though."

Later, Barrett pulled his laptop into bed and pulled up the bird cam admin panel. "You've got an eye for detail. Ready to help out my piss-poor vision?"

He'd told Ambrose the story about Gemma and what she'd seen and his idea. Three cameras faced Lake Honor. If they were lucky, maybe they'd catch some detail leading to a break in the case.

"I don't know if the boat's connected," Barrett said as he logged into the camera admin panel and began scrolling through the archived feeds.

"Kinda feels personal."

"Yeah, it does. Almost everyone out here has a boat and a lot of 'em are like mine. Just little motorboats for fishing and puttering around the lake. But you and I have the properties furthest south of the main road, and they would have passed ten, maybe twelve other boats just out there." Barrett huffed and ran his hands through his hair as the system retrieved the feeds. "And anyone looking at the public reports would see I'm lead on the case. And the only reason for that is because Jacques has my back."

Ambrose wrinkled his nose. "I know it's very spy-movie like but did you mention anything to Jacques yet? About all of this?"

"No. Shit. Maybe I should have." Barrett's sigh was heavy, like lead in water. "This whole thing is so insane. Most of the department brass wants it settled, tucked away in a file and chalked up to random acts of criminal mischief. But a fire lit in the dead of a damp winter isn't easy and the...*viciousness* behind the whole fire tower door? The bridges, damaging them to a point where two people were seriously hurt? Someone could have died." And then he shook his head, leaning into Ambrose with an arm wrapped around his middle. "It's a little Bond villain-esque, huh?"

Ambrose leaned in, too. "Kind of. Like the person doing it watched too many of those movies and combined it with some grudge they have."

"Yeah. Speaking of grudges, I checked all the fired employees in the whole department. Everyone's got an alibi and my most likely suspect did move out to be with his family about three years ago. So no go there."

The archived feed report beeped and pulled up all three feeds from the day Gemma had spotted the person in the fog. With the feeds set to start an hour before the sighting and end an hour later, they had a solid place to start.

"Which one's first?" Ambrose asked as he dug his feet deeper into the covers. Barrett never minded his cold toes.

"The goshawk camera sits just off Gemma's property. But it points more north, so if the fog's too dense, we won't see them." Barrett started the video, cracked open a wide yawn. "You sure you wanna sit here for hours and do this?"

"Yes." Ambrose grabbed his phone from the bedside table and pulled up the natural history podcast he'd just found. "There's no sound on these videos, so I thought we could at least listen while we're watching."

They were in the middle of the second episode when the first bit of movement that wasn't a goshawk head or wing or bit of its dinner took up most of the camera. The goshawk fluttered to the right side, leaving the left open on a lovely shot of the fog rolling out over the lake.

And there was someone in a boat, quickly motoring across the lake. The camera's focus was the bird, so the pixelation and lengthy distance between the boater and the camera weren't helping. But Ambrose could see pretty damn clearly that the person was wearing a dark grey hat and dark blue puffer vest.

"I hate those vests," Barrett muttered. "Gemma was right. It's probably some rich idiot who thinks his gear will save his ass."

"And keep him from getting caught stealing your boat."

"And that." Barrett rewound the footage and hit play again, then chuckled. "You know, I've said that about my ex-brother-in-law. The whole 'rich gear won't save your ass' thing. He thinks like that, too."

Ambrose leaned up to kiss his cheek. "Lot of idiots in the world."

"Yeah."

"Your ex-brother-in-law have a dark blue puffer vest?"

Barrett's bark of laughter was tempered by drawn down brows. "That'd be a hell of a thing."

"You said he hated you."

"He does."

"He knows where you live, where you keep your boat." He wanted to ask but it still felt so personal. But on the other hand, Barrett had shared with him his nephew's story, tales of him and Val stealing from convenience stores because their parents never left enough food for two hungry, growing children. But all he knew about the brother in law was that he was a rich, selfish prick.

"This is getting pretty conjectural. Ken and I do not get along but why steal my boat?" Barrett was now rubbing his thumb over the back of Ambrose's hand; the movement was soothing even as his mind scrambled to make connections. "Val divorced him years ago."

The writer in Ambrose began to fire up a plot. Vengeful ex family member finally takes revenge for some slight injury to their ego. Thrillers had been sold on much less. "Okay, okay. We've no proof, I get that. But!" Ambrose got to his knees, easily slipping into Barrett's lap while his lover watched with amusement. "Has anything changed recently?" Ambrose kissed Barrett softly, slinging his arms around his neck. "Has Val mentioned anything? Anything different? With Forrest..."

He trailed off, looking away as the heat of embarrassment flashed through him. But Barrett tugged him back down to kiss him. "The move. But Ken gave up his visitation rights. He was only interested in Forrest as a trophy, something to show off and attract single moms. And now that Forrest is sick...well, a sick kid's not a good look, I guess. And his only other concern has only ever been money and how much he can make." Barrett frowned. "He was really pissed when Val filed for divorce. Accused her of all kinds of nasty shit, total lies. But he was stuck on the money, and how much he'd lose and he hired these smarmy attorneys."

"Nice guy."

"The fucking best." Another kiss, this one teasing the corner of his mouth and Ambrose let those warm lips slide over his. Felt big hands span his back. "I'm not sure. I can ask her, though. She's been putting up with Ken's bullshit for so long she might have forgotten something. Just chalked it up to whatever move the asshole thought of for the day."

"Okay. So we've got a person in a vest with your boat." Ambrose pointed at the grainy figure on the screen. Barrett took advantage of his turned head to nip at the hinge of his jaw. "*Barrett*. We're trying to solve a mystery."

"I'm aware." Now those warm hands were sliding up, under his shirt. Ambrose sagged against him and Barrett took his weight with ease. "I just wanted to touch you like this before we went back to it."

They watched the footage a few more times. It was easy to see it was Barrett's boat; all the boats were numbered at the lake, per registration and licensure rules. His was number eighteen and the boat had a spiffy flame decal on the side. "Let's try the other cameras."

A waning gibbous moon hung bright in the sky as the night wore on. But after a few hours they were able to rule out the osprey and red tail hawk cameras. One was too far west on the lake to capture any movement near Barrett's house, and the other was mostly the fog and muted sunrise of that morning.

"Damn." Barrett yawned again and, pulling Ambrose with him, leaned back on the pillows. "Well, the boat thief is on there. It's something."

Ambrose snuggled into Barrett's arms, enjoying the man's warmth. "Got a wild thought."

"Hit me."

"Any bird cameras near the entrance to the lake?"

"Two, actually. But that would just catch the road and a bit of where the roads split. One side goes to the recreation areas....and, oh, *fuck*, you're a bloody genius." Barrett was scrambling for his phone and Ambrose watched as he texted his boss. "The other road goes to the residential areas. Jacques is probably up but I should check."

"I love how your mind works," Ambrose said as he watched the rapid fire text conversation. Jacques had access to those cameras at the ranger station, since they were also tied into the new security camera system that had been set up after the supply station fire.

Eventually all the bird cams would feed into the security admin panel, but money was tight - as always in useful government - and the current system only allowed one admin login at a time.

"Jacques will pull it in the morning," Barrett said while setting his phone aside. "And I love how your mind works, too."

They stared at each other, in the dark, for a long moment. The words were *right there*. Waiting. Ready to be spoken aloud but Ambrose so desperately didn't want to sound like a cheesy buffoon. But he wanted to be sure, and having that promise spoken out to the world felt like something he needed. A little bit more surety after having his world rocked again.

"I'm going to say this and hope it's what we're both up for." Ambrose swallowed hard, tasting anticipatory bitterness. "But I want to be exclusive. So exclusive we can get tested and then toss those condoms in a deep drawer."

His grip on Barrett's flimsy tank top tightened. Ambrose watched Barrett's gaze sharpen, his lips part. A big hand cupped his jaw, drew him closer. Whatever lingered in the darkness of Barrett's eyes made Ambrose's blood heat. "You want to be boyfriends," Barrett whispered, his touch lingering. Caressing. A moment later, Barrett's thumb pushed a little into Ambrose's bottom lip and he let his mouth drop open.

There was no reason for this to be erotic and yet...here he was sucking on Barrett's thumb like it was his job and he loved every second of it. Ambrose nodded his answer to Barrett, letting his own gaze go butter soft.

"Christ, what you do to me." Barrett rolled them, then yanked Ambrose back until Barrett could spoon him. The unmistakable ridge of Barrett's erection pressed against his ass made Ambrose moan.

But Barrett wasn't done. He flung an arm over Ambrose's middle, pinned his palm to the mattress. His other arm was under Ambrose's head. He was being gently, lovingly held in place with Barrett's even breathing right next to his ear. Gooseflesh rose over every part of him and he wanted to whimper with how good it felt to be held. Taken. Pinned and trapped on his rules, not someone else's.

"I would love to be your boyfriend." Barrett's words were in his ear, pitched so low Ambrose swore he felt them in his ribs, down his spine. "I would love to show you how much I would love that. Would you like that?"

Ambrose arched against him. It was too good, the tight but not too tight grip and the press of Barrett's body and that *awareness* of him. No need for fight or flight here, where he was safe and cared for. Ambrose wanted to relent. He wanted to give everything Barrett asked of him because he trusted Barrett wouldn't go too far.

"Please," Ambrose whispered.

CHAPTER TWENTY-TWO

B arrett leaned forward in the too-small chair and nodded at Jacques. "I take it you recognize the car that came in."

"Yeah, but I want to make sure I'm not seeing things." Jacques' weather-beaten face didn't show a flicker of emotion and somehow that made the worry in Barrett's gut churn more. "That's why I asked you to come in before we let the others take a look."

Well, that wasn't good. The parks had their fair share of general mischief makers but usually it was a bit of graffiti on the housings of the composting toilets. A few repeat public nudity offenders. No one so deeply invested in their own antics that they would do something like switch out cars to come back and tag another outhouse.

Whatever little voice of instinct had been held at bay by confusion and disbelief started to get louder. All he could hear was *Ken*. But Val had said he'd dropped off the radar after signing away his rights as Forrest's father.

"Except for the nasty letter he left, but I let the lawyer have it. Future ammo if he decides to step into our lives."

"Letter? Val."

"You've been busy, Bear. It's just a letter. I took a picture of it and then handed it right over to Matthew."

"Glad you have a good lawyer. Christ." *Barrett tucked the phone under his chin and shifted his glass to the other hand. After a few seconds, his phone beeped with a text message. He scanned the letter, seeing the normal Ken-style bullshit saying Val was a horrible mother and an even worse wife, glad he was done with them, blah blah blah.*

But the final paragraph was a doozy, and it made Barrett's blood run cold.

"I wish you could see what you've done to me, what you've reduced me to. You were right. I'm not the same man you married. I'm angry

and hurt and most importantly, I want back what you took. So since I can't have that, I'll figure out a way to take something else. Maybe not from you. But I'll figure it out. And no matter what, it'll hurt someone and you'll feel it, too."

It was all still conjecture until Barrett watched in stunned silence as Ken's car passed down the road leading to the lake. To his neighbors and to his home and to Ambrose. Ken's car was unmistakable; right bastard had to take a bright blue sports car deep into the woods. There were two people in the car; a car with Ken's plates.

"No fucking way." He reversed the tape and watched it again. "What the fuck does Ken think he's doing?"

"You always did say he hated you," Jacques said quietly. "Then again, this isn't proof. Could be shitty coincidence."

"He lives hours away. Why come here? Who is in the car with him?" But something nagged at him, that same feeling that another piece was missing. "But he didn't set the fire and damage the FL and steal the generator."

Jacques pursed his lips, gaze lasering in on Barrett. "You sound sure."

"Dead sure. He probably....fuck. Maybe the person in the car with him. Maybe he hired someone. Someone down on their luck that needed cash."

"That's awful down, Barrett."

He frowned. They'd all been tossed at the ass end of desperate before. He knew the stretch of the dusty remains of rice and old cans of beans, of splitting the cost of a tank of gas between four or five people in the carpool so someone had a running vehicle.

"I know. But things don't jive. If it was desperation, they would have taken the supplies, not torched them. Broken into Alpha FL, not boarded it up." Barrett shuffled through the papers on the desk and pulled out Oz's last report. "The investigator made official documentation of my comments about some of the vandalism being *rage-filled*. I still don't think I'm wrong on that."

"Ken's rich, yeah?"

"Filthy. Or, last I knew he was."

"So you hire someone desperate, or tell them to make it look like desperation or rage. Throw us off the scent a little."

Barrett wanted to scoff at it, but he'd heard Ambrose espouse something similar. "It's just so..."

"Blatantly absurd?"

He had to laugh. "I was gonna go with far-fetched but yeah."

Jacques pulled Oz's report over, scanning it again. They'd all practically memorized the paperwork by now. "And you don't think Ken did all this himself."

"That bastard has never gotten his hands dirty, ever. When Val filed for divorce and they went into mediation, Ken sent a proxy. Which you're allowed to do." Barrett tapped the table with a finger. "But he sent someone who looked like him, dressed in his clothes. Even had the guy comb his hair the same way. He hired some actor off an online job board but took the time to make sure the look was right."

"To intimidate Val. Shit, I'd almost forgotten that."

"So yeah, I think he'd never do all the dirty work himself, and he'd go out of his way to fuck with me if he thought I'd wronged him. I'm not discounting what you're saying, Jacques, but it's a long way to go to come after me."

Barrett thought of himself as a laid-back person, someone who's easy-going nature worked well in jobs like forest ranger. He was fine alone, he was fine with people, and he was good in a crisis. But the *thought* of Ken doing anything that even remotely involved Val and Forrest set him spiraling into a seething rage.

"Done anything to piss him off lately?"

"You know I testified against him in the divorce. That was years ago, and he's never done anything remotely like this. And I even helped get her half of his cash, and other than flip me off, Ken never did anything. So something else has happened." Barrett sighed and pushed back from the table. "He sent Val a letter after he'd signed away custody, made some stupid mention of how hurt he was or some nonsense."

"Did she keep it?" Barrett let Jacques see the photo of the letter on his phone. "Yeah, it's too vague. But it kind of sounds like he's still got a bone to pick with your family. Rage doesn't always make sense, especially not when it runs that deep." With a swift swipe of his hand, Jacques put all the paperwork back into his folders and tapped them on the table to even them out. "Well, the police have all of this so far, but I need you to file a report on your boat and make a statement for our records and the cops. They'll talk to him, try not to worry about it."

The anger in his chest lessened and took with it the red-hot, tooth-gnashing parts. But he could feel it like the heartbeat pulse in his temple. He was going to have a headache after this. "Yeah. I'll do the reports now."

Jacques clapped him on the shoulder, his gray mustache twitching. "Good man. Don't know what I'd do without you and Meredith." He paused in the doorway. "Heard there's someone in your life, maybe."

Barrett tried not to flush. "Yeah."

"Good. Bring him 'round during the summer picnic, if you want. No pressure, but you know he'd be welcome."

Jacques left that comment hanging in the air and Barrett scooped up the other paperwork, stood, and walked out into the main ranger office. His head was pounding and his jaw ached with stiffness. He knew the next step was to let the police handle talking to Ken. But he felt like he should give Val a head's up. Then again, she hated Ken enough to round on him, maybe even call him up. She wouldn't be doing it to wreck the investigation, but it could. Shit.

Val had enough to deal with. He'd keep this quiet for now, until it inevitably blew up after the police contacted Ken. He'd be pissed, Val would get the brunt of it....

Barrett pulled out his phone. Rock and a hard place and he hated not having better options. He typed out the text but didn't hit send. Stared at the screen. Deleted the text. He'd just be poking the hornet's nest and as satisfying as it might be to see if Ken would wriggle on the hook he baited, he couldn't do it.

It didn't take long for Oz to show up with a cop in tow after Barrett filed the paperwork. He'd gotten a text first from Oz, asking him to stay put at the office and with a sigh, Barrett had made another pot of coffee and waited.

"I'm just here to observe, since the investigation was swept out of my hands already," Oz said as he sat across from Barrett. The officer, a younger guy with full cheeks, dark blond hair, and the last name Reeds, had Barrett go through everything once again.

"At first, did you all just think it was random vandalism?" Reeds asked, scanning the early reports again.

Barrett shrugged. "A hunch isn't evidence."

"Right, but you told Oz that it looked like someone was angry, whoever nailed up the tower door." Reeds' stare was intense and Barrett didn't like the look in his eyes. "What made you say that?"

"Now, to be fair, Scott, I did say Barrett was just thinking out loud. It's not like it was part of the official statement at first." Oz spared Barrett a glance but his face was carefully blank. He knew Oz had to be impartial but so far Barrett's hunches had paid off. This was no different, except now they had proof Ken had been in the area.

Barrett leaned forward and pulled out the photograph of Alpha's door when it had been nailed shut, the night the generator had been stolen. "Stealing the generator's one thing. It's a pain in the ass and an expense for the department, but we've had folks round here get down on their luck and raid our buildings for scrap metal, copper, supplies. It happens." He tapped the photograph. "I think the generator was convenience, or just a way to spit in our eye. But the door....those nails are a mix of things. The bigger the diameter, the harder they are to bend. Some of these are roofing nails, flooring nails. Taking that time and effort to bend nails like that?" Barrett leaned back and sighed. "It was a hunch."

Reeds frowned and examined the photo again. "Seems like it's someone handy, with the nails and the saw used to cut through the bridges. Feels like a grudge."

"And that's why I said that in my report," Oz said. "But we've ruled out all fired employees. No one had motive or was physically around to do all this over months."

"So what's this about your boat?" Reeds asked Barrett. With an internal sigh, Barrett relayed that story - his search, remembering the bird watch cameras, Jacques finding Ken on the footage the day his boat went missing.

"But a chicken coop roof isn't a footbridge, Barrett. But I admit these marks look the same." Oz held up one of the pictures of Gemma's coop. "Yeah, they might be identical. Good catch."

The look Oz was giving him felt strangely condescending and it made him frown. "No, a coop isn't a footbridge. But so far all the damage has been on state property. My boat and Gemma's coop are private property."

Reeds was nodding now. "It's amping up. Damaging state property's one thing, but private residences call in a whole other set of laws. Plus then the homeowners can sue. Why do you think Ken would do all this? I know the report said it's your ex brother-in-law, but I'd like to hear it from you, Barrett."

He was suddenly rather uncomfortable having Oz hear all this. It was a little too personal. "He's my sister's ex-husband and a prick."

Reeds shrugged. "A lot of people are pricks."

With a sigh, Barrett said, "He's a rich prick who used his kid as an accessory to attract women, he was abusive to my sister, and I helped get her more of his money in the divorce."

"Sounds like a winner," Oz muttered. "But if it is him, and I'm not saying it is, what does he get out of it?"

Like Barrett hadn't rolled this around in his head over and over again. Like he could explain Ken's narcissism and greed, his desire to always be *the best*. How he treated Val and Forrest, how he demanded everyone bend to his every whim. How obsessed he was with appearances and money and how nothing else outside of that mattered.

"I don't know. It could all be coincidence." He waved a hand in the air, voice growing louder. Barrett could feel his anger building like a flightless bird trapped on the ground. "I don't care about my boat. For all I know it's at the bottom of the lake by now. But someone took out bridges people use every day, bridges people depend on to be safe. Someone damaged a fire watch tower we use to spot wildfires and hopefully stop them before they wipe out homes. They burned our supplies, the things we use during emergencies. And they came onto my neighbor's property, just a few yards from her house. She's older and alone and I can guarantee you she can defend herself, but she shouldn't have to be ready to do that."

If either Oz or Reeds was shocked at his outburst, it couldn't compare with his own surprise. "Understood," Reeds finally said.

"I got shit to do, you need anything else?" Barrett needed to leave *now*. He needed to get back home, call Val, make sure everyone was okay. He needed to see Ambrose and pull him close and bury his face in those auburn waves and wait for his breathing to slow down and for the earth to right itself again. He never lost his temper. Ever. But he'd come dangerously close just now.

Reeds waved him off, saying he'd do some follow-up but to not expect anything. And by the time Barrett had hit the front doors to the building, his head didn't feel quite so full of ringing anger but the cold aftershocks left him numb.

"Barrett."

Fuck. "I've gotta go, Oz." Barrett didn't turn around and he didn't stop.

"Wait." Oz put a hand on his arm. Barrett gritted his teeth, sucked in a breath, and turned. "Hey. Been a minute."

"Yeah."

Oz gave him the up-and-down examination but instead of flirty, it felt too clinical. "Sorry about all that. Not much I can do when the cops have the case." He hooked a thumb toward the street. "Want to get a drink? Been thinking I should call you up."

"Sorry, no time. I'm jammed all day."

He moved toward his truck but Oz was there, hands out but not touching him. A little smirk on his face. "I've got a big backseat and a few minutes to spare if you do."

Finally solid ground again. An easy no. "Not interested, Oz. I'm not single anymore. And I've got some planning to do for my boyfriend's birthday."

To his credit, Oz took the news with a nod and a smile. "Let me guess. The neighbor."

For whatever reason that rankled him. "Good guess."

Oz shrugged and jammed his hands into his pockets. "I might have looked him up after you said he watches the dog every now and then. Good looking guy. Lucky you."

Lucky me is right. With a nod and a small smile, Barrett said, "See you around, Oz."

He left Oz standing in the parking lot, watching his truck disappear down the road.

A quick call to Val while he was on the road told him everyone was all right, but she was not letting him get away with just a check-in. "What's going on, Bear?"

He had to be careful here, but he also wasn't going to lie to his sister. Shit. "Okay, what are you doing right now?"

"Just reading while Forrest naps." Barrett could almost see her eyes narrow, her mouth turn down. Val wore every emotion on her face and right now she'd be a combination of worried and suspicious. "Why?"

"Because I need you to promise me you'll keep this away from the kid, and you'll not do *anything*. I mean anything."

Silence, and then, "Okay."

"No, Hopscotch, I'm so serious right now. I need you to focus on you and the kid. Nothing else. Got it?"

"Fuck. You're worrying me here."

Barrett tightened his grip on the steering wheel. "I know, and I'm sorry. But I just had to say that, because you cannot get mixed up in this, no matter how pissed you are. Promise me one more thing."

"Bear."

"Promise me."

"I promise." He heard her inhale shakily.

"You see Ken, you call the cops and you call me. Because he might be mixed up in this sabotage shit in the parks and he's about to get a call from the police here."

"Motherfucker -"

"Val. Don't. I know. But let them handle it. You see him, you call the police."

"Okay." She sucked in a deep breath. "Okay. I hear you."

"No, I need a promise."

"I promise. You know I hate his guts and with him giving up custody, I don't have any issue calling the police. He's not supposed to be around us anyways, he has no legal ties to us anymore."

Barrett hadn't really thought about it that way. But she was right. By law, Ken was a stranger to them. Giving up his parental rights meant Val also lost child support, but between her job and the money Barrett sent every month, they were okay. Stable but never rolling in it. Val said it was a sacrifice she was willing to make to ensure Forrest was safe and away from Ken's influence.

He took the final turn leading home and felt the fog from his mind begin to clear. There was his house up ahead, the roof and siding dappled with late afternoon sun. The lake beyond, sparkling and still. And Ambrose's house next to his, separated only by a large yard now bright with green grass and the tiny yellow puffs of dandelions.

Home. The thing he'd wanted for so long. Buying a house was a legal transaction and a massive goddamn headache. But only in the last few years had it started to carry the warm apple pie feeling of *home*. And with Ambrose in his life, the final pieces were clicking into place. Warmth and safety and stability and four walls that meant more than shelter and a place to sleep.

"Okay. I'm gonna hold you to that promise," he said softly. "I don't think you're in any danger. I just think Ken's somehow wrapped up in all this and I don't know why. Focus on you two, and you call me whenever."

"I will." The shakiness was gone from Val's voice, replaced with a steely resolve. He could see her once again, jaw set, fingers unclenched, her gaze fixed on Forrest. "I love you, Bear. Please be careful."

"I will."

"I'm sending you dates for our picnic, too. I want to move forward. Forrest feels a little bit better every day, and he's stubborn."

He had to laugh. "Shocking."

"Shut up." But he could hear the smile in her voice. "And he'll be okay to get out of the house for a nice afternoon. Bring Ambrose, bring Dandi, and be with us for a weekend. Together, as a family."

That's all he wanted. "Absolutely."

He hung up with Val just as he pulled up. Ambrose was outside with Dandi and Barrett felt instant relief seeing his boyfriend's pink cheeks and bright smile as his dog bounced around the yard. Barrett was out of the truck in an instant, striding over to Ambrose and gathering him up in a hug.

"Well, hello," Ambrose said into Barrett's shoulder. "Bad day?"

"Fucking sucks. Fucking Ken. Shit." He sighed hard and pressed his temple to Ambrose's. "Sorry. It's all just bullshit. I don't know what the fuck is going on and now the cops are involved."

"Hey. Hey." Ambrose's voice was soothing, his touch calming. He pulled back to nestle Barrett's face between his hands. "What do you need?"

Barrett kissed him, hard and fast and it made Ambrose go pliant against him. He spun them so he could press Ambrose up against the door of his truck and lean into that warm, lithe body. "Just this. Just a minute."

Ambrose shivered against him and looped his arms around Barrett's neck. The scent of him, his warmth, the gentle way he rubbed Barrett's back all pulled him into focus. Slowly Barrett's mind cleared and he was able to smile down at Ambrose. "Yeah?" Ambrose asked.

"Yeah."

Beginning of May, the weekend of Ambrose's birthday

Friday afternoon

It made no sense to be nervous. He'd known Raf for almost fifteen years. And Barrett, bloody stupendous man, had taken a week off work timed so conveniently around Ambrose's birthday. He'd protested and waved Barrett off, but Barrett swore up and down he was owed almost a full year of vacation, so a week wouldn't hurt. And whatever time Ambrose and Raf spent off doing their catch-up, Barrett could work on his never-ending list of chores around the house. "I'm also going to fix that shutter on your eastern side," Barrett said as they watched Dandi muck about in the shallow end of the lake.

"You don't have to do that."

"I don't. I want to. Big difference."

"Twist my arm."

Instead, Barrett tugged on his arm until they were pressed together. Barrett dipped his head for a kiss just as the sound of tires on gravel made them pause.

"Oh, please. Don't stop on my account." Raf's head poked out of the window of the car for a moment before withdrawing, then the man himself stepped out, bags in hand.

Barrett chuckled and thrust a hand out just as Dandi galloped by. "Down, girl." Then with a wink, he stepped back to wave at Raf. "I'd come over there and greet you, Raf, but until the beast calms the hell out, I'll stay back here."

Barrett nudged him forward and Ambrose needed no further encouragement to close the distance and wrap his best friend in a hug. "I thought I said dress down," he teased, eyeballing Raf's understated but still very stylish black jeans, black hiking boots with dark purple laces, and wine colored sweater with too many buttons.

"You know me," Raf shot back with a grin. And then in Italian said, "I can't help myself. Besides, these are my outdoor clothes. Didn't want your *boyfriend* to think I was a slacker."

"I know you're teasing but you're an idiot," Ambrose replied back in Italian. He'd learned the language from Raf, whose mother was Italian and insisted her son learn to be multilingual from a young age. Ambrose had a head for languages, so when Raf grew bored of speaking it except when around his mother, Ambrose would come up with insults or bad jokes to keep Raf's skills up. Dragging a begrudging best friend through the translations of several colorful phrases could only be done not around Francia, of course, but it also gave them both ammunition to use on the playground.

"You'd better let that beautiful dog go, Barrett. I want to be absolutely knocked on my ass."

Barrett's eyes widened. "You will regret that the moment she charges you."

With a kiss to Ambrose's cheek, Raf smoothly stepped around him and walked about twenty feet away before crouching. "Let her go."

Eyes still comically wide, Barrett looked to Ambrose, who shrugged. "I told you he's mad."

"As a wax banana, my friends. But wait, let me just..." Raf pulled a hair tie from his pocket, spun his thick, black hair up into a bun on top of his head, and said, "Now I'm ready."

"Sweet Jesus," Ambrose heard Barrett mutter. Dandi was being good so far, but Ambrose could tell from her little butt wiggles that she was *eager* to greet the new person in her midst. And by greet, she would fully knock Raf into the mud, step on him, and lick him.

"I can't believe I'm doing this," Barrett said more loudly.

"Raf will sign any waivers you want!" Ambrose said back.

By now, Dandi was dancing in place too much and Barrett's grip was visibly slipping on the leash. Barrett grit his teeth and let go.

Dandi was off like a bolt, but as soon as she got within two feet of Raf, she started turning circles, tongue lolling, tail a blunt force object. Laughing, Raf put his hands down and let the dog sniff him to her content. Soon, Raf was up and moving toward Barrett, Dandi prancing at his side.

"I should have told you I grew up with Bull Mastiffs. They're calmer than Great Danes but have about the same kind of energy when they're young. I kind of get them." Ambrose watched as Raf bypassed Barrett's hand. "Are we too gay to hug?"

The smile Barrett gave made Ambrose sigh. He welcomed Raf's hug, easily dwarfing the shorter, lither man. Raf was built like a runner and he was several inches shorter than either Barrett or Ambrose. And as if they'd practiced it, then Barrett and Raf turned toward Ambrose. "We might have out-gayed Ambrose!" Raf said, voice pitched higher in faux shock. "I never thought I'd see the day."

Laughing, Ambrose went to them. Dandi gave his fingers a cursory lick. "You are very stupid," Ambrose told Raf fondly.

"And that's why he keeps me to this day," Raf replied in a breezy tone. "But seriously, it's really nice to meet you, Barrett."

Watching his best friend and his boyfriend interact so easily together made Ambrose fully understand the meaning of a few things. Loyalty. Love. Confidence, but not jealousy. How at ease Barrett was in something that could have been a high stress situation; he did this thing with his hands balled in his pockets when he was nervous or worried. But Barrett was starting to tell Raf about Dandi and the casual gestures he knew that came with Barrett were there. A gesture to Dandi, a scratch of her ears. Barrett pointing east without having to consult his phone. The way he rocked back on his heels as he listened. The little smiles he sent Ambrose's way.

Confidence was attractive. Competence came hand-in-hand with that. Barrett's wasn't intimidating or weaponized. From the stories he'd told Ambrose, Barrett fought hard to be able to stand on his own two feet, and it could have made him a gratuitous jerk who took everything for granted and looked down on others. But he was genuine and kind.

Ambrose was definitely falling in love. And he was more than okay with it.

"So we're heading out in the morning. Ambrose said you know all the non-touristy areas and I am not looking to get in a proper hike while dodging people." Raf tipped Barrett a small salute. "Much obliged for that, by the way. This is a much better spot than anything we've gone to in the past."

"That waterfall from...five years ago? That was quite something," Ambrose said, immediately opening his photo app on his phone to find the evidence.

"Oh, Southward Falls!" Raf sighed. "That was pretty. I also got hit on by a completely charming woman."

Barrett's eyes widened, a smile spreading on his face. "And how'd that go?"

Ambrose and Raf exchanged a look and then burst out laughing. "He turned her down, and when we got back to the car, she'd put her number on *all the cars*. I hope she found someone with all that effort."

"It was truly one of those times I was sad she wasn't my type. She was very pretty and even better, very funny."

Ambrose shook his head. "See what I put up with?" he asked Barrett, tone teasing.

Raf slung his arm around Ambrose's shoulders, the movement easy, unforced. And with Barrett grinning at them and Dandi bouncing around their heels, Ambrose could feel his anxiety melt. Even with everything going on, these two men made him feel more relaxed and at home than anything else possibly could.

Ambrose took them inside and let Raf get settled in his guest room while Barrett puttered around the kitchen. But when Ambrose came back from helping Raf with his luggage, Barrett was standing by the kitchen island, hands jammed in his pockets. "I should go, get out of your hair," he said quietly, gaze meeting Ambrose then flicking away. "You and Raf catch up."

"Barrett." He drew closer, close enough to put his hands on Barrett's arms and slide them down until he could pull those hands from worn jean pockets. "I want you here. And trust me, Raf absolutely wants you here. You're not in any way at all. Please stay."

The moment Ambrose pulled Barrett's hands out, the other man linked their fingers together and dipped his head. His kiss was soft and his breath warm on Ambrose's lips. The gentleness made a lump form in his throat and his heart hammer against his ribs. "Make you a deal," Barrett said, sliding his mouth across Ambrose's jaw and pulling a shiver from him. "You two catch up, relax. And I'll make all three of us dinner." The worry had bled off Barrett's face, thankfully. "Kinda my way of meeting in the middle. If that's all right. I know how important Raf is and you two need your time together."

Barrett couldn't see it, but every syllable of his sweetness and care was poking holes in all of Ambrose's defenses. And boyfriend or not, there were parts of Ambrose that had to contend with how much his life had changed for the better after moving out to Lake Honor. "Okay," he whispered back, stealing another kiss. "But promise me something."

"Anything."

"That's a dangerous promise."

"I know." Barrett combed Ambrose's hair away from his face with gentle fingers. "Maybe I like a little danger when you're involved."

He tried to huff but Barrett just laughed softly. "Raf's an early to bed kind of person. So around ten he'll start yawning. We should light a fire in the pit outside, have some drinks, and then let him wander off to bed."

One dark eyebrow went up ever so slightly. "And then?"

Ambrose kissed him, harder now, urgency thrumming in his veins. "I'll get on my knees and you let me do the work."

"Playing with fire, Ambrose."

Ambrose nipped at his jaw, dragging a breathy moan from Barrett. "I've always been good with fire, Barrett."

CHAPTER TWENTY-THREE

The blue painter's tape stood out in stark relief against the grey of the wall, but Barrett stepped back anyways. He wanted to make sure the lines were centered and equal, since the tape was creating diagonal lines, corner to corner, and they needed to be exact. Painting walls wasn't his idea of a good time; it made his neck and back hurt and he'd have to keep Dandi and her tail of death away from the wall. But the nervous energy that had been building for days - hell, weeks - was at a crescendo. He had plans, big ones, for Ambrose's birthday and he wanted it to be right.

Ambrose and Raf were out for their usual hike. They'd invited Barrett along but there was no way he was going to crash their tradition. What lay between he and Ambrose was new and they were learning, but he would never step into something as precious and important as the best friend slash brotherly bond those two shared. He knew Raf was important, maybe *the* most important person in Ambrose's life and seeing them together had only cemented that understanding.

He spent the morning approving the last page spreads for Perry's book. Easier to hand them off to Raf in person. And looking at the spreads reminded him how much his life has changed in just a short amount of time. Maybe the cliché idea of holding tighter to what you had after experiencing a loss was really true. Barrett was certainly determined to cling to the good things a little tighter now.

That frame of mind had then driven him into the work shed, looking for the old plans he'd made to paint a few lines on the wall outside the kitchen. He'd tossed the paint and tape into the shed after Perry died. It just didn't hold any importance or interest then. But now with the spring air heavy with damp and the flowers in full bloom, he saw a chance to plug some holes, as it were. Finish a few things and leave room for the new. That's what spring was about, right?

Dandi was outside, on a long lead attached to the front porch. And she was the reason Barrett's attention was drawn to something outside; he heard her barking over the podcast Ambrose had recommended to him.

His hackles were up as he set down the brush and peered out one of the front windows. Someone in a black jacket and grey slacks stood a few yards from Ambrose's front porch, their face hidden by a scarf and hat. From the angle he had, he couldn't see any identifying markers. That strange tingling sensation of awareness had him eyeing the axe he'd left outside with the intent to chop wood later.

He stepped out onto his own porch and said, "There a reason you're hanging outside my neighbor's house?"

The figure turned and Barrett saw droopy eyes and a slightly red nose. They pulled down their scarf to say, "Making sure I had the correct house. You're Barrett, right?" The man gave him an up-and-down that was a little too invasive for curiosity.

Barrett dipped his head slightly. "I am. You lost?"

The man smiled and withdrew a business card from his pocket. "Adam Waine, private detective."

Barrett took the card, leaning forward slightly but not stepping down off the porch. Forcing the man to approach him and Dandi. ..and come on his property. "All well and good, Mr. Waine, but you didn't answer my question."

The man smiled, big and genuine, and Barrett instinctively wanted to punch him. He knew that was a strong reaction to someone smiling but this man oozed like an oil slick. It must have been a job requirement for smoozy private dicks or something. Waine rocked back on his heels, not stepping away from Barrett's proximity. "Your neighbor's mother hired me to look after him. She's worried about him."

Barrett bristled. "You make a habit of spying on grown adults for their overbearing parents?"

"It pays the bills." The man's smile grew wider. One of his front teeth was crooked. "And I'm good at it."

"And you're talking to me because..."Waine gave Barrett an up-and-down that made him want to crawl out of his skin. "I'm guessing you're more than just the neighbor."

"I'm a friend."

"Right."

At the edge of the porch, Dandi was watching them and she barked once. "I think that's her lunchtime notification, Mr. Waine. So if you don't mind, you can get off my property and stay off my neighbor's as well." Barrett narrowed his eyes and let his arms drop from where they were crossed over his chest. "I'm assuming even private dicks have to learn what constitutes trespassing."

Waine chuckled. "You, I like. You're tough, or you look it."

"Good for me. Now fuck off."

Barrett didn't bother to watch Waine leave. He unclipped Dandi from her lead and took her inside, seeing Waine back off his property from the corner of his eye. But he definitely watched the man walk down the little lane leading to he and Ambrose's homes, and then disappear around the bend and into the trees. He'd clearly parked up the road as to not make noise, likely hoping to sneak onto Ambrose's property and peer in windows.

Unease gathered in his belly and he wanted to text Ambrose to let him know, but he was out with Raf on their hike. The last thing he wanted to do was interrupt that. Barrett quickly made notes of the interaction with Waine (*just in case*, his gut instinct whispered) before turning the podcast back on and returning to his painting.

There in the middle of his stick-straight lines was a dribble of yellow paint. "Motherfucker," he muttered.

"Look at you."

Ambrose raised an eyebrow at Raf. "Look at me what?"

"The flush of early love looks good on you, my friend."

A few responses flitted through his mind but what came out of his mouth was not denial. Ambrose in the past would have denied, rebuffed, maybe even made a joke. "I'm guessing it's pretty obvious."

"On the contrary." Raf turned and those deep hazel eyes gave him a once-over. "It looks natural."

"Oh." That was not what he'd been expecting. "Not going to tease me about being moon-eyed?"

That got him a laugh. "I don't think you have the ability to look moon-eyed, my friend. But I do think you're standing taller. You walk with a confidence I've never seen before. And you clearly adore that man. In short..." Raf stopped and faced Ambrose, putting his hands on Ambrose's shoulders. "It looks right. Good. I like Barrett and I think you're good for each other."

His lips twitched. "So is that the best friend speech?"

"Trust you to mock my sincerity."

"I'm not mocking, I'm checking."

"Check all you want. But I'm serious." Raf squeezed his shoulders and then let go, waving him forward. "Now come on, I want to see this river."

Ambrose was taking Raf up the same trail Barrett had a few days prior. He remembered the way fairly easily and following their trail map past that river would lead them to an overlook. "Best view on the western side of the forest," Barrett had said.

The overlook was half-hidden by a thick copse of pines. Traces of snow clung to the lowest branches, glistening in shadow as the sun's rays were kept away by higher branches. Up this high, the wind's teeth tried to gnaw through his thick fleece. They pushed through the trees and stopped.

"Wow." Ambrose's eyes weren't big enough to take in all that sky. Clear as cobalt and dotted with frothy white clouds, the early afternoon sky was so bright it made him squint. Raf flipped down his sunglasses, slowly turning his head from side to side. Trying to give himself the panorama of a view that actually took Ambrose's breath away. "He didn't show me this when we were up here."

There was a knowing curve to Raf's smile. "He saved it for you."

"For us." Ambrose pulled him over and held up his phone, camera ready. "Like always."

Like always. From the night of their first and only date and every year since, one picture together. The first one was grainy and square, from a flip cell phone with the numbers thumbed off and a cracked case to last year's, outside a bar, with flushed faces and jackets flung over their shoulders.

"Best one yet," Raf said as he smashed his face against Ambrose's.

"Ow, brute."

"Smile, you oaf."

On that overlook they unpacked trail mix and fruit and water and Raf's leather-wrapped flask. Neither said anything for a long time, content in each other's company, watching hawks wheel by.

"I'm only gonna ask this once." Raf was leaning back on his hands, long legs in grey hiking pants stretched out in front of him. "And you better be honest with me."

"Okay." Ambrose turned to sit cross-legged at Raf's left side. "On a scale of one to a gay makeover show, how emotional are we about to get here?"

There was no hiding Raf's smile. There was delight, of course, but a flare of recognition. "I almost don't need to ask anymore."

"What?"

"You have a wicked sense of humor. It's quick and dry and far too delightful to hide behind all that red hair and frowning. But it's been muted for a while."

The smile dropped from Ambrose's face and he looked down at his boots. Raf wasn't wrong. It had been buried. Raf said muted because every time Ambrose was around him, his spirits flew higher. That's what a great friend - a best one - did for one's composure and sanity. But most of those other times, during the harder, darker years after (hell, even before) Preston, Ambrose was buried. Some part of him tucked into a neat little hole over which an unmarked mound of dirt sat. Even the sunniest days couldn't help uncover it.

"I feel more like me. Finally." The admission left him in a rush.

"And we both know why."

Ambrose's flicker of a smile was back. Softer now, steady. "Yeah, we do."

"Do you love him?"

Did he love Barrett? Well, that was insane, right? It'd been six months since he'd moved to Lake Honor, five since he and Barrett started really talking. Four since their weekly dinners. Dates, as they were. And two since they'd first kissed.

It was insane. But maybe love was a little insane, too.

"Slowly, yes. Some piece of me does."

"Does the quantity of those pieces grow with your affection for him?"

Ambrose threw a grape at his head, which the fucker caught and popped into his mouth. "I love you. You're stupid."

Raf shrugged. Ambrose watched the end of his black scarf flutter in the wind. Cashmere, expensive. Raf had excellent taste and the income to support it. "Love is rather stupid, darling. Exposing yourself to all those glass case emotions." He gave an overexaggerated shudder. "Terrible."

"Ha." Ambrose leaned forward, slipping onto his back so he could put his head in Raf's lap. Long, dexterous fingers combed through his hair. "It's not the quantity of the pieces. It's the weight of a single one that grows. My affection for Barrett."

"Your love."

"Slowly blooming, like a particularly stubborn flower."

That got him a laugh. "Trust the writer to get poetic about new love. But you mean like a weed, my friend. Weeds are tougher."

Ambrose closed his eyes. "Trust the artist to recognize bad poetry."

"Purple prose, really. A poem would have better flow."

"Cruel."

Raf sighed. "The worst. Absolutely."

"I shouldn't."

"But you will."

Raf sighed and threw Barrett a dramatic eye roll. "He knows me too well."

Barrett was already a few glasses of wine in, red-cheeked and grinning. "I think this is the part of the night where you tell me all of the embarrassing shit Ambrose won't."

Ambrose groaned while Raf laughed loudly. He finally accepted the glass of wine Ambrose had set near his now empty one. "Well, if I'm drinking, I'm talking." That sharp gaze narrowed, giving Ambrose the once over. "I'm thinking the costume party."

"Oh ho ho, do tell." Barrett stood and wobbled only a little. "Or, wait until I get back at least. I've got something good for dessert but it'll take a minute."

"Please don't use sharp implements when drunk, Barrett." Ambrose was on his feet instantly, following Barrett over to the kitchen. The main floor of the cabin was mostly one large room encompassing the kitchen, living area, and fireplace. Two short hallways branched off of it, leading to guest rooms and Barrett's office and bathrooms. The second floor was a large loft, the landing a small reading area and then the master bedroom and bathroom beyond that. One could look down from the reading area and see the open main floor. Ambrose had watched Barrett cook from that very spot on occasion over the last few months, poking about the bookshelves between hisses of steam or the quick, steady rhythm of a knife.

But just because Ambrose could see Barrett didn't mean he wanted to sit and watch him do all the work. "Here, let me help," he said, slipping behind Barrett with his hands out.

Barrett's grin was loose and bright, and it echoed in Ambrose. He was feeling that way, too. He could hear Raf cooing at Dandi in the background, and the kitchen smelled like roast chicken and thyme and some smoky candle flickering softly on the mantle. It was the most relaxed he'd felt in a long time.

"Here, you start the oven," Barrett said, pulling Ambrose out of his thoughts. "Four hundred degrees. And I'll get the pie."

"Pie?" Raf called from the dining table. "I'm now officially spoiled and it's not my birthday weekend."

Ambrose let out a snort as he turned the oven on and bumped the temperature up to four hundred. "Behave, Raf."

"Never."

Barrett pulled a pie out of the freezer and set it on top of the stove. "Last one from the previous summer."

Ambrose eyed it through the gauzy plastic film covering the top. "I thought I was your pie maker."

Barrett laughed. "You are. On top of a lot of other things." His kiss was soft and sweet, lingering only long enough to make Ambrose sigh. "Val makes these every year from the rhubarb patch in the back." His smile turned sadder. "Every summer they come out for a week. Fish, swim, hike. Forrest won't be up for that this year but I was thinking of taking her some pies when we visit."

His breath got stuck somewhere between his lungs and his mouth. "You want us to go together?"

"If that's okay." Barrett sighed and ran a hand through his hair. "Sorry, I should have handled that better." He put his hand on Ambrose's, his thumb tracing a tendon. "Got something on my mind, and then we can go back to costume parties and visits with my family. While we wait for the oven, can we chat about something?"

A wariness settled in his stomach and made the thought of pie turn sour. Ambrose glanced at Raf, who was watching them, his expression now carefully guarded. Barrett must have realized they were both now on edge, because he led Ambrose back to the table and sat down with a heavy sigh. "Barrett, what's going on?"

Barrett put a business card on the table and then handed Ambrose his phone. The picture was of a shorter man, probably in his fifties, with a ruddy nose and perpetually sad eyes. "Mid afternoon, this guy shows up. Dandi got my attention and I went out to find him just standing there." Barrett relayed the conversation he had with the PI, only to pause midway through his last sentence. "He said your mother hired him."

Ambrose froze with his wine glass halfway to his mouth. Raf instantly put a hand on his shoulder, but he barely felt it. The sheer weight of the *anger* pulsing through him made his next words hoarse. "So she's not going to leave me alone."

"I don't know if he's going to come back. But I told him to fuck off and that he was trespassing." Barrett's mouth thinned and he scratched at the stubble on his jaw. "I'm so sorry, Ambrose. Whatever you want me to do, just say so."

That anger he felt was making his heart hammer in his chest, but there was no spike of anxiety, his vision narrowing into a tunnel and his chest feeling tight. The anger was *good*. It felt *right*. He took it, balled it up, and held it close, and slowly let his fists uncurl. "You don't have to apologize, Barrett. What you did was more than enough." Ambrose said slowly, looking between his best friend and his boyfriend. "I'm not entirely surprised by any of this, sadly."

"What can we do to help?" Raf leaned into him, putting his arm around Ambrose's shoulders.

He'd already chosen his path. He just needed to take those first steps. "Do you still have a Rolodex of lawyers?"

Something wicked glinted in Raf's eyes and Ambrose caught Barrett's nod of approval. "Oh, I've got someone for you, my friend. Newer client of mine at the gallery. She could make your mother's head spin with a *look*." Raf pulled out his phone and fired off a few texts. "Trust me on this. You want a restraining order, she can get it."

"I want whatever will keep her and anyone associated with her off my property." But even as the words left him, he felt that old, ugly bitterness rise in him again. Out of sight, but still not out of mind. Not healed, and maybe not for a long time. If ever. "So she's got enough gall to send someone else but won't come back out herself. And I know I can't control what others do."

"You said you wanted to be free of her." There was a soft rush of air at his left and when he turned, Barrett was seated beside him. He was being held up by Barrett and Raf, their presence at his sides comforting, calming. "I'm not about to give a bunch of unwanted advice here, Ambrose. But maybe you should think about it a little. Consider what free looks like to you."

Raf's arm tightened around him. "Still want the lawyer?"

Ambrose nodded. He wanted the lawyer and the paperwork for a leg to stand on, if it came to that. He wanted the security of those papers. He wanted to see the part they'd play in his freedom. But he knew there was more than just paperwork and court orders to pursue. He needed to schedule another session with Dr. Fielding. "Very much so. But later." He pulled Barrett's hand into his lap and let his head fall back against the chair. "Let's go outside so Barrett can tell me more about this picnic we're going to have."

Once the pie was consumed, they went outside to set the fire pit roaring, drinks in hand. Ambrose felt some of the tension ease from his muscles. It used to be when he got anxious, his entire body would seize up and then he'd ache for days, muscles twitching. But with the clear, dark sky above and a thick glass tumbler of whisky in hand, the desire to tense up and sit ramrod straight all but faded. Barrett sat against the low stone wall around the patio, a blanket under them as Ambrose reclined in the vee of his thick legs. Raf was close by in a rickety camping chair, his face tipped up and one hand tracking a constellation.

"Beautiful out here," Raf murmured, getting noises of agreement from he and Barrett. Ambrose saw him shiver a little when the wind whipped by, but Raf closed his eyes and curled tighter in on himself. With every easy breath his best friend took, Ambrose took one of his own.

"You okay?"

Barrett's voice, a rumble in his ear, made him grip his glass. "Better now," he replied softly. "I'm sorry you got dragged into all this."

"You kidding? You didn't drag me into anything, Ambrose."

Guilt roiled in him. His fucked up past, his fucked up mother, were getting in the way of the best thing to come into his life in a long goddamn time.

"Hey. Ambrose. Look at me." Barrett's fingers were warm under his chin, turning his face until their eyes could meet. "I need you to stop apologizing for your family stuff. Apologize to me if you accidentally eat the last piece of cake or you hit my rear fender. But not for this stuff." He huffed and his breath tickled Ambrose's cheek. "We haven't even gotten into my bullshit, and trust me, I'm gonna be the one apologizing then."

"But you just said..."

"First one's free." Wind chapped lips kissed the delicate spot behind his ear and he bit back on a moan. Barrett *knew* how tender that place was. Ambrose cut his eyes to Raf, but the other man was already asleep.

"If we wake him up and send him to bed," Ambrose said, tipping his head back to rest on Barrett's shoulder. "Then I'm taking you in that chair."

"You're the perfect kind of filthy." Oh, that voice was pitched low in his ear and it sent ripples of awareness, raw and delightful, across his body. "Go."

When Ambrose looked back as he escorted Raf off to bed, Barrett was still sitting against the wall, legs spread wide and watching Ambrose with the darkest eyes reflecting only firelight.

When Ambrose returned, he was alone but not empty handed.

"Can't have you...waking Raf up..." He barely got the words out between wet, open-mouthed kisses along Barrett's jaw and neck. Barrett's eyes were even darker now and Ambrose was happy to sink into them as he gently put the clean, folded washcloth between Barrett's lips. As he pulled his hand away, Barrett snatched it back and pressed his cheek into it. "I changed my mind. Up. Against the wall."

Barrett didn't groan until his back hit the wall, helped along by Ambrose's roaming hands. The sound was muffled but it hit him just the same; a bolt of hot lust down his spine to leave a crater in his belly, open and throbbing. He kissed Barrett's stubbled cheek and sank to his knees. Those big, rough fingers gently combed through his hair.

"Be quiet, Barrett. Can you do that?"

A fervent nod. He couldn't let his gaze linger too long lest he get pulled completely into black, black eyes. Ambrose kissed the top of Barrett's jeans, right above the button, then slid his hands down Barrett's already trembling thighs. He squeezed the muscles under worn cloth and Barrett groaned, the sound muted by the washcloth. "Shhh, Barrett. I have a guest."

With great care Ambrose popped open the button and pulled down the zipper, listening to every hitch in his boyfriend's breathing. The power of this. The *trust*. It made his head spin. "Barrett,

Barrett. God." Ambrose buried his face in the cut of Barrett's hip and breathed. Overwhelmed, overcome, happy to drown. His briefs were soft against Ambrose's cheek and he could *smell* him, that salt-sweet scent of lust rising.

Above him, Barrett made a concerned noise. "I'm good, I'm good." Ambrose squeezed his thighs again. "You rattle me. It's a good thing."

The hands in his hair were even gentler now. He was dizzy with desire, that coil of need tightening in him as he shoved Barrett's briefs down. Barrett had gotten tested earlier in the week and while his results were clean, they were still waiting on Ambrose's. Waiting seemed like a small price to pay when he could lean in and suck Barrett down, no barrier between them. Just skin and warmth and the feel of coarse hair under his fingertips and the sound of Barrett's muffled cries above him.

The next day brought three calls in succession while they lingered over breakfast. Raf and Ambrose were going shopping; a "necessity", Raf said, when Ambrose rolled his eyes.

The first call, the best one, was from Val, asking how things were going. Forrest popped up on video, waving and grinning and looking a little bit more like himself. He sang Ambrose happy birthday in a warbling, high voice and Barrett couldn't help but grin at the blush on Ambrose's face. They made plans for a video picnic before the end of May, before Barrett's fire watch started.

Val ended the call with a wink to Ambrose. "I have so many things I can tell you about Barrett as a kid. Just text me and I'll spill my guts."

"Val." But he was smiling, and so was everyone else.

The second call came only ten minutes later, just as Barrett was pouring more coffee. He set the pot down to fumble with his phone, his heart kicking up when he saw the station's number. Jacques or Meredith wouldn't call without good reason while he was on vacation. But it was Oz's voice on the other end.

"Barrett."

He flicked his gaze over to Ambrose, who was watching him over the rim of his mug. "Oz. What can I do for you?"

"Wanted to give you the head's up. The police talked to Ken and he admitted everything."

"What?" Now Ambrose and Raf were looking at him with concern, Ambrose leaning in over the kitchen island and reaching for him. He took that proffered hand and squeezed tightly.

"Yeah. Said he was....hold on, I have his statement. I'll send you a copy. Ken said, 'Barrett helped ruin my life and I held a grudge for years after I divorced his sister.'" Barrett had to grumble at that; Val was the one who filed for divorce after years and years of Ken's mistreatment and cheating and shady business bullshit. "'But the divorce did a number on my finances and I owed people money. I've been robbing Peter to save Paul and it finally came to a head in the winter. I lost everything in a business transaction. Barrett helped take all of that from me, and since I couldn't lash out at my ex, I decided to harass Barrett. But it got out of hand. The man I hired has his own agenda and I can't stop him.'"

Oz sighed and Barrett heard papers rustling on the other end. Confusion was a fog over his mind. It was one thing to figure Ken was involved, but it was another to have it put so plainly before him. Ken's rage and pain, his stupid ass getting in over his head with money. Barrett could only guess who he owed; Ken had always been secretive about his *business*. Val had only found out he was cheating when Ken left a file cabinet unlocked and she stumbled onto statements from accounts he'd kept in secret.

But this...

Real concern, the kind that had Ambrose abandoning his coffee and squeezing Barrett into a side hug, was now heavy in the air. Raf was quietly watching them, dark brows drawn down. "That's...honestly, Oz, I don't even know what to say."

"Yeah, me either. I've done some stupid stuff in my life but endangering people because you lost some cash?"

Barrett managed to choke out, "Knowing Ken, it was probably a small fortune."

"Figures. Fucking rich assholes." Oz cleared his throat. "So the cops are gonna handle Ken and the charges against him. But this guy he hired to help him is in the wind. We have a description and a last known location, but I'm gonna beg you to be careful. He's the one who hammered Alpha tower's door shut and cut the bridge supports and set the fire. Ken claims he hired this guy, this Marvin, to cause general mischief, steal supplies, maybe slash your tires. Apparently the guy's unhinged."

The last part of Oz's sentence buzzed in Barrett's ears. "Marvin what?"

"Marvin....hold on. Ah, here. Marvin Gilbert."

Marvin Gilbert. Fucking hell.

"I'm guessing you know who that is," Oz said not unkindly.

"Yeah." He steadied himself on Ambrose, wrapping an arm around that lean torso and pulling the other man close. Ambrose came willingly, melting into his side. "Marvin owned the house next door to me before Perry or Ambrose. He built it, actually. Built quite a few of the houses around here. When the city pulled some imminent domain shit to expand the zoning for homes around the lake, Marvin fought them. Lost a lot of money on the properties, from what I understand. I moved in about a year later and Marvin was already in foreclosure on the house next door. He went a little mad before he disappeared into the wind." He sighed and felt the weight of the situation pull him down until he could sit at the counter. Ambrose sat next to him, a silent pillar of support and strength he really needed.

"Mad how?"

"Pacing outside at all hours, yelling on the phone." Barrett flashed back to those early days as he was just getting settled into his place and would watch Marvin rant and rave into his cell. The times Marvin showed up at his house, smelling like cheap whiskey and cigarettes, asking Barrett for money. He'd given him a little here and there but every interaction with Marvin started to unnerve him. And then one day, when he came back from a long shift out on the trails, Barrett found Marvin's place empty. Windows boarded up, doors chained shut, an angry screed pinned to the front door. How he'd lost everything, how the people around the lake never bothered to help, how he'd come back one day. Years ago, and still Marvin was out of his mind.

"So two guys who lose everything and nurse grudges decide to take revenge and hurt a bunch of other people." Oz grumbled something unintelligible into the phone. "Fucking assholes. The cops will find Marvin, Barrett, but I'd keep an eye out just in case. If he hears Ken's been charged, he'll probably flee."

He won't. Barrett knew it instantly, as sure and swift as the lead weight of guilt in his gut. "I don't think so," he managed to say. Something in his voice or on his face made Ambrose lean in harder and rub small, smoothing circles into Barrett's lower back. "Marvin was so angry all those years ago. People who hold anger like that....s ometimes it just grows. Not saying it's logical. And it's all speculation but that kind of rage leaves a mark."

"You said something like that when we were looking at the door."

"I did. I hate that I was right."

A rustling sound, and then Oz said, "Well, you were. Your instincts are good."

"Somehow that doesn't help."

"I know, and I'm sorry for that."

"Shit."

Oz paused and Barrett listened to him breathe. "Stay safe. You see anything at all, call the police. Don't do anything heroic. Please."

There was sincerity in Oz's words and Barrett took it to heart. "Not planning on it."

"And try not to worry."

That made him laugh, the sound bitter on his tongue and even worse in the air. "I always worry." He glanced at Ambrose. "Especially now."

"Take care, Barrett. And if I hear anything, I'll call."

When they hung up, Barrett told Ambrose and Raf everything. And by the end of his retelling, he couldn't look Ambrose in the eyes. On some level he knew none of it was his fault, but at the same time it was. Ambrose was involved because of him and his family and his connection to Lake Honor.

"Don't you dare." Ambrose turned Barrett's face to him, forcing their gazes to collide. "I can see you blaming yourself and don't you dare."

"Better listen to him, Barrett," Raf said from across the counter. "He's got that look on his face like he might chain you down if you don't."

"I will. I swear to everything I have that I will." Ambrose's mouth was a thin white line, pale in an already pale face. "If we're playing the blame game, look what I dragged you into."

"That's not the same, Ambrose."

"Yes, it is. On some level." He got a poke in the chest from a bony figure as Ambrose pulled up to his full height, putting them eye to eye. "Listen to me. We're safe. We'll keep it that way."

The words were *right there*, on the tip of his tongue and begging for release. He wanted to scoop Ambrose up, take him to bed, and pull him close, knowing the scent and feel of him would ground the wild, tangled mass of his mind. Barrett wanted to say those words in

Ambrose's ear between hot, slick breaths and the feel of sinking into him.

Later. Later, he would.

But he chickened out. "Go shopping. Tonight, we're going out. I don't want this to ruin your day."

"Our day," Ambrose corrected. "And it won't." A smile lit up his face. "This all started because of that damn bridge. So really, we should be thanking this Marvin."

"Absolutely not."

Behind them, Raf chuckled. "You can send him a card in prison, if that'll ease your conscience, Ambrose."

Reluctantly he let Ambrose go so he and Raf could gather their boots and jackets. He flung open the back door and Dandi bolted outside, instantly churning up mud and grass as she ran between the trees, darted into the shallow end of the water, and then back to run the circuit again.

Barrett's mind roiled. Ken and Marvin. The PI. Ambrose's family. Val and Forrest. What happened to his quiet life? The silent nights looking out at the stars, the mornings where he was greeted with mist off the lake. But when he reached for what he missed, he found that it wasn't the same anymore. Imagining those mornings alone felt awful, as did nights in an empty bed. His life *wasn't* the same, and it never would be.

As Ambrose walked by, Barrett snagged his arm and hauled him into a kiss. "I love you," he whispered as they parted only enough to breathe. "I'm taking you out tonight and going to embarrass myself on the dance floor and we're going to drink. And then you're going to come visit me on my fire watch and we'll spend the summer hiking and reading and fucking and every moment will be perfect."

Watching all the worry drop from Ambrose's face was better than anything he could have wanted. He definitely didn't expect reciprocation.

"I love you, too."

"You are dangerously close to having your day stolen so I can keep you here." Barrett kept his voice steady even as his heart squeezed tightly in his chest.

Ambrose licked his bottom lip. "I'm guessing naked and in your bed."

"I'm shockingly transparent and easy to anticipate."

Ambrose kissed him then, pulling a short, sharp groan up from Barrett's chest. "Raf's outside."

"Go on. I'll see you later."

"Six sharp."

"Not a second later."

The third call came after Ambrose and Raf left. Barrett had pulled up Val's number and was ready to dial when her name showed up on his screen. "Hey."

"Hey. So...just got a visit from the police. About Ken."

"God." Barrett leaned hard on the counter, letting its sharp edges bite into stomach. "Fucker."

"Agreed."

"Hold on, let me put my big brother hat on here." He paused dramatically as she snorted. "You okay? Cause I can still go beat him up if you want."

"Nah. Fuck him. The best thing I could have ever done was to cut him off completely. Now we won't get wrapped up in his shit." Val took a couple of deep breaths. "How the hell did I ever wind up with him? What was I thinking?"

"You were in love."

"With a narcissistic asshole who risked our livelihood to make a few more bucks. We have a son." Val huffed. "I have a son. Forrest isn't Ken's. He's mine. I gotta remember that."

She was putting up a good front, but Barrett knew her well enough to hear the pain in her voice. "You're the best thing for Forrest, and you always will be. He needs you."

"One problem there, Bear."

"Yeah?"

"We need you, too."

As if he hadn't already been punched in the heart enough today. Ambrose's soft *I love you* was still echoing through his bones, leaving him shaky but elated. And now Val went right for the solar plexus. "We're coming out this summer. I swear."

"I know you are. And Forrest is gonna lose his mind. He's already talking about showing Ambrose his art and going fishing and all these things and I just...I don't want to disappoint him. He hasn't quite realized how limited he is, yet."

Immediately Barrett was digging in the drawers for a pen and a pad of paper. "Then let's make a list. Everything he wants to do, and if we run out of days on the schedule, we'll figure it out. Or find another way to make it happen."

"Bear." Val was definitely choking up, trying to stay strong.

"I got this, Hopscotch."

"I know you do. You always do. But you don't have to do everything. Let us help."

Barrett heard her, and her message.

Let us help. Let us love you the way you love us. With everything you have, every fiber of your being and every part of your soul.

Chapter Twenty-four

T he music was loud and incomprehensible beyond the heavy bass that shook through Ambrose's rib cage. There was sweat across his brow, along his hairline, and he was a little bit drunk. And Barrett was behind him, his grip on Ambrose's hips tight.

He did not need to get an erection in public. But the club was dark and packed and he doubted anyone would notice. It's not like he could help it, with the way Barrett was pressed up against him, his breath on Ambrose's ear. For such a big man, he could *move* and Ambrose wasn't the only one paying attention.

"You have an admirer," he said as he turned in Barrett's arms.

Barrett shook his head. "Drunk. Like us."

"I don't think so. He's been staring." Awareness rippled down his spine and Ambrose shivered.

Barrett grunted. "He can stare all he wants. You're mine."

That made Ambrose smile. "He's not looking at me."

"Still don't care." Barrett's hand snaked down his back and when Ambrose shivered, a firm palm cupped his ass briefly before sliding back up.

"You never struck me as the jealous type."

"I'm not." Barrett's words were growled in his ear and Ambrose had to bite down on a moan. Something about this side of Barrett - mussed and sweating, flushed from the right side of one too many drinks, his hands eager on Ambrose's body - made desire swirl in him. He wasn't one for blind jealousy and all that stupid macho bullshit that some men pulled. But seeing Barrett slightly *possessive* sent a thrill through him.

Ambrose ground his hips against Barrett's. "Show me later."

"Show you..."

"How you feel about another man staring at us."

He got a short, sharp grin in response. "Oh. We can definitely play that game." Barrett's hands shot out and then Ambrose was spun, back pressed against Barrett's chest so they were both looking in the direction of the man ogling at least one of them. He was hidden in the shadows of the booths lining the dance floor, so Ambrose had only seen a flicker of dark hair and a bit of black leather. That could be a hundred different people.

But earlier in the night, as they'd made their way down the sidewalk to the club, he'd swore he'd seen Preston from the corner of his eye. Just for a moment. But when he'd turned and looked, whoever it was had disappeared.

"I bet he's thinking about us right now," Barrett purred in his ear. "More than just who tops and who bottoms. If I were him, I'd be thinking about sliding my hands up your legs, feeling that soft skin behind your knees." Ambrose groaned and tried to turn but Barrett held him fast, grinding up behind him. He wasn't fully hard but there was a distinct ridge pressed into the small of his back.

His pants were way too tight for this.

"If I were him," Barrett continued, that low voice rumbling through him, "I'd want to know how you'd look in my lap. Then under me. How you'd sound as I took you from behind and grabbed that gorgeous hair. How many little bites I could leave along your shoulders, your abs. I'd want to know how you sounded as you broke apart, split in half on my cock."

Ambrose was panting, eyes screwed shut, his whole body twitching. He grabbed one of Barrett's hands and pressed it to the front of his pants. Barrett squeezed him and he nearly shattered right there. "Goddamn you."

"You love it."

"I do, but I need you to fuck me."

"Pretty sure we'd get arrested for that." And then Barrett was tugging him over to an empty booth, far away from the floor where the bass was more muted, like distant thunder. They left the mystery man behind and he didn't matter, because all Ambrose could see and feel and taste was *Barrett*. They weren't even fully seated when he crawled into Barrett's lap, shoving him down the rest of the way. Barrett's mouth was hot on his, his tongue slick and questing, diving into Ambrose's mouth, teeth sharp on his bottom lip. Ambrose wanted to cry with how *good* Barrett felt under him.

He was damn near close to begging when Barrett's big, broad hands spanned his back and then slid down, fingers digging into his ass. Couldn't they just be at home and naked and rolling around together, kissing and teasing? Need ached within him and he wanted *more*. Always more, never enough. He couldn't get enough of Barrett and his kindness and the way he cooked and how he looked when he was concentrating.

"Let's go home," he said as Barrett pressed kisses into his jaw. "Please. I need you."

For a big man, Barrett moved fast. He was soon dragging Ambrose through the club, dodging the crowds and the drunks and shoving a bill into the bouncer's hand. The world spun on its axis a little - too much vodka - but the night was cool on his skin as they waited for a cab to pull up. Barrett kept him close, their bodies touching at the shoulder and chest and hip, and when the cab arrived, he helped Ambrose in and gave the driver directions.

"Behave now," Barrett said in his ear, making Ambrose shiver. "We're not too far." So Ambrose tucked his face into Barrett's neck and closed his eyes.

His phone buzzed just as the cabbie dropped them off in the middle of their shared driveway.

From: Preston *I'm so sorry. I know you deserve more and I don't expect an answer. But you have something better now, something real. I've seen it. It's my fault, all of it. The cheating, our breakup, your pain, your mom. All of it's mine. I'm not looking for your sympathy. I deserve you hating me. But I see it now, and I know. And I wanted to apologize one more time. I told her you were gone. That there was a new you and it wasn't interested in us, and that if that changed, you'd come to us. But I know now. I'm glad you're happy, I'm glad you have him. And she won't bother you again, hopefully. I'll do what I can to stop her.*

Ambrose silently passed his phone over to Barrett and then tipped his head up to suck in a lungful of cold air.

"Sometimes things fall apart for a reason," Barrett said softly. He handed the phone back and then let Ambrose burrow close. "I think he means it."

"I think he does, too." When he looked up at Barrett, he saw nothing but trust and love. That expression took his longing, his heated, aching desire, and turned it softer, sweeter. Ambrose moved in just as Barrett did and their kiss was full of a meaning neither had words for.

The next morning they planned to see Raf off with plenty of hugs and teasing. Barrett hadn't felt so strongly about a person in a long time, outside of his attraction to Ambrose. Raf made being friendly - and becoming friends - so easy. He was casual with his touches, but not invasive. He teased but didn't cajole or insult. And he seemed utterly oblivious to his looks or money, but not in an obnoxious "I'm like everyone else" kind of way.

It made complete sense that Raphael Lutz was Ambrose's best friend. They were, on some level, two sides of the same coin. And it helped that Raf was endearingly genuine and funny.

"So there he is, stumbling around in the bottom half of a horse costume, asking where his head went." Raf could barely hold in his laughter. "Oh, I haven't been able to tell this story in so long."

"Great. Yay," Ambrose deadpanned but despite the fierce blush on his face, he was smiling.

"So did you find your head?" Barrett asked, poking Ambrose in the side while Raf grinned over his coffee cup.

"Turns out, yes he did." Raf's face was a picture of delight. "Because I stole it and put it in the backseat of the car, so when we dumped his rather drunken butt in there, the scream he let out got the cops called on us."

Barrett lost it, picturing a twenty-something Ambrose, eyes crossed from drink, stumbling around in the dark only to land in the backseat of a rustbucket car where Raf had stashed the head part of his horse costume. He and Raf were howling with laughter while Ambrose grumbled and half-heartedly slapped at Raf's shoulder when the ride they'd called pulled into the drive.

"Oh, my dear darling friends, it has been a complete and utter delight." Raf hugged Ambrose long and hard, his eyes fluttering shut. The sight made Barrett's eyes prickle. "And you! Wonderful man you are." Despite their size difference, Raf was strong and Barrett let him yank all three of them into a hug that nearly crushed the air from his lungs. "You are amazing. I couldn't ask for a better partner for Ambrose."

"Jesus. If you're trying to make me cry..." Barrett sniffed and looked away.

"Not at all. But sometimes the truth hurts in a good kind of way." Raf kissed Barrett's cheek. "And you will never get anything but the truth from me." He bent down as Dandi pranced over. "And you, sweetheart! I will miss you. Be good."

"You hear that, Dandi? He said be good." Barrett grinned down at Raf and the dog. "I doubt she'll listen, though."

"I think she will."

They broke apart slowly, mindful of the car idling behind them. "Text me when you get home," Ambrose said as he wiped his eyes on the back of his hand.

"I will." Raf hefted his bags over his shoulder, waved, and got into the car. They watched it leave, disappearing around the corner and into the trees.

"I wish he lived closer," Ambrose said quietly, his breath a cloud of mist in the air. Despite the warmer days, the mornings were still sometimes chilly. "Maybe one day."

"Think he'd be up for cabin life?"

Ambrose snorted. "Not unless he gets hit on the head and loses his memory."

"I'll take that as a no."

"Sadly."

Barrett led them back into his house, whistling for Dandi to follow. There was an air of ease around them once more. He and Ambrose were creatures of habit and, despite Raf's very welcome visit, things had been too hectic to get back to what they enjoyed. The peace and the quiet and now, the slow entrance of their lives into each other's. Barrett doubted they'd be bothered by Preston or Ambrose's mother again. When the shock of Preston's message had worn off, he and Ambrose had sat on the couch and stared at it for a good, long while before acknowledging its' finality. A chapter closed permanently. The ability to move on, move forward.

Jacques had called that morning to let him know that they were actively on the lookout for Marvin Gilbert. The man was, as expected, in the wind. If he turned up, he'd be handled. Jacques was sure of that. It had taken Barrett a near physical effort to contradict his boss. That gut feeling was back and he could just tell that drama wasn't over yet. But he didn't want to scare Ambrose, didn't want him to feel unsafe. Because they weren't in any danger, as far as he could tell, but Ambrose felt *everything* and Barrett didn't want to burden him.

"You're thinking very loudly."

Barrett grinned at Ambrose and shut the front door. "I'm always thinking. I'll try not to be so noisy."

Ambrose patted the couch and Barrett sat beside him, pulling the notepad off the table and flipping it open. "I was thinking about a few things, speaking of thinking."

"Oh?" Ambrose leaned forward, trying to peer at the notepad. "What about?"

"Mostly about you coming up to Alpha tower and how you'll look when I have you sprawled out naked in bed as the sun rises."

Ambrose's eyes widened. "Are you allowed to do that?"

"Think about you naked? I sure as hell hope so."

He got a punch in the arm for that quip. "Smartass. No, having me in the tower during your fire watch."

"Yeah, sure. People take their spouses or kids up there all the time."

"Barrett."

"I'm serious."

"So am I." Ambrose put a hand over his and closed the notepad. "I don't want you to get in trouble."

"I won't, trust me. I wanted to take Dandi for the whole time, but those stairs don't exactly make having a dog that high up easy. I think we can manage you for some visits."

Those grey eyes narrowed but he saw the smile Ambrose was trying to hide. "I see how I rank. Below giant dog."

"Well, if you want to move up in the ranks..." He breathed Ambrose in, let his other hand drift down a jean-clad thigh. "Kiss me."

"You're so easily swayed."

"By you, yes."

Summer

Four weeks later, the first weekend of Barrett's fire watch

"How's it looking up there, Bear?" Meredith's voice was distant through the radio but it was nice to hear her. She was good company during the slow, quiet evenings as the sun set and his active watch ended for the day. He still had to keep an eye out for bonfires and fireworks, but he could rest his eyes as the darkness settled around him. "Pretty good. Haven't seen any campfires and it's been a little on the cool side."

"Wait for mid next week. Supposed to get hot fast."

He groaned. There was also supposed to be quite a bit of rain next week, and the tower got humid quickly. He'd have to pop all the windows and run some fans to keep from sweating to death. "Well, I guess I have that to look forward to."

"What about the boyfriend? The one you promised to bring out this summer?"

Barrett grimaced. "Been a little busy, Mer."

"Doing what, I wonder."

"Ugh."

She laughed. "I'm fucking with you. But I know you'll bring him out."

"After I take him out to see Val and Forrest. If Val finds out I let you lot meet Ambrose before her, she'll have my head."

"I would never get in the way of your sister. She's terrifying."

"You've met her once, Mer."

"Yup, and she scared the fuck outta me."

He snorted. "Okay, I'm getting off of here. Holler if you need anything."

"Will do, Bear."

Barrett clipped the radio back into its little socket and pushed his chair even further back, until the purples and pinks and oranges of the setting sun were all he could see. His body felt heavy after a long day of staring into the woods, and his eyes drifted shut.

A thump outside had him sitting upright, his mind foggy from an ill-advised nap. The tower was now pitch black save for a slice of moon rising over the trees. Shit. He'd fallen asleep, and he had maps to finish for Jacques for the new trails they were extending into acreage that had been gifted to the parks service. Barrett knew the tower like the back of his hand but discombobulated as he was, he lurched forward and bumped into the radio table. It rattled as he regained his balance. "Shit."

Another thump. This one louder, duller. Almost like something hitting wood. But now it was closer. Barrett wheeled, his heart hammering in his chest. He turned once, twice, catching sight of all the windows. Sweat ran down the back of his neck and suddenly the tower felt stifling, closed off. Rangers didn't carry weapons outside of stun guns and bear mace (sadly both were sometimes needed), but in the tower there was a locked gun safe with a shotgun and a box of shells. Why his thoughts immediately went to the gun, he wasn't sure, but something prickled at his senses.

A warning.

Barrett quickly, silently moved to the western side of the tower, pressing his back into the corner and sliding down the wall. This angle gave him the best view of the tower's windows. Reinforced glass meant to withstand high winds and heat and the battering of ice and snow they got every winter. He scanned the darkness, searching.

Minutes ticked by. In the dark. In the humidity. His breaths evened out but he still pulled the gun safe key off his belt and gripped it tightly. Its little teeth bit into his hand.

Barrett didn't know how long he sat there, but when the prickling at his neck went away, he stood, unlocked the gun safe, and drew out the shotgun and the box of shells. He'd checked the gun, cleaned it, kept it unloaded, per their safety regulations as part of his opening procedure for the tower. And he wasn't a *gun guy*. But the security of having it near and unloaded made turning on the lights less daunting.

Horror movie scenarios straight out of the nineties flooded his brain. A message in blood on the windows, maybe, or a hang up phone call. Thank god there wasn't a garage door with a doggie flap. When he got the lights on, there was no message, nothing jamming the doors. No evidence of anything except his own rampant imagination.

"Fuck." He ran a shaking hand down his face and thumbed on his phone with the other. He hit the speakerphone as it rang. "Hey you."

"Hey." Ambrose's voice was soothing his jangled nerves with just one syllable. They weren't far apart physically, but they hadn't been out of each other's company for months. A few miles felt like nautical leagues. "You sound out of breath. You okay?"

"I...I think I just spooked myself. Happens sometimes, up here in the dark." He laughed. "I feel so stupid."

"Well, first of all, it's not stupid. And secondly, did anything happen?"

Barrett relayed the story and at the end, he said, "I seriously went through every horror movie I've ever seen in my head."

"Hmmm. Killer set on fire only to come back from the grave?"

"Definitely."

"Running up the stairs with no exit strategy?"

"Considering I'm up six flights, yep."

"Oh no, not the doggie door."

"Sadly."

"You mean fabulously gruesomely."

Trust Ambrose to make him laugh and stave off a panic attack. "I didn't know you were so bloodthirsty."

"Get me doing something competitive and you don't stand a chance."

Barrett flopped down on the bed and stared up at the ivory mosquito net. He wanted to see Ambrose under it, shadows and sunrise playing about his pale skin like brushstrokes. He wanted to take his time, take Ambrose apart way up here where the sky felt touchable and the breeze always smelled like pine. "Hmm, I'll have to think of something good."

"Well, Dandi and I already have competitive eating down. She wins every night but you can't expect me to compete with something as cute as her."

In the background, Dandi boofed in acknowledgement and they laughed. "I miss you," he said softly, letting the words curl into the speaker.

"I'll be up in two days."

"That's a very long forty-eight hours."

"Well, I do have a favor to ask. Is Miss Sparklepants still half done?"

Barrett's mind screeched to a halt. "What?"

"The coloring book. The one we did together when I twisted my ankle?"

"Fuck. Holy shit, I forgot all about that."

The past came rushing up at him. It had been years since then, right? Surely. Barrett glanced at his screen. June fifteenth. Eight months, almost to the day when he'd seen Ambrose at the dock, and about seven since that night in the tower. "I thought you could finish it and I'll put a frame on it, hang it somewhere."

"Yeah, the bathroom."

"Hush, you. I'm serious. I'll hang it in my office, so every time I'm stuck in a spreadsheet and I hate everything, I can look at it and smile."

Barrett went over to the bookshelf and rifled through the atlases and books on leaves and insects. "I still have that book on fish here, by the way."

"*Brochis splendens.*"

His fingers curled around the coloring book. "Hmm, okay, you got me."

"Emerald catfish. Brazilian."

"Is it actually emerald colored?"

He could hear Ambrose's smile. "Actually, in a way, yes. The scales shimmer bright green. I think it's on a postage stamp in Brazil."

Barrett found the fish ID guide and took it and the coloring book over to the map table. He settled on the stool and flipped the coloring book open until he found Miss Sparklepants. "Well, here she is. Poor Miss Sparklepants, half colored in."

"Ah, the poor dear. I'm sure you'll do right by her."

"You really gonna hang this up?"

"Absolutely! She deserves a nice place. As a reminder."

Barrett smiled. "It makes for a good story."

"The best."

Two days later

Barrett scooped Ambrose up in a hug that threatened the stability of his lungs and he didn't care. Barrett was here and big and warm and he smelled like coffee and Ambrose melted into his arms. Dandi danced around them. "I am terrified of how she's going to get up the stairs," he said into Barrett's shoulder.

"She'll do all right. It just wasn't practical to keep her here the whole month. Plus if there's an emergency, I can't leave her alone in the tower." Barrett crouched and accepted Dandi's licks with ease. He didn't even flinch at the slobber; and admittedly, Ambrose had gotten used to it, too. A dog that big put out *buckets* of drool, and yet he simply didn't care. He also didn't care when Barrett kissed him smelling like sunscreen and sweat, or when Barrett slid big, rough hands up his body, his calluses catching on sensitive skin.

He *reveled* in it.

Because it was Barrett. Because he was in love, helpless to it.

They gathered up Ambrose's bags and the supplies for Dandi and made the slow trek up the stairs. Dandi didn't mind the steep stairs at all, her massive body graceful as she followed Barrett. Ambrose was close behind, just in case.

When they rounded the fourth landing, a flicker caught Ambrose's eye. Fire in the distance. "Barrett?"

Barrett stopped, turned, and swore. "Shit. All right. I'll help you get Dandi up. We can let her have the spot by the bookshelf. Then I gotta go stop 'em."

They shuffled gear and hurried up stairs so Barrett could grab his supplies and rush back down. "Is that fireworks?" Ambrose asked, concerned, as Barrett dashed about.

"Yeah. Not as dangerous now because of the rain this week, but in the middle of a drought..." Barrett gave him a swift kiss and a wink and then was gone, thundering back down the stairs to his truck.

Ambrose sighed and turned slowly in a circle, taking in the frog kettle and the neatly made bed with mosquito netting draped above. On the battered coffee table was a book about fish and the coloring book. Miss Sparklepants was fully colored and, in the corner, signed with a heart.

Chuckling, Ambrose sat on the couch and pulled the fish book into his lap. Dandi was snuffling near the bookshelves. A breeze blew in from the open windows, warm and fragrant with summer. Now that he was in the tower and not in pain, Ambrose saw the appeal immediately. The quiet was satisfyingly peaceful. He let his head fall back against the couch and closed his eyes, enjoying the way the wind caressed his bare arms and face.

After a few minutes, Ambrose got to his feet and put the kettle on. There was no way he'd let Barrett drink that foul bagged blend. Out came the small bag of darjeeling he'd packed for the weekend, ignoring the bottle of wine he'd stowed between rolled up shirts and shorts. That was for later, after the sun went down and the dark cocooned them and they were high up above the forest. After preparing the frog kettle, Ambrose leaned against the counter and looked out over the treetops, smiling at how the wind teased the lush, dark green leaves. It was beautiful up here. Inspiring, even.

His phone buzzed as the kettle heated.

> **From: Barrett** *Damn kids. Lighting fireworks near brush piles, like that shit won't catch on fire. I should be back up soon.*

Ambrose grinned. Maybe he should greet Barrett shirtless, kiss him hard just as he entered the tower. Encourage his boyfriend to slide his hands over his body, beg for Barrett to kiss his neck, suck on his nipples. Ambrose shifted, restless. It was a nice daydream and he hoped Barrett would be in the mood.

> **From: Barrett** *Are you okay? These kids are telling me someone gave them the fireworks. Paid them to set them off. I found a bunch of cut trees nearby, too. Fuck, I'm being paranoid.*

Outside came a thump. Distant, muffled, but distinct against the soft breeze and the sound of Dandi snoring.

Strange.

But Barrett had heard a few odd noises in the night two days ago. Ambrose was instantly on alert, scooting closer to the corner where Barrett had told him a baseball bat was stashed. He found it lying at the bottom of a footlocker, under a few spare, tattered blankets.

Just in case, he told himself. It was daylight and lovely outside and there was nothing to worry about this high up.

Right?

He quickly texted Barrett back, assuring him he was all right but letting him know there was an odd noise.

From: Barrett *I'll be back as soon as I can. Get the bat from the footlocker and make sure Dandi's close. Just in case. I love you.*

He wanted to weep with how sweet that man was, but it pushed and pulled with the worry in his gut. And his hackles were raised, as were Dandi's. Her big head was swiveling to and fro, brown eyes tracking to Ambrose every few seconds, as if she were waiting on his command. "It's all right, girl," he crooned, coming to sit beside her on the floor. Her tail thunked against the worn floorboards. Her velvety head under his palm, her warm breath on his arm, and he breathed in time with her.

There were no more strange noises and slowly Ambrose relaxed. He leaned against the wall, his hand stroking Dandi's back, and closed his eyes. An untold amount of time passed, the breeze lulling him into a hazy kind of sleep.

Shadows settled across his face. The sun slowly sank into the horizon.

Ambrose was warm and comfortable, almost on the edge of too hot. But he didn't want to move, not with Dandi's soft, short fur under his palm and his mind floating. The quiet seeping into his bones, his worries melting away.

But another noise startled him awake untold minutes or hours later.

Thump

Thump

Thump

Dandi was on her feet immediately and the growl she let out had Ambrose scrambling for the bat. He was sweating and breathing hard, could feel his shirt sticking to his back. He wanted to pull at the neck of his t-shirt but it felt like wasted movement.

Fuck. Fuck.

Thump

Thump

Crack

In his mind, Ambrose imagined a giant tree being felled somewhere deep in the forest, its death knell echoing for miles. *If a tree falls, how far out can you hear it?*

But Dandi was having none of his speculation. She barked and growled, dashing for the door and then turning back to almost yell at Ambrose. As if to say, *Get your ass moving, human*. Ambrose shot to his feet, barely able to grab the bat in his sweaty hands, and flung open the door.

They pounded down the stairs, driven by instinct and fear. Dandi's growls were the stuff of nightmares, as if she were the long lost descendant of Cerberus himself, and willing to protect what was hers. No matter the cost.

More thumps came, and the sound of splintering wood echoed around them. His skin was on fire, whatever danger near them driving him to run faster.

His gaze swung wildly, trying to watch his footing while they fled, unknown and unseen fear driving them down to the ground. And as they neared the first story landing, Ambrose looked up to see a massive tree crash into the roof of the tower.

Glass rained down on them and he dove for Dandi. He had to protect her. She was Barrett's. She was precious. And he wouldn't let her get hurt.

They tumbled and Ambrose felt every bit of wood and metal bite into his skin as they fell. He yelled, Dandi yelped, and then everything went black for a long moment.

But he was still conscious, right?

The hard ground was no comfort to his back and his left arm was on *fire*. But Ambrose was able to force his eyes open just as a wet tongue graced his cheek.

"'Sokay Dandi," he muttered. "Give me a moment."

Dandi barked, ending the noise on a snarl so vicious it made Ambrose want to back away. He knew she'd never hurt him. But whatever had her upset, he couldn't see it. Hell, he couldn't even lift his head off the ground. Slowly, as if dragging his eyeballs through mud, he looked over to see boots racing toward him. Dandi's paws shot out of the line of his vision.

His head felt heavy. Couldn't he just sleep? That sounded so good right now.

"Ambrose. Ambrose. I'm here."

CHAPTER TWENTY-FIVE

It happened so fast.

Barrett drove up the long service path to Alpha tower, flicking on his headlights to help navigate the way up. It wasn't quite twilight yet, but the heavy tree cover cast long, deep shadows over the dirt path. He was trying not to grumble at the kids he'd had to lecture on fire safety. Teenagers, really, but it wasn't their fault. Someone had given them the roman candles and some cash and that was...weird.

Sighing, he took the last corner a little faster. All the quicker to get back to Ambrose and spend the night curled up together, gloriously naked, sweat cooling on their skin after taking each other apart.

But it happened so fast.

He caught a flash of grey fur and auburn hair running pell mell down the fire tower stairs. Heard Dandi barking, then growling. He saw the tree smash down on top of the tower and Ambrose and Dandi roll the rest of the way down. Too far down, too fast, but Ambrose (foolish man, what was he thinking) had his arms around Dandi to cushion their fall. He took the brunt of it, landing hard on his back while Dandi rolled up to her feet and charged at his truck, furiously barking and whining.

Barrett was out of the truck in a flash, bolting over to Ambrose, his boots crunching on metal and glass and gravel. And Dandi was snarling toward the eastern woods. Without thinking, he shouted, "Dandi, tackle!" Because his only concern was Ambrose and the blood on his arm and his heavy breathing and the glint of glass in his hair.

"Fuck, fuck, Ambrose." Barrett slid in the dirt, ignoring the shards biting through his clothes. Instinct kicked in and he checked Ambrose's breathing. His panic wasn't quelled by seeing his chest rise and fall. "Ambrose. Talk to me."

"Barrett." Gods, he was a mess, glittering and bloody and streaked with dirt but his eyes were fairly steady as he stared up at Barrett. "There was someone -"

"I know. I know." He fumbled for his phone, barely able to dial the station with the way his hands shook. When Meredith picked up, he rattled off commands. "Mer, I need an ambulance and fire & rescue up at Alpha, immediately. A tree crashed into the roof and Ambrose is hurt."

"Fuck. Got it." Meredith snapped into emergency mode and he wanted to kiss her. "Putting in the calls now. Are you safe?"

"I think. But that tree didn't come down on its own -"

There was a scream from the woods, and loud barking. A yelp.

"Go. Barrett. I'm okay, I just think my wrist is broken."

Shit. Shit. Panic threatened to overwhelm him, but Ambrose pulled the phone from him. "I'll talk to her, she'll keep me company."

Barrett took off like a shot, grabbing the bat Ambrose had dropped in his fall and bolting toward Dandi. The trees were thick here, but he was experienced with hard terrain. Even as branches snapped at him, snagging his hair and clothes, Barrett pushed forward.

Another bark. A growl.

"Dandi, come!" he yelled, hoping to get a better idea of where she was. He got a bark in response and breathed a little easier. The sound of paws rushed at him, then the sight of his big, sweet, brave dog loping toward him nearly took him out at the knees. She had a cut above her eye but otherwise seemed unharmed.

As he moved to her, Barrett spotted movement between the trees. Dandi growled in warning. As the man appeared before them, she dove right for him, teeth bared.

A yell.

A familiar face, more wrinkled than the last time he'd seen it, cursing the name of Lake Honor and everyone who lived there. One who took his ire out on Barrett with harsh words but never violence. Marvin had a mad gleam in his eyes as Barrett scrambled to his feet and after Dandi.

"Dandi, down!"

She skidded to a stop, nearly halfway between them. Barrett had the advantage of panic but Marvin had momentum, and they collided as Barrett threw himself in front of Dandi.

Marvin's fist was there and Barrett reacted.

He hadn't played baseball since high school, but he was nearly six and a half feet of hard won muscle. Barrett swung the bat and connected.

Later, he would think of it as arm for an arm. It wasn't the most charitable line of thought for certain, but Marvin had done a lot of damage. The protective parts of Barrett, the ones that rose up in that moment, bat in hand, weren't too fussed about his thoughts, either.

The scream Marvin let out as his elbow shattered echoed around them. Dandi snarled and barked, angrier than Barrett could have ever imagined. Barrett took Marvin to the ground with a tackle and the older man didn't put up a fight. He was likely blinded by pain.

"The tree?" Barrett was screaming in his face. "Did you?" Marvin was half screaming, half moaning in agony and unable to answer. "Where?"

"Back...back behind me," Marvin gasped. "Wasn't supposed to fall that way."

Barrett was pure instinct and adrenaline now. He was up again, yelling for Dandi to guard as he ran into the woods, following Marvin's footsteps back. Yards ahead he caught the glint of an axe, so he scooped it up and ran back, now armed twice over.

As the whine of sirens echoed in the distance, Barrett stood over Marvin. "Get the fuck up. *Now.*" As Marvin stood on shaking legs, he said, "Dandi's gonna watch you. You move, she will take you down. Understand?"

He didn't give Marvin a chance to answer, because all he could think about was *Ambrose*. Barrett had never run so fast in his life and when he burst out from the treeline, he saw Meredith and a paramedic rushing toward Ambrose, who had propped himself up against Barrett's truck. He was cradling his jacket-wrapped arm; Barrett recognized it as his own jacket, the one that had been on his passenger seat.

Ambrose was alive, awake, and talking to Meredith as she leaned down.

"Fuck. Mer. In the woods, Marvin Gilbert and Dandi." He handed her the bat and she was off, two police officers close behind. All he could see was Ambrose and the blood and the cuts on his face and the paramedic gently handling a pale arm.

"Pretty superficial but you've got some glass in here." The paramedic was checking Ambrose's vitals and Barrett nearly forgot how to breathe as he knelt in the dirt. He wanted to pull Ambrose to him but couldn't. It physically ached to be unable to do such a simple thing.

"Ambrose."

Ambrose smiled softly at Barrett. "I'm okay."

The paramedic, a woman named Honey, with dark, curly hair and green eyes, nodded. "You'll need to have some tests done. Likely concussed and this cut's gonna scar. But your blood pressure's okay and you're breathing all right."

"Barrett." Ambrose held his good hand out and Barrett took it. His skin was turning cold and his heart felt like it was straining with every beat. *Probably shock*, he thought dimly. "You're coming with me."

"Yes. Absolutely."

Always

A week later

"You're fussing."

"Sorry. I am."

Barrett's flush was far too adorable, but Ambrose didn't want to tease him. Too much. "You're all good." He craned his neck up and was rewarded with a soft kiss. When he tried to deepen it, Barrett gave him a flicker of tongue but then pulled back. "You're supposed to be resting."

"I am." Ambrose sunk deeper into the pillows. "Because someone is taking such good care of me."

Barrett kissed his forehead before whisking the lunch tray away. "You good? I was gonna take Dandi on a run."

"A run?"

Barrett shrugged. "Thought I'd pick it back up. It's good stress release."

"So is sex."

"Which you are in no condition for."

He grinned. "Enjoy your run."

In the hour while Barrett was gone, Ambrose pulled over his laptop. He couldn't type, not with his left wrist broken and the entire arm in a sling, but he could dictate some emails.

The first was to the lawyer Raf had recommended. He'd given a lot of thought to a restraining order and decided it was the path that would give him the best closure. But after talking to Barrett, he left Preston out of it. On some level, he could understand Preston's state of mind and Barrett's gentle support of how Ambrose was feeling made things more clear. The lawyer, Juniper Belgrade, had immediately slapped his mother with a restraining order. And he'd heard nothing since. With any luck, he wouldn't hear anything ever again.

Marvin Gilbert was in jail awaiting trial. He'd have to testify, as would Barrett. And there was a lot of uncertainty about the severity of the charges. The district attorney had filed for attempted involuntary manslaughter. Ambrose thought it fit, and not just in his situation. The bridges Marvin had sabotaged, the supply shed fire that could have gotten out of control? The man hadn't needed to crash a tree down on Alpha tower in order to put people's lives at risk. And some selfish part of him wanted the man punished. Marvin had nearly crushed him under a massive old oak.

Selfish. Selfish and money-hungry and driven by revenge. Marvin was cutting down old trees and carving them into lumber. With so many acres and so few rangers, the thefts went unseen for months.

Until now.

Marvin had started his quest to sabotage Lake Honor and its most valued asset, the state park, with cutting down those old trees and stealing them to help build his new cabin several towns over. "The town owes me," he'd told police. But when his lumber thefts didn't provoke the reaction he'd been hoping, he'd upped the ante.

All because of money.

Pride, too. And while Ambrose could somewhat sympathize with how life-altering it would be to lose hundreds of thousands of dollars in investment when the town forced him out, nothing was worth staking lives on. And Marvin was the perfect partner for Barrett's brother-in-law.

Then things got out of hand. Ken didn't want to do anything violent, but Marvin did. They argued, then split ways. Marvin's anger grew.

Thinking on that made rage bubble in his chest, so much that his hand trembled as it hovered over the laptop keys.

Raf's face appeared on screen. "Hey."

"Ambrose." Raf was a picture of worry, brows drawn down and nearly hidden behind his tortoiseshell frames. His gaze flitted to the sling, then back to Ambrose's face. "I'm coming out there."

"Raf, it's okay. It's a bunch of bruises and cuts and a broken wrist." He smirked. "Seems all those tumbling classes dear old Mother enrolled me in as a child imprinted a little."

"You are..." Raf's nostrils flared and his mouth thinned. He looked away, voice tight. "You could have been hurt badly. I'm overjoyed you're all right but if you wanted me to come back out, you just had to ask."

Oh, Raf. Trying to inject levity in a situation where emotions were high and tight. He'd love to have Raf back out at the house, but his friend had a business to run and a life to live and a few bumps and bruises weren't worth flying across the country for. "Hey. It's okay."

Raf shook himself and refocused on Ambrose. "I know. I was having a moment."

"Quite a moment."

A flicker of a smile. "Even my moments are spectacularly dramatic, you must admit."

"Daytime awards worthy."

That smile grew. "Well, since you're making jokes at my expense, you must feel better. And that means you can hear my news and promise to keep it under wraps from Barrett." Ambrose opened his mouth to protest. "For now. I had a thought in that regard."

He held up his hand in surrender. "Do tell, and I will try not to reflect on how my best friend asked me to keep a secret from my boyfriend. The man who saved my life twice."

"Message received, acknowledged, and heard. And it's only so I can make sure all the details are in place before I let *you* do the big reveal."

When Raf was done laying out the plan, Ambrose was grinning so widely it hurt. "He's going to be in shock, you know that?"

"That would make me so happy, you have no idea. It's the waiting that's going to suck." Raf sighed and leaned forward, curling a fist under his cheek. "And it's going to be on you to get him there."

"I don't think that will be an issue. I already told him we ought to go somewhere for his birthday, and he won't be the least bit suspicious if I mention adding in a visit to you."

Raf seemed to breathe a sigh of relief. "Well, when you get everything confirmed, let me know and I'll start ordering everything we'll need. And Ambrose?"

"Yeah?"

"I love you. You're my best friend and my brother and my platonic soulmate and I'm so, so glad you're okay."

The words got stuck in his throat, leaving him to rasp, "Raf."

"I know, darling. And now you've found your *one* and given me hope that mine's out there somewhere. I am so happy for you."

"Love you, too."

Raf signed off, leaving Ambrose nearly in tears, heart fit to bursting. He felt loved, safe and warm in his little house by the lake. It was even better when Barrett came back, sweaty and grimy and grinning, Dandi bouncing at his heels. "Hey, you," he said, coming up behind Ambrose in the kitchen.

Ambrose leaned back until he could kiss the underside of Barrett's damp jaw. "You're gross."

"So gross."

"Eugh, go shower." The grip Barrett had on his hips belied other thoughts. "You know, we haven't tried it in that chair by the fireplace."

"Hmmm." Barrett's right hand slid in, then down, squeezing Ambrose's thigh. "And I said you're injured and we shouldn't."

"Shouldn't, not couldn't."

"Found a loophole?"

"I'm more crafty than most think."

A final squeeze to his thigh while Barrett's lips lingered on his neck left Ambrose leaning hard against the counter. "I'll mull on that while I'm in the shower, then."

"Fucking tease!" Ambrose shouted at his back while Barrett laughed. If Barrett was surprised by Ambrose following him into the shower, he didn't show it. Instead, he dropped to his knees and let his mouth and hands worship Ambrose's body, leaving him shaking before Barrett ever touched his cock.

"Fuck, Barrett." Ambrose whined as Barrett bypassed his aching prick *again* to mouth at the thin skin on his inner right thigh.

The water beating down was almost too hot, but it felt heavenly on his body. The contrast of sharp teeth and smooth lips was setting his nerves on overdrive. "Gorgeous," Barrett murmured before licking the head of Ambrose's cock. He pushed Ambrose's fingers into his hair. "Hold on."

Chapter Twenty-six

Late Autumn

B arrett awoke from his nap to find a hand on his shoulder and drool on the jacket he'd balled up under his head. "Wha...where are we?"

"Stopped for gas about an hour ago, and now we're five miles out," Ambrose said as he glanced at the GPS display in their rental. "Wanted to wake you up before we pulled in."

"Thanks." Barrett swiped at the drool on his face. "Laughing at me on my birthday?"

Ambrose was still snickering as he said, "Does it help if I say it's out of love?"

Barrett glared at him but it had no heat to it. "Seems like an easy excuse."

Ambrose only laughed. "You ready?"

"Absolutely." He stared out the windshield as office buildings whizzed by. Val and Forrest lived outside Camden, a large city a few states over. The plan was to spend several days with them, then drop off the rental and fly out to California. Another week of sightseeing and relaxation, on top of visiting Raf, and capped off by attending Raf's new gallery exhibit. His biggest one yet, apparently. Art galleries weren't really Barrett's vibe, but he wanted to spend his thirty-nineth birthday somewhere warm, surrounded by people he loved.

Time didn't mean the same now, not like it had before. Barrett used to pass time between his shifts fishing, reading, trying to play guitar (and usually failing). He would sit in the silence and let his thoughts wander. And he thought that was what he wanted. Steadily alone in the quiet, in the wilderness, simply moving from one day to the next. But he wasn't beholden to it, tied down by an ideal life and upset that it had been upended. He'd always counted himself as someone who rolled with the punches, but *so much* had happened. And it was only now that he had the time to look back and wonder at how much had changed.

Starting with the man beside him.

"I can feel you staring," Ambrose said quietly, a small smile on his lips.

"I like staring at you."

"And oddly, I enjoy being stared at by you." He threw Barrett a wink. "Okay, they should be just up ahead."

Ambrose pulled into the parking lot of a small townhouse complex with neat hedgerows and what looked like fresh grey paint on the shutters. The days were growing shorter and even though it was late afternoon, the sky was gathering the colors of dusk already. Lights glowed behind shades and blinds in many of the units, including Val's.

They weren't even in park before the door to her home swung open and there were his sister and nephew, grinning ear to ear. Barrett swiftly kissed Ambrose and was out of the car, running over to scoop up his family in his arms. He needed to hug them, kiss their foreheads, muss the fringe Forrest was slowly regrowing.

His heart was in his throat but he was so happy. "Missed you too, Bear."

"Uncle, Uncle!" Forrest was still thin and pale, but his eyes were bright and his smile made Barrett's chest constrict painfully.

"Hey, kid." Barrett leaned down and carefully scooped Forrest up.

"Ambrose!" Forrest yelled it in his ear and they all laughed. The sound was the very thing Barrett needed to hear.

Ambrose put a warm hand on the small of Barrett's back. "Nice to meet you both, in person."

Val's smile spoke volumes. "Please, get over here. We're huggers, if Barrett hadn't told you that already."

And Ambrose, his sensitive, sweet, sometimes grouchy boyfriend, accepted Val's hug easily. He knew that might be tough for Ambrose and had told Val to be prepared for a gentle *no, thank you*, but Ambrose walked right into her arms. Forrest reached out and with a nod from Ambrose, touched that dark red hair, wonder on his face.

"If you're trying to make me tear up, you're doing good so far," Barrett murmured, getting a pleased grin in return. He could feel the prickle of tears in the corners of his eyes and sniffed hard, hoping they'd fade away. If he started crying now, he'd not stop for a long time.

They bustled between the townhouse and the car with bags and when everyone was settled in Val's cozy living room, Barrett video called Meredith. "Hey Mer. How's things?"

Meredith was outside her house, leaning against faded wood siding. "Gimmie a sec, she's already got her nose in something. Dandi, c'mere!"

There was some scuffling and then there was that big dolt of a dog, panting and doggie-grinning. Forrest squealed in glee when he saw Dandi on the screen. "Sorry I couldn't bring her, kid. Maybe we can do a winter trip, you come out to us?"

"I think we can arrange that," Val said as she handed Ambrose a cup of tea.

The softly pleased look on Ambrose's face was made all the better when he took a sip. "This is amazing."

"I heard you're a bit of a tea connoisseur, so I wanted to make sure I did it right."

"Hey Forrest!" Meredith was rubbing Dandi's ears and making her drool. "Did your uncle show you Dandi's new trick?"

"No!" Forrest leaned in, his nose almost touching Barrett's phone.

"Okay, let's do it, doggo!" Meredith stood and motioned for Dandi to sit; a command she knew well and always obeyed. "Okay now, hug!"

That massive dog sprung up on her hind legs and gently (as gently as a one hundred and fifty pound dog could) put her front paws on Meredith's shoulders. Dandi was taller by almost a head but Meredith leaned in and let Dandi lick her face. "Apparently the face lick needs some work," Barrett said, chuckling at Forrest's giggles and the bright smile on Val's face. "We'll get there."

"She hugs! That's so cool. You taught her that?" Forrest asked, watching Dandi sit back down and Meredith give her treats for good behavior.

"I didn't." He pointed at Ambrose. "Someone was encouraging her to always knock him over, so we compromised."

Ambrose's face was the picture of innocence, except for the roguish lift to his brows. "I have no idea what you're talking about."

With Barrett's hand on his arm to steady him, Forrest got to his feet and walked over to Ambrose. "Uncle Bear said to ask. Can I have a hug, Ambrose?"

Val sucked in a breath and that prickle was back at the corners of Barrett's eyes. "Jesus Christ," he muttered, hoping Forrest didn't hear him.

Ambrose made eye contact with him over Forrest's head. "Absolutely. Just show me what's okay? I know you have a port and I don't want to bump it."

Forrest nodded sagely and pointed to a spot below his right collarbone. "Just not there."

Barrett watched, heart in throat, as Ambrose got on his knees and held his arms out to Forrest. His nephew launched forward and wrapped his little arms around Ambrose's neck, snuggling in immediately. There was no panic in Ambrose's eyes, only gentle hesitance as he carefully hugged Forrest close. "It's nice to meet you, Forrest. Your uncle has told me a lot about you and your mom."

"Yeah? Uncle Bear said you paint and play guitar and write and do math stuff!" Forrest pulled back to look at Ambrose, his gaze unwavering in the way only a child's could be. "Can you teach me something?"

"I would love to." A smile like sunshine spread over Ambrose's beautiful face. "What should we start with?"

"So, it's no fire tower, but I think it'll do."

Ambrose clung to Barrett's lapels, an expression of faux shock on his face. "You would dare."

"I did dare."

Ambrose kissed his cheek. "And it's your birthday, so we go wherever you want, darling." He sucked in a deep breath and grinned. "It is beautiful."

He'd taken to calling Barrett *darling* and his big bear of a boyfriend liked it, so it stayed. He tried not to overuse it but Barrett made that difficult sometimes; for all the things he did worth a *darling*, Ambrose wanted to add on *sweetheart* and *my love* and maybe another dozen endearments. He was pretty sure Barrett would take them all in stride, like he did ninety-five percent of things.

The rooftop bar Barrett wanted to visit was an open-air space twinkling with strands of solar lights amidst curling ivy and the scent of dying summer flowers. Their little table was in the far corner, away from most of the crowd and situated so they could see the blues guitarist who was due on stage any minute. It had been a whirlwind few days and now they had a chance to stop and relax. To be with each other and celebrate in their own, quiet way.

They ordered specialty cocktails, knees touching under the table, hands curled together on the marble top. Barrett looked spectacular in a dark blue sports jacket and matching pants, a pale pink shirt underneath, open at the throat despite the chill in the air. Ambrose had thrown on a thick sweater with faux leather patches and a diagonal zipper at the neck. Raf had "suggested" the sweater to him and he'd bought it without thinking. He wanted to look good for Barrett during their celebration at the bar and from the expression on Barrett's face, he'd done well.

The tight, *tight* black jeans were probably helping, too.

Overhead the stars glittered in a velvet black sky and Ambrose looked up, trying to track a few of the constellations he knew. But the hand on his knee was distracting in the best possible way. "So, this is kind of where my plan ended," Barrett said in his ear. "I just wanted to come here since Val talked about it after her work party."

"I think it's lovely. And we don't need a plan besides enjoying the night and our drinks and the music." A few people carrying guitars climbed onto the small stage and the crowd quieted down. "And each other. It's perfect."

The night took on a dream-like quality as they sipped their drinks and listened to the live music. The blues guitars were smoky and deep, the riffs making Ambrose's fingers ache for his guitar back home. The two men and one woman on stage were technically skilled, but they infused their music with a chaotic energy that swung from somber to playful and back. It tugged the audience along with it, leaving the air thick with emotion like raw nerve endings. Ambrose could feel his hair stand on end.

"They're really good," Barrett said in his ear. Ambrose shivered and snuggled closer. "We should dance."

"No one else is dancing," he pointed out, but there were definitely a lot of people wiggling in their seats.

"Then we'll start it up." And Barrett tugged him from the stool, swooping them into the space clearly meant for dancing but sadly abandoned as of the moment. Ambrose loved the way Barrett swung into action, clear and confident and willing to misstep or fuck up completely. He wasn't afraid of failure, and he wasn't afraid of new things. Barrett said Ambrose gave him that confidence, and maybe that was true to an extent, but Ambrose saw Barrett fully in moments like these. Smiling and laughing, his grip sure but not too tight. The press of his body, the warmth of his kiss, the deep rumble of his voice in Ambrose's ear.

"You are divine," he said, lifting a hand to Barrett's jaw. "I love you. I hope your birthday's been good so far."

Barrett's answer was immediate. "The best. I love you, too. You're too good to me."

"I think we could both say that to each other until the end of days and it would never not be true."

The way Barrett's face crumpled, the shine to his eyes, almost made Ambrose tear up as well. He choked it back, not wanting to ruin the moment. "Looks like we started something," Barrett said in his ear as they watched other couples wander out to the dance floor, the music carrying them into a soft sway against the somber guitar notes.

"That just means they have good taste," he replied, grinning.

When Barrett leaned in to kiss him, Ambrose cast his gaze up for just a moment to take in that sky once more. "It's no fire tower," he said, playfully kissing Barrett. "It's better."

Chapter Twenty-seven

"You're here!" Raf sang as Ambrose and Barrett walked into the gallery. The massive open space wasn't traditional in any way. It sang of color and taste, the walls painted a beautiful dark blue and the floors white marble that gleamed in the glare of the overhead lights. But taking all that in after walking through the rotunda entrance practically dripping in flowers was almost a balm on the eyes. Raf immediately hugged them both and then with teasing fingers straightened Barrett's tie. "You look fantastic."

"Are you saying that because you helped pick out the clothes?" Barrett was barely able to suppress a grin.

"Pish, hardly. I know for a fact if you didn't want to take my suggestions, you wouldn't. Ambrose is a stubborn mule and you listen to him. That's all the evidence I need of any potential recalcitrance." Raf stepped back to eye them at arm's length. He was resplendent in a velvet jacket the color of mulberries, paisley shirt and yellow scarf gorgeously contrasting with his dark hair. "You look perfect. The party's about to start, so feel free to wander, order at the bar, and then just take it all in." He squeezed their arms. "I'm so glad you're here, both of you."

Raf flitted off to attend to the rest of the preparations and greet guests upon arrival, leaving he and Ambrose to wander. The new gallery exhibit was "The Science of Art", focusing on natural landscapes, glittering galaxies, and even paintings and models of DNA strands. It was like nothing Barrett had ever seen and he found himself gawking open-mouthed at the beautiful pieces on display.

"I did say Raf had unique taste," Ambrose said quietly in his ear as they walked arm in arm, sipping champagne. "But he's even outdone himself here."

"And these are all local artists?" Barrett leaned in to get a closer look at a mixed-media piece depicting the solar system. The colors curved and sang in his vision and he had to blink a few times to refocus on the piece as a whole.

"Most of them. Some Raf found through his many, many connections. And some of them are his new marketing manager's doing." Ambrose looked around, as if trying to spot Raf's mysterious new employee, the one they'd only heard about a few times when Raf called. "But they must have called in some favors, too."

"I can only imagine."

Ambrose snorted. "He's always been good at networking. I remember him brokering peace between clubs on campus several times."

"Good lord."

They continued to walk, pausing often to admire the complexity and skill with which the art pieces were crafted. They read the description cards and circled around the gathering crowds. Neither one of them wanted to stand in the middle of a bunch of "critics" sneering over their champagne glasses. But even as they passed others and overheard snippets of conversation, the general opinion seemed to be awe. It really was like no other gallery show.

Raf caught up with them later, his cheeks slightly pink from excitement. His ascot was gone and the little gold medallion he always wore glinted below the hollow of his throat. "You two! Here we are, my loves." He neatly inserted himself between them and guided them over to a door on the east side of the building. Barrett shot Ambrose a curious look and his boyfriend shrugged. "My little surprise for the night. I wanted you to see it first, before I let in the gaping masses."

With a nudge from his hip, Raf opened the door, then ducked back out. Barrett turned to ask what was going on, but that's when the centerpiece of the room caught his eye.

"Happy birthday." Ambrose was staring at him, naked vulnerability on his beautiful face.

"You didn't."

"Raf and I did."

Before him on a massive easel was a compilation of Perry's illustrations. Each one expertly, perfectly printed and backed on soft white to let the viewer focus on the drape of foxglove petals and the beauty of fragile honeysuckle. Weeping wisteria graced one corner, its lavender hue stunning the eye and drawing the gaze down to the colorful dots of a wildflower field. That field had been one of

Perry's last pieces. The same field Barrett had taken Ambrose to in the spring. Perry had found that spot and showed it to Barrett, and they'd tucked it away like a secret well kept.

Now it could be shared with everyone.

Barrett couldn't speak. He tried, but the tears falling down his face must have been a sign of his gratitude, because Ambrose reached up to wipe them away with his thumb. He swallowed hard and pulled Ambrose to him. "You did this," he managed to say.

"I love you. I wanted to do this. Perry was special to you, a good friend when you needed one." Now Ambrose's eyes were damp and he was trying to blink the tears away and failing. "Without him, we would have never met."

"Oh god, you're right." Barrett didn't know whether to laugh or cry. His heart didn't fit in his chest and he thought he might need to sit down. And at the same time, he wanted to see all of the illustrations. Because the room was nothing but Perry's art.

The door behind them opened and Raf stuck his head in. "Ready for the world to see or do you need another moment?"

Barrett shook his head, laughter bubbling up out of him. "Send them in. They should see this." And then he marched over to Raf and drew him into a hug. "I know you did this," he said quietly, pulling back to look at the other man. "And I love you for it."

"Anything for a friend, you big sweetheart." Raf's blush deepened, then he stepped back and straightened his lapels. "All right, let's do this."

The door to the gallery opened and the crowd swarmed in. Books were sold at an alarming pace. They heard remarks about the gentle beauty of the illustrations and wonderings at the artist. None of the illustrations were for sale but several people tried to negotiate with Raf or his staff.

In the middle of the chaos, Ambrose handed Barrett a copy of the book and turned it to the back flap. There, in black and white, was a photo of Perry and the bio Barrett had given Raf for print. "He would have loved this," Barrett said, tracing his finger over Perry's face. "He would have been incredibly embarrassed, but he would have loved it, too."

"He deserved to have his art displayed like this." Ambrose leaned close and Barrett pulled him in. "You're a good friend, darling."

"He was a good man." Barrett kissed the top of Ambrose's head. "Hopefully I'm a good boyfriend, too." He was trying not to be too vulnerable in a moment where emotions swirled in him, caught in the tide of everything happening around them.

"The best."

The kiss they shared was only the start of something new. Something wonderful and bold and different. Exciting and a little frightening. And at the same time, so peaceful that Barrett felt it echo in his bones. This was the right path for his life. "I love it here, but I can't wait to go home with you."

"Me too, darling. Me too."

ACKNOWLEDGEMENTS

My sincerest, sweetest thanks to:

Daze, for a cover that defied every expectation and brought Ambrose and Barrett to life. And for reading and replying and for being a friend, and for your incredible suggestions.

My beta readers, for giving me wonderful feedback and ideas, and for loving these two as much as I do. Cayla, your insights were invaluable and I owe you about ten drinks when I eventually visit.

Agu and Kei and James, for helping me kick my own ass. For your friendship and love.

All those who gave advice and assistance, from teaching me about ranger life (no matter how much I then twisted it for my own uses and made plot armor out of it), to sharp eyes that caught mistakes and inconsistencies. All other mistakes are mine, and mine alone.

ABOUT THE AUTHOR

Halli Starling (she/they) is a queer author, librarian, gamer, editor, and nerd. *Ask Me For Fire* is her third book. Her work can be found on hallistarling.com and she's on Twitter and Instagram @hallistarling.

Printed in the USA
CPSIA information can be obtained
at www.ICGtesting.com
LVHW022113011123
762552LV00082B/222/J